Hyacinth Brown

Bitter
Desire

A NOVEL OF ABUSE, REVENGE AND REDEMPTION

HYACINTH BROWN

Bitter Desire

A NOVEL OF ABUSE, REVENGE AND REDEMPTION

MEREO
Cirencester

Mereo Books

1A The Wool Market Dyer Street Cirencester Gloucestershire GL7 2PR
An imprint of Memoirs Publishing www.mereobooks.com

Bitter Desire: 978-1-86151-436-3

First published in Great Britain in 2015
by Mereo Books, an imprint of Memoirs Publishing

The address for Memoirs Publishing Group Limited can be found at
www.memoirspublishing.com

The Memoirs Publishing Group Ltd Reg. No. 7834348

The Memoirs Publishing Group supports both The Forest Stewardship Council® (FSC®) and the
PEFC® leading international forest-certification organisations. Our books carrying both the FSC
label and the PEFC® and are printed on FSC®-certified paper. FSC® is the only
forest-certification scheme supported by the leading environmental organisations including
Greenpeace. Our paper procurement policy can be found at
www.memoirspublishing.com/environment

Typeset in 9/13pt Bembo
by Wiltshire Associates Publisher Services Ltd. Printed and bound in Great Britain by
Printondemand-Worldwide, Peterborough PE2 6XD

For every book sold I will donate twenty five per cent to charities for of cancer, diabetes, abused victims and sick children. My reason for choosing these charities is that I'm having treatment for breast cancer, and I have family and friends suffering from diabetes. A loving great-grandson was premature and passed away. Also, because this story has been based on abused teenagers and women, I would like to help them in any way I can.

Hyacinth Brown

Chapter 1

Petra Jackson was having her bath one Tuesday afternoon when her mother shouted from the bottom of the stairs, "Pet honey, Arden and I are leaving to see your grandma. We'll be back in a few hours."

Petra was listening to I Will Survive and her headphones were covering her ears, so she didn't hear her mother.

"Petra!" her mother shouted twice, and getting no reply she made her way up the stairs. Her husband Morgan, a police officer, met her halfway and held her hand saying, "Ann love, I'll let Petra know you and Arden are going out."

She looked hard into his eyes. "No, it's best that I go and tell my daughter that her brother and I are going to see her Grandma." She tried to pass him to go upstairs, but he grabbed her hand, saying, "I said I would tell her, as soon as she gets out of the bath."

"Honey, you know what Petra's like, so let me go and tell her. Besides, she might have a message for me to give her grandma or want to come with us as it's her day off school."

"Look honey, Petra is fifteen and a big girl and I am sure she wouldn't mind if you leave her. Besides, she might not want to be disturbed when she's having her bath. You and Arden go. Petra and I will be fine. When you get to your mother's and you want to phone her, please do, and give your Mum a kiss from me." He led his wife towards the front door. "I think it's time you and Arden left. I'll let Petra know you've gone as soon as she's out of the bath."

Arden looked at the floor and smiled. "Okay."

"Well, you take care of your mother for me honey," said Morgan and grinned.

"And you take care of our Petra for us too, honey," she said.

"That's my job, sweetheart."

Mrs Forbes smiled. Before she walked out the door, he said again, "Don't you forget to say hello to your Mum for me and don't hurry away from her as you haven't seen her for a while."

Mrs Forbes' smile faded; her face suddenly looked puzzled.

"Honey, don't worry over Petra and me," he said, smiling.

"Morgan Forbes, is anything going on between you and our Petra?" She looked serious.

"Ann honey, don't be silly. What can be going on between Petra and me? She's my stepdaughter and I love her as I love my son."

She looked hard at him.

"Why has that bright smile suddenly been wiped off your face?" he asked.

"She grinned. Well, I was thinking of coming back within an hour to cook supper, but since you told me not to hurry back, I won't. And I won't forget to tell mother you said hello. Morgan honey, I don't feel good leaving without telling Petra."

"Ann, as I told you, Petra and I will find our supper. You drive safely and spend some time with your mother."

"Are you sure you won't need me to cook your supper?" She asked.

"Yes, of course I'm sure. As I said, you and Arden have a good time with your mother and don't worry about us."

Mrs Forbes forced a smile and kissed him on his lips, then she and Arden left the house. Her husband watched them get in her car and drive away, then he dragged the back of his hand across his lips and closed the door quietly. He stood at the bottom of the stairs looking up, then he drank some whiskey from the bottle. He marched upstairs facing the bathroom door, smiling broadly. He guzzled down a good amount of whiskey and turned the bathroom door handle, but it was locked. He knocked a couple of times on the door.

"Yes, is that you Mum?" she asked.

"No, it's me. Your mother wants to speak to you," he said.

"I'll be out soon," Petra said, getting out of the bath.

"Open the door. Your mother is in a hurry and she wants to see you now," he said. "And I want to speak to you."

"What do you want with me? I'm getting dressed. Tell Mum I'll be with her as soon as I'm ready. And as for you, you go to hell," Petra said, hooking her bra.

"Open the damn door now!" He shouted, pounding on the door. "I need a shirt ironing."

"Go away and leave me alone. Why can't you ask Mum to do it?" Petra said, slipping into her knickers.

He laughed, then kicked the door open and walked. "I have watched you growing up into a beautiful petal and now you have, I think it's time we have some fun." He ran the back of his hand down her face.

"Get the fuck out of my way. Mum! Arden!" She shouted from the top of her voice, but as he knew they were gone, he laughed.

"Where's Mum?"

"She asked me to look after you, they've gone to visit your grandma. So, it's just you and me, honey."

"I'm not your honey. Mum…" She yelled.

"Shout harder, honey. Your mother might just about hear you as she's on her way to your grandma." He laughed then grabbed her hand, struggling with her to take her down on the bathroom floor; she slipped on the wet floor and fell on her bottom. As he went to touch her, she kicked him in his chest and his bottle of whiskey dropped on the tiled floor and shattered. She rooted backward on her butt to prevent him touching her, and her right heel engaged on a piece of the broken bottle. He saw blood, and said, "You brought this on yourself. If you had given in to me, this wouldn't have happened." He grabbed her hair dragging her out the bathroom and when she kicked and screamed, he slapped her face.

"Shut up, bitch!" he said. He stopped at his bedroom door and kicked the door wide open, then forced her into the room. She bit his hand and he punched her on the side of her head, knocking her to the floor. She was dazed. She scurried away on all fours trying to escape from his grasp, but he grabbed her and his grip became stronger. With the force from his body he pushed her against the bedroom door, shutting it with a bang.

"Let me go!" she cried, begging him, but he laughed.

"Please dad, please don't hurt me," she pleaded.

"Petra, why can't you be nice to me, I'm sure we would get on much better and nobody needs to know we're lovers," he said pressing against her.

"Fucking get off me!" she shouted and scratched his face with her fingernails.

He grabbed her by the throat; she spat on his face. He wiped off her saliva and flung her to the floor and jammed his foot on her chest. Panting for breath, as he lifted his foot off her she kicked him between his groins and quickly got up. In agony, still gripping her with one hand, he pulled her down then thrust his body onto her.

"Get off me! You fucking bastard!" she cried and he laughed in between painful groans, "I'll get up after I get what I want."

Petra sunk her nails in his face; he felt burning pain. "Do you think I reared you because I had to? I did it because I knew it would come to this. I wanted you from the very beginning."

"Please get off me, my foot is bleeding and hurting."

"My face is bleeding and hurting too and I'm not complaining. So the sooner I get what I want the sooner I let you go," he said, trying to force her legs open with his knees, but she bit him on his arm.

He rolled off her and she got up quickly and ran into her room, struggling to shove her bed to barricade the door. He gave a hard push with his shoulder and in a rage he pushed the bed against her, knocking her so she staggered back unbalanced. He then charged into her, but she managed to get steady on her feet trying to fight him off. He thumped her on her chest, then flung her on the bed, tore her panties off and dropped on her. As he carried his lips to hers, she kneed him in the groin. He rolled off her and went down on his knees with his hands in his crotch, groaning. She grabbed some clothes, ran to the shower room and bolted the door. As she was hurrying to put her clothes on, he stood up and looked in the wardrobe mirror, staring and patting his seeping, bloodied face. Then he went and kicked the shower room door open and asked, "Where are you going to run to now?" He pulled the shirt out of her hands, slapped her face and watched her stagger back. Then he dragged her out of the shower room, holding her hand, and tossed her on the landing floor.

"Dad, please leave me alone. If you hurt me, I'll tell Mum and go to the police."

"I'm the police you stupid bitch! And I'm not your dad. As for your mother, she's as thick as a fucking plank."

Petra grabbed the plant pot and hit him on the forehead. But as she was going to hit him again he grabbed the pot from her hand and tossed it over the landing, shattering it. He then felt his forehead before punching her on her breast. Then he grabbed her throat and she croaked out, "You're choking me!" He took his hand away and watched her coughing, then said to her, "I just want you to catch your breath." She screamed at the top of her voice, shouting, "Get away from me! You sick bastard!"

"Petra, you're young and beautiful and I will look after you" he said. "We can leave here and live elsewhere. I would ask for a transfer far away from here."

"Please let me put my clothes on!" she begged him, crying.

"Damn you Petra, why can't you understand, I'm in love with you. If you're afraid of your mother, don't be, as she wouldn't find out until you want me completely, then we would leave here and find a place. Petra, I don't love your mother anymore. I stayed with your mother only to be with you."

"What about your son? Have you no respect for him to want to fuck his sister as well as his mother?"

"As I said, I love you and I'm sure your mother would understand when we told her our reason for leaving."

"And will my brother understand too?" Petra asked.

"I don't give a damn. All that is keeping me here is you!" he shouted and faced her. She kicked him on his leg. He grabbed her by her shoulders and shook her roughly. "Petra, I don't want to hurt you."

"Please don't!" Petra cried, exhausted.

His breath reeked of alcohol and he slurred, "I wouldn't hurt you babe. All I want is a little pleasure and to have you to myself."

He grinned, then tried to kiss her. She bit his lips. He dragged the back of his hand across his lips to wipe the blood away. He looked at his smeared bloodied hand, then said in anger, "You little slut, I love you." He pulled her into him, squeezing her. She bit his chest so that he would let go, and she ran into her brother's room, bolted the door and grabbed Arden's football towel, wrapping it around her up to her shoulders. Forbes kicked the door open and stood at the doorway laughing. "Now, where are you going to run to? Your mother's and my room again? Oh shit! I forgot the spare room."

"Why are you doing this to me? I'm your stepdaughter. I was six years old when you married Mum," Petra cried.

He gazed at her. "You don't know how long I've waited for you to be a young woman."

"Let me go, you sick bastard!" she said and hit him on his head with Arden's bicycle pump. He pulled the pump away and slapped her face, saying, "Now why do you want to fight me? Do you think I live with your mum because I loved her? Petra, you're the reason why I'm still here. From the moment I saw you, I fell in love with you, even though you were a child. I've waited patiently for this time. Now I think the time is right. You are becoming a mature woman."

"I'm only fifteen. How can you look at me and say that, you perverted dirty old man! I've looked at you as a father and all this time you were planning to have your way with me. Have you no respect for me knowing that I'm your stepdaughter?"

"What has that got to do with what I want?"

"You're my mother's husband, my brother's natural father."

"What has that got to do with me wanting you? Your brother was a mistake. I didn't want to have children with your fucking mother. I was desperate for somewhere to live and she took me in when I needed help. I didn't love her then and I don't love her now. It's you I love. Now why don't you give in and stop fighting me?"

"Get the fuck away from me, otherwise I'll go to the police."

"You stupid little fool, I am the police!"

Petra tried to hit him with her brother's tennis racket, but he ducked, grabbing her by the leg, taking her to the floor and pinning her down with his knees in her chest. "I can't breathe," she said, gasping for breath and crying.

"You give me what I want and you'll be okay to breathe." He raised his knees off her chest but still had her hands pinned to the floor.

"Get off me you fucking sick bastard!" she cried, trying her hardest to shake him off.

"Don't fight me." He grinned, then lay on her, moving his hands to her breast. She sunk her nails in his face again. He hit her face and straightened up, sitting on her tummy then slackened his trousers; she was trying her hardest to push him off.

"No no no!" she yelled loudly, still struggling hard to throw him off and crying. Then she felt his penis rubbing against her legs, and cried, "No dad.

No, no, dad! Please don't. It's not right. It's incest."

"You're not carrying my blood. So let me show you how much I love you." He entered into her. She screamed terribly with her eyes closed feeling his penetration, exhausted from fighting and crying from tiredness. Then, feeling him ejaculate, she managed to hit him on his chest. He eased off her and she pushed him off and ran into the bathroom to shower. As she rushed past him, he dragged the towel from around her, but she kept going and didn't look back. She got into her room and latched the door.

He talked softly outside her door. "I love you," he said.

Petra was clenching her stomach and heaving. She was so enraged with anger and frustration that she took a pair of scissors to her hair.

That evening Mrs Forbes arrived home to meet her husband eating a sandwich and drinking a can of beer. She looked hard at him, then asked, "Where's Petra?"

"Where's who?" he asked smiling.

"I asked you where my daughter is. You told me you'd look after her and I haven't seen her. So I'm asking you again, where is my daughter?"

"How was your afternoon with your mother, is she okay?" he asked, still smiling.

"My mother is fine. She said to say hello. Now, I don't have to ask you how you spent your afternoon as I can see you're okay. But I would like to know where Petra is."

"Well honey, if you would like to know how your precious daughter is, I suggest you march up those stairs, into her room where you'll meet her snug in bed under her quilt."

"What's the matter with her? Is she sick?"

"Honey, I don't know what's the matter with her. All I know is that she went to bed," he said, grinning.

"I don't know why you're grinning so happily when you can't tell me why my daughter is in bed. I know I should have taken her with me. I wouldn't trust you again to even look after Arden's dog," she said, then turned away from the cooker to face him. She saw the scratches on his face.

"What happened to your face?" she asked.

"Oh, I went to get a packet of cigarettes and saw a young couple fighting. While I was trying to separate them the woman scratched me."

"Morgan, when did you start smoking again?"

"The cigarettes weren't for me. My brother phoned and asked me to take him some to work."

"Well, I think you should look after those scratches before your face gets infected. And don't think I will let you off so lightly. I haven't finished with you yet. Has Petra had anything to eat?"

"Look Ann, I offered her something to eat, but she told me she wasn't hungry. Where's Arden by the way?"

"He stopped off at Stanley's, he will be here soon. Your silly smile is giving me the creeps. However, you sit there with your stupid smile while I go and tell my daughter I'm home and her Grandma sends her love."

"You do that."

She looked hard at him and stood at the bottom of the stairs calling "Petra". No answer. She marched upstairs, knocked on the door and then entered her daughter's room. She switched on the lights and shook her on her shoulder. Petra moved the cover off her head.

"What are you doing in bed? Are you not feeling well?"

Petra moved the cover further down to her shoulders and looked up at her mother, blinking.

"Didn't you hear me calling you?"

"No mum, I was asleep."

"Have you been crying?"

"Yes, I was having period pains and my tummy was hurting so much, but after the pain eased, I fell asleep."

"Are you still in pain?"

"No."

"Would you like something to eat? What happened to your hair?"

"Oh, I was trying out a new hairstyle. It turned out wrong so I chopped it."

"Well, would you like something to eat now?"

Through sobs, she softly answered, "No."

"Petra, it doesn't look that bad and it will grow back in no time. Well, you rest and I'll bring you a light snack."

"Thanks Mum, but I'm not hungry."

"You have to eat something. Hasn't your dad given you anything to eat?"

"I told him I wasn't hungry."

Mrs Forbes left Petra and met her husband standing on the landing in front of their bedroom door smiling. "I don't know what you're smiling about, but I'm dog tired and I have to go and prepare supper, and you're still wearing that silly grin on your face," she said, very annoyed.

"Well, what's happened to Petra, why can't she help you cook supper? She's a young woman now. If you always have to look after her like a five-year-old child, she will always expect it. I think it's time she helped with the housework. Well honey, I have less than two hours to get to work."

"Morgan, our daughter is lying in bed not feeling well. So let's leave her for now. Oh, Eldridge phoned to say he wants to see you before you go to work."

"What did you say?"

"I said, your brother Eldridge wants to see you before you go to work."

"Is he coming here?" he asked looking worried.

"I don't know. Why don't you call him and ask him, seeing as you have his cigarettes to give to him?"

"Ann, I'm sure Petra's feeling better by now."

"Why do you say that? What do you know? Has Petra told you what's the matter with her?"

"No. I guess she slept it off. I hope she's okay as she had a long sleep. Ann, you shouldn't worry about her, I'm sure she's fine."

"Morgan, what the heck do you know about women's troubles? I understand the pain she's having as I usually go through the same, so shut up, come downstairs and help me cook. That is, if you want to eat before you go to work."

"Okay, I'll be down soon." He looked over the landing to check she had gone, then went into Petra's room and said, "Not a word to your Mum about us, otherwise I'll kill her and then you. Remember what I said sweetheart. I'll only lose my job and spend a few years in prison."

"Don't worry, you evil bastard, you'll get what's coming to you in full," replied Petra.

"What did you say?" he asked, squeezing her around the mouth. She pushed his hand away and said, "I'll keep your secret for now, but I know what I'll do to you and no one will find out. It will be the deadliest secret of all and you won't even have the strength to beg for mercy.".

"What is that supposed to mean? You're mine, every part of you. And if you know what is good for you and your mother, you'll keep your big gob shut." He laughed again and went down to the kitchen and sat at the table drinking a can of beer.

Mrs Forbes took supper up to Petra. "Here, eat this." She touched Petra's forehead and then said. "Thank heavens you haven't got a temperature."

"Mum, I'm not hungry. I just want to be alone."

"Honey, I know what you're going through, but you have to eat."

"Mum, I might eat something later."

"Petra, I think you need a sanitary towel and your sheets need to be changed. You go the bathroom and tidy yourself."

Petra went to the bathroom, showered and on returning to her room she saw clean sheets on her bed. Her mother took the bloodied sheets and left the supper. Petra forced herself to eat, then shutting her eyes, she lay back falling asleep.

Long after, Arden took her leftover supper into the kitchen.

"At least she ate some," Mrs Forbes said and emptied what was left into the bin. After tidying the kitchen, she looked in on Petra, but found her sleeping. She turned the lights off before she went and had her bath.

An hour later, Forbes left to go to work. Arden turned off the downstairs lights and went to his room feeling sad, knowing Petra wasn't feeling well.

Chapter 2

The following morning, Forbes was home at six-thirty from work. He found Mrs Forbes and Arden sleeping, so he went into Petra's room, startling her with his touch as he woke her.

She faced him. "What are you doing in my room? I want you to get out, now!"

"Honey, this is my house and I'll get out when I'm ready. In the meantime, I'll keep clear until I'm ready for you again and you won't be putting any more locks on this door," he said and left.

For the past two weeks, Arden had noticed the atmosphere between his sister and his father, but he said nothing except to give his father the cold shoulder all the time and only speak to him if he had too.

Two weeks later, on a Tuesday afternoon, Arden got home from school and walked into the house singing and looking happy. His father was watching football on the television. Arden looked at him and turned to walk out the room.

"Hey son, we're enemies now are we?"

"I don't know what you mean dad."

"Well, for a couple of weeks now, you and your sister have hardly spoken to me. Did she say anything about me?"

"Why should she say anything to me about you, have you done something wrong to her?"

"No son, of course I haven't. I love both of you equally. I wouldn't hurt either of you."

"I'm glad to hear that."

"Look son, how about us going to watch our favourite team play Saturday. It would be my treat to you, what do you say son?"

"I don't know dad." Arden walked away.

When Petra walked into the house, she went straight to her room and sat on her bed. Arden knocked on her door but she didn't answer.

"Pet it's me."

"I know Arden. What do you want?"

"To speak to you."

"Come in."

Arden walked in. "Are you all right sis?"

"Yes, I'm okay."

"Sis, I notice you're unhappy since the day Mum and I went to see Grandma. Did anything happen while we were away?"

"No Arden. Nothing happened."

Arden smiled cheerfully. He left, went to his father and said, "Dad, I'll go with you to see the match."

"Thanks son. I won't be working Saturday. After we've seen the match, I'll treat you to a burger."

Arden smiled and went and had his dinner. Mrs Forbes walked in.

"Arden is having his dinner and Pet, I think she's in her room and your dinner's in the pot," Forbes said.

"That girl, I wonder what's wrong with her?" Mrs Forbes looked hard at him then went to Petra and asked, "Honey, why are you up here? Have you had your dinner?"

"No Mum. I'll have it later."

"Okay, but you should eat your dinner, your dad cooked your favourite, mixed vegetables, rice, prawns and chicken."

"I will eat Mum. But I'm not hungry at the moment."

Later that afternoon Petra heated her dinner, ate it in her room and stayed there for the rest of the evening.

Forbes took a screwdriver and put some holes in Arden's left trainer, then threw it in the doghouse smiling. He watched the dog ripping it before letting him out.

Arden got home to meet his dog roaming around the yard. He put the dog back in his kennel and saw the trainer. "Oh no, my brand new white trainer!" he said to his dad. "Did you let my dog out?"

"Yes son, as the morning was warm, I let him out for a walk around the garden."

"Dad, he's chewed my left trainer almost to pieces."

"I'm sorry son. Here's a hundred pounds, go and get another pair." Arden rushed out of the house to go and buy a new pair of trainers. Forbes smiled and went to his room to wait for Petra; he knew Mrs Forbes was at work and Arden had gone to buy his trainers.

Petra got home from school and as she couldn't see Arden, she ran up to his room, but he wasn't there. She went to her room and sat on her bed. Forbes quietly left his room, pushed Petra's door open and pounced on her back, ripping her panties off and hitting her nearly unconscious. He proceeded to rape her a second time leaving her crying and in agony.

"Petra Jackson," she said to herself, "I vow that there will not be a third time when I'll be raped by that sick-minded bastard or anyone else". And so, Petra dealt with stepfather Forbes in the most careful and unique way.

Petra and four of her friends had felt defenceless fighting their rapist families. They also felt they couldn't trust anyone to talk to, so the five of them, Petra Jackson, Faith Randall, Jenny Greave, Elizabeth Grey and Stanley Marshall, dealt with their problems. They were sexually assaulted and physically abused by their father, stepfather, brother and uncle.

Stanley Marshall was white and thirteen when his stepfather buggered him a Monday night when his mother went to babysit her sister Marjorie's two children. Four days later Stanley cried to his twelve-year-old friend Arden, "Why has my stepfather hurt me so much knowing he's a high court judge and I love him?"

"In what way did he hurt you? Well, I'm sure you'll get over it," Arden said and left Stanley standing by his gate. Tears flowed heavily on Stanley's chest while looking at Arden as he went home.

That night Stanley was crying blue murder and next morning, his mother took him to see Dr Wilding. After the doctor examined Stanley she said, "Mrs O'Neil, can I have a word with you please." She took Mrs O'Neil away from Stanley. She looked into Mrs O'Neil's eyes then said," Mrs O'Neil, I'm sorry to tell you but Stanley was molested."

Mrs O'Neil stared at the doctor in disbelief trying hard to take in what she had just been told.

After Dr Wilding quizzed Stanley in the presence of his mother and got no answers, she asked Mrs O'Neil to excuse her and Stanley for few minutes. Mrs O'Neil left her and Stanley. She then pleaded Stanley to tell her who had sexually molested him. Stanley told her that he didn't know as his attacker had his face covered and forced him into his car when he was giving him directions. The doctor looked hard at Stanley, then asked his mother in again telling her, "Stanley has told me that when he was giving directions to a man wearing a hood that mostly covered his face, he was pulled into his car, taken somewhere and raped."

Tears came to Mrs O'Neil's eyes. Dr Wilding looked at her remorsefully and said, "Mrs O'Neil, I'm so sorry that Stanley doesn't know his attacker. All I can do is to treat him and report this to the police."

Mrs O'Neil shook her head remorsefully, feeling strongly that her son had lied about the hooded man, but she said nothing. She took Stanley home with treatment for him.

That Friday night Mrs O'Neil ran to Stanley when she heard his screams. She knocked at the toilet door. "Stanley, what's the matter?" He kept quiet. "Stanley, I heard you cry out."

"I was a little constipated but I'm okay now," he groaned.

Mrs O'Neil stood at the toilet door to hear Stanley crying. That night she rang Dr Wilding to tell her that Stanley's pain seemed unbearable.

Later that night Dr Wilding knocked at Mrs O'Neil's door. Judge O'Neil answered the door and looked hard at the doctor. "Please come in, doctor," said Mrs O'Neil.

Judge O'Neil looked at his wife and then at the doctor. Mrs O'Neil asked Dr Wilding up to Stanley's room telling her, "My Stanley, I know he's suffering greatly. He went to the toilet and I heard him scream. He must have been passing excrement but when I knocked on the door he went quiet. Doctor, his scream had sounded horrendous and I know he was in pain. I watched him stifle his screams with his hand over his mouth. He told me that when he forced excrement out, his back passage bleeds and hurts so much." After Dr Wilding listened, she booked Stanley into a private hospital of Mrs O'Neil's choice.

Stanley spent ten days getting well before his mother took him home.

The hospital doctor arranged to have a counsellor to help her and Stanley come to terms with what had happened.

Two weeks later, Mrs O'Neil and Stanley had counselling and Stanley was feeling much better and comfortable, but anytime his stepfather went near him, he shivered dreadfully. One time, however, when Stanley went to the toilet and found he was constipated, he screamed violently, passing excrement with drips of blood. The following day, his friend Arden called to see him. He cried to Arden telling him, "I went to have a shit and my bottom burst leaking blood in the toilet."

"Stanley, what's going on with you mate, have you turned the other way?"

"Arden, I can't tell you what happened."

"Why can't you?"

"I just can't," Stanley said as his eyes became moistened with tears.

Arden left Stanley's room and went downstairs to wait for him to go to the football match. As Arden heard Stanley's screaming, he ran upstairs to him pounding on the toilet door. "What happening Stanley?"

Stanley kept quiet for a moment, but screamed out saying, "Oh God." Then he opened the door, his face saturated with sweat."

"What's the matter?" Arden asked.

"It's just shitting is painful Mon."

Stanley went back into the toilet. Arden stood outside the toilet door and was listening to every groan Stanley made. When Stanley finished, he gave a long hard sigh of relief but could hardly stand up straight as he was trembling, with sweat pouring off his face and his hands were shaking while washing them. Nervously, he opened the toilet door to see Arden with his back against the landing bannisters with his arms folded. "Stan, you almost gave me a fright. I thought a rat climbed up the toilet and got hold of your dick. Anyway, why were you screaming?"

"Arden, my stepfather …"

"What about your stepfather, what were you going to tell me?" Arden asked looking hard at Stanley.

Stanley dried his eyes and turned his back on Arden.

"Stanley, we've been friends since we started school, I won't tell anyone what you told me. You're stepfather beat you?"

"Worse than that, he jumped on my back unexpectedly when I was on my bed doing my homework, ripped my pyjamas off and shoved his dick up my bum. I tried to fight him but I failed. Arden, he hurt me badly. I'm so afraid to have a shit and I don't want to tell Mum he raped me. I don't want to cause any trouble between him and Mum."

"Stanley, you have to tell your Mum otherwise he'll do it again."

"Arden, I can't. I shouldn't have told you."

"Stanley, my sister is always in her room since me and Mum went to visit grandma. Ever since that day, she has never been the same happy sister. I'm not sure what happened but dad's being cool to me. I suspect something happened and I'm yet to find out."

"Come on let's go play football." Stanley said.

Arden's team won the football match by four goals to one. Arden went home from football looking happy and said to Petra, "Sis, our team won by three goals. But as he saw his dad coming their way, he kissed Petra's face and walked away. His dad looked at Petra smiling, then walked in the kitchen. Arden went back to Petra and said, "Can I ask you something?"

"What do you want to know?"

"I saw dad squeeze your breasts yesterday when Mum was putting out the rubbish. You looked uncomfortable. What's going on?"

Tears welled up in Petra's eyes as she said, "Your stinking dad hurt me but I will get my revenge."

Arden tried to hug her, but as she stared at him, he walked away looking sad.

"Arden?"

"Yes Pet." He faced her. She hugged him. "Arden, can I tell you a secret? You must promise not to tell anyone."

"I promise."

"Your dad raped me."

"What are you telling me sis, I'll kill him." Tears now welled up in Arden's eyes.

"Your dad hurt me so much and I have to deal with him in my own way." Petra took time to hug her brother again. "You know what little brother? It's up to me to do what is best to protect myself."

"Sis, I want you to promise me not to tell anyone what I'm going to tell you."

"I'll take it to the grave."

"Sis, Stanley told me his dad abused him."

"In what way?"

"He raped him."

Petra turned facing her brother. "Are you sure about that, Arden?"

"He told me and I believed him. Pet, I heard him scream when he was having a shit."

Petra's face went sad. "Our monster families must be stopped doing evil things to us." She sounded bitterly anger.

Arden smiled between tears.

"Keep strong little brother. They hurt us, but what's in store for them will be shocking."

Arden nodded, then fixed his eyes on Petra. She hugged him and said, "I'll be okay little brother." He smiled, then went to his room in tears.

Five weeks later Petra's mother stuck a note on the fridge for her. I have gone to a cosmetics meeting and I'll be home about eight. Officer Forbes got home first. After reading the note, a wide smile came over his face. "Ann," he said, "I thought the meeting was next Tuesday."

"It was, but I had a call asking if I minded going tonight as the hall had been double booked."

"Well, you don't go to work Fridays, so you go to your meeting," Forbes said. He was thinking of Petra.

"Well, I left Petra a note and some money for her and Arden to get fish and chips."

"It's three o'clock. I'm sure you have time to prepare something for them."

"I would Morgan Forbes but the time I have, I would like to go and spend it with Mum."

"Fair enough."

"Well, I should go now. You behave yourself and let Petra know I left her a note."

"I will Ann." He kissed her face, she left to go and see her mother before going to the meeting. Her husband smiled and pulled the note off the fridge and went into the living room. That afternoon Petra went home to meet her stepfather sitting at the kitchen table. She turned to walk out when he asked,

"How was your day beautiful?" She looked at him with cutting eyes, went to her room and bolted the door.

Sometime later she heard him and Arden talking. She left thinking it was okay for her to get something to eat. She went into the living room looking for Arden, but found her stepfather sitting alone. She rushed out the room and went into the dining room, but Arden wasn't there.

She turned to see the note on the coffee table her mother left her. Panicking and feeling scared, she returned to her room but didn't bolt her door, seeing Arden feeding his dog from her bedroom window. Then her stepfather opened her door and walked in.

"I want you to get out of my room now!" Petra yelped.

"Why do you always have to fight me?"

"Oh, I mustn't forget you told me this house is yours. So I think I should leave and go to the welfare and beg to stay there."

"Petra, don't be stupid. You and I could be lovers without anyone knowing."

Petra pushed past him and ran downstairs. He ran halfway down the stairs and jumped over the banisters in front of her. She tried to push him out of the way but he barred her. "You get out of my way!" she bawled.

He smiled, "If you are looking for your little shit brother to come and rescue you, he left after feeding his dog. Well my sweet pea, it's nearly six weeks since we had fun."

"You know what, you're right. Just let me get something to eat as I'm hungry."

"Okay, let's go get something to eat first." Petra took the lead. He followed and sat at the table watching her. She gave him a nasty look and filled the kettle with water. He went over to her. She looked at him. He turned. She hit him on his head with the kettle, then dropped it and ran out the house.

At nine o'clock Petra got home to meet her brother and mother. Officer Forbes had gone to work.

That night Petra sat on her bed and typed fifty notes about rape and abuse. She put the notes in her school folder after showing one to Arden and told him. "I typed fifty of these."

"Petra what do you intend to do with these notes?"

"I'm going to take them to school on Monday morning and give them to my classmates during recess."

"Please be careful sis, I wouldn't want you to get into trouble."

"Don't worry little brother. I will be very careful and discreet as I want my plan to work and to help others who are disadvantaged like me and Stanley."

Arden smiled. "Sis, I will help you in any way."

"Arden, I'm sure two of my friends are troubled."

"How can you tell Petra?"

"Arden, trust me. I know it's up to me to help them."

Arden felt pleased for his sister and compassion for his friend Stanley. Petra sat on her bed while Arden sat on a chair. Smiling, she jumped down off her bed and hugged Arden around his shoulders and said, "Arden dear, I have been raped by dad. I was a virgin and I'm sure you know what I mean. Little brother, I'm not afraid or ashamed to tell you as you're my only and loved brother. I know you wouldn't tell a soul. However, if you're a true friend to Stanley, as you said, you should work with us. Arden, I don't want you to feel sorry for what dad has done to me. You're not responsible for his wicked doings. I honestly thought I could trust him as my faithful dad. Arden, he abused my trust towards him. Little brother, he owes us a decent upbringing but instead he's wickedly abused me. The trust and respect I had for him is now dead and buried. I was just little more than a baby when he married Mum." Tears welled up in Arden's eyes. "Believe me little brother, the evil good-for-nothing will pay for what he's done to me."

Arden phoned Stanley and read one of Petra's notes to him. After Stanley listened with interest, he dried his tears.

"What do you think, Stan?"

"That's good man, but I don't want anyone to know about me."

"Stan, I told my sister. She won't say anything. My dad raped her. So she typed these notes to give to her classmates. Are you with us?"

"Arden, I'm in. Let me know what Petra wants me to do. I want my stepfather dead!" Stanley said.

"We'll help you Stan. You're my best friend. You stay cool," Arden said and put the phone down as his mother was coming his way. Arden went to Petra smiling.

"So, why are you smiling?" Petra asked.

"I have watched you and I could see through you. You haven't been happy since that day when Mum and I got home after seeing Grandma."

"Well that day your dad raped me."

Sunday afternoon Stanley went to Arden's home. Petra asked him if it was true his stepfather had raped him. "Yes, he did," he said, then tears followed. Petra hugged him, and he smiled. "Arden told me about your notes."

"Stanley, I want to help you and others," Petra said. Stanley smiled.

Petra gave him one of her notes. "You can keep this one and whatever you decide, please mark 'CUY' for 'completely understand you' at the bottom of the note. Meaning 'clearly understood' and 'yes' for raped or no. Stanley, I want you to keep that note and be sure you want revenge on your stepfather. Then please return the note to me at the end of our school day. We should meet at my Grandma's house at six o' clock tomorrow evening. I will take some of these notes to school tomorrow and whatever the outcome, we'll take it from there."

Arden lifted his head smiling and looked amazingly coolly into Petra's eyes, then commented, "Not bad at all sis. A note like this would shake the shamed shivers out of whomever it concerned." Stanley smiled then put the note in his jeans pocket. Arden took Stanley into the kitchen and treated him to cake and a glass of pop before he went home.

On Monday morning, Petra took most of the notes to school and passed them to twelve of her friends at break time. When school was over, she received four of the notes from Elizabeth Grey, Faith Randall, Jenny Greave and Stanley Marshall. The four returned notes had 'CUY' written at the end just as Petra had asked them to do.

At six o' clock Elizabeth, Faith, Jenny and Stanley met Petra at her Grandma's gate as arranged. She took them into the dining room. "Thank you for coming. My Grandma is at a meeting. Please take your seats. My friends as of now, I have invited you to this, our first meeting, as we have to decide what to do with our rapist families."

"We should kill them!" Stanley shouted.

"No!" Elizabeth replied. "Killing is too good for such animals."

"Then what do you suggest, Elizabeth?" Faith interrupted to ask.

"We should burn them alive until their bones crumble to ashes," Elizabeth said in painful anger.

"No!" said Faith, "That's too cruel, even though they are animals."

"So what do you suggest then, Faith?" Elizabeth asked.

Jenny interrupted. "We should..." she held her words, then paused for a moment. "I think we should cut their balls off after we knock them out cold with a strong dose of morphine. So they would never look at another person again."

"You're forgetting one thing Jenny, if we cut their balls off they might turn into killers. Don't you think so Jenny?" Petra asked. "Still, I do agree with you Jenny, but, as I said, cutting their balls off might do more harm than good. If I had it my way, I would put these perverts in the worst jail permanently and throw the key away in the depths of hell. Youths like us suffer because of these family incestuous bastards. I know we've all suffered deeply and the after-effects will haunt us more than a Freddie Krueger film. I hope that someday soon girls, we might just be able to get over the horrors of what's happened to us. However, I believe it will be so hard for our friend Stanley to forget easily what his wicked stepfather has done to him."

Petra directed her look at Stanley. "Stan, I'm glad you did not tell your mother. I admire you for that, as you didn't want to ruin her reputation bearing in mind that she has so many decent friends that respect her. Stanley, sometimes we have to lie to protect ourselves and our caring loved ones. You thought by telling your mother and doctor you were attacked by a hooded man was best for all. Stan, as it was bitterly painful for us girls, I know how hard it has been for you." Tears welled up in Petra's eyes so much so that she ended the meeting and they went home.

Arden looked at Petra and saw her in tears. "Sis, are you crying?"

"I was thinking about Stanley's screams that you told me about when he went to the toilet. Arden, my crying wasn't for me but for Stanley. I'm feeling hurt and dirty deep inside from what your dad has done to me; what he did will haunt me. But as I said, it will take a damn long time for our friend Stanley to block out what has happened to him, and I know he will never forget his wicked stepfather."

That Monday night as Petra spoke to her brother she cried. "Arden, I haven't felt so happy in a very long time knowing I'm not alone. But I'm still feeling hurt."

"I'm happy that you're happy sis."

Petra danced with her brother when he said, "I'll stand shoulder to shoulder with you, big sis."

"I know, little brother." Petra danced by herself for a long time to Brown Girl in the Ring before she went to bed.

The following Tuesday, Petra held another meeting at her Grandma's house.

"Well my friends, I told my brother what we're up against and what we ought to do. However, we have five infected bugs to dispose of indefinitely. All in favour please raise your right hands," Petra said. Seeing her four friends' hands raised, she nodded smiling and said, "Then whatever we do must remain top secret. We'll start with my stepfather. We must destroy him first as he is the police. When he is out of the way, our chances will be greater with the rest of the lowlife shits."

"That I would agree with," Elizabeth said.

"We all agree with you, Petra," Jenny said.

Elizabeth and Faith smiled while Stanley's tears flowed heavily on his shirt. Petra looked at him in such a remorseful way and said, "Okay friends, we'll chop off their dirty fingers from the evil hands that they touched us with! Then we'll poke their evil eyes out of the filthy heads that they looked on our bodies with. We'll swipe the dicks off that they viciously rooted into us. However, we'll need morphine, hypodermic needles, surgical gloves, scalpels, mouth caps, sharp razors and fine salt to throw over their wounds. From there, it's up to the bastards if they survive or not. So this means we'll have to get our mothers and whoever else out of the way so we can carry out our jobs. When our mothers get home, they'll find their bastard husbands neatly wrapped in bright red bloodied sheets." Petra smiled in relief and contentment.

Stanley, Jenny, Elizabeth and Faith stood up in respect and applauded Petra. Petra smiled triumphantly. Then she stood up and said, "My good friends, here is where we should end our second meeting. I will show you out now and please go straight home. I'm going to wait for my Grandma before I go home."

Petra showed her four friends out, then prepared a cheese and ham salad for her and her Grandma's supper.

An hour later, her Grandma returned home to find Petra sitting watching television. "Sit yourself down Grandma, I've made us a ham and cheese salad," Petra said.

"Oh my dear granddaughter, I'm so glad to see you."

"Well Grandma, I'm very happy to see you as well and I love you," Petra said.

"I know you do, my darling Pet. I know you do."

Petra put their salad suppers on the table. "That looks so inviting, but I must wash my hands before I eat."

Petra smiled.

Her Grandma sat down and started eating. "Mmm, this is very tasty. Petra, you should come and do this for me more often as well as cook me a hot meal. I'm really enjoying this. However, when you have finished eating, I think you should go home as it's dark and before your mother starts worrying."

"Yes Grandma."

"You're growing up to be a very beautiful young woman. I just want you to look after yourself."

Petra smiled as her Grandma looked at her. You and Arden are the only two loving close relatives I have apart from your mother. I will leave my house to you and your brother."

"Grandma, you still have plenty of life left in you! However, I think I should get ready to go as I've got school tomorrow. I will come and stay with you Friday night. You don't mind me staying over, do you?"

"Not at all my dear, I would be glad for your company any time. Now finish your ice cream and be off before your mother sends your dad out with a search party looking for you."

Petra smiled and carried the used plates to the sink.

"Petra, leave the plates, it's time you went home. I'll wash them."

"It's only a couple of plates, Grandma. It will only take me a couple of minutes to wash them."

"I know and it won't take me long to wash them either. Leave them and go home. Take some money from the kitchen drawer to buy a bus ticket."

"I have a bus pass." Petra kissed her. "You go straight home honey."

Petra set out running and as she disappeared her Grandma closed the door and returned to the kitchen, washed the plates, then showered and settled down in bed reading Denyah.

When Petra got home, she rang her Grandma telling her, "I'm home now, grandma."

"Thank God. Now I can sleep peacefully." Closing her book, she yawned, then fell asleep.

That Friday night Petra slept at her Grandma's as promised. The next Tuesday at school, Petra told her four friends that they should have another meeting the following Monday at six o'clock as her Grandma would be out for the evening. Her friends agreed. Stanley went home while Petra, Elizabeth, Faith and Jenny stayed after school to play netball. After the game, Petra went home feeling happy, until she met her stepfather sitting at the dinner table smiling. She looked hard at him with cutting eyes.

"Honey, we were waiting for you to eat," he said.

"I'm not hungry, I had some chips."

"Petra, you have to eat a proper meal."

"Mum, I'm really not hungry. I need to go to my room to do my homework."

"Okay Pet, I'll leave your supper in the oven for when you're ready. I will be going to parents' evening. We won't be too long, but please make sure you lock all the windows and doors after your father leaves for work if we're not back by then."

"Okay Mum."

Minutes later, Petra's mother and brother left the house. Outside, Arden said, "Mum, I don't feel well."

"What's the matter with you? You were okay before we left the house. Well, we won't stay long. We can just show our faces and leave."

Arden and his mother got into the car. He was thinking about Petra, knowing his dad raped her when she was left alone. Arden forced a heave. "Stop pretending you're sick. All day yesterday and today you were happy to come with me so that I could see your work and now you're pretending to be sick. What's going on with you son?"

"Nothing Mum, I just don't feel well."

"Arden, you have to be at school to see your teachers and to show me your work. We'll only stay a short time. Anyway, you should feel proud about your work."

"I am Mum."

"So why the hesitatio, have you done something wrong?"

"No Mum. I... I don't like leaving Pet on her own when she's sick."

"What makes you think your sister's sick?"

"I heard her telling you her tummy hurts."

Mrs Forbes smiled, "Arden that was last week. Things about your sister, you'll never understand. We'll be home before she misses us. Besides, she wouldn't be alone. Your father will be with her."

"That what I'm afraid of," Arden mumbled.

"What did you say?"

"Nothing."

"Buckle up, let's go and then we can get back quickly since you are so worried about your sister; I'm sure she will be okay."

"It's not my sister I worried about."

"Are you trying to tell me something?"

"No Mum."

That same Tuesday evening, Petra left shortly after her mother to go and play netball at the community centre in Sparkbrook. Her stepfather rushed after her, shouting, "Where are you going now?"

"To play netball."

"Does your mother know?"

"I told her yesterday and she was okay with it."

"Well your mother didn't say anything to me. So I think you had better get back in the house." He grinned.

Petra snarled, then ran to catch the bus. "Petra, you get back here!" he shouted. Petra ran faster, leaving him at the gate. "Damn you, little bastard! You haven't heard the last of me yet. Your arse is mine!" he said furiously, going back into the house. Angrily he continued, "You little fuck! You have to come home." He took a can of beer out of the fridge and prised it open with anger, causing the beer to foam. He drank deeply, belched hard, dumped himself on the settee and kicked the cat in temper. The cat meowed, running away. He tossed the can of beer against the wall saying, "Petra! You little fuck, you think you can get away!"

Some hours later, Petra returned home to find her stepfather sitting in the living room. He smiled broadly, looking her up and down before getting up. She ran upstairs looking for her mother and brother. As they weren't there she rushed downstairs to hear her stepfather laughing. "You thought your mother was upstairs," he said. He laughed again. She rushed to the door, where he grabbed her hand, pulling her into the front room. She fought him, but he knocked her down with a blow to her chest and tore her skirt and knickers off. While he was raping her, however, she bit the end of his right ear off. He punched her face, threatening her, "You make a sound and I'll kill you." He wiped the running blood off his face while she groaned, then as he ejaculated he got off her and felt his burning ear to realise that a quarter of it was missing.

Mrs Webber, who lived three doors up, knocked at the front door. Forbes answered, "What do you want?"

"I've brought your cat home. The poor thing is limping." She put the cat down in the doorway and left; Forbes pushed the cat out again.

Mrs Forbes drove through her gate to find her cat lying outside the doorway meowing. She picked it up, trying to open the door with her key; Forbes rushed to the door jamming his body against it to stop it opening. Mrs Forbes saw him behind the glass door. "Please move out of the way Morgan and let me in," she begged. He moved. "Why were you barricading the door and why is your ear wrapped in plaster?"

"I tripped over Arden's school bag and banged my head and cut my ear. I think I'm still bleeding."

"You'll find some bandage in the bathroom cabinet."

He rushed upstairs saying to Petra, "Not a word."

"Fuck you, Morgan!"

"Oh, it's Morgan now then, since we got this little thing going?"

"You raped me, three times, so what the hell do you expect? I want you to keep well away."

"And if I don't?"

"I'll kill you."

He laughed teasingly. "I wonder what your mother would say if I told her you came on to me. Anyway, you keep my secret and I'll keep yours." He blew Petra a kiss then went to the bathroom when he heard Mrs Forbes walking up the stairs. She cleaned Forbes' injury. You're becoming prone to these accidents. And Morgan why is a piece of your ear missing?" "Arden's dog had the cat; he bit my ear when I tried to intervene."

"Well, I think you should go to the hospital and get it seen to." She washed her hands and went to Petra. "Why are you upstairs?"

"I was feeling tired."

Arden opened the door and ran up to Petra. I was so worried about you."

"I'm okay Arden. Oh, and Stanley phoned to say please take his mobile phone to school tomorrow."

Arden hit his forehead. "I forgot to give it to him on my way to school this morning. I better ask Mum to take me now."

"Arden, he said tomorrow."

"Petra, have you been crying?"

"No, do I look like I've been crying?"

"Your eyes look weepy."

"That's because I'm very tired."

Arden smiled. He went to his mother. "Mum can you give me a lift so that I can give Stanley his mobile phone?"

"Arden, if you must, take his phone to him now, it's only three streets away. Pet, come down for your tea."

"I've already had something to eat Mum."

Forbes went and changed into his uniform. He opened Petra's door saying, "I'm not hurting you. I'm simply showing you the outer world and I can never get enough of you my sweet young pea."

"Mum..."

"You say anything to your stupid mother or anyone else about me and I'll kill you as I said. Anyway, no one will believe you." He laughed, then left and went to work.

Arden knocked on Petra's door. "Pet, can I come in?"

"Arden, I'm very tired. I'll speak to you tomorrow."

"Can't I see you for a couple of minutes?"

"Okay, but only for a couple of minutes."

Arden pushed the door open and stood in the entrance. "Can I turn the lights on?"

"Why? You only want to talk, so say what you want and go."

Arden walked in, turned the lights on and looked in her face. "Pet, I think you should tell Mum."

"Look Arden, all I want now is sleep. I'll see you in the morning."

"Pet, you looked stressed. Has dad troubled you again?"

Petra didn't answer. Arden asked again. "Has dad hurt you?"

"No, no. He didn't. Now please go."

Their mother was walking past Petra's door when she heard Arden then say, "I know he hurt you. I'll kill him."

Mrs Forbes asked, "Who is it you're going to kill, Arden?"

"No one Mum."

"Well, I think it's time you went to bed."

"Yes Mum."

"Arden, I heard what you said about your father. He would never hurt any of us. Your sister might be having boy troubles. That's something you'll experience with girls when you get older. Anyway, it's time you go and see if your dog's all right before you go to bed."

By this time, Petra was in pain from the blow her stepfather had given her, but she was too scared to tell her mother. Her strong-minded ego was encouraging her to deal with her stepfather in the worst way and she did not want to jeopardise her chance of getting even with him. Arden fed his dog and gave him fresh water after cleaning the kennel. He was heading for the bathroom as his mother was going downstairs.

"Arden, have you cleaned your dog house?"

"Yes Mum, I saw him eat and drink and I left him lying down in his basket. Mum, he needs more plastic bags."

"Arden, you're getting enough pocket money to buy your dog bags. I hope you don't put his mess in my bin. I made you the cheese sandwich you asked for. Go and ask your sister if she wants anything to eat."

Arden went to Petra, but she was asleep. He said to his Mum, "Petra is sleeping. Thanks for the sandwich Mum, but I need to go to the bathroom first."

"Well, I'm going to my room. Turn off the kitchen lights after you've eaten and no loud music playing in your room tonight."

The following morning, even though Petra felt bitter towards her stepfather, in the presence of her mother she pretended that everything was normal. At the breakfast table, she joined in making conversation with her stepfather and mother. He laughed happily, feeling confident and thinking all was well. He gave Petra the eye. She smiled and went to school.

That evening Mrs Forbes said to Petra, "I'm so happy to see you and your dad getting on well." Petra looked hard at her.

"Pet, I'm really happy to know we're a loving family. He may not be your biological dad, but he's a good one to you and Arden. So please try to respect him."

That Saturday afternoon, Officer Forbes bought Arden a wristwatch and Petra a gold chain. He gave Arden his wristwatch, but wanted to hook the chain around Petra's neck in the presence of her mother. "I will hook it myself," Petra said.

He gave her the chain and smiled. "You look after that chain honey, your father loves you."

Petra grinned at her mother and went into the kitchen to have a drink and then went up to her room.

Forbes went to Petra and whispered, "Your mother looked jealous." Petra looked hard at him and went downstairs to the living room to be by herself.

"Mum, Dad hit Petra," Arden told her.

Mrs Forbes stared at Arden before confronting her husband. "Tell me Morgan, what the hell's going on with you and my daughter."

"What? Why are you asking that?"

"I'm asking you. What's going on between you and my daughter?"

"Look Ann, Petra's my daughter too and you mind how you talk and act around her. We don't want her to hate either of us. Is it so wrong to give gifts to my daughter for the first time?"

"No Morgan. I'm happy for our family to be close. But you can't blame me for feeling over protective about my daughter."

"She's my daughter too, Ann."

Petra went to her room and savagely tore the gold chain to bits, threw them in the bin and dumped herself on her bed saying, "I'll do worse to you, you evil son-of-a bitch!"

Forbes left his wife in the kitchen and went to his room to change into his uniform. Mrs Forbes followed him to their room to see him in plain blue boxer shorts looking at himself in the full-length wardrobe mirror. "Who's that handsome man in the mirror?" she asked. He smiled. Mrs Forbes slapped his bottom.

"Don't do that!" He snapped and quickly put his uniform on. "I'm going for a drink, then to work," he said.

"I thought you were on a week's holiday?"

"No, I only had a couple of days off."

"Morgan Forbes, are you seeing another woman?"

He smiled, "Don't be silly. Of course I'm not. Why do you ask?"

"Morgan, when was the last time you showed me that you love me?"

"Ann, we're not teenagers anymore."

"What have teenagers got to do with you making love to me? From a few months ago you've changed towards me. I need a little attention sometimes. If you're having an affair I want to know. I don't think I could sleep with a deceitful husband not knowing what he would bring home to me."

"Woman, shut you're blasted mouth, I won't be bringing anything home to you because I can't bear to hear your groaning when having sex with you."

"You cheating bastard, I knew you were up to no good. You can fuck all the dogs you want and see if I care. I think its best you move into the spare room. I will have to let the children know about us."

Forbes looked hard into his wife's eyes and burst into laughter. He dropped onto the bed and said, "You silly jealous woman. You are the only woman in my life. I wanted to make love to you a few weeks ago, but I found a rash on my testicle so I went to the doctors and had it seen to. It was a sweat rash but I scratched it and it became infected. I didn't want to bother you, as it wasn't serious. But you know I love you." Mrs Forbes smiled and believed him.

Officer Forbes is six foot two inches tall. He's English born, very good looking, has a good muscular body and short-cropped curly black hair; his dimples show clearly in both cheeks when smiling. His eyes of sea green suit his clear complexion and were often mistaken as lenses. In fact, everything about Forbes is very attractive.

After that night fighting with his wife he was very careful about what he said and did around her, as he didn't want to spoil his chances of taking Petra at any opportunity. From that night, he and Mrs Forbes became closer and he would make love to her for peace's sake.

The following Friday evening Arden was going downstairs, he saw his dad block Petra's way and trying to kiss her. Arden attacked him, punching him on the chest telling him, "Leave my sister alone!"

He looked crossly at Arden, went to his room and lay face up smiling until Mrs Forbes walked in. He stopped smiling and turned his back on her still smiling.

The Sunday morning Mrs Forbes was in the front garden cutting flowers. Forbes saw Arden going into the garden, he left his tea on the counter and rushed in the garden telling Arden, "Go and feed your dog."

"I've done it." Arden watched him with hate.

"Well I want to speak to your mother in private."

Arden sucked his teeth and went to his dog then to Petra.

"Ann honey, I didn't want to tell you this, but you know our Petra is now growing up and becoming a young woman ..."

"Yes Morgan, I know. Just what are you trying to tell me, and, what about my daughter?"

"I slapped her one day last week after she tried to kiss me and again yesterday although I'd warned her. I pushed her away and threatened her never to try anything like that again."

"Why didn't you tell me before now? What the hell is the matter with her?"

"I don't think she'll try anything like that again as I made it clear to her I'm her father and I love you. I'm sorry I hit her, but I had to let her know I was serious, so that she wouldn't attempt to kiss me ever again."

Mrs Forbes threw the cut flowers on the ground, rushed into the house to find Petra, but she was in her brother's room playing Frustration and eating ice cream with him. Mrs Forbes rushed upstairs and called her. "I'm in Arden's room Mum." She rushed into Arden's room and started throwing punches towards Petra's face, knocking the ice cream out of her mouth. She only stopped flying punches when she saw Petra's face bleeding and then she fell hopelessly in a corner of the room.

Arden held his mother's hand as she fired another blow cutting Petra over her left eye. "Mum, Petra has had more than enough beatings." His mother pushed him away.

Petra was bleeding from her mouth and over her left eye as her mother's rings had cut her.

"Mum, what has my sister done so wrong for you to beat her so viciously?" Arden asked crying.

"Your sister is becoming a slut! And the two of us won't be living in the same house sharing my husband. Your loving sister tried to kiss your dad again even though he had smacked her for doing the same before."

"Mum, my dad is lying to you."

"Shut up! Your dad wouldn't lie about her. I've watched her playing with him. If I catch her too close to him, she'll find herself out on the street with her kind. Since she's acting like a slut, I'll treat her like one."

"Mum, that's not fair. I've watched my dad try to kiss Petra and she tried to fight him off." Arden cried harder wiping his nose with the back of his hand.

"Arden, I told you to shut up, or you will find yourself living on the street with your sister." Mrs Forbes then turned and looked at Petra saying, "As for you miss trollop, get out of Arden's room and get into yours and stay out of my way."

Petra cried and went to her room bleeding. She held the paper handkerchief over her cuts and curled up on her quilt.

Arden went to see Petra later and asked her if she needed anything. "No," she said softly. Arden became teary-eyed looking at her swollen lips and eye, and then he kissed her forehead. "I'm sorry sis for Mum beating you and not believing us."

"That's okay. Thanks for supporting me."

"That's okay sis. I love you." He left her room in tears.

At dinner time Mrs Forbes pushed Petra's door open, "Food's in the pot if you want it and I hope you choke on it."

Petra stayed in her room for the remainder of the day. During the night, Arden took a chicken sandwich to her and a can of coke. She ate and drank then showered. On her way back to her room, her stepfather eyed her and blew a kiss. Arden saw him and warned him. "Keep away."

"What will you do if I don't?"

"You're not my dad any more," Arden told him and went to his room in tears. Forbes followed behind him and pushed his door open. "Get out of my room. I hate you. You're no longer my dad."

He picked Arden up by his throat and said, "You little shit bag, you keep your mouth shut about me or I'll make you, your sister and that stupid mother's life a living hell." Arden was kicking and struggling for breath before he dropped him. Arden stared at him holding his throat and coughing. Forbes pressed the point of his shoe into Arden's chest saying, "You see me with your sister, you just look the other way and say nothing!" He then left Arden's room and shut the door with a bang.

"Your time will come soon bastard when you'll pay!" Arden said under his breath.

Chapter 3

One Tuesday evening Petra accompanied her Grandma to her local church. She was one of the speakers and a strong supporter for collecting donations for third world charities. While Petra and her Grandma stood at the church door, her Grandma faced her and grabbed her hand. "What's the matter Grandma?" Petra looked very concerned.

"I don't think I'm feeling too well."

"Grandma, did you take your tablets before you came out?"

"Yes dear, I think I have, but earlier on as I had a terrible headache and a touch of diarrhoea."

"Grandma, I think I should take you home to rest."

"I think you're right Pet, but I have to be here as this meeting is so important. I think I know why I just went dizzy. I'm wearing my two-year-old glasses." She laughed. Petra laughed as well. "Look dear, you can leave me now. I'll be all right. If I need you, I will give you a call. Will you be okay getting home?"

"Yes Grandma. What about you? Would you like me and Arden to come and pick you up?"

"No dear, I'll get a lift home."

"Grandma, if you need to come home before the meeting finishes, just ring and I'll ask Mum to get you."

"Thanks dear, I know you mean well, but I think I'll be okay. Since I joined the savers meeting, I can't remember missing one. I would especially regret missing this meeting. It is so important that even if I didn't feel well, I would try and stay to till the end."

"Okay Grandma, respect to you, but as I said, if you need me, call." Petra kissed her. "Well, I will leave you to attend your extremely important meeting."

"Yes Petra dear, it's for a good cause and some of us have to be concerned for the less fortunate parents and children." Petra saw her Grandma settle in her front seat, and then she raced back to her Grandma's house to let her friends in. Short of breath and smiling, she let out a big sigh before saying, "I'm sorry for being late."

"That's okay Petra," Faith said. "We've only been here for a couple of minutes."

Petra smiled before opening the front door with her key and letting her friends in. Smiling, she looked around making sure the neighbours didn't see her letting her friends in. She took her four friends upstairs to the room she slept in when she stayed over. "Are you hungry?"

"I could do with a sandwich," Jenny said.

"I'll be right back." Petra left and made turkey sandwiches for her and her friends before their meeting started. As they settled down eating and drinking coke, Petra made it extremely clear to them what she had in mind. "It might be stomach churning." She paused a moment. "Well, when you hear what I have to say, if any of you don't want to go any further, I would understand and I won't hold any ill feelings against any of you." Petra smiled then said, "Whatever you decide, I'll respect your decision."

Liz looked at Jenny, Stanley and Faith with a wondering expression and with her sandwich to her mouth. The five of them went silent. Liz bit her sandwich. Jenny raised her bottle of coke saying, "Petra, I clearly understand. I don't care what it takes, I want my bastard uncle to feel the pain that he has inflicted on me." Jenny smiled. She gulped down her last drop of coke and shoved the last of her sandwich in her mouth then faded into silence with her friends.

Petra broke the silence by banging her coke bottle on the dressing table asking, "May I have your attention please?" Her friends looked at her. "Now," Petra said. "If we're to take action, we should tell the truth. Just the truth of what our rapist bastard family has done to us! Stanley, you are a lad, would you be so kind to tell us what happened between you and your stepfather. Don't feel ashamed, or afraid. Just remember we're here for the same cause. After you have spoken, it will be our decision to lay down the penalty on each of our family rapists. My stepfather sent me to hell, but I'm back to deal with him. I know the pain you went through."

"Well?" said Petra. "I'm glad you're the strongest of us," Faith recited. Petra hugged Stanley and gave him a reassuring smile.

Stanley forced a smile before he took the stand. Pressing his right palm against his chest, tears rolled down his white pale face. Petra got up from her seat and put her arm around him. "Stan, you tell us when you're ready." He nodded.

"Just know this Stan, you're not alone," said Jenny.

As Stanley looked at Petra, she said, "We are here for the same reason. Please Stanley, start when you're ready and do take your time. We have at least two hours before my Grandma comes home."

Stanley wiped away sweat and tears with his cap and smiled. "I don't know my natural father. I have never met him. My mother told me that they divorced a couple of months before my birth. Four months later Mum met my stepfather at his daughter Caroline's wedding party. He and Mum's eyes met. He eyed her up, she smiled. He asked her to dance. She then mingled with some friends, but when walking to her table, their eyes met again. He showed her an inviting smile before beckoning her to sit next to him. Mum said she smiled and ignored him at first, but he came to her, held her hand and said proudly, "I couldn't keep my eyes off you." Mum said she smiled and he took her from the wedding party to his gallery to show her his paintings. She said most of the paintings were done by his daughter Caroline's mother when she was alive.

"Mum said she wasn't really interested in him, but at the same time she did not want to hurt his feelings by not excepting his invitation when he offered to escort her to his gallery, so she went with him. He is at least fourteen years older than Mum. This is why I think she wasn't interested in him and especially because he's a judge. Mum said after that evening he asked her out for dinner, which she accepted and many times after that. They went to dinners as well as travelling abroad and visiting places together. They went to the theatre, went dancing and to so many more functions. Mum developed a taste for going out with him to expensive parties and dinners and their friendship grew stronger. She eventually fell in love with him. Eight months later he proposed to her and they were married in the tenth month. I was five months old then.

Two weeks ago I saw him playing with himself. I told Mum that I didn't like him, but she asked me to give him a chance and that I would get to like him. I asked her why she had married him. She told me that his first wife had died in a car accident. Then she asked why I had waited until now to decide not to like him. I told her that I would like to know my real dad. Well she said, he was a gambler, a thief and a two-timing rat and I must not ask her about him again. By then my stepfather had shown up and he smiled as he winked.

"Anyway, I became very suspicious of him, as every time I had a shower he would want something from the bathroom. When I didn't let him in, he would be waiting by the door until I came out. He would have a white bath towel to give to me like a sign, even though I had my own. I would take the bath towel from him as a son to a father and I'd wrap his towel over mine just so he would go away.

"There was one time when Mum was downstairs and I had just got out of the bath. That time he wasn't anywhere to be seen. I thought he was out, as Mum said he'd rung to say he would be home late. But when I went to my room, I was so shocked to see him sitting on my bed. He pulled the towel from around me and smiled widely. His deep sunken eyes were focused on the lower part of my body. As I asked him to leave my room, he carried on smiling. He didn't want to make a sound. I turned to leave. He grabbed my left hand, smiled and then touched my bottom. I called out to Mum, that's when he let go of my hand. I ran to the bathroom, got dressed quickly and I was out of the house faster than lightning. I heard Mum calling me but I ran faster.

"That evening when I got home, Mum asked me where I had gone. I told her to the cinema with friends. Then Mum shouted upstairs to my stepfather telling him I'd come home and there was no need for him to go looking for me. He came downstairs and looked at me, then said that I should let Mum know where I am going in future. Mum went outside. I was going upstairs and the next thing I knew he felt my bottom. I punched him in the face and ran outside to meet Mum talking to our neighbour Mrs Slater. Mum told me to get in the house. I went in to see the bastard grinning before he went upstairs. Mum came in shortly and said supper was ready. She called him to come down.

"As I sat down at the table, he came and sat next to me. As Mum was putting the food on the table he was squeezing my left leg in different places up to my groin. I stabbed his hand with my fork. As Mum went into the kitchen to get the wine, I told him that if he ever touched me again I would tell Mum he raped me. He laughed, tapped me on my leg then dropped the fork and asked me to pick it up. By this time Mum was sitting at the table. As I had refused to pick the fork up he asked me again, please pick the fork up. I looked at Mum and then at him. His smiling made me realise he had dropped the fork deliberately, anyway, I bent down to pick the fork up, and I saw his dick sticking out of his trousers. It was stiff. I shuddered. I gave him the fork and pretended that I saw nothing. Mum said thanks and then she went and got him another. I wanted so much to tell Mum what her bastard husband had done to me, but somehow, as I looked her in her face, the words got stuck in my throat and no matter how hard I tried to tell her, I just could not.

"The following Tuesday night Mum went to babysit for my Aunt Marjorie again as the usual babysitter had flu. The rain poured down bringing darkness with thunder and lightning. I didn't like to be left in the house with him since he showed me what he was; I felt so scared, alone and uncomfortable. As I kept silent in bed listening to the rain, I heard the howling wind as my window was partly open. Then the son of a bitch came racing in my head before I heard a knock on my door. I jumped from fright and began shivering.

"It's me," he said. I kept quiet pretending I was asleep. He said from outside, "I'm so very sorry and ashamed of what I have done to you. Please let me in. From this day forward I'll be the best father to you. I will not make you feel uncomfortable again."

"Well you have said what you want, so you can leave now," I told him. He cleared his throat. "If ever I get too close to you, you tell your mother or anyone," he said.

"Remembering what he had done to me, fear took over. I stared at the door with the intention not to let the bastard in, but as he sounded so convincing, I believed him and opened the door. "You okay?" he asked. I looked at him. He smiled standing at the head of my bed with one hand down his tracksuit, and then an evil smile came over his face. I will never forget that smile. He then shadowed over me. I felt as if my whole body had crumbled. Shivering, I remember the horrific pain he inflicted on me; I was so frightened.

I pulled the sheet over my head. Sweat instantly covered me as I felt him sit on my bed. I could not think of anything to do, but cried "Oh gosh! No!"

"He pulled the cover off me with one tug. He was only wearing a black string vest and his tracksuit bottoms were on the floor. His dick was hard. I jumped out of the bed and tried to run, but he grabbed me and flung me back onto the bed. I kicked and punched him in his face, busting his nose. As the blood came, he grabbed me. I struggled with him to get free, but he was too strong for me. I screamed, he grabbed my throat, ruffled me on my belly, pushing my face down between the pillows making it hard for me to breathe. I must have been dazed after he punched the side of my head. The next thing I knew was I felt his heavy weight and a hard push up my bottom. I cried out to him begging him to stop. But the harder he pushed up me the stronger he was breathing out his alcoholic breath on my neck. The pain was excruciating. It was like a screwdriver ripping into me.

"I had to tell Mum a hooded man had raped me as the brute left me in so much pain. She did not believe me. Instead, she slapped me around the face and said I was telling lies. For her to take me seriously I told her that I was going to the police. Her son of a bitch husband put me in hospital. I hate that bastard so much that it would be a pleasure to kill him for hurting me."

Stanley broke down in tears. Petra comforted him before he took his seat.

"Now Liz," Petra said. "Would you please take your stand and tell us the truth about what happened to you. As I said, it will be our decision to lay down our laws after we've heard your story."

Elizabeth stood up and swallowed deeply before moving into the centre of the room to take the stand.

She faced Petra, Faith, Jenny and Stanley and grinned emotionally then breathed out deeply, wiping tears from her eyes before telling her story.

"One sunny Monday afternoon, August 16th, my best friend Yvonne called for me to go with her to the four o'clock matinee. As I was upstairs in my room getting dressed, my father told her that I'd already left. As I heard what he said to my friend, I rushed downstairs, but she'd gone. I looked out of the kitchen window to see her getting into her brother's car. I ran out after her barefoot, but her brother had driven off. I went back into the house and put my shoes on. I then asked my mother for some money, but she didn't reply. Dad said, "She's drunk." He was right. She was dead drunk. Well, as I took her purse out of her shopping bag to take some money out, my dad pulled the purse away and hit me across my face. He then called me a thief. I raised my hand to hit him back, but he knocked me to the floor with a heavy blow to my chest then fucked me right beside my drunken mother. Can you believe that my own dad, who is a social worker, fucked me and took away my virginity?"

Elizabeth burst out crying. Petra comforted her and gave her a tissue to dry her eyes. As Elizabeth sat down, Petra asked Faith to take the stand.

Faith also forced a smile saying, "I'm fifteen years old now. My nightmare began when I was fourteen and a half. Anyway, last year on Christmas Eve night, I went to take presents for Aunt Laura, who is my mother's sister, my step uncle Charles and my cousin Daniel. I was happy taking part in the celebrations, eating peanuts and drinking coke. Suddenly, my mother rang and told Aunt Laura that my father was on his way to take me home. This news left me angry and unhappy, but I was very careful not to let Aunt Laura see it. Aunt Laura looked at the clock when we heard the doorbell ring. She answered the door and walked into the living room with my father. "Well," Aunt Laura said to him, "You lost no time getting here." My dad smiled and said he came early, as he wanted to get off the road before the drunkards left the pubs. Aunt Laura smiled then said, "My sister rang to say you would be here in ten minutes and ten minutes exactly you're here." Smiling, he said to Aunt Laura, "I've come to get Faith. I hope you've no objection?" Aunt Laura said that she had no objection at all. Aunt Laura looked at me and said, "Faith your dad has come to take you home."

"I turned to dad and told him how happy I was to be taking part in decorating my Aunt's Christmas tree and helping to wrap the presents. He smiled. "Can I spend the night here, and you can come and get me in the morning?" I asked. "No", he said, "Your mother would like you to come home. There will be other nights you can spend with your Aunt." Aunt Laura looked at him; I wanted to cry but I didn't. Then Aunt Laura turned and looked at me. I said nothing. Then my dad told her that I had to be home to open my presents as I always did every Christmas morning. Aunt Laura's face turned sad. She looked at me and raised her shoulders smiling. She gave me my present and one for Mum. I said thank you and kissed her goodbye, and then said goodbye to my cousin and step uncle. As I walked out of my aunt's house, my dad took my hand into his. My blood ran cold followed by the most sickly and horrible feeling. As we got to his car, he let go of my hand. As I was getting in the back, he opened the front door saying, "I'm your dad, do you think that I will bite you if you sit in the front with me?" I forced a smile and sat next to him. As Aunt Laura was standing at her front door I waved goodbye. As my dad drove away my aunt closed the door.

"My dad drove some distance away then I caught him looking at me very strangely. I felt very frightened and tense; I had the feeling he was up to no good. He looked at me again. I wanted so much to punch him in the eyes and jump out of his car. Anyway, he drove us to some derelict place that I don't think I could identify. He groped my breasts before he fucked me in the car while holding a knife to my throat. He left me feeling so dirty and sickened that I'd have knocked his fucking head on the steering wheel cutting his forehead if I could. I wanted to grab the wheel so we would crash, killing us, but I told myself I would kill him and enjoy doing so. My friends, I will never forget that night. I wanted so much to end my life. When he saw blood running down my legs, he pulled out a handful of tissues from the box on his dashboard, flung them on my lap and told me to clean myself as if I was one of his pick-up whores and I had offered."

Stanley, Elizabeth and Faith's faces were saturated with tears. Petra swallowed deeply as though she had a lump in her throat. Before she asked Jenny to take the stand, she gave her a tissue to dry her tears. Jenny closed and opened her eyes in a disgusting expression. The room went silent, and then Petra asked Jenny to take the stand.

Jenny wiped her tears, forced a grin then covered her mouth with her palm. Petra went to her and said, "Jenny, my friend, we listened to our friends Stanley, Liz and Faith. It leaves you and me to tell ours. Are you ready?"

Jenny shook her head smiling then began. "My Uncle Keith..." She started to cry. Petra went to her and said, "I know what you have been through Jenny, we've all been viciously robbed of our virginity by our evil families. We're here to tell what happened, so that we can set a nasty punishment for our disgusting bastard rapist parents. So please Jenny my friend, we would like to hear your story. It does not matter how nasty or painful it is. Remember those animals are on trial. We can only carry out sentences according to their crimes."

"You're right Petra," Jenny said, then she gladly continued. "Four months ago, 17th August, I was just about to go to the school disco with three friends when my Uncle Keith came to see my Mum. Both my Mum and my dad were out visiting friends. He looked at me strangely with those fiery, piercing looking eyes as if I was lying. He grinned fiercely sending the shivers up me. I had to convince him that Mum and dad went out every Wednesday evening to play bingo and had a meal afterwards. "Well," he said, "I'm here to borrow twenty pounds."

"Uncle Keith," I said, "My parents are not at home, but I can lend you twenty pounds." During the time I was speaking to him, he was standing at the kitchen door. I was giving him the money, but he stood staring at me. I asked him again if he wanted the money. He did not answer. He touched my dress and left a dirty mark, and as the dress was light pink it showed clearly. I went and got changed into a pair of jeans and a dark blue blouse. As I was coming out of my bedroom, I was shocked to see my uncle outside the door with that stupid grin on his face. I tried walking past him, but he pushed me back into my room. I was petrified, as I knew he was drugged up. "If you really need the money, I'll give it to you," I said. He laughed loudly as his cold-looking drugged eyes were assessing my body. Thinking I would get rid of him, I gave him thirty pounds from my birthday money I was saving to buy a new computer. He grabbed the money out of my hands and shoved it in his jeans pocket. "Well, I'll see you," I told him, but as I passed him at the door he grabbed the back of my hair and forced me to kneel until I was on my knees facing directly towards his jeans fly. He unzipped his jeans and pushed my face into his crotch. If that wasn't enough, he held a knife to my left eye. I was crying, "Please uncle, please uncle don't do this to me." He laughed hilariously and moved the knife from my eyes to the tip of my neck. He pulled his dick out of his boxer shorts with the other hand and told me to suck it just like his woman does. Tears were rolling down my face like the Niagara Falls. I was drowning in my own tears and my own screams were starting to sicken me. I could not believe my own uncle was doing this to me. I kept thinking why me or why him! As I refused to suck his dick, he pierced my neck with his knife; I thought he was going to slit my throat. He kept saying, "Do it." As he was digging his knife deeper into my neck, he didn't move it from my neck until my lips were fully around his dick."

Jenny paused from telling her story as she wiped her lips in disgust, sniffed the snot back up her nose and spat the phlegm out of her mouth in the tissue. She continued speaking. "He said he had more respect for me so he wasn't gonna cum in my mouth. I felt like a cheap inexperienced whore who had just been pulled off Hagley Road." Jenny smiled trying her hardest to hold her tears back, and then she continued her story. "He threw me on the floor and told me I should be ashamed of myself and what I had just done. As I watched, his eyes dimmed to a change of shame. He asked me if I knew how much my mother would be hurt if he told her I had seduced him. The way he said it, it was like I offered or encouraged him. As I was screaming, he put his right hand over my mouth to dampen my screams and pushed me to the floor. He then held me by my throat before he thrust his hard cock into me until my insides were feeling sore. I felt paralysed, the bottom half of my body was left numb. He pulled out of me and I thought it was all over, but then he climbed further up me and pinned my arms down with his knees. He put his dick in my face and started masturbating until white stuff dripped all over my face and chest. Then laughing, he had the nerves of the devil to say thanks for the cash and maybe next time, when he returns my money, he will let me go on top! Then he left still laughing like a crowing cock." Jenny cried bitterly then went to her seat.

"Well friends," Petra said smiling as she looked at her friends, Stanley, Faith, Elizabeth and Jenny. She put her arms around Jenny's shoulders smiling saying, "Just like the four of you, my stepfather raped me. When he should be guiding me in the right direction, instead, he took advantage of me, tore me apart and wanted to mould me into his whore. I cried bitterly about what he put me through. He left me feeling so ashamed and feeling dirty. I swear to God and myself the time would come when he would pay! My friends, now is the time! Before I say anymore, I must begin. Well, this is what my evil stepfather has done to me.

"My stepfather raped me three times, once when my Mum and my brother went to visit my Grandma, the second time was when I got home from school, and the third when I got home from netball and met him alone. The cunning bastard grabbed my hand the next evening and I slapped his face. Mum was walking past my room when she saw him feeling his face. She looked at him and went to her room. The bastard crept into my room saying that my mother would be annoyed with me if she knew I had been to bed with him. My brother overheard him and threatened to kill him if he didn't leave me alone. Well the bastard then told my mother that I tried to kiss him and he had warned me to keep away from him. My mother believed him and she gave me the worst beating. I was trying to tell her that he raped me three times, but she didn't even give me a chance. She slapped my face as she beat me and called me a slut.

"I was so shocked to know that my mother had left the opening for the son of a bitch to have me when he wanted. Well, I shouldn't expect anything better from her as she left my real dad and took in that bastard after he showed her a few pounds. Dad didn't have the money for her flashy lifestyle. That creepy bastard tempted her with expensive clothes, shoes, perfumes and jewellery from drugs money. Well, my real dad's only a carpenter. I didn't really want her and my dad to separate; it hurt me when they did. However, that's another story.

"Well, as my mother did believe her evil bastard husband that I'd tried to kiss him, she sent me to my room that evening without dinner or speaking to me. The following morning, she forbade me to eat at the table with them or at any time until I had learned to respect her bastard husband. She stopped washing my clothes, giving me pocket money and stopped my friends coming to the house. This made the bastard so very happy that he offered me money several times, but I refused every time. My brother Arden would share his money with me to help as I needed to buy Tampax, deodorants and chewing gum. Whenever I tried to speak to my mother, she would avoid me. Mother and I are not close any more."

"So my friends, should we become fuckpots to our rapist families? Well, I don't think we should. If we don't put a definite stop to these animals that they are, we will definitely become their fucked pots and maybe end up with pups for the bastards. Incidentally, I wouldn't wish for any other young person to be used like we were. How can our own families take advantage of us? Rapist families are so cleverly cunning, vicious and undetected. They let other members of their family see them as loyal and not as abusers. Well people, see their outside appearance and think that they're human, but we know better. This is why they should be permanently put down like aggressive animals. We have to stop them! So, it's up to us! Raise your hands if they're to be forgiven and allowed to go on taking advantage. So my friends, if they should be punished keep your hands down." When Petra saw no hand was raised she smiled and said, "Thank you. We should meet here again for our final meeting". She proposed they meet on Tuesday in two weeks at five o'clock when her Grandma would be at her charity meeting. Her friends Stanley, Jenny, Faith and Elizabeth agreed and Petra ended the meeting and they went home.

Two weeks later the Tuesday evening at five o'clock Petra and her friends had their final meeting at her Grandma's house. Stanley said to them, "I will ask my friend Martin to get what we need from his father's chemist."

Petra looked at him with excitement and smiled before she said, "The four of us would be so appreciative."

Their final third meeting was brief and cleverly planned.

A week later, on Saturday morning, Stanley asked his friend Martin if it was possible for him to help get some items from his dad's chemist, giving him a list of what he needed. Martin had a good look, passed the list back to Stanley then scratched his neck and shook his head. "I understand," Stanley said.

Martin looked Stanley in the eyes with wonder and told him, "I will try but I can't promise you anything." He took the list back.

Stanley smiled, "I understand," and they both went their separate ways.

The following Sunday lunchtime, Martin went to see Stanley. He met Stanley's mother sweeping her yard tiles.

"Good afternoon Mrs O'Neil."

"Good afternoon Martin. What brings you here?"

"I have come to see Stanley." He looked nervous.

"Well Martin, to say you were looking so happy a second ago and now you're looking very tense. Are you not feeling well?"

"Yes Mrs O'Neil. I'm good. Is Stanley at home?"

"Yes, he is. Go right in."

Martin pushed the door and walked in. "Stanley!" he called.

"Come up to my room."

Martin climbed the stairs to meet Judge O'Neil standing at his bedroom door.

"Good afternoon Mr O'Neil."

"Hello Martin. You should come more often to see Stanley, he sometimes looks depressed and that's not good for a boy of his age," Judge O'Neil laughed.

Martin knocked on Stanley's door. "Come in," Stanley said. Martin opened the door but before he walked in, he looked back at Judge O'Neil to see him still standing on the landing with his arms folded and smiling.

"Close the door," Stanley said.

Martin closed the door. He and Stanley remained silent for a while as they thought Judge O'Neil could be listening outside the door. Then Stanley shouted, "My king took over your queen," and they laughed. Judge O'Neil tiptoed away from Stanley's door. As Stanley heard his car start, he went into his mother's room, looked out of the window to see him driving through the gate. He went back to Martin. "Do you think you could get what I asked for?"

"I'm sorry Stan." Martin got off the bed and turned to walk out of the room. Getting to the door he looked back at Stanley.

"We need those items to use on our rapist families because they robbed us of our youth."

Martin faced Stanley and said, "My stepfather has raped my sister Kay at least five times that I know of. She cried for me to help and I couldn't do anything to help her. When I approached him he knocked me down, told me not to interfere and broke my nose. As my sister asked me not to say anything, I lied to Mum that I was in a fight when she asked what happened to my face and she took me to the hospital. My sister was just fourteen years old then, but she's going on sixteen and our stepfather is still blackmailing her by telling her he will let everyone know that she sleeps with him if she refuses him. Stanley, I'll get what you need." Martin sobbed. Tears came into Stanley's eyes as he said, "We'll get your stepfather out of your sister's life, but I thought he was your dad?"

On the Saturday night a week later, Martin went into his stepfather's chemist whilst he was at the casino and got what Stanley had asked for. As he was giving Stanley the items, he said to him, "I want my stepfather out of the way."

"Martin, we will do that for you, but you have to swear to us that you'll keep silent no matter what."

"I swear to you Stanley, on mine and my sister's lives that I shall never tell anyone about us," Martin said.

"Us?" Stanley asked looking puzzled.

"I want to join you five. I want to watch my stepfather's wicked face cringe with pain like he put my sister through."

Martin smiled with contentment. Stanley hugged him. Joyously, Stanley and Martin sealed their friendship with a handshake then Martin said, "I shall never tell a soul about what we are going to do to our rapist families."

Stanley smiled.

Martin sat on the bed and said, "Stan, I want him dead or badly crippled so that he can't hurt my sister again. In fact, if he's not dead, I want him to be worse than senile so that he won't be able to recognise he's living. But I'd rather him dead, and in the worst way. I want to hear the bastard beg to end his life."

"Martin, I understand what you're saying but I think you should leave it to us," Stanley said.

"Well, I really would like him to suffer and to let him know the cause for his execution before he died. I would like to tell him he will never be in a state to interfere with my sister again," Martin said.

Stanley agreed with Martin and Martin swore to keep Stanley and his friends' secret to himself. Sighing with relief, Martin shook Stanley's hand once again. After Martin left, Stanley phoned Petra, but Officer Forbes answered. Stanley breathed out heavily and stayed silent with the phone to his ears.

"Who's this?" Forbes asked. Stanley remained silent. Forbes shouted down the phone, "Who the hell are you? If you can't say, get the hell off the phone and don't phone my house again." He banged the phone down and went to Petra shouting, "Tell your friends never to ring my house phone again."

Petra hissed through her teeth, walking away. "You tell your blasted friends not to phone here again." Petra looked back at him. He blew her a kiss and smiled.

Petra had the feeling Stanley had phoned, so she went to see him. "I phoned you but your dad answered. I said nothing though."

"Stanley, he's not my dad as you know and he'll never be. You know how much I despise the bastard. So never link me to him again, ever!"

"You're right Pet. However, Martin's got all we need and everything seems to be okay."

"Thanks Stanley, you are making me feel so happy now."

"I'm happy too Petra."

Stanley showed the items to Petra.

"Stanley, I think you should put them in a safe place out of sight until tomorrow night."

"Okay."

Petra left. Stanley hid the chemist bag containing the items behind his wardrobe.

The Monday morning before Stanley left for school, he kissed his mother and his stepfather goodbye. His stepfather had a bright and happy smile on his face. Stanley met Petra outside her gate and told her that they should operate on the five of their family, one at a time but in the same week. Petra thought deeply and said to Stanley, "You should leave everything to me."

Stanley agreed. He went to school feeling happy.

That Monday afternoon during break time, Petra told Stanley, Faith, Elizabeth and Jenny, "We'll operate on my stepfather first as he's the police."

They agreed. Then Faith said, "What do you know about operating?" Petra replied, "I learnt from the internet and you'll learn from me."

After school, Petra told her friends that they all needed to act normally. She then set the time for six thirty that same evening for them to carry out their task on her stepfather as her mother would be at work.

Petra phoned Stanley telling him to give Jenny, Liz and Faith a call and to meet at her house. Stanley did just that and he and the others went to Petra's. As she saw them walking through the gate, she opened the front door and let them in. She led them into the lounge and told them to be very quiet so as not to disturb her sleeping stepfather who was on night shift. After they delivered the items they left.

The following night Petra's mother rang her while at work. "Tell your father I will be going to my mother's after work and I don't think I'll make it home to see him off to work." Petra was more than happy to know her plan was falling into place. She didn't give Forbes the message as she had planned his execution that evening.

Petra played her favourite song, I Will Survive.

"She called her friends telling them, "You must be here by eight thirty sharp"."

"We will Petra," Liz said.

Meanwhile, Mrs Forbes and her mother were having a meal. After they had eaten, she kissed her mother goodnight, ready to leave when her mother said, "Ann, would you mind changing a bulb on the stairway please?"

"Okay Mum."

"Thank you dear."

After changing the bulb, she asked her mother if there was anything else she needed before she left. Then she asked her, "What about your cake, don't you want it?"

"No Ann my dear. I really have to be careful what I eat lately."

That evening Stanley phoned for Jenny, Faith and Liz. He asked them to meet him outside Petra's house. When they got there and rang the doorbell, she let them in and checked to see if what she needed was there. Petra left her friends in the dining room with the lights off and went to her stepfather's room to find him not there. "Shit," she said.

She went down to her friends and said, "The bastard must have slipped out when I was on the phone talking to Mum."

Forbes was in fact drinking with friends at the Red Lion pub.

"Shit, shit, shit!" retorted Petra, but before she sent her friends home she told them, "I'll be in touch so we can decide our next move."

Chapter 4

One week later, Tuesday night, Stanley and his friends made plans to carry out the amputation on Judge O'Neil. Stanley rang Petra telling her, "My stepfather has taken the week off work to go to Spain to see relatives. Instead, I want them to visit him in his coffin."

Petra smiled, "I know what you mean Stan, but we have to move very carefully."

"I understand," said Stanley.

Petra put the phone down.

Late that Tuesday evening, Stanley's mother went socialising with friends leaving a note saying that she would be home late. Stanley went to Petra and told her. After leaving Petra he went home to meet his stepfather sitting at the kitchen table drinking vodka. "So, you decide to come home now," his stepfather said.

Stanley looked at the clock. "I'm sorry. Mum said your supper is in the oven."

"Would you mind putting it in the microwave for me?"

Stanley looked disgustingly at him before putting the food in the microwave. "Are you going to sit and watch me eat?"

"I have to go and do my homework."

Judge O'Neil smiled as he watched Stanley leave the kitchen. He ate his supper and left the house without telling Stanley.

Later that evening it was raining heavily. Stanley fell asleep over his homework and woke up when he heard the front door shut with a bang. Rubbing his eyes, he left his room and stood on the landing looking down. As he saw Judge O'Neil coming up the stairs, he rushed downstairs to make himself a cup of hot chocolate as he'd intended to do earlier. His stepfather followed him to the kitchen. Stanley boiled the kettle. Judge O'Neil stared. "Is that a brew?"

"Yes, would you like one?" Stanley asked.

"Oh yes, if you are making."

Stanley took a small bottle of liquid out of his trouser pocket, emptied it into the cup and mixed it with the coffee. "Are you taking a shower?" Stanley asked.

"Oh yes, I think I should." Judge O'Neil left to go to his bedroom. "I'll bring it up to you in a minute and leave it on your bedside cabinet," Stanley said.

"Bring it up and I'll drink it now," the judge said, and he waited in his room sitting on his bed in his birthday suit. Stanley was so shocked that it caused him to spill some of the coffee. Judge O'Neil took the coffee and drank some. Licking his lips, he stared at Stanley with confusion. Sipping more coffee, he licked his lips again, looking more confused. He took another drink and mumbled, "This tastes a bit sweet, but it's not a sugary taste, it's smooth, sort of creamy nearly to the bottom." He leant back tipping on his right side and sprawling on the bed face upright, the ceiling spinning and room going around. "What's happening?" he groaned. He slowly realised what Stanley was doing to him.

When he was almost in a coma, Stanley read him his rights and left him asleep before he went to his room smiling.

Later that night, when Judge O'Neil woke out of his deep sleep, he went to Stanley's room and asked him, "What did you give me to drink?"

"Just some coffee liquor. I had some and I fell asleep after we did it. You know what I mean."

"Well, I can't remember."

"That's because you fell asleep as we were groggy."

"I still can't remember any of that." He smiled and went to his room feeling confused.

The following afternoon, Stanley got home from school to meet his stepfather alone. Stanley became paranoid and went to his room. Judge O'Neil knocked on his door and opened it at the same time. "I didn't tell anyone about us. Please go away."

O'Neil smiled. "I would like you to see what I have bought for your mother. But you'll have to come to my room."

Stanley followed him and stood outside the door. "Come in son, I won't do anything to you. I only want you to see what I've bought."

The judge moved further into the room. Stanley moved in but stood near the door. O'Neil showed him a diamond bracelet. "Do you think your Mum will like it?"

Stanley nodded.

"I'm doing all this for you."

Stanley gave him a nasty look and left the house, but when he returned home he went to his room and turned the lights on, and saw his stepfather lying on his bed. "What you doing in my bed?" he said.

"Turn the lights off and lie next to me," O'Neil said and moved to the other side of the bed, making room and patting the bed. Stanley sat on the edge of his bed.

"I'm starving," O'Neil said.

"You're still hungry after eating your supper?"

"Not for food, honey."

"Don't call me honey," Stanley shouted angrily.

"I thought we'd become lovers?"

"You thought wrong! I only wanted to be your son."

He touched Stanley's leg.

"Don't touch me. If you touch me again…"

"You'll do what? You will kill me, take me to court and have me put in jail?" Judge O'Neil laughed. "Look Stanley, I've had younger than you and I set them free in exchange. What I mean is that you'll soon get as used to me as the others."

"Why did you marry Mum when you know you're attracted to men?"

"Son, you're very bright. I love your Mum. I also love men as I get more enjoyment."

Stanley stared at him. "Oh, I was referring to young men like you," he said.

"What kind of man are you? How can you use young defenceless boys like me?"

"You're different, but the others are animals. As I said, I free them and they serve me well. Well enough of this. You won't feel any more pain as you're matured to sexual intercourse by now, having done it twice." He laughed.

An angry expression showed on Stanley's face.

"I love you, Stan."

"You're out of your fucking evil mind. I have loved and respected you as a dad, but now you are nothing but a pile of stale shit. The respect I had for you is long gone and forgotten. My mother will know about you and what you've done to me."

Judge O'Neil laughed. "Have you ever heard about frog style? Well you say anything to your mother or anyone else and you'll be serving tosses in prison frog style."

"Fuck you!" Stanley shouted at him and moved to the door.

O'Neil got off his bed and grabbed Stanley by his shirt collar saying, "You little tosser, not even your mother would believe anything you tell her about me. She told me she despised you. I'm the one who stopped your mother from putting you into a home. Your mother was willing to post you off to some faraway school."

"I would have been better off if she'd sent me. At least I wouldn't have been destroyed by you."

O'Neil reached out and touched Stanley's bottom. Stanley kicked him in the face, ran down to the kitchen and took one of his mother's vegetable knives from the draw. He raced back upstairs in anger and raised the knife to O'Neil's chest saying, "I'll kill you." But, remembering he'd left the back door open for Petra, Liz and Jenny to sneak in and go to the spare room and hide, he put the knife down and walked out. Judge O'Neil watched as Stanley left the room leaving the door open. "You little shit!" he said.

Stanley smiled and went back to him saying, "You know what? You're right. I love you but I'm still angry with you for taking me without consent. But I'm okay now and we should go to your room."

"Do you mean that Stanley?"

"Well, you don't have to if you don't want. I can always turn to someone else who would appreciate my body. I thought being that you were my first, I could get to like you and keep it in the family without Mum knowing. But it's up to you now, as I won't ask you a second time. Well, I will be in my room instead if you change your mind."

Stanley left him smiling and went quickly to the spare room to see his friends standing in the walk-in wardrobe before getting into his bedroom. Meanwhile Judge O'Neil had a large shot of vodka before he followed Stanley to his room.

Stanley looked at him with his hand down his trousers playing with his penis until it was stiff, then he dropped his trousers at his feet, grinning.

Stanley sat on the bed. He put one hand around Stanley's shoulder, masturbating with the other. "I only want you to give me a blow job," he said and stood facing Stanley telling him, "Down on your knees." He moved his hand from his penis and relaxed looking down into Stanley's face smirking. Stanley turned his face away then faced him showing a pretend smile.

"I'm going for a drink of water as I feel thirsty," Stanley told him. "I'll get it for you, you relax until I get back," he said to Stanley.

Happily O'Neil left and in seconds he was back with a glass of water for Stanley.

"Thanks."

He kissed Stanley on the lips and slipped in bed under the quilt smiling. "Wouldn't you like us to be in my room?"

"Dad, I would feel more comfortable if we move to the spare room."

"I agree."

As Stanley and O'Neil left his room, Stanley rushed to the spare room to see his friends quietly hiding. "I will cough to tell you when," he whispered.

O'Neil then walked leisurely into the spare room. Stanley turned his back on him. O'Neil got undressed down to his waist. He drank another shot of vodka and told Stanley, "I want you on your knees." Stanley coughed. Petra, Jenny, Liz and Faith burst out of the walk-in wardrobe. Judge O'Neil was in shock, staring at Stanley and his friends.

"Aren't you amused, Dad?" Jenny said.

"You little bastard!"

Liz stabbed the judge in the neck with a general anaesthetic and made him fall asleep in seconds. Then Stanley chopped three of the judge's fingers off from his left hand, slit the tip of his tongue and hocked his penis off with a Stanley knife. Then he and Petra took pleasure in wrapping the lifeless judge's body in a sheet, dragging him downstairs and bundling him in his car. "Stan, you stay here," Petra told him and she drove the car down the road while her friends washed their hands with their gloves on. When Petra returned, Stanley embraced her as he did with Elizabeth, Faith and Jenny before he saw them out. He smiled and sat at the kitchen table and waited for his mother to come home.

An hour later, his mother arrived home and met him eating a slice of cake and drinking a glass of cold milk in the kitchen.

"Hi Mum."

"Hello son." She looked in the living room and went back to Stanley.

"Where's your father?"

"I don't know."

"It's not like your father to be out at this time."

"Well, he didn't phone to say anything."

Mrs O'Neil was thinking about her husband. She rubbed her forehead staring at Stanley. Stanley smiled, "Oh," she said and reached in her handbag for some aspirins and swallowed two with some of Stanley's milk.

"You sure your father didn't phone?"

"I'm sure Mum." Stanley moved to the living room leaving the unfinished milk on the table. His mother swallowed more milk and poured the remainder down the sink and washed the glass. She then took a bottle of gin from the mini bar and filled two glasses and took them up to her bedroom where she planned to wait for her husband to come home. She placed one of the glasses on the banister outside her bedroom door, then she opened the door and turned the lights on with one hand. She turned back to the banister and reached for the glass and placed both on her cabinet. She then went and had a shower. Petra rang Stanley. "Everything is okay," she said. Stanley smiled.

His mother returned to her room waiting for her husband. She rang him on his mobile and got no answer. She rang him again. "Come on Basil, answer me," she said frustrated. She drank the two glasses of gin and fell into a dozed sleep.

When she woke, she saw that the time was approaching ten to ten. She got out of bed and paced the room. Stanley knew that this was the right time to go to his mother. He ran upstairs and first went into the spare room and had a good look around to see if his friends had left any incriminating evidence. Everything was in place as they had all been wearing gloves, but he still took time to clean the walk-in wardrobe with soapy water and furniture polish before he went to see how his mother was. He sat with her and turned his face away so she couldn't see him smiling. Then he looked seriously at his mother saying, "I wonder where dad's got to."

The front doorbell rang loudly.

Mrs O'Neil answered the door. Three police officers were standing on the doorstep.

"Mrs O'Neil, it's about your husband."

"What about him?"

"We found him in his car. We think he may have been murdered but we can't rule out anything for sure at the moment."

Mrs O'Neil screamed out.

Stanley went to her. "Mum, I heard you screaming. What's wrong?"

She stared in Stanley's face, crying. Stanley ran to the bathroom, got her a large piece of toilet tissue and gave it to her saying, "Wipe your nose Mum." His mother took the tissue, tossed it on the floor and wiped her nose on her blouse. The police took Mrs O'Neil and Stanley to identify her husband's body. As she saw his naked body covered in blood, she hugged her husband and never wanting to let him go. Two police officers took her away.

"Mum, we should get home as you need to change your clothes." His mother stood facing him with her mouth wide open and her face saturated in tears with snot running out of her nose and her bottom lip trembling.

"Mum, we should go home."

"My husband's dead!" she shouted. "Someone has murdered your father, Stanley." She stuttered, getting her words out. "Oh Stan, someone killed your dad."

"No Mum, he probably fucked with the wrong person and they took revenge. He probably raped someone..." Stanley paused as he realised what he said.

His mother looked at him in a trance way and asked, "What do you mean when you said he probably raped someone? Stanley, are you trying to tell me your father was a rapist?"

"No Mum," Stanley said. "I meant he must have messed with someone and they killed him. He tried to do it to me."

His mother pulled him away from the police. "You're a damn liar and I don't want this to get out. Do you hear me? I don't want you to breathe a word about what you told me to anyone. Tell me Stanley, did you do this to your father?"

"No Mum. But what he had done to me, I hated him. He was the one who molested me and I lied to you about a hooded man." Stanley broke down crying and hugged his mother whilst smiling behind her back.

After Stanley's mother took her arms from around him, Superintendent Peterson said to her, "A driver found him naked in his car. He was dead when we got to him. I'm so sorry." Superintendent Peterson took her and Stanley home.

Mrs O'Neil cried all the time.

"Someone has done a nasty job on the judge," the superintendent said to his fellow officers.

"They sure did, yes," Officer Melbourne said. "They murdered him in the worst way I've seen in a long time. In fact, in my thirty-two years working in the force, I haven't seen a mess like this."

"Why? What has the judge done to end up dead with his fucking dick in his mouth? What the hell is happening with this sickening world of people? What has he done to end up like he has? Someone did not agree with the way he tried their case. So they made sure they put him out of their fucking case for life."

"Super, the way he was killed, do you think it was an act of revenge?"

"Possible, Officer Melbourne, quite possible. But I tell you this, when I catch the son of a bitch, their arse belongs to me," the superintendent said very angrily.

Forensics taped around the car and blocked off the road after taking pictures of the body.

"Well Super, we have a difficult fight on our hands," Officer Melbourne said.

"These bastards who have done this are maniacs and we have to stop them. They must be stopped from killing someone else!"

A few minutes later a coroner came and examined the body. He reported three of O'Neil's middle fingers on his left hand were amputated, the tip of his tongue was slit and he had also been castrated.

"I'm worried," the coroner said. "I've never seen such wicked work before."

"I see what you mean," Superintendent Peterson said.

The ambulance arrived at the murder scene and took Judge O'Neil's body to the morgue. Superintendent Peterson and officers went to Mrs O'Neil and asked, "Is there anything that you or Stanley can tell us that could lead us to your husband's killer?"

"No! Nothing! I can't tell you anything. I mean my husband was an important man. He worked on many cases, but I don't think he had any enemies to that effect."

Superintendent Peterson scratched the left side of his head in thought and said, "Whoever has done this knew exactly what they were doing. I put this down to someone who's in the medical field."

"That I'm agreed with," said Melbourne.

"I think this was done by amateurs who held a grudge. Even so, they had an idea what they were doing. However, I'll make out a full report for the inquest. Well, I must be off. Good night to you sirs," as the coroner looked at his watch and saw how late it was.

"To you too doctor," Superintendent Peterson said, wiping sweat off his face.

Before the coroner left, he took his gloves off and sprayed his hand with antibiotic lotion. Forensics took the car away and moved the tape.

The next morning, four officers including Detective Inspector Hanson and Superintendent Peterson had at least five officers searching both sides of the road and where Judge O'Neil's car was, but they found nothing. Detective Inspector Hanson and Superintendent Peterson took two police officrs with them and went to Mrs O'Neil's house. They asked her if they could search the house inside and around the yard to see what they could find to lead them to Judge O'Neil's killer. Mrs O'Neil nodded her head and the police carried out their search but again, nothing was found. Stanley and his friends had been wearing gloves and plastic on their shoes and had then hidden the items carefully, ready to use on their other rapist family members.

Meanwhile, Mrs O'Neil made a call to Mr Aston, Judge O'Neil's half-brother, to tell him the bad news that his brother had been murdered.

Tears welled up in Mr Aston's eyes before he woke his wife. As she looked at him, he shook his greying head. He sat up in bed with the phone in his hand and said, "Chena dear, Kathleen just rang to say that my brother has been murdered."

"Are you sure that's what she said?" his wife turned lazily facing him.

"I'm quite sure my dear. I have to go to Kathleen now. Will you be all right?"

"Yes, I will. We'll have to let the girls know later, poor Kathleen."

Mrs O'Neil put her phone down and turned to Superintendent Peterson and two of his colleges to see them just leaving with the judge's gloves in a small see-through plastic bag. As Mrs O'Neil stared at Superintendent Peterson, he said, "They will be sent to the lab to be checked for evidence." Mrs O'Neil was still staring in the superintendent's eyes when he took her to one side saying, "Don't upset yourself too much. We'll do whatever it takes to catch his killer."

Just as the superintendent was about to ask Mrs O'Neil some questions, she burst out crying, seeing the criminal investigator carefully take the bag that contained the bloodied sheet from an officer and to his car. But before Officers Baldwin, Mathew and Superintendent Peterson accompanied the criminal investigator, Officer Dennis arrived on the scene and said to Mrs O'Neil, "Mrs O'Neil, I'm so sorry to hear that your husband has been murdered. We shall do our best to find his killer".

"We will call on you the minute we hear anything," the superintendent said.

Mrs O'Neil nodded her head and wiped her nose with the back of her hand.

As Superintendent Peterson, Detective Inspector Hanson and his officers left, Mrs O'Neil burst out crying.

"Who did this to your father Stanley?" As Stanley didn't answer she shouted at him. "I'm talking to you Stanley."

Stanley faced her and stood firm, looking at her as tears rolled down her face. She held on to the bedroom door as she could barely stand up on her own.

"Who the fuck did this to your father?" she stared widely at Stanley.

"He is not my father, I hate him and I always will. He was dirty. How could you let him do this to me! He deserves what he got and to burn, burn in the fire of hell." Stanley hit back at his mother with words.

"How dare you!" she shouted. "After all he had done for you. Rearing you from a baby and giving you his name. Get to your room!"

"Will you be okay, Mum?" he asked.

She didn't answer and just stared at him in a trance. Stanley smiled in her face, she slapped him hard before he went to his room and slammed the door shut behind him making her jump.

Mrs O'Neil phoned Caroline, her stepdaughter. Dillon answered. "Hello."

"Dillon, it's me Kathleen. Can I speak to Caroline?"

"Sure of course, have you been crying?"

Mrs O'Neil blew her nose. "Will you get Caroline now?"

"Kathleen, you sound upset is anything wrong?"

"Dillon, will you please get Caroline for me;"

"Hold on a sec Kathleen I'll go and get her," he left Mrs O'Neil holding the phone and went upstairs to Caroline. Looking at her with a confused expression, she asked, "What's the matter?"

"Your Mum would like to speak to you. Hurry, she sounded serious, like she was crying."

"I'll take it from here." Caroline rushed out of the bath and picked the phone up on the landing.

"Hello Mum."

"Caroline, I came home to find your father dead." Caroline went silent.

"Caroline, are you there?"

"Yes Mum I am. Dillon and I will be with you soon." Caroline went to her husband with the bath towel around her crying. "Dad's dead."

Dillon stared at her before he asked, "Are you sure that's what your Mum said?"

"Of course I'm sure. We need to go to her."

"Well you get some clothes on and get Abby, then we'll go."

Caroline got dressed then fetched Abby out of her room saying, "Honey, we have to go and see Grandma now."

"Why Mum?"

"Something happened to your granddad and your nan needs us. Put your shoes on honey and meet me downstairs."

As soon as Abby was ready her father drove them to Mrs O'Neil to find her sitting in the kitchen in darkness. Caroline turned the lights on.

Mrs O'Neil burst out crying. "Your father's been murdered. I was asked by the police to identify him and then they took him away." Caroline hugged her.

"Mum, is nan going to make tea?" Abby asked.

"Honey, nan is sick. I'll make us something." Caroline touched Mrs O'Neil's shoulder. "Mum, have you and Stanley eaten?"

Mrs O'Neil shook her head. "How can I eat when my husband has been murdered? He was mutilated."

"Mum, you have to eat to keep strong. I'll make us something."

"Caroline, your father was mutilated. His private part was chopped off and rammed down his throat."

Caroline went silent and leaned against the cocktail bar. Tears filled her eyes.

"Honey, you stay with Mum while I order some food." Dillon turned to Mrs O'Neil, "Where's Stanley?"

"I sent him to his room."

"Where was Stanley when dad was murdered?" Caroline asked.

"He claimed he was with friends. The police say that a driver stopped after becoming suspicious when seeing your father's car parked without lights on. He was found with a sheet wrapped around him."

"I don't know what to say. We'll just have to leave everything to the police," Dillon said, before he ordered food for them. Meanwhile, Caroline made tea, but Mrs O'Neil found it difficult to swallow hers.

"Mum, please drink your tea," Caroline said.

"Oh honey, they murdered your father in the worst way. I loved him so much." Abby hugged her nan telling her "Me and Arial love you."

"Mum, would you like us to spend the night with you and Stanley?" Caroline asked.

"No honey, I want to be on my own tonight."

"Are you sure about that Mum?"

"Yes Caroline, I'm quite sure. Stanley and I will be all right. The police have just left and I'm really tired."

"Okay Mum. The food is here, when you've eaten we'll leave, but not before I see you eat and settled down in bed."

Mrs O'Neil ate nearly all her food. Caroline tidied the kitchen and saw her to bed. Abby hugged her nan goodnight."

"Goodnight honey, where's your sister?"

"She's with Aunt Delia. Nan will you be coming to her party, Arial and I would love you to very much."

There was a knock at the door; Caroline answered it. "Hello Uncle Aston." She hugged him and let him in. She led him upstairs to Mrs O'Neil.

He sat beside her and hugged her without saying a word. "Thanks for coming."

"Cat, we're family and we have to be here for each other."

"Uncle, we just ordered some food. Would you like some?"

"No thank you dear, but I'll have some coffee, black with two sugars and I'll rest in the living room until morning."

Caroline took his coffee to him. "Well Mum, we have to leave now as I have to go and get Arial, but I'll be here in the morning after I take them to school. You try and get a good night's sleep."

"I'll try. You give Arial a hug for me."

"Goodnight Mum. I'll go and say goodnight to Stanley before we leave."

Uncle Aston went into the living room. Caroline closed Mrs O'Neil's door on her way out and went to say goodnight to Stanley. "If you and Mum need us, just call no matter what time."

"I will Uncle Dillon."

Dillon drove to Delia's home to fetch Arial. "I phoned you but you didn't answer. I was just about to put Arial to bed."

"Delia, I'm sorry I didn't ring to let you know that I was going to Mums. She rang to tell me that dad has been murdered."

"Dad's been murdered, when and where?"

"Mum said the police called round after they found his naked body in his parked car. He was mutilated." Caroline blew her nose. "It's up to the police now. Arial, your dad and sister are waiting in the car. Kiss your aunt goodnight and let's go."

Arial kissed her aunt and left with her mother.

"Caroline, call me tomorrow and let me know what's happening, will you?"

"Delia, I will, as soon as I know more."

At home Abby asked, "Mum, what's the matter with nan?"

"Honey, your granddad is in heaven with your other nan."

"Is granddad dead?" Arial asked.

"Yes sweetheart, granddad's dead."

"Honey, I'm so sorry about your dad. You see the children to bed then I'll bring you up some coffee," Dillon offered.

After Caroline put the girls to bed, she began crying. Her husband gave her a cup of coffee. Here drink this honey."

Caroline took the coffee and put it on her side table. Her husband hugged her and said, "Honey, I'm so sorry. Your father was a good person."

"Too good that someone hated him so much to kill him, Dillon, who'd hate dad?"

"I don't know. In his line of work, anyone could hate him. Drink your coffee then try and get some sleep. I'll have a look in on the girls to make sure they're okay."

"Dillon, we'll have to postpone Arial's birthday party until all this horrible happenings are over."

Dillon sat beside her, she looked at him, "Oh Dillon."

"Go to sleep Caroline. We'll speak about this in the morning. I know Arial will be fuming, but we'll have to make her understand."

"How can we tell an eight-year-old child that she's not having her birthday party, Dillon? She has already invited her friends. I can't go back on my word; we'll give her her party."

"You're right. Arial will have her party."

The following morning, Arial went to her parents' room. "Good morning daddy."

"Good morning precious."

"Where's Mum?"

"She's gone to the bathroom. Arial, I think you should get back into bed. It's not time to get up yet."

"But I'm not sleepy anymore dad." And just as she sat down by her dad, Abby came running into the room crying, "Mummy!"

"Come on sweetheart, daddy will take you back to your room."

"Let them stay here, Dillon," Caroline said as she walked back into the bedroom.

"Honey, Arial's nearly eight and should be okay sleeping in her own room."

"I know that, but maybe they're a little restless. So please let's leave them till she drops off to sleep. That's all I ask."

"Okay honey. I'll be in the spare room if you need me."

In bed Dillon found it hard to sleep. He went back to his room to see the girls sleeping.

Caroline and her husband then went to the spare room together to sleep.

Mrs O'Neil stayed awake partly through the night crying. After she'd cried for so long, she fell asleep on the bedroom floor and woke up at five thirty in the morning and started crying again. She barely got dressed and drove to Sutton police station without wearing make-up or combing her hair.

"Can I see Superintendent Peterson please?" she asked a policewoman.

The officer took her to a waiting room and asked her to have a seat while she rang the superintendent.

Before the officer spoke to Superintendent Peterson she looked at her watch, then realised the superintendent wouldn't start until six o'clock that morning. The officer went back to the waiting room and informed Mrs O'Neil saying, "I'm sorry. The superintendent is not due in until six. Would you like some tea or coffee while you wait?"

"No, no thank you." Just as the officer introduced herself as Officer Warren, she smiled and then turned to walk away, Superintendent Peterson walked in and saw Mrs O'Neil, he smiled.

"I did not expect you to be here so early. Have you been waiting long?"

"No superintendent, but we need to hurry as I've left Stanley at home alone."

"Of course, would you be kind enough to follow me? We shouldn't be that long, just a few questions."

Officer Warren smiled and Superintendent said, "Thank you Officer Warren."

Mrs O'Neil followed Superintendent Peterson into his office, which had two chairs, a table and a tape recorder. He offered her a seat before he took his. Just then an officer walked in. Before Mrs O'Neil could ask who he was, the superintendent introduced Todd as Officer Vincent Todd. Then he said, "Mrs O'Neil, I think you should go home to your son as you're not charged with anything. I'm so sorry. We will contact you as soon as we find out anything and we hope you will do likewise. If you need my help, please do not hesitate to get in contact with Officer Todd or me. Your husband was a good man and we will not delay in finding his killer. In the meantime, keep yourself safe."

"I will and do not worry Mr Peterson, if I find out anything I will get in touch," Mrs O'Neil said as she sniffed up through her nose and wiped her eyes with the piece of tissue she had in her hand. She then left the police station and returned home to see Jenny and Stanley at the front door about to leave.

"Uncle Aston has left. He said he'd see you later," Stanley told his mother.

"Don't be late home Stanley. I cannot believe you're going out," Mrs O'Neil said. "You be home for breakfast before eight and remember you have to go to school."

Stanley smiled and left with Jenny to meet with Faith and Elizabeth outside Petra's house. Petra phoned her mother, pretending she was someone else by disguising her voice and telling her mother that her Grandma had been taken ill and wanted her. Without any questions asked, her mother went to see her. When her mother got there, however, she met her mother in good health. "Mother, I thought you were ill?"

"You must have heard wrong, Ann my dear."

"No mother, I heard what I told you. Someone phoned and told me that you feel sick and so I rushed here to see you."

"Why didn't you send Petra or Arden instead of coming?"

"Mum, if I'd sent Petra or Arden and they found you really ill, what could they have done?"

"Well, thank you for your urgent attendance, but someone is playing with you. I'm okay and I think you had better get home to the children and your husband."

"Mum, Petra left the house to be with her friends and as for Arden, I left him snoring like thunder. Well, as for my husband, he too might be sleeping like a log. So since I'm here, I might as well cook us breakfast."

Mrs Forbes cooked a gammon steak and boiled egg for her and her mother. As they were having breakfast, Petra let her friends in with her key and told her friends to be very quiet as her stepfather was already in bed getting an early nap, as he'd just come home from his night shift. Petra sneaked up to the top of the stairs and quietly opened her brother's door checking to see if he was sleeping. As she was sure, she invited her friends upstairs.

After Petra gave her friends the all-clear, they put their gloves on and plastic bags on their shoes, tying them around their feet up to their ankles before creeping into the bedroom where Officer Forbes was lying with his face in the pillow. Jenny said to them, "If we are to carry out our job, we should dress in our surgical clothes."

They got dressed in their surgical clothes, black plastic bags and left their other clothes on Petra's bed, and then they went into Forbes' room, tiptoeing quietly. Petra pulled the needle filled with the sleeping dose out of a brown paper bag and stuck it into Forbes' vein, which showed clearly in his neck. He let out a little scream before he was knocked out cold. She dragged the needle from the bottom of his neck up, until the tip of the needle snapped off inside him. She then took the razor and slit him across his throat, so that the insides were hanging out. Then she took his penis out of his shorts with pliers, swiped it off with the sharp razor and left it beside his body. They left him on the bedroom floor saturated in blood.

They all had a quick shower, got dressed and then left the house carrying everything they had used. Petra went with Jenny. After she saw Jenny burn the plastic bags and bin the ashes, she returned home to meet her mother crying.

"What's wrong mum?" she asked pretending to sound concerned.

"It's your father. He's dead! He's dead!" Mrs Forbes sobbed.

"What? How's that mum?" Petra asked pretending to be in shock, but with a hidden smile.

"After you left, I had a call telling me Mum was ill, but when I got there she was okay. If only I had been at home, my husband would be alive now."

Just then three police cars arrived with Superintendent Peterson and three others taking the lead. They parked behind each other, got out of their cars and following behind the Superintendent and Officer Todd went into Mrs Forbes' house like a swarm of bees. Following closely behind was the coroner and the criminal investigator. Mrs Forbes led them up to her bedroom, but in the half an hour they took to search the room, they found nothing that was linked to the crime.

"Some smart-arse genius really hates my bastard friends to send them off in such style," Officer Todd said as he shivered coldly.

"You can say that again," Superintendent Peterson replied, looking as mad as a vicious dog.

"Officer Forbes a rapist, can you believe that? Shit!" said Superintendent Peterson as he recognised the sign that Forbes had been accused of rape.

"Every one of these bastards deserves what they get!" Officer Hodge said to Detectives Paul, his brother Scott Hanson and Superintendent Peterson.

The superintendent looked coldly at Hodge and said, "Hodge, whatever your reason is, I want the cold-hearted people who killed Judge O'Neil and Officer Forbes. I want them before the end of this month. Such killings must be stopped."

Officer Hodge spat on the ground and walked away.

After Todd and the superintendent went back to his office, the superintendent was looking through his window in thought over the death of his two colleagues, Judge O'Neil and Officer Forbes. He faced Officer Todd and asked him, "Will you call my daughter Julia and tell her I will be home late tonight. You know my number don't you?"

"Yes, yes of course," Todd replied, looking strangely at Superintendent Peterson.

"Todd, why are you looking at me like that?"

"Super, I'm sure Julia is at work by now and I don't want to disturb her."

"If you don't want to call my daughter then I will."

"I'll ring her right away sir," Todd said looking confused.

But before Todd could ring Julia, the superintendent said to him, "I heard you're still dating my daughter. Personally, I have nothing against you except that I don't approve that you let her down twice. However, she is over the age of consent. But, if you only want my daughter to have a good fling, you should pitch on some other fly-by-day and whore-at-night. If you hurt her, you'll have me to deal with."

Todd looked at Superintendent Peterson holding the phone and shook his head.

"You just remember that I'll break your fucking neck if you hurt my Julia!"

"What is worrying you pops, is it because I'm white?"

"No Todd, but some of you white blokes only want a bit of black on the side and not to be seen with."

"Well, don't worry about me pops. I'm deeply in love with your daughter. I've asked her to marry me again."

"What about the woman you were dining with in the Frog Leap Hotel?"

"That woman is my sister, her name is Cynthia. She is happily married with two kids, seven and three years. Her husband went to the gents when you saw us. I took them both for a meal as it was her birthday."

"So why were you looking in her eyes like lovers?"

"Now I see what's eating you up. Super, if you'd come over to us you would have known she's my sister. However, I was telling her that I took an exam to be a PI investigator and I passed. I also told her that I'm in love with your daughter and I want to marry her. Anything else you would like to know?" Todd smiled.

"Well, I'll be damned," the superintendent smiled. "I'm sorry to jump to conclusions. However, when are you planning to marry my daughter? Is there anything you'd like as a wedding present?"

"Just the house you live in, as it's too big for an old busybody like you!" Todd joked and laughed.

"Get the hell out of my office, you…"

Todd quickly left leaving the door wide open. The superintendent moved from the window, smiling from ear to ear, and closed the door. He sat at his desk reaching for a pencil and a sheet of plain paper and happily sketched a bride and groom standing in front of a priest. He smiled before he happily kissed the sketched bride and said, "Honey, you don't know how much I love you. You're everything I need in a daughter." He looked proudly at the sketches and then rang his friend John, a housing agent.

"John?"

"That's me. Is that you buddy?" John asked as he recognised Superintendent Peterson's voice.

"I'm the one."

"Hello buddy. You old brute, when are you going to play a game of darts with me?" John laughed.

"Very soon buddy. John, have you still got that four-bedroomed house for sale?"

"Yes, yes. May I ask why?"

"I want to buy it."

"Any special reason?"

"Well yes, a wedding present for Julia and my son-in-law."

"It will cost you."

"John, I don't care how much; I need to buy that house."

"Well the price is four hundred and forty-seven thousand. Have you seen the house?"

"No, I'm going by what you told me."

"Well, the house is in a nice area in Sutton, but it needs decorating. If it's too expensive I would be happy to fix you up with a three-bedroomed house not too far from that one."

"John, the four-bedroomed house would be just what I need for my daughter and her husband as they're young and they'll have a family."

"Okay buddy, my friend. The house will be Julia's. I will need you to come to my office so that we can go ahead with the purchase and do what needs to be done. "

"John, I'm ready to buy the house outright. You get someone to do what's necessary and let me know the excess cost. Meanwhile, I will find a solicitor and surveyor next week."

"Okay, and I will call an interior decorator and have it fully decorated, but I think Julia should choose her furnishers."

"I think you're right John. Will you keep this between us as I don't want her or her future husband to know yet?"

"I'll see you soon buddy. Don't worry, everything will be fine and kept undercover."

"Buddy, I will add a conservatory to the house as a gift from the mrs and me to our goddaughter. If we get a move on now, the house will only take two months to repair."

"John, what about the kitchen, is it a good size?"

"Buddy, why don't you visit and take a look for yourself and let me know what will suit my goddaughter."

"You're right, I think I will. I'll see you Sunday about two o'clock?"

"Okay, that time suits me."

"Well, goodbye for now John." He put his phone down and rang Caroline, Judge O'Neil's daughter, but Caroline and her husband had first taken the children to school. Then he went to see Mrs O'Neil. As Mrs O'Neil heard the door shut she left the living room and went into the hall. Then seeing Caroline and her husband she smiled and walked up to meet them. Caroline hugged her saying, "Dillon and I came as soon as we took the children to school. Mum how are you now? How did you and Stanley get on last night?"

"Well, he's a very young strong boy and his father's death hasn't got to him yet. He's at school. As for me, I hardly slept. Anyway, have you both had breakfast?"

"Yes we have. How about you Mum, have you?"

"I couldn't eat even if I wanted to; your father's death is circling around in my head."

"Mum, you'll have to eat as you have to keep strong for Stanley and your grandchildren. They need you. I'm going to cook you some breakfast. You get back in the living room and rest while I go and see what's in the fridge."

Mrs O'Neil went in the living room and lay on the settee with a sheet over her.

Caroline returned with a nice sausage, egg and tomato breakfast and coffee, but met Mrs O'Neil sleeping. She shook her, "Mum, here's your breakfast."

Mrs O'Neil sat up rubbing her eyes. "Try and eat Mum. It's a difficult time for us, but we have to be strong."

"Kathleen, Caroline's right. Try and eat."

"Dillon, it's so hard for me to swallow. I'm missing my husband so much."

"I know Mum, just try and eat as much as you can."

While Dillon went to make some coffee for himself, Caroline sat with Mrs O'Neil watching while she ate. Caroline smiled to see the plate clean. "I was hungry after all. Thank you."

Caroline took the plate. "Mum, would you and Stanley like to spend some time with us?"

"Honey I can't. I have to be here for anyone when they come to pay their respects. Besides, I can't be anywhere but here until I bury your father and things settle."

"I understand. Mum, do you think you'll still be able to look after Arial next Thursday? If you can't, I'll ask her other nan."

"Caroline, of course I will be able to look after my granddaughter. Honey, as you said, I'm here for my family. I lost my husband but I still have my family. What about Abby?"

She will be in school, but Arial's school will be closed for teachers' training day and I promised Maggie to be with her at the hospital. One other thing Mum, will you let Dillon and I take care of dad's funeral?"

"I can't let you do that, he's my husband."

"Mum, I'm not asking you for anything. I only want to help."

"Okay, but you let me know if you need anything, and the cost. Oh yes, your father left a considerable amount of money to you, Delia and Stanley. His will will reveal how much."

"Mum, I don't need dad's money. You know I have more than I will ever need. Dillon is supporting the children and me very well and he's very wealthy. Besides, dad has given me quite a lot and my paintings have earned me millions. You keep what dad left to me as Stanley will need it for further education."

Mrs O'Neil looked sincerely hard at Caroline.

"Kathleen, Caroline's right again. We don't need the money. Caroline and I are making more money than we need. But we'd like you and Stanley to consider spending some time with us after the funeral."

Mrs O'Neil nodded her head and moved into her husband's reclining chair. "Oh, Delia rang to say she's coming later."

"Kathleen, I meant it, that you and Stanley have to come and spend some time with us. Your grandchildren will like that as they're very fond of you. They would be so happy to see you."

"Yes of course, it's time I spend some time with them as its long overdue."

Dillon smiled, then he joined Caroline in the kitchen as she was preparing dinner before they had to leave to get the children from school.

Early the next morning, the police went to the crime scene where Forbes had been murdered, but found nothing that would give them a clue. The police were baffled. They were also receiving calls praising the killers of Judge O'Neil and Forbes. One caller rang the police to say that thank God someone cared what happens to abused people. The police were so furious over these calls that Detective Myers banged the phone down saying, "Someone is making a mockery of the law."

Superintendent Peterson shook his head in disgust. "Even the damn newspaper branded our colleagues rapist animals and stated that someone's cleaning out the filth."

As Todd watched Superintendent Peterson he said, "Todd, what the heck is happening to our society? Right on this morning's front page a Madame Stall sent her message to the police saying, 'Thank heaven for people who care about abused people' as her fifteen-year-old granddaughter was raped and murdered, and she would give up to one million pounds to find the brute and dispose of him."

Officer Kelly took the paper, read it, and then turned to the superintendent saying, "These two crimes relate to the same pattern."

"Tell me about it. How fucking clever you are."

Officer Kelly hissed through his teeth, shook his head in disgust, tossed the newspaper on the ground and walked away.

Jenny and Petra were mingling amongst the officers, gathering information. They smiled, knowing everything was working in their favour.

Officer Kelly was one of the officers who went into Mrs Forbes' house to watch the two paramedics put her husband's body in a bag. He went outside again and watched as the paramedics carried their colleague's body to the ambulance.

"Damn!" Officer Kelly said in anger. "Two members of our society in one week and they're labelled rapists as well as being mutilated! What the hell is going on?" he bawled out so that everyone looked at him.

"Does this mean Forbes and the judge were rapists?" Officer Hodge asked.

"How the fuck would I know?"

"Take it easy Kelly. This is a bloody time we all didn't want to happen. It's very upsetting, Detective Inspector Hanson," Hanson said.

"I would have loved to be there to shake the revenged hand," Officer Hodge said in anger.

"You keep your filthy mouth closed and your remarks to yourself. I don't want to hear you say anything like that again," said Kelly, pointing his finger into Hodge's face.

"Get your fucking finger out of my face before I break it off and shove it up your arse," said Officer Hodge furiously as his face showed anger.

"Look Hodge, you might have a point, but it wouldn't do you or me any good steaming up and ripping out one another's throats. We've been mates for a long time and I would like to keep it that way if you want us to remain friends. I'm sorry to fly off the handle," Kelly said, and touched Hodge on his shoulder.

"Well mate, from one officer to another, maybe the sons of a bitch deserved what they got. They're filthy rapist bastards! I still think they got what they deserved. I wouldn't want us to fall out either."

"I'm glad to hear that Hodge, but what have you got against Judge O'Neil and Forbes?"

"They were not people. In case you don't know better, they were fucking animals that preyed on defenceless weak people."

"Look Hodge, I can tell you're feeling hurt, but remember we're a team. I realise you have your reasons to be angry. But at the same time, let's have a little respect for our two colleagues."

"I'll tell you what Kelly. I'm sure you have enough respect to share for the two of us. So you show their family you care about what happened to them, but leave me out."

"Come on mate, don't be so bitter. I had no idea that you hated our colleagues so much." .

"I only hate rapists. Any rapist," Hodge said, his face contorted with anger. "I've developed a nasty taste for rapists. I would like to squash fuckers like them under my boots like lumps of shit!"

Kelly smiled looking at Hodge in disbelief.

Hodge wiped his sweaty face and said, "My sister's daughter was raped three years ago. She was only fourteen years old. The bastard ripped her insides to pieces. Four days after she was raped, her mother found her in a bath of ice cold water dead, with her wrists slashed and a suicide note stuck on the basin saying 'Sorry Mum, I love you so much and please forgive me for what I have done. I've been raped twice and I couldn't go through the pain again.' Those were my niece's words. The bastard that raped my niece is still out there somewhere and hasn't been caught, as she didn't say who he was. The bastard might still be going on raping people. So you tell me Kelly, should I have any sort of sympathy for bastards such as rapists? I say good luck to those who are making this a safer place."

"Okay Hodge, you've made your point."

"Kelly, I don't think you will ever understand what is going on in the world, even though you're a cop."

Kelly joined the rest of his colleagues.

Hodge frowned sadly and joined Superintendent Peterson, Officer Todd and Detectives Paul and his brother Scott Hanson.

"What's up with you two?" asked Detective Paul.

"Well, the fellow has reason to be sore headed," Kelly said, as he patted Detective Paul Hanson on his shoulder and said, "I'd no idea that his niece had been raped and it made her commit suicide!"

"Yes, I know. Go easy on him, seeing what happened to our two friends, it has brought back memories of his niece," said Detective Paul Hanson.

Superintendent Peterson took Officer Todd aside and said, "Todd I want to crush the bastards that murdered my friends under my boot."

"Superintendent Peterson, I believe you have to catch the killers first."

"Todd, shut your fucking trap. Forbes and I were good friends and I am hungry for our mates' fucking murderers. I won't rest until I get them!"

"Yes sir!" said Detective Todd.

As the superintendent and Detective Todd struggled through the crowd to get to their car, a Detective Mike Ives rushed up to them and stared the superintendent in the face.

"What now, Ives?" asked Superintendent Peterson.

"Well sir, I've checked for fingerprints but we found none," Ives said, rubbing his forehead in wonder.

"Shit, that's all we need," said Superintendent Peterson.

"Super, you don't suppose they raped their victims and their victim murdered them?"

"Todd, shut your big white lips."

"Have you got something against my big white lips? Or, are you one of those black fathers who doesn't want their daughter to be with a white man?"

"Are you saying that I'm racist? If I was, you wouldn't be coming to my house every night to convince my daughter to have you. She is my only daughter and I don't see what the fuck she sees in you. I asked you to call her and you were not even capable of doing that without me pressuring you."

"You really do fucking hate me don't you? If I didn't love her so much, I would stop seeing her on the account of you," said Detective Todd.

"So you do love my daughter? Well I don't want to know the rest, but if you let her down I will screw your fucking head from your body."

"Super, I want to ask her to be my wife."

"So you should Todd. You're going to marry my daughter next month before she shows. I will do all the spending; you and Julia do the inviting. I want my only daughter to be happy. I want her dead mother to dance in her grave on her wedding day. I want my grandchild to mash my bunions every day to let me know I'm alive. Todd, you don't have to worry about anything and especially somewhere for the family to live. I will take care of all that."

"Why do you want to do this, Super?"

"Todd, I love my daughter."

"I know you do, but it should be my responsibility to take care of my family," Todd smiled. Superintendent Peterson looked hard in his face and then Todd said, "Super, I'll let you choose a room in your house since you will soon be my dad, except Julia and I will be having the one you're sleeping in now ."

"You don't expect me to live with you and Julia once you're married, and surely you don't expect to take my daughter and my grandchild to live in your one bedroom flat, do you?"

"Super, when Julia becomes my wife everything will fall into place. I will support my family the best way I can."

"Todd, you can call me Rodney or dad, but don't expect me to call you anything but T or Todd. Vincent is too long to call."

"That suits me fine."

"How about us going for drink later?"

"Okay, I will meet you at the local about eight."

"Oh Todd, have you anywhere special to go tomorrow evening apart from meeting my daughter?"

"No sup. Why do you ask?" Todd grinned.

"Good! Would you like to go with me somewhere before we go for a drink tomorrow? I have something to show you. But I don't want you to breathe a word to my daughter."

"Okay Super, but tomorrow is Sunday."

"I know."

Before the superintendent and Todd drove away in their own cars, Todd said to the superintendent, "I'm truly in love with Julia."

"I know."

Meanwhile, Petra phoned Stanley and asked him to call their friends to arrange to meet in the next two hours.

Stanley phoned Elizabeth, Faith and Jenny and asked them to meet him outside the Stingray Fish and Chip shop. Within ten minutes they met Stanley as he asked. He bought fish and chips for them including Petra's. He left his friends waiting around the corner while he went to Petra's and rang the doorbell. She answered the door and as she saw him, she walked out, closed the door behind her and left with him. "I asked our friends to wait around the corner. Here, I brought you some chips."

"Thanks."

They met up with their friends, all eating chips.

"Look friends," said Petra, "The reason I asked you here is because if we want to take revenge on our rapist and our wicked families, we'll have to work on them quickly, and most of all we have to be extremely careful about not giving the police any clues that could lead back to us now or later. We also won't give the police time to think. So, while they are looking for evidence of the two bastards we've done in, we will strike on our next victims. Jenny, it's got to be your uncle, Elizabeth's father or Faith's stepfather. I don't mind or care which one, but we've got to put down one of them tonight and the three of them if possible by Monday."

"Petra, we understand what you're saying, but don't you think we are pushing our luck too much?" Faith asked looking nervous.

"Faith, what are you trying to tell me, that you don't want to go any further?"

"No Petra, I'm not saying that at all. I'm simply saying that we'll have to be extremely careful."

"Yes Faith, I totally agree with what you're saying, but at the same time, we have to strike the iron while it's hot. We stop now and we might get caught. We've already disposed of two of the fleas who now cannot ever harm decent human beings such as us. This is why we must act now, or never! I don't enjoy any of this, but the other three must have the same punishment. Then we'll decide what we should do with Martin's sister's rapist. We at least owe him that much for what he has supplied us with. Now shall we continue or not?" Petra asked seriously.

After a moment of deep thinking Petra broke the silence between them saying, "Your faces are telling me you're having regrets about what we have done and are about to do." Jenny smiled, looking into Petra's face. Petra turned looking at her other friends and waited patiently for their reply.

"Well," Faith said, "You're right Petra. The quicker we act the more chance we'll have. As soon as the police come to one of our houses, we should move onto the next."

"I agree with Faith," Elizabeth said.

"Me too," said Jenny.

"And me," Stanley said.

"Well, that's settled then. I'm glad you agree with me," Petra said, smiling.

"So when should we work on any of them?" Stanley asked.

"I would like us to start tonight or any other night, but to end our task next week. We've four days to complete our task," Petra said. "Well as tonight is Saturday and it's raining, Faith, I think we should have a good chance taking your daddy as he's always sweet after leaving the pub. Oh one other thing I forgot to mention, I've dealt with my abuser, and so should you, and then we won't have anything over each other. The five of us will be present to witness justice being done, so that we should feel the satisfaction of taking care of our own problems all by ourselves. I felt as if I was the judge, jury and executioner while dealing with my stepfather; it hasn't left me feeling devalued. I'm sorry to have left my mother a widow, but there's no way I could have left her husband here on earth to use me as a bedpan. I know there will be a time when I'll have to give account to God for what I have done, but at the same time, I had to protect myself from his abuse. Anyway, for what I have done, I am left with no regrets and especially for the way he forced into me." Petra forced a sad smile behind her tears.

"Yes Petra! We should carry out our work, we all agree with you. If we stop now our chance may never come again. We will operate tonight on one of the bugs. Preferably, my evil dad," Elizabeth said as tears came into her eyes.

"Well thank you my bosom friends, I'm glad you all see my point. Now, I want you all to go home then meet me in an hour. Better still, Stan, I want you to wait at home for my call. You may all go home now," Petra told them.

Petra's four friends looked at her with gladness and smiles and went home.

Later that evening when it was dark, Faith decided as it was raining so heavily that it would be a good time to act on her father. She phoned Petra to say, "My father's home and my mother is as drunk as a rising ball of dough. I think this is my chance as the wicked brute is sleeping."

Petra summoned Stanley, Elizabeth, Faith and Jenny to come to her house as her mother was in bed sleeping.

Within ten minutes they were with Petra. While they were discussing whether it should be Faith or Elizabeth's dad to be castrated and executed, Petra said, "Actually, Faith, Liz, I don't care which one of your dads goes down, but it has to be one or both tonight. Even you Jenny, your uncle might even be the first out of the three. However, the other four of us will be with the accused to witness justice being carried out. So, there should be no scrabble over which of our rapist family will go down next. All we want is to see justice carried out on our evil poisonous abusers with the other four of us there to assist and to ensure that this justice is done. When it comes to the amputating and castrating, the five of us take part in binding the brutes in plain double sheets, then watching as it soaks up the deep red blood while death takes over." Petra smiled brightly and her friends laughed joyously.

Meanwhile that night, Superintendent Peterson was tossing and turning in his reclining chair, busting his brain thinking of who could have carried out such an operation on his colleagues Judge O'Neil and Officer Forbes until he dropped off to sleep, snoring.

An hour after their meeting had finished, Faith texted Petra on her mobile phone saying "My father has just left to go to work. So, I'm afraid, it won't be him tonight."

"Well, he escaped tonight but there will be other nights. He won't escape, so don't take it too hard," replied Petra. As she finished texting Faith, she phoned Stanley telling him to get the girls and bring them to her house at ten. At half past nine Stanley and the girls were already there. She saw them and just about got to open the door before they rang the doorbell. She smiled and let them in. By this time Petra's mother had woken up, so disappointed, they went with Jenny to her house and she treated them with cakes and pop. Twenty minutes later, Jenny saw her friends out, then closed the door and double locked it before she took her bath and went to bed. Before Petra and her friends went home, Petra advised them to do nothing unless all five of them were present each and every time they decided to carry out the work on their rapist families.

"Well Petra, we knew what we were up against and as you usually warn us, of course we should all be on the scene to support each other. I'm sure the rest of us will respect your opinion as we have become friends and acted as one," Elizabeth said. Petra nodded with a smile and they went home.

Later that night, Jenny's uncle pulled up outside her house. He got out of his car and walked up to the front door. The outdoor light came on followed by a heavy knock from him on the door. Jenny turned slowly, and getting out of bed she went to her window, lifted the curtains and looked outside to see her uncle leaning against his car looking up. She began shivering with fear. Climbing back into bed, he again knocked on the door but harder. She panicked, knowing he was only there to rape her again. As his knocking got louder, it disturbed the neighbours so much that Mrs Joseph shouted at him, "You're waking everyone up."

Jenny left her bedroom and went down to the living room and sat in the two-seater settee curled up with fright. Her eyes and ears were on the alert looking and listening for her Uncle Keith to knock on the door again. Eventually he knocked on the door softly and then stopped. After a couple of minutes, he knocked at the door again but harder as before, alarming the neighbours so that they peeped through their windows. Jenny's eyes widened and fixed on the door in fright.

"Open the door Jenny!" her uncle shouted through the door latch. But she sat tightly and nervously with her eyes still transfixed on the door. She blocked her ears by pressing two cushions firmly over them and her face pressed against the edge of both cushions. He lifted the door latch again and shouted, "Jenny, I'm going, but I'll be back soon."

Jenny got up and looked through the kitchen window to see him getting into his car, and then he drove away. She sighed with relief and sat down again. Mrs Joseph closed her door huffing and went back to bed.

Ten minutes later, however, she heard three heavy knocks on the door again. As Jenny knew it was her uncle, she jumped frightfully into the corner of the settee. She felt cold with a look of horror on her face and her eyes were fixed on the door.

Her uncle was knocking so hard on her door continuously that it disturbed both of Jenny's neighbours and made them open their doors and look at him.

"What the fuck are you two looking at? Get the fuck back inside and stay there," he said in anger as he inhaled the joint he was smoking deeply. He rolled his eyes aggressively.

"You should not be here. Your sister and her husband are away and to say you are in no fit state coming around to harass little Jenny is an understatement. You have been smoking that smelly stick practically all year it seems. Young man, why don't you go home, I can see your discoloured eyes rolling," Mrs Thomson said.

"Young lad you want ought to be whipped until you learn how to respect your elders," Mrs Joseph said.

"Get the fuck back inside before I knock both of you in!" Keith said to them.

Mrs Joseph shook her head in disgust and said, "Young man, I pity you." She closed her door and went into her kitchen where she made a cup of tea and sat at her kitchen table drinking it. Then as she heard his knocking again, she said, "Poor Jenny, I hope you don't open the door to your rat of an uncle."

Keith pursued his knocking at Jenny's front door again, but Jenny didn't answer. He knocked louder several times and when he had no reply, he backed away from the door and said, "Jenny, you can't hide from me forever. I'm going, but I'll be back, and you had better open the fucking door when I knock again." He kicked the door hard and left.

As Jenny heard the screeching of his car, she knew he had driven away. She sighed with relief crying and lifted the curtain to see his car wasn't there. She then rang Petra. "My uncle come pounding on the door but I didn't let him in."

"You did the right thing." Petra put the phone down. Her mother was sitting next to the phone and watching her with interest, trying to listen in on the conversation.

"Who's that love?"

"It was Jenny. She just phoned to let me know that she bought me a netball skirt."

Jenny still had the phone in her hand when her neighbour Mrs Joseph knocked at her door and shouted through the letter box saying, "Jenny it's me, Mrs Joseph."

Jenny quickly opened the door and let Mrs Joseph in, closing the door quickly behind her.

Mrs Joseph stood in the hall. "Jenny, your uncle is disgusting and rude. You did the right thing by not opening the door to him. I looked at him and all I could see was that he was under the influence of drugs, and he smells strongly with whatever he's smoking. Anyway, have your parents gone away yet?"

"No, not yet Mrs Joseph. They have just gone to visit friends."

"Well, you be careful with that young uncle. Don't let him into your parents' house when they're not at home and especially when he's high on drugs. Make sure you lock the doors and windows and if you need me while your parents are away, I will be only next door."

"Thank you, Mrs Joseph. Goodbye," Jenny said and saw Mrs Joseph out.

That evening, when Petra's mother went into the kitchen, Petra quickly rang Jenny, telling her, "You've done the right thing. Never let your uncle in the house."

"Well Mrs Joseph told me the same."

"Jenny, I totally agree with Mrs Joseph."

"Me too, that's why I didn't invite him in as Mum and dad weren't at home. Well bye for now Pet and I'll see you tomorrow." Jenny put the phone down.

On Sunday evening Superintendent Peterson took Todd to see the house he was going to buy as a wedding present for Julia and him. Todd was gobsmacked and staring at the house. "Not a word to Julia about this, Todd."

"I promise."

Chapter 5

Uncle Keith took Jenny's mum and dad to Manchester airport at nine thirty the following Monday morning, where they would be catching the twelve fifteen flight to Canada. At the airport, Jenny's aunt said to her sister Denise, "You and Boyd have a good time and don't worry about Jenny. We will look after her until you both get back". She gave her sister a big hug saying, "This is from me, just a little something for you."

"What is it?"

"Just some loose change so that you and Boyd can have a meal when you're out."

Denise looked at her. "I'm okay."

"Go on sis, its two hundred pounds and the same for our Sister Daniel. Will you give this to her and tell her I love her? Well sis, you and Boyd have a lovely time and take some wedding photos to show us."

"Thanks Marie, but I wish you were coming with us. Sister Daniel would be so happy to see you; we haven't seen her for nine years."

"Denise, I wish I was going with you and Boyd, but I really couldn't afford to after building a new kitchen. Well sister honey, as I said, I'll look after Jenny until you're home."

"Marie, are you sure going to my home to stay with Jenny won't be too strenuous for you?"

"Denise, I think Jenny would feel better at her home?" Marie said.

"Maybe Marie, but I'm thinking about you as well, knowing you have a teaching job. That's why I think it might be easier for Jenny to stay at your house."

"Denise, Jenny will be okay. You and Boyd get on that plane, enjoy your flight and don't worry about her or anything else. I would be more comfortable staying at your house with her until you return."

"Anyway, thanks Marie and I'll see you when we get back. Oh, I left enough money with Jenny for her to buy what she needs, so you don't give her any more."

"Ok Denise." Marie smiled and she bought breakfast for all. Her brother Keith, however, hardly touched his and instead went to the gents to smoke a joint. When he got back, he looked at their faces grinning.

"What about your food?" Marie asked.

"I don't eat junk like that."

"Why didn't you tell me?"

"You didn't ask."

"Leave him, sis," Denise said as she saw his eyes widening.

Boyd touched Marie's hand, saying. "Denise is right, leave him."

While waiting for the plane to arrive, Denise and Marie went to the ladies. "Marie, seeing our brother in that state, I'm so worried that he might bully Jenny for money as he always used to come to me. But when I found out about his habit, I stopped giving it to him."

"Relax Denise, I won't let him do anything wrong to Jenny."

After Jenny got home from school, she prepared her own dinner as she'd told her mother she didn't want a cooked meal.

"Well sis, when I leave here, I will go home and make arrangements with my husband and my two teenage daughters, Joe and Carrie."

"Yes, you should and thank you for looking after my daughter."

Keith was listening with interest to Marie telling their sister Denise that she would be going home first then to Jenny. He smiled happily, then said to Denise, "Take our sister Marie's advice and don't worry about our Jenny. I'll help look after her."

"Thank you Keith. You know, you really should ease up on what you're smoking as it smells strongly on you. Well, thanks for bringing Boyd and me to the airport. We'll see you when we get home." She hugged him, then brushed the smell away smiling.

As Denise and Boyd left to board the plane, Keith said to Marie, "Sis, I think we should be getting home."

"Yes," Marie said. On their way home, she rang Jenny on her mobile telling her, "I will be with you at about eight."

Keith smiled as he said to Marie, "I should buy a takeaway and take it to Jenny."

"No, you do no such thing. I don't want you to go anyway near her while you are still smoking that nasty smelling drug. Besides, she will be okay to make her own dinner."

"What's the fuss about Marie? She's my niece and I'm only offering her a takeaway," Keith said grinning.

"Still, I can't trust you to be with her while you're smoking your filth."

"Marie, are you still going on about the kiss I gave to your friend's daughter? She was the one who kissed me. Besides, she was fourteen."

"Keith, she was just a child. Good thing I saw you otherwise you might well have gone further."

"Look Marie, she was the one that begged me for a fix in exchange for sex."

"Keith, for the love of God, Ashen was just fourteen and just a child compared to a thirty-two-year-old man like you."

"So because of that, you think I will molest my niece? Well if you think that, you don't know me at all."

"Keith, you're okay when you're not smoking your drugs, but when you are, I wouldn't trust you with my cat, let alone anyone else. I have seen you flashing your privates when you come out of my toilet. The only reason why I haven't stopped you from coming to my house is because you're my brother and I can handle you. So you keep well away from Jenny."

But despite Keith pretending to take his sister seriously, after he drove her home, he drove straight to Jenny's house and parked his car in the driveway behind Jenny's father's car. He then injected himself with drugs and inhaled deeply, smiling with his eyes fixed on the roof of his car. He grinned, swinging his long plaited waxed lock of hair from side to side before tumbling out of his car and staggering up to Jenny's door; he knocked at the door at least a dozen times. For every knock, Jenny shuddered with a frightening feeling.

Throughout his knocking, Jenny was upstairs looking down on him through her window. He stopped knocking and rang the doorbell for a good minute; it seemed like he would never stop. With the irritating noise of the doorbell ringing, Jenny blocked her ears with her palms covering them, but the noise was still penetrating her ears, making her very frustrated. She opened her window and shouted to him, "Fuck off!"

Suddenly he stopped ringing the doorbell, lifted the letter flap and shouted into it, "You come down and let me in or everyone around here will know about you." Jenny closed her window, went downstairs and stood nervously behind the door. He rang the doorbell again. Jenny began to tremble and tears came into her eyes. She then stood behind the door and said, "Why don't you fuck off and leave me alone!" She ran up to her bedroom again and sat on her bed crying.

Keith began ringing the doorbell again for such a long time that Jenny got angry. She got off her bed, walked slowly out of her room and eventually she walked downstairs very slowly, still hearing the doorbell penetrating her ears. She stood at the door nervously, considering whether she should open it so that he would stop. She reached for the door lock, but still hesitated to open the door. Staring widely at the door lock, she swallowed deeply as she inhaled and breathed out. Then she slowly took her time, brushing downward on her short denim skirt. She closed her eyes tightly before opening them to stare at the door lock again and hearing her uncle giggling.

"Jenny, I know you're standing behind the door. I can hear you breathing. I was there when Marie phoned to tell you that she would be with you about eight. Open the door. I only want to speak to you. I'm sorry for what I did to you. Please open the door." His eyes were rolling from side to side.

"No, go away! I hate you!" Jenny told him as she was backing away from the door. He rang the doorbell again saying, "Open the door Jenny, or I will tell everyone that you went to bed with me."

Jenny did not want to make a scene and as she saw her neighbour Mrs Joseph come out of her house and seemed to be going somewhere, she opened the door saying, "Uncle Keith, you've made a terrible mistake with me and I told no one. Please go and leave me alone."

Her uncle walked in, quickly closed the door and smoothed Jenny's face downwards with the back of his left hand. She knocked his hand away and opened the door to say hello to Mrs Joseph, as she saw her coming to the door.

Mrs Joseph faced Jenny and asked, "Will you be okay honey?"

"Yes Mrs Joseph, my uncle came to see if I'm okay." Jenny was smiling, but feeling deep hurt within her.

"Well honey, I hope you'll be okay." Mrs Joseph gave Keith a nasty look as he inhaled his fat rolled-up drugged cigarette. He breathed out a thick puff of smoke then smiled widely, looking at her. Mrs Joseph fanned the smoked away with her hand and said to Jenny, "Honey, you shouldn't let him into your mother's house and especially when they are away. I know he's your uncle, but he's also a bad soul and has no respect smoking that stinking drug in your parents' home."

"If you don't fuck off, I'll knock you into next Wednesday," he told Mrs Joseph.

"Young man, with that attitude, you will soon come to a bitter end," Mrs Joseph faced Jenny saying. "Jenny love, you should ask him to leave while I'm here and don't open the door to him again unless someone's with you."

"I'll be okay Mrs Joseph. Uncle Keith brought me a message from Aunt Marie and he was just about to leave when you showed up."

"The truth is Jenny, I would like to see him leave before I leave you."

"If you don't take your grey arse out of here, I'll knock you back the fuck to your house or to where you are going," Keith rudely said, then inhaled deeply and blew smoke in Mrs Joseph's face again.

"Mrs Joseph began coughing then shook her head and said, "You have no respect at all. Jenny, be careful and I'll see you when I get back. Would you like anything from the shop until your Aunt arrives?"

"No thank you. I'll be okay Mrs Joseph, and thanks again," Jenny said.

Mrs Joseph left with a fearful feeling for Jenny being left with her uncle being the way he was. Outside the door Mrs Joseph stopped and thought for a moment, and then she knocked on Jenny's door again and said, "It's me Jenny." Jenny opened the door smiling. "Would you like to take a walk with me?"

"Really Mrs Joseph, I'll be ok. My uncle is no threat to me."

Keith stepped outside the house holding the door and Mrs Joseph quickly left. "You have more sense than I thought," he told her and laughed.

As Jenny was about to close the door, Keith put one foot inside and smiled. Jenny backed away. He walked in and kicked the door shut then laughed. He faced Jenny with staring eyes then smiled as his eyes travelled all over her from head to foot. Jenny stood firmly by the kitchen door and looked straight into his eyes then asked him, "Why have you come here?"

"To take care of you, why else do you think I came?" he replied, grinning.

"Well, I don't need your help! I don't even want to see you," she said, tearfully with her eyes wide open.

"But I want to see you," he said as he twisted her left hand up to her shoulder and shoved his hand up her skirt, feeling her vagina and laughing.

"Please leave me alone Uncle Keith. I didn't tell Mum or anyone what you did to me. Please go and leave me alone," she cried.

"I bought you some chocolates," he said taking a heavy pull from his joint, puffing out with a teasing smile and with his right hand down his boxer shorts.

"Stick your chocolates and get out of here!" she cried, louder. But he grabbed her from behind as she tried to open the door to escape him. "You're not getting away from me. Not now, not ever! I own you. Every part of you, and if you tell anyone about me, I'll kill you."

"Please uncle, let me go as you're hurting me," Jenny pleaded with him.

"How can I hurt you when I'm only feeling your pussy and your breasts? You should be enjoying my touch."

Jenny was trying her hardest to fight him off her, but at the same time she was trying her hardest not to scratch him, knowing she would take revenge on him and leave no trace for the police. He slapped her, she staggered and nearly fell, but he pushed her to the floor and rolled her on her back. He forced his tongue into her mouth as he was squeezing her nipples and making her cry bitterly. "Please Uncle Keith, you hurt me so much before and you're still hurting me. Please don't do this to me again uncle."

"Don't call me uncle!" he said furiously and ripped her blouse off and then tried to shove his tongue in her mouth again. As he raised up to move further down her, she kneed him in his groin and broke free, but as she was running up to her room, he grabbed her right foot and she fell, hitting her forehead on the stairs. He dragged her down the steps, slapped her hard in her face, pulled his penknife out of his pocket and held it to her throat telling her, "You give me any more trouble and I won't fucking hesitate to use it on you."

Jenny froze fearfully before she began trembling. Tears showered her bosom. She stayed extremely silent staring at him.

As his hold was much too strong for her, she pierced him on his left arm with her brooch pin. "You fucking little slut, I felt that!" he shouted. He hit her in the face so hard that she stumbled and fell backwards onto the settee.

He held her back and she cried out for help. He dragged her off the settee, pushed her onto the wooden floor, flung himself onto her and tore her panties off. "No, no, no!" she yelled out, trying her hardest to fight him off. He cuffed her across her temple and pierced below her left ear with his penknife telling her, "Shut up or I'll really shut you up for good."

Jenny lay on the floor quietly, frightened with closed eyes. Her uncle rolled her over on her tummy as he viciously forced himself into her from behind. She screamed out as he was savagely raping her, "Oh God, Mum!" But the more she cried, the harder he pushed into her, holding her face jammed to the floor. Then as he ejaculated he rolled off her, turned his back to her and snorted cocaine. He then raised his face up towards the ceiling, grinning happily. "Honey, I know we're blood related, but from the first time, I could never resist you. You're also still tight, but the more we do it, the suppler you'll become. Jenny, I'm falling in love with you and I will leave my woman for you."

Jenny went into the kitchen and took a sharp knife from the drawer and hurried back to see her uncle on his knees zipping his jeans up. She stood over him holding the knife at her right side with tears trickling down onto her bosom. She then stared at her tore panties on the floor before she rubbed between her bruised legs. She looked at her smeared bloodied hand that she had rubbed on her pierced neck. For an instant she saw him as a giant maggot trying to chew a way out.

She widened her eyes as she stood behind him holding the knife ready to use on him. He faced her still kneeling and burst out laughing saying, "You belong to me. You're the sweetest and softness creature I have ever had. You tell your mother or anyone else and I'll hurt you that bad that you will pray for death." He laughed hilariously.

"Oh no, you won't, you fucking bastard," she said. Then she plunged the twelve-inch blade into her uncle's shoulder with hate and anger.

Her uncle stared at her in shock then froze and he dropped hopelessly onto his left side. She dragged the knife out of his shoulder and backed away to the kitchen door, watching the blood flowing from him onto the wooden floor. He managed to get up on his feet and staggered towards her holding onto her skirt; she stared and smiled, seeing the blood spouting from his shoulder. She burst into hilarious laughing and plunged the knife in his right shoulder, and again dragged the knife out. Blood spouted everywhere. She laughed in his face and plunged the knife into his left leg, her eyes stretched wide with contentment and anger. She laughed triumphantly as she repeatedly stabbed him until his body was covered in blood. She stopped stabbing him when she became exhausted and dropped hopelessly on her knees beside him.

"You're the one that's fucked now. Aren't you? You rammed your stinking dick into me like I'm one of your bitches and growled your horrible sound into my ears. Who's in control now?"

She stabbed him in his left arm. Then she dropped the knife and backed away, screaming in anger saying, "Dead, you bastard, dead!"

By this time her uncle's body was saturated in blood. He seemed lifeless, lying in a pool of his blood.

Even though she stabbed her uncle repeatedly, he was strong enough to pull himself as far as the front door looking for a way to escape. She chained the door and laughed saying, "You're not going any further, you wicked heartless bastard!" Her uncle's groans began to sound faint and his eyes looked dim and lifeless. She looked down on him, smiling triumphantly. "I won. You took my virginity away and I took your life. I cried my eyes sore as you penetrated me with your big razor sharp dick, and now you're crying for mercy now I have taken my revenge. I begged you not to rape me again and you laughed in my face. Now you're dying and your eyes are pleading for mercy. Well, Uncle Keith, this laugh is on me."

Jenny put her mother's gardening gloves on and began laughing hysterically and stripped naked in front of him saying, "Look well Uncle Keith, for this is the last time you will cast your evil eyes on my body." As her uncle's head flopped to the left side, she roughly jerked his head upright so that he could look at her, but his head dropped helplessly. He was dying and choking on his blood. Angrily she asked him, "Have you had a good look at my youthful body that you penetrated? I can't say I'm pure because you took that away from me. But you know what uncle? You won't be around to tell anyone you took my virginity." Her laughing changed into crying. "We could have been a loving family, but you chose to be my enemy by taking advantage of me. I could never be like my cousin Leanne and hide the fact that you raped me. You see Uncle Keith, I'm a little stronger than our Leanne. You raped her until she ended up in a madhouse. Well, I won't be going there on account of you or anyone else, but I know where you will be going - to the depths of hell Uncle Keith, straight down. Oh yes, after Leanne told Aunt Susan, you then fucking threatened her. Leanne was fifteen years old like I am now. But thank God, she recovered. Now she is sixteen and ran into hiding leaving no trace. But guess what uncle, I will search for her, but you won't be around to grin in her face. I don't think I will ever get rid of your stinking revolting smell you have left on me now, but I will work hard scrubbing your filth off me. Well uncle, what I have done to you is for my cousin Leanne and me. If I help you, you'll only move on to raping our next blood relative and I really couldn't take the chance to leave you alive. I do hope you won't hold that against me. You see, Uncle Keith, it's not only me I have to protect, it's the rest of my family, especially my mother, because when you're high on drugs you won't care which hole you ram it in, so long as you satisfy your sexual lust. So I do hope you'll understand what I have said. I really can't leave you to rape my mother. So, it is only right I stop you."

She yanked his head upright and let it drop, then laughed, saying, "Just look at you now, you can't even hold your head up. I only let you go and your head flapped like a wrung chicken neck. However, I'm sorry I'm not in a position to read you your rights as I'm not the law, just your executioner."

Jenny then pressed her right foot down onto her uncle's back as he was dragging himself towards the front door. "Oh my dear uncle, no more trails of blood for me to clean. However, I think it's time for your final dose of medicine," and with that she plunged the knife into her uncle's right eye. Blood streamed down his face and he groaned horrifyingly. She watched him gasping hopelessly for breath and fighting for his life. Then she whispered, "You filthy bastard! I pleaded, I screamed and begged you to stop hurting me and you laughed as you were pushing your stinking dick into me holding a knife to my throat. Now the knife has slipped from your hand into mine and now you're begging me not to hurt you and that I should now feel sorry for you? Now Uncle Keith, the trouble with you, you were under the influence of drugs when you viciously raped me. But for me, I don't have to take drugs to get even with you. You burst me open and left me covered in blood and pain when you first raped me. This time, you have left me with internal bruises between my legs from how you forced yourself into me. You have left my body aching because of what you have done to me. I will always have nightmares seeing and feeling your ugly rasta-head face and smelling your stinking body. You have stripped me of decency and hurt me terribly. Yes I will help – help you go to hell. As I told you, you're an evil bastard! You'll never rape any youth again!"

She got her surgical gloves from her secret place between the bath and cupboard. She put the gloves on, marched downstairs into the kitchen, spread a bin bag over her uncle's belly while he was choking on his blood, sat on him and said, "As I said, let me help you go straight to hell quicker. You evil bastard! You'll never hurt me again!"

As Keith barely held onto Jenny's left foot, hatred covered her face and without remorse she hauled the knife across his left hand, slicing four of his fingers. He let out a long mournful groan. She then unzipped his jeans, grabbed his penis with her father's pliers and with one swift slice she took it clean off. More blood spouted from him, and the floor looked like it was covered with patches of deep red carpet. His groaning faded as pitifully his eyes closed with blood streaming down his face.

Jenny's laughing was hysterical as she rammed his penis in his mouth. She stared at the running blood coming from him. She got off him and spat on his face saying, "Rapist bastards such as you deserve what you get. You're my uncle and you've disrespected me by penetrating me like one of your drugged whores. You made me hate you. You sickening, rotten bastard! Now I shall help you by calling you an ambulance, but I have to get you out of my mother's house first and watch you, sealed in a black bag, go to the morgue. Revenge is so good!" Jenny said laughing heartily.

She looked at the kitchen clock and saw the time was fifteen minutes to seven. This left her with just enough time to clean the place before her Aunt Marie would arrive.

She rang Petra, crying, and asked her to come over to her house immediately. When Petra heard her crying, she knew Jenny was in trouble and needed her help desperately. "Mum, can I take some money to lend Jenny as her Aunt Marie won't be with her until eight."

"Where's Jenny's mum?"

"She's gone to Canada. Jenny said she's hungry."

"Okay Petra, you can go but I want you home by nine o'clock at the latest."

"Yes mother," said Petra and she raced off to Jenny's house three streets away. By this time Jenny was upstairs looking out of her mother's bedroom window overlooking the main road. When she saw Petra racing towards her front door, she ran down the stairs as fast as she could and told her to go round the back where she let her in.

"It's my uncle," Jenny said crying. "He knew I was alone. Mum and Dad left for Canada this morning. My Aunt Marie will be here to stay with me at about eight o' clock. She phoned to tell me. My bastard Uncle Keith knew this, so he came and the fucking bastard raped me again. He threatened that if I told my Mum or anyone, he would hurt me real bad and that I'd never walk again or speak. Petra, I would not become his incest whore, so I gave him exactly what he deserved, the rotten bastard!"

"Oh Jenny, you really have done a first class job on the evil bastard, I couldn't have done better myself. Still, he worked his way up to this. Just one thing though, your mother's hall is in a very bad state," Petra laughed.

"Petra, he raped me after he took his drugs. I begged him to go away, but did he? No, he laughed in my face before he penetrated his dirty dick into me once again. Well the fucker lost this round after a second time, but I was sure he would never be around to rape me a third time!"

"We'll call the police. But we'll have to get him out of here and wash the blood away. Have you been wearing gloves?"

"Yes Petra, I have been wearing gloves. My mother's gardening gloves first, then I used a pair of ours. The police will never know I did this," Jenny said, cool and calm.

"Jenny, he's still alive," Petra said. "But I don't think he will last much longer. One other thing, we'll have to make sure that absolutely no trace of you can be found on him."

"How can he still be alive when he has bled so much from his wounds?" Jenny said. "Well, he won't be for much longer."

She put on her gloves once again and stabbed her uncle straight though his neck with hate. He stretched out, staring. She stared at him and then at Petra and said, "Now he is dead. And if I had the chance to kill him again, it would be in a worse way."

Petra laughed softly and said, "Well, you did what you had to do. And I'm very proud of you for taking on this evil monster on your own."

Jenny spat on her uncle again. Petra washed the spit off with methylated sprit and threw the rest over the stab wounds on the body. "Jenny, we shouldn't leave any evidence on the maggot for the police to trace back to us."

Petra hooked his penis out of his mouth using a wire clothes hanger and made sure it was flushed down the toilet, then she injected a strong fix down his throat and washed his legs clean with vinegar and mentholated spirit. Petra said, "Good."

Jenny smiled and said, "I wasn't thinking straight. All I wanted was to destroy the maggot."

"Jenny, I think you should leave the knife in him," Petra said.

"I can't do that Petra. The police will know it's one of Mum's knives."

"Jenny, you'll have to trust me. Your uncle was a rotten druggie bastard and he stole your mother's knife and then left. Seconds later you heard the sound of a car coming, the horn blowing and you saw your uncle scream into your mother's yard. You went to see what had happened and you saw your uncle with the knife stuck into him. You dragged him out of his car and into the house. Well let's do what we have to do as your Aunt Marie will be here soon and I have to get home by eight or nine o'clock," Petra said.

"You're right Pet. But I think I should go and get someone to help me. Someone who would vouch for me and say that I helped my uncle," Jenny said.

Petra smiled and left. Jenny knocked on Mrs Joseph's door knowing Mrs Joseph had gone to the fish and chip shop. Mr Joseph took his time coming to the door in his wheelchair as he was disabled. He saw the panic on Jenny's face and asked, "What is it, child?"

Jenny stuttered. "My uncle had an accident and I think he's dead."

"Well, I can't come out as I can't walk and the wife's gone to the chip shop. Have you called for an ambulance or the police?"

"Yes I called the police."

"Well you get back to your uncle and wait for the police Jenny?"

"Ok Mr Joseph." But Jenny stood crying her eyes out.

"I knew that boy would come to a bitter end. He had no respect for God or man. I listened to him abusing my wife with his bad language. If I could leave my chair I would have knocked his head off his body. I can't say I'm sorry for him, but I'm sorry for you Jenny having to deal with a louse like him. My wife should be on her way back. Jenny, you leave everything to the police, as you're too young to deal with what happened to him. Many times my wife came home and complained about him either selling drugs or smoking it and using abusive language. You get back to your uncle Jenny until the wife get home and then I'll send her over."

93

"Okay Mr Joseph, and thanks."

Jenny's neighbour Hilda had come out and she hugged Jenny. "You get into your house. I'll call the police."

"I have done," Jenny said crying. Hilda saw her into her house and heated a cup of milk and gave it to her saying, "You drink this honey. It will help calm you. Look, I'll go and lock my door and be back in a few minutes."

"Okay Hilda. Please hurry back," Jenny said and as Hilda left, Jenny smiled.

"Jenny, I brought you some fish and chips as your Aunt Marie hasn't come yet," said Mrs Joseph, who had been sent straight over.

Jenny took the fish and chips and said, "Thank you Mrs Joseph, but I can't eat it," showing her appreciation by smiling.

Mrs Joseph gave her a caring smile and warned her to keep her door locked until her aunt arrived.

"Mrs Joseph, my Uncle Keith was murdered in his car and as you weren't at home, I called my friend Petra here as I was scared."

"Oh dear, was it that uncle who was so disgustingly rude to me?"

"Yes, Mrs Joseph, but he didn't mean to be rude. He was drugged and that's how he behaved when he was in that state. But I did love him," Jenny said in pretence.

"I know you did honey. But you're not to blame for how he turned out and what happened to him. Ah, I knew it would have turned out to be this way. When will your Aunt Marie be here?"

"I don't know. She phoned to say that she would be with me about eight. I so miss Mum," Jenny said crying for real.

"Honey, you try and eat some of your fish and chips."

"Thanks Mrs Joseph, but I don't think I would be able to eat them after what has happened to my uncle." She put a chip in her mouth, pretending to choke on her crying while Petra looked into her eyes and noticed her crying was for real. "Seriously Jenny, I'm sorry for what we went through and have to go through," Petra said.

"All the same, you try and eat," Mrs Joseph said.

"Mrs Joseph, Jenny's really distraught and she's been crying before and since I have been here for the past twenty minutes. Mrs Joseph, have you seen the state of her uncle?" Petra asked her.

"No honey, I can't say I have. But I'm sorry for what has happened to him, even though he might deserve what he got. You should have been here to hear what he said to me. He was so disrespectful, but even so, as I said, I'm very sorry he wasted his life. Well, you encourage Jenny to eat and I'll be back and stay with her until her aunt arrives," Mrs Joseph said.

Petra smiled and Jenny nodded her head. Mrs Joseph went home, Jenny left her door open and shared the fish and chips with Petra, but neither of them could eat.

"Sorry Mrs Joseph to waste your fish and chips, but I blame this fucking rapist of my uncle to sicken my stomach." Jenny threw the fish and chips into the kitchen bin.

Meanwhile, Jenny and Petra carefully planned their story of what to tell the police, and just in time, as they saw at least eight police officers walking towards the house.

Mrs Joseph and Hilda walked into Jenny's house and Jenny put on pretend sobbing. She was really good at it, stuttering out her words, telling the police she was doing her homework after her uncle had left then she heard a car crash and when she went to look she saw her uncle's car and another sped off.

Petra took over telling the police, Mrs Joseph and Hilda, "Jenny phoned to tell me her uncle had been stabbed so I came over." Petra paused, then breathed out and faced Jenny who was sitting next to Hilda and being comforted by two white policemen and a black policewoman. When she saw Detective Inspector Hanson, however, she walked away without him seeing her.

"Well, did your uncle say anything before we came?" one of the police officers asked.

"He tried to speak, but I couldn't understand him as he was just gargling," Jenny said.

Petra faced Mrs Joseph after the police had left the room and said, "Jenny told me she went to put the rubbish out when she saw her uncle's car coming at full speed almost knocking her down and she had to run quickly out of his way. As her uncle stopped the car and he looked like he was hurt, she pulled him out."

"I hope he's all right, even though he was disrespectful to me," Mrs Joseph said.

Jenny shook her head and repeated to Mrs Joseph," I think my uncle is dead."

"That young Keith was so disrespectful to me so many times, but I hope he pulls through. I wouldn't wish to see him around me while he's smoking that nasty drug again though."

"Well thank you Mrs Joseph for the information," the policewoman said after seeing her hearing aid almost out of her ear, but she didn't tell her Jenny's uncle was dead.

Mrs Joseph touched Jenny and said, "Jenny, you take care and I'll just let my husband know I'm with you then I'll be back."

The policewoman then said to Jenny, "We'll leave you for now, but we'll be back if we should need you."

Then the WPC came back to Jenny and asked, "Has your uncle ever tried to molest you?"

"That's my uncle you're talking about." Tears came to Jenny's eyes.

Just then WPC Phipps stepped forward and said, "I heard what you asked her. I think you should be more sensitive about your questions and what you say. She's a young person and she should have an adult with her."

"Officer Phipps, are you telling me that I'm not capable of doing my job?"

"Officer Mansfield, I'm not saying that at all. I'm saying that you should be careful how you speak to Jenny."

"Well thank you for your support Officer Phipps, but I'm quite capable of doing my job."

"Well, I'm glad to hear that Officer Mansfield." Officer Phipps walked off to meet one of the policemen.

Meanwhile, Petra went to a phone box and rang Jenny to remind her. "You tell the police you heard a car scream into your drive that stopped suddenly almost knocking you down. You were frightened and you ran into the house and shut the door as you were on your own and the night was dark. Then you heard a loud knock on your door, you hesitated to open the door but as you thought your aunt was at the door, you opened it and your uncle fell against you covering you with his blood. You struggled to push him off but the force of his body carried you down to the floor. As you were on the floor you managed to crawl from underneath his dead weight. You didn't know what to do. So you rang your best friend and she told you to call the police and an ambulance, which you did."

"Pet, I did, but I think Hilda called the police too, but I did phone for the ambulance," Jenny said.

"The dirty bastard didn't know his end would come and I thought he was insane. The son of a bitch really deserved what he got," Petra said then she went on to say, "Meet your kind in hell, Uncle Keith! Now we have to grant our friend Martin his wish. Ah well, bitterness comes after sweetness, that's what my Grandma always said. What's sweet in the mouth and bitter in the arse? Now Uncle Keith, you and your kind didn't know you'd have to pay for your wicked crimes. Well, at least none of you will sexually abuse anyone again. Justice has been done to three of you and we still have another three to deal with," Petra said. She then went back to Jenny's yard and stayed hidden behind some onlookers. She saw Superintendent Peterson get out of his car followed by three police cars that stopped outside Jenny's gate with at least nine policemen and three policewomen, of which one was black, two mixed race and there were two black policemen. Petra's eyes were on the black WPC all the time as she was very good-looking, tall and had a nice smile. Petra's eyes followed her as she joined her colleagues in the yard.

Superintendent Peterson, Officer Kelly and Detective Todd went into the house followed by Detectives Scott and his brother Paul Hanson. At this time, the crime scene was festered with police and onlookers. Petra left the crime scene to go to the chip shop.

The detectives and their teams of police searched everywhere and for everything that was significant to the crime. As they saw the front yard was wet, a policeman stroked his face in thought before he asked Jenny, "Why is the floor wet?"

"Well I washed the blood away," Jenny said.

Then as Jenny saw one of the police searching the rubbish shed, she asked him, "What are you looking for?" claiming to be naïve.

"Evidence."

Jenny's aunt arrived. She quickly got out of her car and rushed to Jenny as she saw her crying. "It's Uncle Keith. He's dead."

She stared at Jenny. "What do you mean?"

"Yes Marie. Your brother's dead. I'm so sorry. Poor little Jenny had to deal with all this. I'm so glad you're here now to support her," Hilda said.

Hanson showed his badge.

"Detective, Jenny's my niece. Her parents left for Canada this morning and I'm here to be with her."

"Now that you're here, we would like to ask young Jenny some questions about her uncle in your presence. What's your name?"

"Mrs Somers."

"I'm sorry," Officer Kelly said, "This is Detective Inspector Hanson."

'My parents have gone to Canada. Officer, are you the head of your colleagues?" Jenny asked, pretending to be stupid. Officer Kelly looked hard at Jenny and nodded his head, then left with his colleagues to watch the porters put her Uncle Keith into a black bag and zip it up. Jenny smiled watching the porters taking her uncle's body into the ambulance.

"Fuck, who is responsible for such acts?" Superintendent Peterson said furiously.

"Does this mean Judge O'Neil was a rapist?" Detective Todd asked giggling.

"How the fuck would I know!" Superintendent Peterson replied in a bad temper.

Officers Hodge and Kelly looked at each other, then Officer Hodge said, "Those bastards got the right medicine."

"Officer Hodge, keep your fucking mouth closed. I don't want to hear you say anything like this again and especially about any of my fellow colleagues. Take it from me, you ever utter one word that I don't want to hear and I'll ram your fucking badge down your throat!"

"Yes sir!" Officer Hodge said and walked away. Superintendent Peterson looked at Officer Hodge, shook his head then walked away to meet Inspector Carson who was walking towards him. Officer Hodge spat on the ground and said, "The filthy bastards, child molesters, they deserve what they got and I hope they never catch whoever did them in."

Detective Todd heard Hodge, and he asked him, "Have you held a grudge against Judge O'Neil and Officer Forbes?"

Officer Hodge aggressively pushed Detective Todd hard and said, "Yes, I was fucked in my arse by my stepfather when I was eleven and he was a priest, and so was my niece molested. Now you know why I am so pissed off and despise rapists. Now you can go and tell your father-in-law that I couldn't give a fuck if I leave the force."

"Look friend, I had no idea. I'm sorry. I feel the same about rapists. I'm sure what the killers did was out of anger, hurt and hatred, but that doesn't give them the right to murder their victims and think they can get away with it scot-free. There's a law for rapists or any other crime," Detective Todd said and left Officer Hodge by their car. He left to join his other fellow officers before most of the police left the crime scene.

Petra returned from the chip shop and stood well away and was very careful not to be seen by any of the police. When she saw Jenny's aunt, she went home.

"How come you're home so early?"

"Mum, her aunt is with her."

Meanwhile, Detective Inspector Hanson told Jenny's aunt, "Jenny will have to come to the police station for an interview."

"I will see that my niece helps you in any way."

"I will arrange transport for you and Jenny to get to the station."

On arrival, Jenny and her aunt were taken to the interview room where Jenny was asked to tell her story.

"Jenny, was your uncle dead when you found him?" Detective Scott Hanson asked. Jenny looked at her aunt. Her aunt nodded.

"He must have been barely alive when he got to me."

"Had you noticed anything else about your uncle?"

"Yes, there was blood everywhere."

Superintendent Peterson looked on at the detective with his lips slightly pushed forward. "Well, that will wrap us up for now."

"Thank you Jenny."

"Just as Superintendent Peterson and the detective were about to walk away, Officer Kelly said, "Mrs Somers, would you mind my asking Jenny another question?"

"What would you like to know Officer Kelly?" Jenny asked.

"I don't know how to ask you this about the wetting of the yard."

"Officer Kelly, I washed away the blood out of the yard as I didn't think it mattered," Jenny began crying. "I didn't know I shouldn't have washed the blood away. I didn't know what your Officers would have wanted. I'm sorry. I'm sorry."

"That's okay Jenny, you wouldn't have known," Officer Kelly said.

"Calm down Jenny. Mrs Somers, you're free to go with your niece," Detective Inspector Hanson said.

"Detective, was my brother dead when you got to him?"

"Yes, Mrs Somers. I'm afraid he was," Officer Kelly answered quickly with a faint smile.

Detective Inspector Hanson and the superintendent moved away.

"Officer Kelly, I'm sorry that I couldn't have done more to help my uncle. I asked my neighbour Mrs Joseph to stay until the police came."

Chapter 6

Two nights later, Petra, Jenny, Stanley, Elizabeth and Faith performed the same operation on Martin's uncle for raping Martin's sister. He had after all supplied them with the tools and morphine they'd used on their rapist families. That same night they operated on Elizabeth and Faith's fathers in their cars, away from their homes.

The police were called to the crime scenes. They were confused and disgusted, not knowing who was responsible for the six killings. The only motives and clues that Detective Inspector Hanson could come up with was the fact that the six killings were linked by the fact that they were rapists and that their victims had murdered them.

Superintendent Peterson smiled, but was still full of anger. Then he said to Detective Todd, "Again, no motive and still no fucking suspects. So, where the fuck does that leave us? Six fucking murders of suspected rapists who had their dicks hacked off with two of their dicks stuffed almost down their throats, three dicks rested beside their bodies and one missing. What the hell is going on? These hackers think they are fucking clever, but it's a matter of time until I sling the shackles over their fucking necks instead."

After the police had coffee, they all went back to the murder scene where's Jenny's uncle was killed.

Petra was wearing jeans, a dark T-shirt and black baseball cap pulled over her eyes and her hands were in her jeans pockets. She looked at Superintendent Peterson, giggling. "What the heck's so funny?"

"You, super," Petra said. Detective Todd smiled, but didn't recognise her.

"Todd, you can wipe that smile off your face. I'm going home and if I'm not at work tomorrow, don't call me."

Todd smiled, "The same to me mate."

The superintendent touched Todd's shoulder, "It has been a hectic time for us all." He left in his car, went home and took a bottle of beer out of the fridge and kicked the door shut.

"Take it easy dad. Have you had a hard day?" Julia asked.

"Honey, you don't want to know. All I need now is a hot shower and a nap."

"What about your dinner?" she asked

"Honey, I'm not hungry."

"Dad, whatever happened at work, you shouldn't let it interfere with your appetite. I've cooked us a nice piece of hake and rice, your favourite."

"I appreciate your cooking honey, but I don't think I've the appetite tonight."

"Well, I'll put it in the oven for later then and if you don't eat I'll put it in the fridge."

"Okay Julia, leave it in the microwave. I'll eat after I have a shower."

"Okay dad. If you need me, I'll be in the living room."

Her dad kissed her on her forehead, had his shower and then returned and ate his dinner. Afterwards, he went to Julia and said, "Your mother's taught you how to cook a tasty meal."

"I know dad. But I think it's time you find someone."

"Why? Are you getting fed up with me?"

"Dad, I could never get fed up with you because I love you and it's my duty to take care of you even if you have a wife."

"Well you know I'm too old for women now. Besides, I don't think I would ever love any other woman as I loved your mother."

"Dad, that is because you're glued to your desk at work and home. You should get out sometimes and enjoy life."

"I'm too old for that. Honey, I'd rather be at home with you."

Julia laughed and left Superintendent Peterson on the living room settee.

An hour later, Julia woke him. "Dad, it's twenty to ten. I think you should go to bed."

Superintendent Peterson got up, stretched upright and marched up to the toilet and then to bed. Julia turned off all the downstairs lights and then had a long bath before she went to bed.

Three days later, Friday morning, Petra rang Superintendent Peterson at the station disguising her voice with a high-pitched tone and said to him, "It's time you got up off your fat rusty arses, take your officers and look for all rapists. Do your jobs by locking them up and leaving them in a special prison to eat their shit until their flesh is rotten and drops from their stinking bones."

"Who's this?" the superintendent asked in frustration.

"Someone who went through the agony of being raped." Petra giggled and rang off.

"Hello, Hello?" Superintendent said. Petra walked out of the phone box.

When he got no reply, he became very angry and shouted, "Who the fuck are you?" He then banged the phone down and said, "Damn, damn, damn!" He walked over to his office window looking straight into the park where he could see the flowers blooming. He went into deep thought and mumbled to himself, "I'm sure I've heard that giggling before." He thought more deeply, concentrating on where he had heard it. He shook his head slowly and smiled, "No," he said softly, "It cannot be." He was thinking of his sister's son Jules, who was confined to a wheelchair due to a fall from an apple tree when he was seven.

"No, no, no, my nephew has no reason to phone me. It's got to be someone else." But still Superintendent Peterson frowned and was busting his brain thinking of who had phoned him. "My nephew is disabled. Even the voice sounded like his, but I know it's not him," he said, thinking deeply again. He then looked at his wristwatch before calling Detective Todd into his office.

Todd looked at his mates and raised his shoulders in suspense, left his desk and then went to see Superintendent Peterson. He remained standing as the superintendent took his seat and smiled.

"I want you to take some flowers to Julia on your way home," Superintendent Peterson said.

"Flowers, sir?" Todd asked, looking puzzled.

"Yes! Flowers, that's what I said. You know what flowers look like don't you?" Superintendent Peterson asked wiping the built-up sweat off his forehead.

"Yes sir. But I already took some to her less than an hour ago," Todd smiled.

"Todd, I don't care when you last took flowers to my daughter. I want you to buy her some flowers on your way home and give them to her. Do you want the money now for the flowers?" He looked into Todd's eyes.

"Oh no sir," Todd smiled.

"Todd, she asked me to get her some flowers. Oh, and while you're in the florist, order a couple of wreaths for next Monday and pay for them. I want one in the shape of a judge and the other an officer in uniform. You know where to send them. I'll square up with you later."

"Yes sir." Todd remained smiling.

"Todd, are you sure you don't want the money for the flowers now?"

"No sir, what kind of man do you think I am taking money off you for my fiancée's flowers?"

"A real man, I hope. And you let me know how much I owe you for the wreaths. By the way, you remember the exam you took to be a private investigator detective?"

"Yes sir. What about it?" Todd asked.

"You passed. So, you will soon have your team as you will start your new job next month or even sooner. We'll discuss it later. Congratulations. And this cheque is for the wreaths, just fill in the amount. I've signed it."

"Thank you, sir."

Superintendent Peterson stood up and patted Todd on his left shoulder with a smile. "You're a good bloke."

Todd went back to his office smiling.

"Someone came back with their bottom dusted with talc," Officer Kelly joked and all the officers laughed.

"He wanted to see me about the two wreaths for Officer Forbes and Judge O'Neil actually," Todd said grinning.

Officer Kelly got up from his seat, walked over to Todd's desk and put ten pounds on it saying, "This is from me."

Then the others put ten pounds each on Todd's desk, making a total of two hundred and seventy pounds.

"Well thanks mates for your donations," Todd said.

Twenty minutes later, Todd said goodbye to his colleagues and left. He stopped at the florist shop and bought a lovely bunch of flowers for Julia and ordered the two wreaths. He then told Mrs Archer to send the judge-shaped wreath to Mrs O'Neil for the following Thursday morning for nine o'clock, as the funeral was at twelve fifteen and the officer-shape wreath to Mrs Forbes the following Monday morning, as Forbes' funeral would be held at eleven thirty. Todd gave Mrs Archer the addresses for Mrs O'Neil and Mrs Forbes then watched her write the delivery times down, and then she neatly wrapped the bunch of flowers, gave them to Todd saying, "I'll make sure Mrs O'Neil and Mrs Forbes get their wreaths in good time."He paid for the wreaths and the flowers. "Thank you very much," Mrs Archer said. "Officer, I'm very sorry about your friends."

Todd nodded then left with the bunch of flowers. On his way to Julia, he stopped at the Morrison shop and bought a bottle of champagne and a bottle of red wine; Julia's favourite. When he left the shop and got into his car, he looked at the flowers beside him, he touched them and smiled, and then drove away. When he arrived at Julia's, he parked his car in the driveway, took the flowers and the carrier bag that contained the champagne and wine and walked up to the door and rang the doorbell smiling. "Come on Jul. Answer the door love," he said. As there was no answer, he backed away looking up at her window. He rang the doorbell several times and as he was about to leave, Julia walked into the house and heard the doorbell ringing. She dropped the basket of dried clothes she'd taken in on the table and rushed to open the door.

"What took you so long?" he asked smiling. Julia smiled. "I didn't hear the doorbell. "

"I was beginning to think you were not at home. Did you really not hear the doorbell?"

"I only heard it when I walked back into the house; I was getting my washing off the line in the garden. I'm sorry Todd. Were you ringing for long?"

"Long enough to think you were out. However, I have brought you some flowers, champagne, wine and myself. You and I are going to celebrate my new job," he said happily and with such a romantic smile on his handsome face and his big blue eyes sparkling.

He popped open the bottle of champagne, filled two glasses and gave Julia one. He swallowed some and said, "I've passed my exam to be a forensic investigator. We'll get married December, five months from now." He then swallowed more champagne. Julia watched him drinking while holding her glass of champagne.

"Drink up love. We're celebrating my new job and our future."

"Todd, I'm so happy for you, but it's a little too early for me to get drunk and I have to cook dad's dinner. Besides, I don't want dad to come home and see me drunk. I also hope you'll take a taxi home after you've drunk that bottle of champagne?"

"Jul, one glass of champagne won't do any harm."

"Todd, remember you're a policeman and sometimes accidents are caused by the unexpected."

"You're absolutely right Jul. What if I went home, got some sleep and came back later so we can celebrate properly. Would you mind doing me some dinner?"

"Of course, what time will you be back?"

"About five, would that be okay?"

"Sure, I'll keep the wine and champagne on ice until then."

"Julia, will you be my beautiful wife?" He smiled broadly.

"Yes Vincent Todd, I will marry you as you're so handsome and I'm so much in love with you," Julia said, looking happy.

"Well, we have at least five months to prepare and to let family and friends know," Todd said looking into Julia's eyes while smiling. He took her into his arms and kissed her passionately. Julia's half-brother Curtis then walked into the room smiling, wearing only a pair of khaki shorts and a black string vest. Todd parted from Julia and said angrily, "I'll call you."

"Todd…"

But Todd became jealous and turned to leave. "Todd, he's my…" But Todd was so angry that he said, "Julia, I said I'll call you!"

"How dare you speak to me like that!" Julia said, outraged. "You may leave now! And don't bother to call."

Todd rushed out of the house looking hurt and very angry. He jumped into his car then drove away at speed. Julia ran after him shouting, "Todd, Todd, please stop and hear me out. Todd, Todd!" she shouted in frustration. She took several deep breaths then ran into the road hoping he would see her in the wing mirror, but he sped away faster, attracting attention from onlookers.

When Julia realised her neighbours Mrs Brooks and Mr Wells were looking at her, she smiled and walked into the house in tears to meet her half-brother Curtis drinking champagne. She looked hard at him.

"What's the matter with him leaving in such a hurry? He came into your house, saw me and got jealous. When you tried to explain, he left angrily like a whirlwind. Sis, I don't think you should be with him."

"Curtis, what the hell do you know about Todd except his name? You walked in on us half naked and smiling. So, what was he to think after your grinning gave him the wrong impression?" Julia said frowning.

"I'm sorry sis," Curtis apologised.

"It's too late for apologies. Besides, dad did not tell me he had a son, and I'm sure you're not my mother's child. So don't call me sis!"

"Thanks for letting me know how you feel about me. Look Julia, I did not come here to cause trouble. I'm here as I would like to get to know you and my father. Obviously I was wrong to come here. I'll be out of your way as soon as I've seen my father," Curtis said and put the full glass of champagne on the drinks bar then turned to leave.

"Curtis, please wait. I shouldn't have jumped down your throat because of Todd's ignorance. If he can't trust me now, how will he when we're married? Curtis, you're my dad's son and that makes us family. To hell with Todd! This home is as much yours as it is mine. If Todd really did love me, he would have listened to me. Well, he had his chance and he took it. I don't think he'll ever love me. Well brother, we might as well make use of his champagne and his wine." Julia passed a glass of champagne to Curtis saying, "Cheers, welcome home brother."

After they drank a couple of glasses, Julia laughed saying, "You know what Curtis. This champagne is really good." She laughed and fell bottom down onto the settee and began crying over Todd saying, "Oh Curtis, I love Todd so much. But I guess he has finished with me."

"Julia, don't take it too hard, he'll be back when he cools down. So, how long have you two been dating sis?"

"About eighteen months on and off," Julia said sadly.

Curtis gave Julia a downhearted look and smiled. Julia threw a cushion at his head and laughed saying, "I'll get my own back on you one day."

Both Julia and Curtis laughed heartily then Julia asked him, "Would you like me to take you out to dinner tonight?"

"I would like that, but what about dad? I thought you said you had to cook his dinner."

"Well, I was going to cook dinner but I know he would be happy to come with us - it is Friday. Besides, we need someone to pay!" Julia said.

"Well, I'd like to eat out," Curtis said.

"And I don't want you to breathe a word about what I told you as dad thinks I'm pregnant. He adores Todd. In fact, he could take my place and let Todd make love to him instead!"

Curtis laughed.

"Do not tell dad I said that either."

"You really love him, don't you?" Curtis asked. "And have you told dad that you're going to have a baby?"

"No Curtis, but because Todd stayed the night, he thought we'd slept together. A month later he heard me telling a friend about another friend who is having a baby. So he thought I was telling my friend I was having a baby. Oh, I remember the way he looked at me and smiled, then asked me if I had something to tell him. I wondered if Todd had told him we slept together."

"Well, I think you should let dad know that you're not having a baby," Curtis said.

"I will, but not yet. With all that's going on, I don't want him to feel disappointed."

"You love dad very much don't you?" Curtis asked.

"Yes, I do." Julia said. "Anyway, I had better go and wash my hair if I have to take you to dinner." After Julia washed and preened her hair, she and Curtis had a light snack before Superintendent Peterson arrived home.

At three-thirty their father walked in the house and he saw the champagne and wine on the table. He looked at Julia and then at Curtis with a smile and asked, "What are you two celebrating?"

"Julia will explain," Curtis said.

"Oh, Todd brought them for us to celebrate. He said he'd passed his exam to be a detective."

"Oh yes, that's right," Superintendent Peterson said.

"Well, you may as well help yourself dad," Julia said.

"No honey, not for me."

"Dad, would you like to have dinner with your long-lost son Curtis and me tonight?"

"Sure, I don't mind having my dinner now." He looked at Curtis. Curtis tried to give him a handshake, but he hugged Curtis and said, "Welcome home son."

"We will be eating out tonight," Julia said.

"Not for me honey, I'll just grab a sandwich, have a bath and then just rest. You and Curtis go and have dinner. Your brother and I can get to know each other afterwards."

"Dad, I was hoping you would come with us to foot the bill," Julia joked.

"Well Jules, here's a couple of hundred and don't get drunk. Curtis you look after your sister. This is for you Curtis."

"Dad, I have a little of my own."

"Did I ask you if you have money? Here, you hold on to this one thousand pounds and don't get the idea I'm paying you for the past years. However, I'd a good meal today at work and I don't think I can manage another heavy meal. So you and Curtis go and have a good time," the superintendent said and went up to his room.

Curtis booked a table for Julia and him.

At six o'clock that evening Julia and Curtis went to the Ibis Hotel in the centre of Birmingham for dinner. While they were having dinner, Officer Kelly left his table and walked over to Julia and Curtis.

"Hello Julia."

"Do I know you?"

"I think you do. Still let me refresh your memory. I'm Officer Kelly. I work with your father and Todd and I came to your home a few weeks ago."

"Oh yes, that's right. Sorry I had to rush upstairs but my hair was soaking wet. Are you alone Officer Kelly?"

"My sister's with me, but I think she went to the ladies."

"So Officer Kelly, have you ordered dinner yet?"

"Well no, not yet. I was just about to order when I saw both of you."

"Would you and your sister like to join us?" Julia asked him, while Curtis remained silent.

"My sister and I would love to."

Just as Officer Kelly spoke, his sister Estelle walked over to Julia's table and faced Curtis, smiling.

Curtis got up in respect and asked Estelle to have a seat as he pulled out her chair. When Estelle took her seat, she looked up at Curtis smiling. Officer Kelly sat down.

"Officer Kelly, please meet my brother Curtis, my dad's son."

Officer Kelly and Curtis shook hands smiling.

A waitress came to them. Estelle and Officer Kelly ordered their meals as Julia and Curtis had already ordered. Curtis ordered a bottle of the best wine. At the end of their meals, Curtis paid the bill. After they had finished the wine, the four of them left the restaurant. Outside they said goodnight. Officer Kelly and his sister thanked Julia and Curtis for their meals and an enjoyable night before they left.

As the night was still young with the a warm gentle breeze blowing and scented flower blossoms filling the air, Julia was looking happy as she got into the car and said, "Brother, I feel like going to a club. Any club," she laughed as she flicked her long curly hair backwards.

Curtis smiled.

"Curtis, do you find me attractive?"

"Sis, you're very beautiful."

"I'm happy you're my brother. So let's go and hit the clubs. Just look at how many people are going to enjoy themselves. Did you notice the way Estelle looked at you?"

"Sure, I noticed, but I'm sure it doesn't mean anything other than politeness. I'm happy you're my sister too, but the only club you will be going to is in your bed. Besides, I don't want dad to say that I'm leading you astray."

"Curtis, dad is always telling me to go out and enjoy myself. Besides, I'll be with my brother. So why don't you just turn the car around and drive us to the first club we see on Broad Street. I promise you we'll have a hell of a time. I might find a husband and you a wife," Julia laughed.

Curtis smiled broadly. "The first time I had sex was at a nightclub in a filthy toilet poking some woman I had only met once. She followed me into the toilet, dropped her panties and I had her from behind. She was hot with alcohol and I was sexually frustrated. She wanted me so badly that I did the job by cooling her off. Every time I went to party after that, I screwed a different woman until I caught the crabs and that put me off dating any women. That was about four years ago; I'm all clean and new now. So my dear sister, I wouldn't want you to lose your identity or catch what I did at any club. So, you're going home to your bed as I care about you. I wouldn't want to answer to your dad or that jealous Todd of yours. By the way, if Todd's so jealous of you, how come he left you for so long after he thought he scored you? He might be playing as clever a game as you are. I bet he knows he didn't score you. That is why he hasn't attempted to make love to you since."

"You know what Curtis, now that you mention it I believe you might be right. Todd and I decided not to make love until we're married. That night when he was pissed and fell asleep at our house, I wondered if he thought we had done anything," Julia said.

"Even so, he is still slow and a fool. If you were my woman, I would score you every night," Curtis said laughing.

"That's where you're wrong. I wouldn't let you and you could never be my man because you're my brother. As for Todd, we respect each other. Todd's a lovely bloke, but he seems to be very jealous and I don't think I can stand that. So, I really think it would be best if Todd and I weren't with each other for a while, even though I love him," Julia said.

"How old are you sis?"

"I'm twenty-five. Isn't it a shame that I'm still untouched?"

"Well sis, that's how things turn out to be sometimes. I love you as a sister. Even so, I won't come between you and Todd," Curtis said.

"Oh, as we're on the subject of virginity, let me give you a little advice. I want you to be very careful around here as men are being castrated and murdered, and if that wasn't enough, the killers pierced their eyes and slit their tongues. Judge O'Neil and Officer Forbes were two of the six. Judge O'Neil will be buried on Thursday at twelve thirty at Witten Cemetery, and then the following Monday it will be Officer Forbes' turn. We'll have to get you a suit."

"No Julia, I hate going to funerals," Curtis said.

"Dad would like you to come with us. I'm sure he would like to show you off to some of his buddies."

"I won't be going to any funeral."

"You can't let dad down. We'll get up early in the morning and go into town to buy you a suit; I think the one suit will do."

That Saturday morning, Julia took Curtis to town and bought him a nice designer three-piece grey suit of his choice, a black satin long-sleeved shirt with matching black and grey striped tie, black shoes, and a dozen pairs of socks and boxer shorts.

That evening, Superintendent Peterson took Curtis to his local pub to have a drink. He introduced Curtis to his workmates Detective Elves, Officer

Hodge and detective brothers Paul and Scott Hanson. The Superintendent and Curtis spent three hours drinking with their mates, then they went home to find Julia sleeping.

On Sunday morning over breakfast Julia said, "Dad, I didn't hear when you and Curtis came home last night."

"That's because you were out cold. However, we got in after eleven. Sorry we stayed out late."

"And what made you think I was asleep, dad?"

"Because I looked in on you and you seemed to be in dreamland, so I didn't bother to wake you."

"Dad, I wasn't sleeping. I heard when you and Curtis came home and you came into my room."

While Curtis was picking at his breakfast, the superintendent asked, "Do you want your bacon?"

"I do, but I don't think I have the strength and appetite to eat."

"Well, I hate to see crispy bacon get thrown in the bin."

The superintendent scraped the bacon off Curtis' plate and onto his, leaving the egg and tomatoes. Julia smiled, "Dad, you're eating like a pig this morning. As for your brother, you shouldn't put into your body what you can't control. Dad, you shouldn't let him drink more than he can handle."

"Julia honey, your brother's a man and not a teenager."

"Yes I know dad, but not all men can handle drink. Besides, I don't think you should pull him into your bad habits, going to pubs."

"Sis, I know I had a little too much. All I need right now is a strong drink of Andrews liver salts to cool my thumping headache and a beautiful chick to rub my upset tummy."

Superintendent Peterson laughed.

"Brother, you'll be better off with a feather pillow and a strong drink of Andrews and remember what I told you about men around here."

"What your sister is trying to tell you is that someone in this area is hacking off men's dicks and then leaving them by their drained bodies. So you've been warned."

"Yes dad."

"And as for you dad, I think it's time you found a lovely woman and married her."

"Julia honey, I've loved only one woman and that was your mother. So there's no other woman out there for me."

"So my mother wasn't good enough for you to marry dad?" Curtis asked.

"Son, your mother ran out on me before I found out she was having you. Yes, I loved your mother very much and I do hope you understand that."

"Sure, I understand. But why didn't you go after her?" Curtis asked interestedly.

"Son, if I'd known you existed, I would have been searching high and low to find you. I'm also sorry about what happened to your mother."

"Dad, I'm sorry to cross-examine you. I'm happy to know you and my sister."

"I know you are, son. I know you are." The superintendent smiled.

Curtis hugged him.

Julia gave Curtis a glass of Andrews' liver salts saying, "Here is your Andrews brother, but I can't promise you that beautiful young chick you would like to rub you up."

Superintendent Peterson laughed, so did Curtis before he drank the Andrews. "Come on brother, I want to see you drink this down before I go and cook dinner."

Curtis finished his drink. Julia took the glass and said, "I think you should go for a walk in the fresh air. I know you'll feel better and have a double helping of dinner."

"You know sis, I think you may be right," Curtis said and he went for a long walk, returning an hour later.

"Over dinner Curtis said, "Sister, you were so right. I'm feeling great since I went walking and breathed in fresh air. Do you mind me making a cup of tea?"

"Curtis, you don't have to ask. Make this the last time you ask me. We're family and this is your home and what we have in this home is ours. So you want anything, I repeat, you don't have to ask."

Curtis made a cup of tea, then went into the living room and lay on the settee. After an hour he was feeling much better and he went to church with Julia and Superintendent Peterson.

At the church Julia nudged Curtis and whispered to him, "The girl on the other side keeps looking at you and smiling."

"Believe me sis, I'm not in the least interested. Anyway, I'm not ready for any woman yet."

Julia smiled. She said nothing more but just kept looking at the young black attractive woman looking at her brother.

After the service the pastor waited at the door to shake everyone's hand, thanking each person for coming. As she came to shake Curtis' hand, she looked deep into his eyes and it seemed that she didn't want to let his hand go. Curtis smiled and slid his hand slowly out of hers. As Julia and her father were standing waiting for Curtis, the pastor smiled and Curtis walked away. Julia shook her head still smiling. As they were walking to their car, she said, "Brother, you go to church another Sunday and you'll surely find a wife."

Curtis laughed, Superintendent Peterson asked, "What is the joke about?"

"Dad, it was just a simple joke between me and my handsome brother. Anyhow, the service was nice."

"Yes, it was," the superintendent said. They got in their car and as Curtis was about to drive away, the pastor walked up to them and said, "Mr Peterson, Julia thanks for coming. As for you, Mr Handsome, I do hope you'll come again. It's always great to welcome fresh faces."

Curtis smiled and looked at his wristwatch. The pastor said goodbye and left. Curtis drove away smiling.

"What was that all about, son?"

"I have no idea dad."

"Well, brother, you have a choice between an attractive black young beauty and a white beautiful middle-aged pastor. Now brother it's up to you." Julia laughed, then the three of them stayed silent for a while, but as soon as Curtis turned in the gateway, the superintendent burst into laughter then said, "So you lucky devil, I saw the way the young pastor looked at you with her lovely blue eyes."

"Dad, I can't help it if I have your handsome looks and am attractive to some of the most beautiful chicks." Curtis giggled.

Julia looked deeply in Curtis' face and said, "Curtis you are really a handsome bloke, but dad is miles in front."

Julia had put a bright smile on her dad's face and he said, "I gave you half of my looks and I kept the other half." The three of them had a good laugh.

"But Curtis, you really are very handsome," Julia said again.

"Are you sorry I'm your brother?" Curtis asked, laughing.

"You two cut it out," the superintendent said with straight face.

Curtis parked in the garage, Julia opened the door with her key then left the door open. As Curtis walked into the house, he went for a glass of whiskey.

"Whiskey?" Julia asked.

"Just to settle my nerves. You want a little one dad?"

"No. Not for me son."

Julia changed her clothes and then went to cook the dinner. Three-thirty in the afternoon, over dinner, Julia said, "The service was enjoyable."

"Julia, are you teasing your brother again."

"No dad. However, I should look about myself."

Curtis helped Julia with the washing up while Superintendent Peterson went in the garden to fork up the ground to sow vegetables. Curtis went to help him leaving Julia cleaning the kitchen. Sometime later, Julia rang Todd at his flat. As she couldn't get him so she rang his mother. "Hello. Dorothy, it's me Julia."

"Julia, if you're looking for Todd, he left about twenty minutes ago. Is everything okay?"

"Yes. Sure, of course." Julia's voice sounded dull.

"Julia, you're talking to me honey. Come on, what's wrong? Did you and Todd have a fight?"

"No nothing like that. It's just a misunderstanding between us."

"Well I hope you both sort out whatever went wrong," Mrs Todd said.

"Well goodbye Dorothy."

"I'll see you soon Julia."

Julia put the phone down and went to her room in tears.

Todd's mother shook her head smiling as she put her phone on the receiver.

Some hours later, Curtis woke Julia from her sleep. "Sis, I made supper. Not as good as yours, but its edible."

Julia faced him smiling. "I best go freshen up first." She left then returned shortly looking cool. "You changed your hairstyle."

"Well yes, I'm getting a little weary of the old style." She sat looking at Curtis as he put her supper on the table in front of her. She raised her eyes to his and tucked in. After eating, she recited, "Brother, I give you ten out of ten. You are an expert cook."

"That is because I had a great-grandma that taught me. She also taught me how to wash, darn, iron my clothes and tidy a house. Bless her," Curtis said.

"Where's your grandma?" Julia asked.

"She's living in Scotland. She's a lovely old soul."

"So why don't you buy a house here in Sutton and bring her down to live?" Julia said.

"Well let's see how I get on with you and dad first. Besides, I don't think she'll want to live anywhere else after living in Scotland for forty years. Besides, all her old friends and relatives are there."

"Well son, you will have no problems with me if you need help to buy a place, you can count on me."

"Thanks dad."

The following Thursday morning at eleven thirty, Curtis drove his father and Julia to the funeral of Judge O'Neil. At the service, the late Judge O'Neil's sister sung the Lords' Prayer; she had a powerful voice.

The church was so packed with mourners and officers of different ranks that people were standing at the back and sides with so many more standing in the churchyard. It was a spectacular scene to have so many officers turned out in uniform.

Julia's eyes were searching for Todd amongst the officers, but she only saw him when leaving the church after the service. As her eyes met Todd's, he smiled, but she noticed how moist his eyes looked. She wondered if Todd's tears had been over their breaking up or over the death of his two colleges. At the burial, she watched him take a woman's hand in his. She lowered her head before backing away behind some mourners then tears welled up in her eyes.

After Superintendent Peterson saw Todd holding the woman's hand, he went looking for Julia. Julia saw him walking towards her and she dried her tears quickly. He hugged her around her shoulders saying, "Jul love, let's go and find your brother as the burial is nearly over."

"Dad, you go and find him. I'll wait here."

"Were you crying?"

"Not really dad; it's been so emotional that tears came in my eyes. You go get Curtis. I'll be okay."

"Have you seen Todd?"

"Yes dad. I saw him."

Superintendent Peterson smiled then left to find Curtis chatting to Officer Kelly and couple of officers. "Hi mates," the superintendent greeted his colleges. Officer Kelly respectfully nodded smiling. The superintendent faced Curtis, "Son, your sister and I are ready to leave."

"Okay dad." Curtis said goodbye before they left to get Julia.

Just as the superintendent was getting in the front seat, he saw an old retired friend, Superintendent Stock. "I'll be right back after I say hello to an old friend." Curtis smiled.

Superintendent Peterson went to his old friend. They shook hands as they chatted. Julia blew her nose so hard that Curtis looked at her. She burst out crying. Curtis went and sat in the back with her. She hugged him. "Come on Jul, why are you crying?"

"I saw Todd holding a woman's hand."

Curtis squinted. "I'm sure she meant nothing to him."

Their dad came back and sat in the front seat; Curtis got in the driver's seat, belted up then looked back at Julia. She smiled. Just as Curtis was about to drive away, Todd rushed up to the car and knocked on the window. Curtis wound down his window. "Julia, can I speak to you later?"

"Sure, of course."

Todd walked back to the young white woman.

"Dad, let's stay for the burials," Julia said.

"Are you sure, love?"

"Yes dad. I saw some friends I would like to say hello to too."

Curtis went to talk to some friends he met in the pub while Superintendent Peterson mingled with his colleagues as he watched Julia talking to her boss and workmates.

"Well Julia, we'll see you at the wake," her friends told her. "Well, I'm not sure as I have to be somewhere, but I'll see you four tomorrow at work." She hugged her friends then went back to Curtis. "Curtis, please take me home as I don't want to go to the restaurant."

"Why not, aren't you feeling well?"

"Curtis, I just want to go home, then you and dad can go to the restaurant if you want."

"Julia, what's the hurry to go home. If you don't want to speak to Todd, you don't have too."

"Curtis, are you going to take me home or shall I call a taxi?"

"Julia, what's the matter with you and Todd?"

"Curtis, I really don't want to talk about Todd, now or any other time. Since he came into our home and saw you, he rushed out of the house like he was on fire. Curtis, if Todd wants to be stubborn, then so can I be. I won't be a doormat for him. So would you please take me home?"

"Okay. Just let me get dad." Curtis smiled, then left and shortly he returned with his dad. They took Julia home, saw her in the house. "Sis, will you be okay?"

"Yes Curtis, you and dad go back to show your respect. Curtis, see dad is okay will you and don't let him stay out too late as he has to go to work tomorrow morning."

"Okay sis, I'll be sure to bring him home early."

Julia watched her dad and brother drive away. She closed the door then had some wine before sitting on the settee.

The superintendent and Curtis walked into the restaurant; Mrs O'Neil went to him. She smiled then hugged him. "Thanks for the lovely wreath."

"It's from the team."

"Please be sure to thank all for me."

"Well you take care, Mrs O'Neil." The Superintendent said goodbye then went to Mrs Forbes to say hello. After spending four hours and with the darkness creeping in, Curtis took his father home to find Julia sleeping.

"What's up with your sister? It's only ten past five and she's in bed."

"Dad, I worry about her. I really think she loves that Todd. But he doesn't seem to care a damn about her. He doesn't deserve her," Curtis said furiously.

"Son, you keep out of Julia and Todd's business. They have been courting for the past four years, they have broken up hundreds of times and then got back together. Those two belong with each other. They will end up together, I'm sure," Superintendent Peterson said.

On Sunday morning, Petra gave her mother a card with a freshly-cut red rose in the middle saying, 'I will forever love you Mum'. Her mother hugged her and told her, "I love you and Arden more than life itself." Petra smiled.

That morning, Petra's friends Stanley, Faith, Elizabeth, Martin and Jenny went to pay their respects to Mrs O'Neil, but with fake smiles as they told her they were sorry about her husband.

That Sunday morning, Julia rang Todd. He picked the phone up but it dropped. Julia hung up in anger. For the next three hours she tried phoning him, but every time she could not get hold of him.

Eventually that Sunday afternoon Todd did answer the ringing phone.

"Hello,"

"Todd, it's me."

"Julia I understand if you don't want to see me any more." He hung up. Tears welled up in Julia's eyes. She coiled herself on the settee crying softly and then sobbing. The superintendent heard her. He stood over her. "Are you crying Jul?"

"Dad, Todd broke up with me. We're no longer engaged. I'll post the engagement ring back to him."

"Well love, it might be for the best."

That evening Superintendent Peterson went to see Todd at his flat to talk to him before they both started the night shift. After Superintendent Peterson knocked at Todd's door for so long, a Mr Weeks, Todd's neighbour, told him Todd had left about an hour ago.

"Thanks," Superintendent Peterson said to Mr Weeks and he drove to see Todd's mother. Before he got out of his car, he smiled, shaking his greying head. He knocked at Mrs Todd's door.

"Well Super, what brings you here?"

"Is Todd here?"

"No, he's at his flat."

"I just came from there and he's not at home, which is why I'm here."

"Is anything wrong?"

"No, no. I'll see him later."

"Would you like to leave a message?"

"Not really, as I said, I will see him at work."

"Well, I'm going to do some cleaning for him later and I can pass on your message to him. Really, it won't be any trouble," Mrs Todd said.

"Anyway, why are you really here Superintendent Peterson?" Mrs Todd asked and then went on to say, "I know you're here for a good reason."

"Oh, I came to have a word with your Todd."

"Superintendent Peterson, I'm very sorry that the relationship between your Julia and my Todd didn't work out."

"Don't worry about them Mrs Todd, it's just a misunderstanding. I asked Todd to take Julia some flowers and he met my son Curtis in the house. So, your son flared up and stormed out of the house and didn't want to listen when Julia tried to explain the situation."

"So my Todd thought your son was Julia's boyfriend?"

"Exactly."

"Mr Peterson, I thought Julia was your only child," Mrs Todd said smiling.

"I thought so too, until I got a phone call from my son saying that he wanted to get to know me and that I'm his father."

"But did you know he was coming to see you?"

"No Mrs Todd," Superintendent Peterson laughed.

"Well, the same day he phoned me, he turned up while I was at work and Julia let him in. Todd saw him before I did. He's thirty-two. Seven years older than Julia and he's quite a lad. I didn't even know he existed until he phoned me."

"And why is that Mr Peterson?"

"I wish you would call me Rodney."

"Only if you will call me Dorothy."

"Well Dorothy, when I got to know her, I was hoping she would be my wife but it wasn't to be. Anyway, I was twenty-eight when I met Curtis' mother. She was a singer in the Double Star Night Club. I was just an officer then."

"So tell me Super, I mean Rodney, where's Curtis mother and why had she never told you that you were going to have a son or had a son? Would you mind me asking if your relationship was brief or long?"

"Well Dorothy, where she was working as a singer and a dancer, a gang fight broke out which led to a young man being killed and seven others wounded. I was one of the officers that went to the club to investigate. That is when I met my son's mother. That night she was singing. I went to her aid when I saw her lying on the floor in blood; she held onto me so tightly that I offered to take her to the hospital. She looked frightened, but she smiled widely and said she was wearing someone else's blood. I laughed, she laughed.

From there we became good friends. That night I took her home. Her home of course." He laughed. "She got changed and asked me to stay for a while. Before I knew it, it was morning. She gave me her phone number. I called her and for three weeks we were an item and I started spending a lot of time with her. Three months later her regular club opened again. That Saturday night I was off duty and I called at the club to pick her up ten minutes later than she asked. I was told by another dancer that she had just left. I rushed out to catch her when I saw her getting into a car. The driver said something to her and she looked at me smiling before they drove away. The following morning I met her in the newsagent but as she was trying to explain, I walked away. A month later, I saw her mother and she told me she had sent her daughter away from me as her daughter told her that I didn't want to have anything more do with her. Well, her mother told me it was just a couple of flings that had happened between her daughter and me. Then, after trying so many times to get in touch with her, she told me I was wasting my time and that her daughter was in love with someone else. Even if it was not so, there was no way she would have let me see her daughter as they were moving to Leeds. I didn't even know her daughter was carrying my son. I fell in love with Julia's mother and four months after we had been together I married her.

"For twenty-five years I thought Julia was my only child. Like Todd, I played ignorant. I didn't want to know who the other man was. Two months later I saw Mrs Barton, Curtis' Grandma's sister, and I asked her to tell me where Curtis' Grandma lived, but she refused, and then told me that she had made a promise to her sister never to tell me where she lived. Anyway, I went to Leeds looking for her, but I had no luck. A week later I came back home sad and mad as a tiger that had lost his meal. For four months I was pining over Shana but as I realised there would never be a Shana in my life anymore, I told myself, Peterson, pick yourself up and get on with your life; stop dreaming and wake up to reality. Well, as I told you, I met Julia's mother at a friend's wedding party and we got to like each other, so I dated her and soon we were married. But each time I lay in bed beside Julia's mother, I saw Curtis' mother. Well I fought desperately hard not to think about her – Curtis' mother of course. But the harder I tried not to think of her, the stronger I could see her face that at one time I became so aggressive to Julia's mother telling her how much I had loved Shana. It took Julia's mother five months to forgive me and share our bed. As I said, I had to move on and start showing Julia's mother how much I loved her; it took some time for Shana to wash out of my thoughts. Then Julia came along and I was so happy.

"Eleven years later, I lost Julia's mother to a tumour. However, two years later, Shana's aunt told my sister, Shana and three friends went sailing somewhere in Miami and their yacht collided with another and sank. Shana and her three friends drowned. Strangely enough, I had a feeling something wasn't quite right because I often used to have nightmares, night after night, of a little boy crying. Curtis was the nightmare and that boy."

"So Curtis' Grandma didn't tell you about Curtis?"

"No Dorothy. She didn't even give me a clue. I missed out on bringing up my son." The superintendent's face showed sadness.

Mrs Todd smiled before she said, "Funnily enough, did Julia tell you that she's going to have a baby?"

Superintendent Peterson looked into Mrs Todd's eyes in surprise before he said, "No. She hasn't said anything to me."

Mrs Todd smiled gracefully. "Well Julia's friend Rita told me she thinks Julia may be a couple months pregnant. I think you'd better tell Todd before he makes the same mistake as you as he's a strong-headed lad. I really want him to marry Julia and I want my grandchild to know me. So, I think it's up to us to see that Todd and Julia patch up their differences. Don't you think Rodney?"

"Yes Dorothy. I think you're right. Where is Todd now?" the superintendent asked.

"I think he went to the gym if he's not at home," Mrs Todd said.

"Okay, I'll see him at work later or tomorrow." Superintendent Peterson smiled.

"By the way Rodney, did you find out who that man was?" Mrs Todd asked dying to know.

"Yes Dorothy, he was her brother. You take care and tell Ernest hello for me." Superintendent turned to leave.

"I will Rodney. You take care too."

Superintendent Peterson waved goodbye and he got into his car and drove home. He let himself into his house to find Curtis drinking a can of beer.

"Hello dad. I fancied one of your beers."

"Help yourself Curtis, where's Julia?"

"Somewhere upstairs I think. Do you want me to go and get her?"

"No, no, no. You finish your beer son. I'll go to her," Superintendent Peterson said.

Curtis widened his eyes as he shrugged his shoulders in thought. Superintendent Peterson looked at him, smiled, and then marched upstairs to find Julia in her room lying across her bed face downwards. He cleared his throat with a soft cough made Julia lift her head up to look at him.

"Hello dad. What are you doing in my room?"

"I just came to have a look on you. I thought you were sleeping."

"I was just about to, when you sneaked into my room."

"Jul, I didn't sneak in your room. I walked in."

"What do you want dad?"

"I see Todd's bought you some flowers," the superintendent said to make conversation.

"Look dad, I told you how nasty Todd was to me. I don't care if I never see him again and as for the flowers, he told me they're for the price of a kiss. That was before he rushed away."

"Superintendent Peterson laughed and then asked, "Todd knows you're carrying?"

"Carrying what? Dad, I hate to ask you to leave my room as I'm very tired. I'll speak to you later," said Julia and she pulled the quilt over her head. Superintendent Peterson left her room. He quietly closed her door and stood outside the door for a few seconds in thought before he went downstairs into the living room to have a chat and a beer with Curtis. Ten minutes later Curtis went to work.

That evening Superintendent Peterson had his dinner at about seven o'clock in the evening, then went to the pub to have a drink. After Curtis finished his evening shift, he met Superintendent Peterson in the pub and had a drink with him and three of the superintendent's mates. At ten-thirty Curtis and Superintendent Peterson said goodnight and left. Curtis drove behind Superintendent Peterson all the way home. They parked their cars in the garage then Curtis said, "Dad, I hate to see Julia look so unhappy. I don't think Todd deserves her."

"Son, she is twenty-five and we can't tell her what to do. So let's keep out of her way eh?"

"Dad, I know what you're saying, but I can't sit comfortably while my sister is pining away over some man that doesn't deserve her."

"Son, I hate to disturb that overworked brain of yours, but Todd isn't some man. He's the man your sister loves and wants to be his wife, so you and I will have to tread carefully and give her space. I don't want you to say anything to her concerning Todd. This is a problem they both will have to work out."

"I understand, dad."

As Superintendent Peterson and Curtis walked in, Julia got up from the settee and said, "Goodnight dad. Goodnight Curtis."

"Are you going to bed now honey?"

"Yes dad. I was only waiting to see you home safely. I left you and Curtis some chicken supper. I'm so tired so I'll see you both in the morning." Julia walked out the living room yawning.

"Honey, haven't you heard from Todd?" Superintendent Peterson asked anxiously.

"Dad, I don't want to talk about Todd now or anytime, so please don't mention his name to me again," Julia said sadly and went to bed. In bed she cried softly. Before Curtis ate, he knocked on her door. She dried her eyes quickly and said, "Come in." Curtis walked in smiling.

"Sis, I know it's none of my business, but seeing you looking so unhappy makes me feel bad. It's since Todd saw me and became jealous that he drifted away. Well it's up to me to get you two back together as you were," Curtis said looking guilty.

"Curtis, don't feel bad, nothing's lost forever. When Todd saw you, he left like a puff of wind. If he'd really loved me or cared, he would have asked why you were here or who you were. I asked dad never to speak to Todd about me. I'm asking you to do the same. If Todd loves me, he has to come to me."

"Sis, do you love him?"

"Yes Curtis. I love him very much but I won't be crawling to him."

"Sis, I respect what you say and I'm very proud of you. Goodnight."

"Goodnight Curtis."

On Monday morning at Officer Forbes' funeral, the church was packed with mourners and officers who turned out to pay their respects. Superintendent Peterson and Curtis were amongst the mourners.

On Tuesday morning the Superintendent went to work before Curtis and Julia got up. At work he saw Detective Todd and asked him in his office.

"Todd. Do you know Julia is carrying?"

"Carrying what?

"Julia is going to have your baby?"

Todd looked at Superintendent Peterson in surprise.

"You mean you didn't know?" the superintendent smiled.

"Super, I didn't go that far with your daughter, moreover to be having a baby with her. Did Julia tell you she's having my child?" Todd looked shocked.

"No. She didn't. But your mother told me."

"My mother told you that Julia is having my baby?" Todd's blue eyes stretched open wide.

"Well yes, but not deliberately. I called to have a word with you concerning Julia over what you told her about the flowers."

"Superintendent, if Julia is having a baby, it's not mine."

"What do you mean my daughter's child is not yours?" Superintendent Peterson raised his voice in anger. Todd raised his eyes to the ceiling and said, "Because I have not touched Julia, I went no further than a kiss."

Superintendent Peterson fisted Todd in his face and knocked him down. Todd got up in rage and pushed the Superintendent Peterson away and then said outright, "I didn't fuck your daughter. Not even once." Then he walked out of Superintendent Peterson's office. Peterson sat at his desk deep in thought then shoved the pile of documents off his desk to the floor in temper. A few minutes later, he drove himself home to meet Curtis sitting on the settee. "Where's Julia?" he asked.

"At work, I think." Curtis said. "She hasn't come home yet."

"I thought she was on her holiday," Superintendent Peterson said.

"Oh, I don't know," Curtis said looking surprised.

As Superintendent Peterson was getting into his car, he saw Julia getting out of hers. He walked up to her with a serious look on his face.

"What's the matter dad?" she asked standing by her car.

"I just left Todd. I told him you were pregnant and he told me he hasn't touched you in that way."

"Dad, Todd has told you the truth, I am not pregnant. Todd and I did not sleep together, we only kissed. I told Todd I would sleep with him only if we were married and not before. He agreed with me. Dad, I'm still a virgin if you must know. Todd hasn't touched me! I told you when Todd saw Curtis he thought I was having an affair. Todd refused to hear what I had to say. He accused me of being unfaithful. He broke off the engagement and I saw him at Judge O'Neil's graveside with a white woman's hand in his. I haven't seen Todd for four days. I tried to get in touch with him by phoning him to explain about Curtis but each time his phone rings out. Dad, I can't keep up with Todd. He has given me the impression he never wants to see me again. Even if was pregnant, I would just have to learn to live with my bastard child."

"Don't say that! Just don't. I'll see Todd later and I will explain."

"No dad. Don't! Todd's the one that walked out on me and broke the engagement off. I will not beg him to consider having me back! No way will I creep to Todd. If he did really love me, he would have listened to what I had to say. Dad if you ask him to come here, I will move out and you'll never see me again. If Todd comes to see me, it must be of his own free will and I'll be expecting an apology."

"Julia…"

"Yes dad?"

"Oh nothing honey, I'll see you later," the Superintendent said and left for work.

Three o'clock the same afternoon, the Superintendent returned home and invited Julia and Curtis to dinner at the Albany Hotel as Julia was still crying over the break-up with Todd.

Curtis got changed. He went to Julia. "Are you ready sis?"

Julia lifted her head from under her cover and said, "You and dad go and have dinner." Curtis and Superintendent Peterson looked at her and saw tears in her eyes. "I'm having period pains." The Superintendent smiled, but looked confused. "Okay. We'll order in dinner and we'll eat out another night."

"No dad, you and Curtis go and have dinner. Some rest will do me good."

The Superintendent went downstairs to Curtis. "I hate to leave your sister knowing she's not feeling well."

Curtis said nothing. The Superintendent went back to Julia. Looking at him she said, "Dad, you and Curtis please go for dinner. I will be all right soon. I just need to stay in bed and rest for a couple of hours." The Superintendent touched her head and went back to Curtis saying, "Let's go son."

"Well, we booked for seven o'clock," Curtis said as he saw his watch saying ten past six. Just before they left, the superintendent went to Julia and asked her, "How are you feeling now?"

"I'm still in pain."

"I really hate to leave you in this state. We can always cancel and have dinner another time."

"No dad. You take Curtis to dinner. Both of you have a good time. I think I will feel much better after I sleep."

"Okay. We will. But if you should need me, just call."

"Okay dad. I will and don't worry about me."

"We'll see you when we get home."

"Okay dad, you and my brother have a good time."

The superintendent and Curtis left and got to the hotel at five to seven.

After dinner, on the way out of the hotel, the superintendent and Curtis watched Todd and a young woman get into his car.

Todd saw the superintendent and Curtis looking at them. He drove away with a faint smile. The superintendent smiled and Curtis got into their car.

"Dad, wasn't that Todd?"

"Yes. But when he saw you, he thought you were Julia's sidekick."

Curtis grinned. "Well, if you ask me, I don't think he deserves my sister. He is nothing but an arrogant jealous rat. I just feel like taking that chick from him."

"Well I didn't ask you and he is only jealous because he loves your sister. And about the chick, she's a cop and stay well away."

"Look dad, I am sorry but I'm only speaking my mind."

"That's okay son, maybe you are right. Now I've found you I do not want to lose you. I am so proud of you being a doctor I would like you to stay with Julia and me. I will have a word with your Uncle Barnes and see if he can help you get a job in his hospital. Besides you would be good company for Julia and me."

"I'm happy living with you and Julia dad," Curtis said.

When Superintendent Peterson and Curtis got home, they met Julia sitting at the kitchen table drinking a glass of milk. They didn't tell her that they saw Todd with this policewoman.

On Wednesday afternoon the superintendent had a pint with Todd and mates in the Lion Pub, but said nothing to Todd concerning Julia. The Thursday morning at work he asked Todd in his office and said, "I think you have done the right thing to push my daughter aside." Todd kept silent and well away from the superintendent for the rest of the day and he did the same for the rest of the week and only spoke to the superintendent if he had to.

One week later, on Saturday morning, Petra was on her way to the newspaper shop when she met Julia by her gate getting into her car.

"Good morning Julia."

"Good morning Petra."

Julia smiled. "Petra, I'm so sorry about your dad."

"I wish I could say the same."

Julia's smile faded. "Did the police find out who killed your father?"

"Your dad's the best person to ask."

"Well, I hope something will come to light."

"Julia, do you mind me asking you a question?"

"Of course not Petra, you ask me what you like."

"Were you in agony when you first gave yourself to Todd?"

"Petra I can't discuss this with you."

"Julia, I only want to know if you were in pain. I'm sorry I asked, that was completely out of order. Still, I am sure you were when you first made love to Todd."

"Petra what are you trying to tell me?" Julia looked puzzled.

"I heard a friend of a friend said when she first had sex it hurt her a lot."

"Well yes, I suppose it hurts but the truth is, I can't tell you because I made a promise to myself that I would never give myself to anyone until we are married."

"Well you have a good and protective father, but you think of other unfortunate young people who aren't as protected as you to be abused and have been raped by members of their families. Tell me if youths are not safe at home with families, where would they be safe." Petra's lovely bright brown eyes lowered to the ground.

"Even so Petra, I think people that have been raped should tell the police or families that care, don't you think so Petra?"

"Don't you think they haven't? Wake up to the wicked people of the world, Julia. So many people have been ignored by the law, families or even social workers after complaining of rape and abuse by members of their families or other folk. I've listened to the television, to friends and read about rapists and abusers. Even some families refuse to believe other families about their ordeals and left them in danger. So Julia, I strongly agree with anyone to take the law into their own hands to deal with rapists and abusive people and eliminate them to kingdom come! If each abuser took revenge, it would be a damn lot less work for the police to deal with as they only have to scrape up the abusive shits and disintegrate them. Don't you think it would be safer to do that?"

Julia watched Petra in wonder as she walked away. She shook her head smiling, still thinking over what Petra had said.

That Saturday afternoon Todd's mother told him Curtis was Julia's brother but Julia or her father didn't know about him until he'd turned up. Tears came sliding down Todd's face. Later that evening he went to see Julia. Shamefully he apologised saying "Julia, I'm so very sorry for not listening to you when you were trying to tell me about your brother. Judge O'Neil and Forbes' death along with everything else has been playing on my mind and it's left me feeling confused. Julia, I won't feel comfortable until my colleague's murderer is caught. But, I'm here to ask you to give us another chance."

"Todd, I love you. Well, as for whatever else, good luck. According to my new founded friend Petra, they must have done wrong to deserve what they got. Maybe Petra is right."

"Julia, just what are you saying, did Petra say anything else?"

"No Todd. But I saw remorse on her face."

"Oh love, I think this ring belongs to you." Todd took Julia's left hand into his, slipped a diamond ring onto her finger and then kissed it. Julia's eyes widened as she stared at the diamond shining under the light.

"What happened to my first engagement ring?" she asked in wonder.

"I exchanged it for the best. Have a look inside – it says VT JP to signify Vincent Todd and Julia Peterson. Julia I love you so much. I didn't know I would miss you so much."

"Todd, I love you very much too."

Todd took Julia in his arms then kissed her passionately. "I got jealous when I saw your brother."

"I know."

"How about us two go out for a meal tonight?"

"Okay Todd, well what time will you call for me?"

"About six. I would also like you to meet my Aunt Doris and family. One of her daughter's Joanne was with me at Judge O'Neil's funeral."

Julia smiled to have heard Joanne was the young woman's hand Todd was holding. "Why are you smiling?"

"No reason Todd." Julia flung her arms around his neck.

"Come on honey, that smile is telling me a love story."

Todd pushed Julia down onto the three-seater settee tickling her saying, "Tell me why your smile pictured a lovely story."

Julia was laughing so much that her prancing showed Todd her panties. But as she felt Todd's erection, she stopped laughing and pushed him off her then got up staring at him.

"Jul, I wouldn't have taken you until you're ready to give in to me. I respect what you told me and I want to look into those beautiful brown eyes when you give yourself to me for the first time. By the way, how come you're having my child without inviting me to take part?" he laughed softly.

"Oh, that came from my loudmouth friend as I told her you and I were pissed one night and I wasn't sure if we had had sex. Oh, that's why dad asked me if I was pregnant as he also heard me telling a friend another of my friends is pregnant. Todd, you're not vexed with me for not giving in to you?"

"No. As I said, I wouldn't unless you come to me."

"Thanks honey. I do love you and as soon as we're married I'm all yours."

"Anyway, before I take you to dinner, I'll take you to meet the rest of my new-found family," Todd said.

"When did your Aunt Doris and her family arrive?" Julia asked

"Yesterday morning. My aunt and her husband arrived from New York. Joanne and Kim are here. You will adore them, especially my aunt."

"Todd, I heard she is very rich. Is that true?"

"Julia, she's as poor as a church mouse. It's Eric her husband who is rich. If he should leave her, I think she would fall facedown and be glad to scoop in a worm for a meal." Todd laughed and went home and at five thirty he rang Julia asking her if she was ready.

"Yes. I'm waiting on you my love."

"I'll be there in fifteen minutes."

Julia put the phone down and faced her brother smiling then saying, "Todd's taking me to dinner."

"You be careful with that jealous bloke."

"Curtis, I have been careful for the last four years and eight months. Todd knows the rules. It's one of his family traditions, so I believe that by being with him I will be one hundred per cent safe as he's the love of my life."

"Until his cock snake rises and becomes uncontrollable, especially after having a few drinks, then who knows what will happen."

"Curtis, Todd's not like you."

Curtis laughed. "You're so right sis, having a beautiful woman like you would be my body warmer every night."

Curtis laughed again. "But be honest sis, do you think Todd's a virgin?"

"Well brother, I don't know. But Todd will just have to be patient with me until the time comes. So my dear brother, let's leave it at that."

Just then Todd's car pulled up outside the gate. Julia told Curtis that she would see him later and she left the house to meet Todd walking up the pathway. As they met, Todd kissed her, then held her hand and walked her to his car. A few of Julia's neighbours watched until they got into the car and drove away.

As Todd drove them to see his parents and family from America, Julia looked nervous.

"What's the matter darling?" he asked her.

"I'm feeling a little nervous about meeting your aunt and her family."

"Don't worry, everything will be all right. We'll just say hello, then leave."

"It may be easier said than done. If your Aunt Doris is anything like your mother, we may be in for a long stay."

Todd pulled up by his mother's gate. He escorted Julia into the house to meet his Aunt Doris and the rest of the family. His Aunt Doris went to Julia and walked around her deeply inhaling her perfume scent. She smiled looking into Julia's eyes saying, "You smell as beautiful as you look. Yes honey, my nephew has chosen wisely. I do like you Julia."

Julia faced Todd with a smile and whispered to him, "I like her."

Then as his Aunt lifted Julia's chin she said, "You're very beautiful."

Julia smiled, then looked at her wristwatch so that Todd would see her.

"We have to go now," Todd told his family, "We've booked dinner for six thirty."

"So soon?" his mother asked.

"They're young and so much in love. Well Todd, you better be off with your future wife. We'll catch up later. We're here for four months. Now take your beautiful lady and run away before I beg you both to stay." Todd kissed his aunt on her face before he and Julia walked out of the house and to his car. He opened the door for Julia to get in. As Julia sat comfortably in the front seat and waited for him to get in, his twenty-year-old cousin Kim ran into his arms and kissed him. He looked more shocked than Julia was. As he stood in shock staring at Kim, she laughed then asked,

"What's the matter Todd, haven't you ever been kissed by a real woman before?"

Todd looked at Julia and wiped his lips with a pale blue handkerchief.

Kim went further to unbutton her blouse showing her pointed hard nipples and laughed when Julia looked hard at her and covered her eyes with her hands while Todd shook Kim by the shoulders and said to her, "Don't ever, ever, try to kiss me again!"

"I'm not your cousin! I was adopted and I'm not a virgin either! You and your stupid family with your old mildew traditions about your wives having to be virgins; well, I spit on that." She turned and faced Julia then said, "Girl, I pity you to be in this crazy family. After you're married to the family, you'll have to report to them you were a virgin. Still, you're very lucky, the sampling of sex ended a few years ago, otherwise Todd's father would be the first to bore your little spyhole and leave it bleeding wide open for his son to walk in and then both will let the family know if you're a virgin or not! Well, go and enjoy your dinner both of you." Kim said and laughed. So annoyed, Todd raised his hand to hit Kim, but as Julia looked at him he dropped his hand at his side.

"Come on Todd, let's go," Julia said.

Todd got into his car but before he drove away, Kim lifted her skirt up to her waist showing her black silk G-string knickers and stuck two fingers up and then went into the house.

"She's something else," Julia said.

"She's a bitch!" Todd said taking Julia's hand into his and kissed her hand saying, "You know I love you and you're the one I'm going to marry".

Julia smiled. "With Kim coming between us, there might not be any marriage."

"Honey, there's no Kim. So you have nothing to worry about."

When Kim got into the house, Joanne was waiting for her.

"I saw what you did."

"Fuck you!"

"The same goes to you too Kim."

"Oh, you're a long way behind the times darling. There's only one man has done that and that is my adopted sugar daddy! Your daddy is giving me what I want. Why do you think I have thousands of pounds in my account? Well let me put you in the picture. I exchanged my body for his money! It all comes from your daddy. Oh, and just in case you decide to tell mother, she already knows. If I leave, your daddy will come with me."

"You dirty, little nasty bitch!" Joanne slapped Kim across the face.

Kim held her face and laughed. "By the way, you can tell your cousin Todd, when I see what I want, that's exactly what I'll get! And believe me, I have my ways." Kim cut her eyes at Joanne and went to her room.

Kim is very beautiful, reckless, strong-minded and gets exactly what she wants. She's twenty years old and a mixed race colour of camel, with white pearly teeth, pout lips, shoulder length wavy dark brown hair, five foot eight in height and has a figure to make men turn their heads to look at her. Joanne is her half-sister on her mother's side. Joanne is white, very good looking and two inches shorter with a beautiful curvy figure.

Meanwhile, Todd and Julia were eating dinner. Over dinner, Julia was looking at Todd. She said nothing, but she looked troubled that each time she took a spoonful of food it seemed as though it choked her.

"What's the matter darling?" Todd asked her. She shook her head.

"Do you want us to leave?"

"No!" she whispered, and then put a small amount of meat in her mouth. Todd was looking at her. He too was also looking troubled.

"Todd, if you should get the chance to make love to Kim, would you do it?"

"Julia, I almost lost you once because of my stupid jealousness. I will not do anything to endanger our future of getting married. I love you too much to be sucked in by a little tramp like Kim."

Julia smiled. "I think she's ruthless and capable of destroying other people's happiness."

"Don't worry about her."

"Todd, how did she become part of your family?" Julia asked interestedly.

"It's like this, Aunt Doris and Kim's mother were good friends for years. Oh, and her mother's black. Anyway, according to my aunt, her husband is Kim's dad. But I believe Kim's her daughter."

"Why do you think that?"

"My other aunt told Mum Aunt Doris had a fling with a dark security guard twenty years ago."

"What's your aunt's husband's job?"

"He's an architect."

"But surely, your aunt should tell Kim the truth regardless."

"Jul, Joanne showed me Kim's birth certificate has her dad's and Kim's mother's name as my aunt's name on it. But she never knew her supposed mother as she was just five weeks when she left her with my aunt."

"Poor Kim, no wonder she acts like a little lost child."

"Well, honey, are you ready to leave?"

Julia smiled. "I will be right back." She went to the toilet leaving Todd to pay the bill. After she returned Todd took her hand into his and they left. He kissed her and took her home. Before seeing her in, he kissed her again. "Thanks for having dinner with me." He watched her going into her house and close the door before he drove himself to his mother's house and let himself in. As he was about to turn the light on in the living room, Kim placed her hand over his hand saying, "Don't. Everyone's sleeping and we wouldn't want to wake them. I knew you'd be back, that's why I'm downstairs waiting for you."

"Where are the others really?"

"Well, they said they've gone to visit friends. But I knew you'd be back, so I stayed in. Since we both know why you're here, let's not beat around the bush. You're here for sex and I'm here to give it to you. Now just take a good long hard look at my sexy slim, beautiful brown body then tell me Todd, can you resist my beautiful body? And, I don't mean just getting a kiss. Todd, you're going to end up in bed with me even if I have to drag you down. I'm willing to let you have me at no charge. If you refuse me, I will kill you." She dropped her housecoat at her feet.

"Kim, put your clothes on and leave me alone."

"Todd, why are you really here? I know you didn't come to say goodnight."

Todd smiled.

"Todd, I know you came to see me and I'm happy as I'm falling in love with you." She took Todd's hand to her vagina.

"Kim, you're crazy. You know that going to bed with you would be wrong."

"Why don't you let me be the judge of that? Now get your clothes off and rest your arse on the settee or on the floor. I really don't care which place you choose. Now strip!"

As Todd looked Kim in the face, she reached for his baton and lifted it threateningly. "Now strip! If I have to tell you again, I will knock your dick off."

Todd quickly stripped himself naked then said, "You're fucking crazy."

Kim pushed Todd down on the settee and jumped on him, kissing him all over his body and filled her mouth with his penis until he could no longer control himself. She moved her vagina onto his hard penis taking control while he was staring in her face. As sexual feelings took him over, he took control and was fucking her relentlessly, not realising she was a virgin. Kim whispered into his ears, saying, "You're my first and I wonder what Julia will say or do if I tell her about us."

"You tell Julia or anyone about this and I'll kill you."

Kim smiled. She tried to kiss him, but he moved his face and forced hatefully within her until he ejaculated. He got up and went to the bathroom to wash her blood off.

Kim followed shortly behind telling him, "I'm holding the handle while you hold the blade. You just remember that. You will come to me whenever I need you."

Todd closed his eyes feeling threatened. She kissed the back of his neck. He got dressed and as he was going downstairs she burst out laughing saying, "Get the hell out of here before your family comes home."

He faced her. "You little senseless bitch." He ran up to her raising a blow to her head.

"I'm a bitch, I admit. But you're the law. I could say you raped me. Now, suppose I make a complaint to the police that you raped me and I shot you in defence. Now, as you can see, I have nothing to lose but my life and I still have your semen in me. As for you my dear Todd, you have too much to lose. So, when I call you, you better be falling at my feet. Don't worry. I know what to do to keep your semen alive just in case. I'll let you get married to Julia. But she and I will be sharing you. You can sleep with her five nights and two with me. I can't be fairer than that. I'm going to buy myself a house in this part so that I can be near you. Don't look so worried. Julia and I will become good friends."

Todd left the house and drove himself to his flat. In bed, he was so restless that he got out of bed, drank some whiskey and tossed the empty glass against the wall in anger.

"Damn! What have I done?" he asked himself, then he closed his eyes for a moment in deep thought before he rang Julia telling her, "I want you to invite Petra to our wedding."

"Why would you want me to invite Petra to our wedding Todd? I don't think that I could do that as I hardly know her. Todd, what's going on with you and her? Do you fancy her?"

"Of course not. I got to like her and because her father was one of my colleagues, I thought we should invite her and her family to our wedding."

"Todd, you haven't told me your reason for inviting them to our wedding?"

"Julia, they're Officer Forbes' family."

"Okay Todd, but if I find out you're messing with her or any other women, I won't have anything to do with you. You sound as if you're in a hurry to get married. Are you in love with her?"

"Julia, I love you too much to get involved with other women. I want us to get married as I'm in love with you and I would really like us to get married in the next couple of months."

"Todd, are you in some sort of trouble?"

"Why do you ask that?"

"Oh nothing Todd, just that you sliced out nine months from our set date to get married and you're bringing it forward, it makes me feel nervous. Todd, I have to know why you want us to get married so soon. I told dad that we're getting married next year and he agreed with that and I don't think I want to change the time. So, I really want to know why you're in a hurry for us to get married sooner. Todd, you told me that we both have to be virgins and I'm willing to wait for that time next year. Are you willing to wait Todd? Are you a virgin?"

"Julia, I can't discuss this with you at the moment and yes, I'm willing to wait until you are ready for us to get married. All I can tell you is I love you. That is why I want to marry you," Todd said feeling guilty.

"Todd, you only had to say yes or no to my asking if you're a virgin. Anyway, what about Judge O'Neil and Officer Forbes' case?"

"Oh don't worry over them honey, their cases will never be closed. And honey, my reason for wanting to get married sooner is because I can't bare the pain of being apart from you for so long. Officer Forbes was my friend, which is why I asked you to invite his daughter. But you don't have to if you don't want. I'm sorry honey. I shouldn't have asked."

"Okay Todd, I will invite her and her family when the time comes. I think Petra is a lovely girl. By the way Todd, I heard on the morning news that a very rich woman has donated one million pounds to a children's home because her granddaughter's rapist has been found dead in bed with a bullet in the middle of his forehead."

"Julia, what the hell are you talking about?"

"You mean you didn't know about Bradley Simms? Well honey, police also found a suicide note in his pocket stating that he raped and then killed Lorie Gaskell, but it was an accident and when he woke up after his drug taking he found her dead lying beside him. Todd, Lorie was the daughter of a head teacher. Bradley's cousin Iron's body was also found in an old demolition meat shop with a bullet hole also in the middle of his forehead. They said Hans killed him for raping a Madame Stall granddaughter.

"Police have claimed that Omari had been heavily sedated with drugs before he was murdered and castrated just like Officer Forbes and Judge O'Neil. Todd, the police think it's the same people that carried out the operation on the Judge and the others. Todd, dad rang you last night and he said he couldn't get you. Todd, where were you at ten o'clock last night?"

Todd hesitated after taking some time to say, "Oh I popped back to see my aunt as we only had a short time to say hello."

Chapter 7

At nine weeks of Kim's pregnancy she fell down the stairs. Some hours later she started bleeding. As she was in pain and crying, her aunt called in the doctor. "Miss Lemoore, you're still pregnant" he said. "You're very lucky. You could have had a miscarriage from the fall. I'll admit you to the hospital now so that they can stop the bleeding and check you. I would like to see you next Friday at ten thirty. Would you like me to call you an ambulance, or would you like to make your own way to the hospital?"

"Thanks doc. I will take a taxi. Would you mind calling me one?"

The doctor called his assistant nurse. "Would you please call a taxi for Miss Lemoore?"

"Right away doc." The nurse left and rang for a taxi. The doctor gave Kim a letter to take to the hospital. Shortly, the taxi arrived and the nurse helped Kim in and watched the taxi drive away.

That same week on Saturday, Petra and Julia became good friends and after that they met most weeks in Muriel's café on Broad Street to have breakfast or lunch.

As time went on their friendship developed so much so that Petra came close to telling Julia about her stepfather, but she got a hold on herself when Julia accidentally knocked her cup of coffee off the table. "You were going to tell me about your stepfather?" Julia said.

"Oh yes, I miss him now that he's gone."

Julia touched Petra's hand. "I'm so sorry."

Petra smiled. Julia went to work while Petra went shopping.

That same Saturday morning Todd called to see Julia. "She has already left for work," Curtis told him. Irene the housemaid looked at Todd and saw how worried he looked. "Son, you look like you just crawled out of a snake pit."

"Believe me Irene, it is worse than that," Todd said. Irene smiled, Todd turned towards the door. Superintendent Peterson looked up at him and said, "Todd, come and sit down and have some breakfast."

"Thank you, but I've already eaten."

"Oh by the way, I think it would be nice for you and Julia to get married three months on Saturday, the twenty third."

"Why is that, super?" Todd asked.

"Nothing, oh nothing really, I just thought it would be nice for you and Julia to get married on your birthday after putting off getting married for three years."

"Oh, that would be great," Irene intervened.

The superintendent looked at Irene in a cheerful manner and cleared his throat. Irene smiled and lowered her head as she put the coffee on the table.

"Well, I'll see Julia after work," Todd said.

"Come on Todd, have a seat and tell me why you're here."

"What made you think I came here to tell you anything?" Todd said as Superintendent Peterson looked in his eyes.

"Todd, I wasn't born yesterday. I can tell by your voice something is bothering you. Is everything all right with you and Julia?"

"Sure, Julia and I are okay."

But Superintendent Peterson had a strong feeling that Todd was hiding something from him. As he watched Todd walk out the door, he shook his head before he got up out of his seat and moved towards the front door. Watching Todd getting in his car, he shook his head again and as Todd drove away, he closed the door and sat down when the phone starting ringing. Curtis came charging down the stairs like he was on fire with his tie loosened around his neck.

"I thought you were with your patients by now," Superintendent Peterson said looking at Curtis to answer the phone.

"I overslept. I had too much to drink last night. Dad, I'll see you later." He grabbed a slice of toast and rushed out the door, got into his car and drove to work at the hospital.

The phone was still ringing. Irene answered, "Hello, Superintendent Peterson's residence."

"Can I speak to Curtis please?"

"Oh, you just missed him. Would you like to leave a message?" Irene asked.

"Oh never mind, I'll come over tonight. On the other hand, can you tell him that Kim called. I was in hospital and was discharged this morning."

"Okay Kim."

Kim hung up. Irene put the phone down and then reported to Superintendent Peterson and said, "Mr Peterson I might not be here when Curtis comes home. Would you please tell him he had a missed call from Kim and she said she would call tonight."

"Okay," said the superintendent. "Well, I'm off to work." He left.

Irene did the housework and cooked dinner before she went to visit a friend.

Julia got home from work and went into the kitchen for a drink of orange juice before checking the answering machine for messages. After hearing Kim's message, she wondered what she had wanted. As she was thinking about Kim and what she did to Todd, Curtis walked in and went for a beer from the fridge. After drinking the beer and looking at Julia, he asked, "Why the sad face, sis?"

"Kim left you or Todd a message on the machine."

"Now I know why the sad face," Curtis smiled. "However, Kim and I have nothing in common."

Julia grinned.

"Well, I better head for the shower," Curtis said after he had drunk the last of his beer. Julia had a bath, then she and Curtis waited on their father to get home to have dinner.

After waiting an hour and Superintendent Peterson hadn't come home, Julia said to Curtis, "I don't know about you, but I'm ready to eat."

"Me too."

"Well I'll just nip to my room to get my unfinished lemonade," Julia said. Coming from her room Superintendent Peterson and Todd walked into the house singing Will Someone Hear My Cry out of tune and they seemed to be well lubricated with booze. Julia stood over the landing looking down on them. Curtis closed his medical file and left it on the side table and went to meet his dad and Todd. Irene let herself into the house and looked hard at Superintendent Peterson. "Mr Peterson, you should be ashamed of yourself to come home drunk."

The superintendent looked up at Irene with eyes half closed and smiling. Irene went into the kitchen and returned to ask Curtis, "Haven't you and Julia had dinner?"

"We'd decided to wait on dad," Julia said.

"You shouldn't, just look at your dad. He seems to be well pissed, if you would excuse my language. And he has young Todd going down the same road with him." Irene crossed over to the superintendent. "Mr Peterson, would you please take your seat while I go and fetch your dinner?"

The superintendent hugged and kissed Irene with feeling. She looked at him in shock. "I've wanted to do that for a long time before now," he said. He giggled, then lightly slapped Irene's butt again. She slapped his face and went into the kitchen smiling. He followed her and then kissed her again. This time, her face glittered. She faced Curtis and said, "A Miss Kim phoned to tell you that she would see you tonight. I told your father to tell you."

"Thank you for telling me. Julia told me, but I don't think it's me Kim wants to see. I hardly spoke to the woman when she was here three weeks ago. All the same, thank you Irene."

"It's okay Curtis?"

Curtis smiled and Julia looked at him in wonder. Irene took the food to the table then left them eating as she went and prepared one of the spare rooms for Todd to sleep the night as he was weak with booze and was unable to drive himself home. The superintendent and Todd picked at their dinner. Curtis helped Todd to his room then out of his trousers and shirt, leaving him in his boxer shorts and T-shirt. He then lay him in bed then turned the lights off, left the room and went down to Julia. He smiled.

"What is it now Curtis?"

"Will Todd be selling his flat when you two marry?"

"I don't know. Why do you ask?"

"I heard he's buying a house."

"I don't think Todd's ready to buy a house yet."

"Whoops, I put my foot in it."

"Come on Curtis, what has Todd been telling you? I'm sure Todd would have told me if he was buying a house."

"I'm sure he would. Anyway, if he's selling his flat, will you let me know?"

"You'll have to ask him."

"Yes, I will."

"Anyway, are you interested in buying Todd's flat? Are you getting claustrophobia around me?"

"No, nothing likes that, I might be lucky to find myself a girlfriend and I would like to be private sometimes. I'm sure you know what I mean sis."

"Yes, I think I know."

"Anyway, goodnight."

"Goodnight Curtis."

Julia went to bed leaving Curtis writing his medical reports.

Early the next morning, Julia saw the superintendent leave Irene's room and go into his. She smiled and went to the bathroom. Coming from the bathroom, she met Irene and smiled, "I guess you know your father slept with me last night."

"I'm happy for both of you." Julia hugged Irene. "Oh Todd left very early this morning," Irene said.

Julia smiled and went to her room and got dressed.

That morning, Todd's mother rang Julia telling her Todd slept at her house.

"Todd slept in our spare room and Irene told me she saw him leave early."

"Julia, what's going on? I heard Kim and Todd's voices. He's now sleeping downstairs on my settee."

Tears came in Julia's eyes.

That morning Kim rang Julia telling her she would like to be her friend.

"Who's this?" Julia asked in panic.

Kim giggled, then put the phone down and then went to her room.

At eight o'clock in the morning Todd had breakfast and then rang Julia on his mobile phone telling her he loved her. He then drove to his flat and rang her again. "I love you."

"I love you too Todd." He blew her a long sounding kiss down the phone and she hung up. That day, Julia didn't see Todd as he spent his time with Kim after he finished work.

On Saturday morning Julia went to work and in the evening Todd asked her to dine out with him. As he was on his way out of his flat he met Kim. I've been phoning you," she said.

"Look Kim. It was a mistake between us. Look, I don't want Julia to know we slept together."

"Todd, as I said, I will let you marry the fool. But when I call you, you best come running to me. As I told you, I've nothing to lose but my life. The fool and I will share you, five nights with her and two with me. I can't be fairer than that. I told you I would be buying a house in this area so that I can be near you. Don't look so worried. The fool and I will become best of friends."

Todd got angry and slapped Kim's face. "Now get out of here," he told her. Then he went into his flat and dumped himself onto his settee and phoned Julia telling her that he had come down with the flu."

"Okay," Julia said. "Let's leave going to dinner until another time. Would you like me to come over?" she asked.

"No, I'll take a couple of painkillers and go to bed. I'll see you tomorrow." He put the phone down and reached for a bottle of whiskey, taking several mouthfuls. He filled the glass, then tossed it against the wall in bitter anger. "Damn! What have I done?" he said, close to tears. He sat on the settee deep in thought, and then rang Julia. "Julia, I've been thinking about us. I would really like us to throw a big engagement party to make it official. Let's make it known to everyone we're in love. Let's spread the word."

"Todd, what has brought this on all of a sudden? In the past three years you may have proposed to me, but you hardly mentioned a word about us getting married," Julia said with a confused expression on her face.

"Jul, I just think it would be nice to spread the word. We could invite all our friends and family to let them know we're serious this time."

"Todd, I thought I told you before I don't want to rush into marriage. I'm not ready for any of this even though I accept your ring."

"I understand what you're saying, but you know that you're the only woman in my life. I'm prepared to wait until you are ready. Whether it's another one, two or three years because what we have is special and no one can come between us," Todd said with disturbing thoughts of Kim on his mind.

"Well enough of your talk about a party. Anyway, what's happening about Judge O'Neil and Officer Forbes' case?"

"Oh, as I told you, don't worry. Their case will never be closed," Todd said.

One month later, Todd and Julia's father planned an engagement party to surprise Julia. That week Todd and Superintendent Peterson sent out invitations to guests stating that it was a surprise engagement party for Julia and Todd to be held three weeks on Saturday, starting at seven, at Superintendent Peterson's house.

Three weeks later on the Saturday in the early morning, Irene the housekeeper and Todd's mother and two friends cooked most of the food at Todd's mother's house so that Julia would not know what was going on. During the afternoon, Julia's friends took her to a wine bar in town to have a drink to get her out of the way.

The food was cooked, the drinks were cooled and a cold finger buffet was also prepared by a restaurant and was taken to Julia and her father's home. The furniture was taken out of the oversized living room and the floor was covered in laminated flooring. A DJ and his sound system took their place hidden behind a decorative screen in the corner of the room. The patio doors were slightly open, which led to an acre and a half of mowed lawn with some enormous trees enclosing it in. Some tables and chairs were set around the swimming pool with ice buckets and boxes of champagne and beers.

At six thirty as the guests started to arrive, Todd went to town and fetched Julia from the Red Lion where she had been drinking with three friends and her boss to keep her out of the house. Todd phoned to say that everything was okay, and the superintendent got everyone ready to hide in the back garden.

Shortly afterwards, Todd and Julia arrived. As they got in the house, Todd held her hand and led her through towards the back door. "Why is it so quiet and where's everyone?" she asked feeling merry and holding onto Todd's arm as she had had a little too much to drink.

"Don't worry about anyone," Todd said.

"Where's all the furniture gone and why's that screen in here?"

"Don't worry about that either," Todd said.

"What do you mean by don't worry about that? Dad would be pissed off."

"I don't think he will be bothered, wait until you see outside. You will have even more to say." Julia then walked towards the back door with a confused expression on her face and as she opened the door, multi-coloured lights switched on and everyone shouted. "Congratulations!" Her confused expression soon changed to a happy smile. She then turned to Todd and planted a kiss on his lips then did the same to her father. As she looked around, she saw the workmates she had been drinking with earlier walking towards her. They smiled. "I should have known y'all were up to something. Now how often is it that you three take me out for a drink? Especially my boss!" Julia said.

"We had to do what needed to be done. Girlfriend, I wish I were you. You receive all this special treatment and he's so handsome too," Sabrina said.

"You go girl, go and hang on to your man for the rest of the night and forever," Cathy said.

Julia then faced her other friend Joyce and asked, "What have you got to say about setting me up like this?"

"Girlfriend, when you're finished with him, pass him on to me."

All three friends smiled and raised their glasses of champagne and said, "Congratulations Julia, our dear friend."

Julia kissed her friends on their cheeks and told them, "I'll see you three later. And thanks for your support."

The party was just beginning when Julia's boss walked in and walked over to her smiling. Julia shook her head and said, "You of all people."

"Well honey, with such a handsome husband-to-be, no wonder it had to be a secret. Anyway honey, this is for you, a couple of hundred pounds. You can get your own present," her boss told her.

Julia took the card and said, "Thanks." Her boss kissed her on her lips. Todd walked her to the drinks and gave Julia's boss a glass of champagne. "Thanks," she said smiling and Julia introduced her to her brother and dad.

The party was raving on, music playing and people were getting down to the beat of Kiss Me Honey, Honey by Shirley Bassey, while others were drinking, eating and socialising. Todd and Joanne went around topping up the guest's glasses with champagne or drinks of their choice when Todd noticed a very familiar face coming towards him. It was Kim. She stood facing Todd. "I can't remember inviting you – no I definitely know for sure I didn't invite you."

"Todd, you wouldn't remember inviting me, because you didn't," Kim said.

"So what the heck are you doing here?"

"I heard all the family and friends were invited and we are friends aren't we? In fact, we're much more than just friends, aren't we?" Kim said, rubbing her tummy.

"Kim, don't start with this madness, this is mine and Julia's day to prove to all like you how much I love her. Don't spoil it for us," Todd said looking very displeased.

"Would I do such a thing?" Kim said smirking, then walked away to meet Detectives Hanson's brothers Paul, Scott and Robin. As Todd looked at her, she kissed Detective Scott Hanson on his lips then looked at Todd and smiled broadly.

"Todd, what is all this about?" Detective Scott Hanson asked.

"Search me mate and you'll never find the answer," Todd said and walked away. Scott smiled.

"Something is definitely going on between Todd and her," Detective Robin said.

"Well, lucky for him mate. He has two, I'm looking for one," Scott said.

As the night went on, everybody was more than merry; the drinks and food were going down very rapidly. As the song Wifey B Next was blasting out the loud speakers, Todd and Julia finally managed to have a dance together. After a few more glasses of champagne and dancing, Todd was feeling very tired and tipsy. Therefore, he decided to go upstairs and put his head down in one of the spare rooms to rest leaving Julia and Joanne to entertain their guests. As this was happening, Kim sneaked out of the back garden and followed Todd upstairs without him noticing her. As Todd was just about put his head down he heard the door creak. He tried lifting his head up and tried to get up but fell down on the bed. She then let herself in and shut the door.

"Look at you, you're all pissed up. Too many drinks Hey, you couldn't handle," Kim said as she was also very tipsy.

"Just get out of the room and leave me alone will you," Todd said with a twisted tongue as he tried to get on his feet before falling backwards onto the bed.

Kim walked towards the bed and slowly stood over him and dropped the straps of her black dress off her shoulders as she looked in his eyes and said in a seductive way, "Come off it Todd, I'm not that easy to get rid of. Just admit it to yourself you want me, don't you? You know you can't resist me and I've got much more to offer you than Julia can."

"Please Kim, don't do this. I'm not in the right state of mind. Put your clothes on. I'm not interested. Get the hell out of here!"

"I've warned you before, when I want something, I always get it. And I want you and the time is now!" Kim said.

"No Kim, I won't give into you this time."

"Todd, I don't want to get violent again. You know I don't like to, but if I have to take such a measure, I will," Kim said.

"What is it?" Todd shouted very angrily.

"I thought I made it clear to you that I want you," Kim said as she climbed on top of him.

While Joanne was walking up the stairs towards the toilet, she stopped as she heard shouting and put her ear against the door to listen to what was going on. She heard Todd and Kim's voice. "My God," she said to herself and knocked on the door. "What the heck's going on?"

"Who's that?" Todd asked nervously.

"It's me Joanne, what's going on in there?"

"Stay there, I'm coming," Todd said and he staggered out of bed and stumbled towards the door and opened it looking shaken up. "What were you doing and who else is in there with you?"

As he was walking away from Joanne to return to the party, he said, "No one special you should worry about."

As Joanne knew it was Kim, she said "Todd, whatever. Whatever." And as she carried on towards the toilet she heard Kim's voice coming from the room. She put her head around and saw Kim standing in the nude. Kim looked very content with herself smiling as Joanne walked towards her. "You bitch! You had to show yourself at the wrong time," Kim said and pushed Joanne against the wall. Joanne knocked her hand off her and grabbed her by her neck and then jammed her against the wall and told her, "I know your kind and what you're trying to do, you know Todd doesn't like you, so why don't you just leave him alone, before you have more than you can cope with. I mean it Kim. Leave him alone otherwise it is going to get very nasty. And that's a promise not just a warning."

Kim didn't utter a word. She put her clothes on very quickly and walked out of the room. As soon as she left the room, Joanne whizzed to the toilet. Kim went back outside and drank a few more drinks that were on the table. She cocked one eye open to notice Todd happily dancing with Julia. Instantly she had forgotten what Joanne had said and went over to Todd and pinched his bottom, then drunkenly whispered in his ear, "Save the last dance for me."

"What did she whisper in your ear? Julia asked. "You look a bit on edge."

"Nothing interesting. Kim is just Kim," Todd said.

"What have you been doing upstairs? You look more distressed than when you left the party."

Joanne came back to join the party. Luckily, Kim was nowhere near Todd when Joanne came back as she was still very annoyed. The party was coming to an end and everyone coupled up for a dance. Superintendent Peterson and Irene, Joanne and Curtis and Julia and Todd all had a dance together, as were many others. Kim was sitting amongst the drunkards who were too drunk to move. You could see in her eyes that she was very jealous as she sat there staring at Julia. She waited until the song Cupid Draw Back Your Bow had finished and stood up. As another song Save The Last Dance For Me was playing, she walked over to where Todd and Julia were and started dancing in front of them flaunting herself. Eventually she got in between them and turned Todd around so he was now facing her and leaving Julia standing alone. Kim grabbed Todd around his waist, pulled him close and smothered him with kisses. He tried to put up a fight, but it looked very effortless to where Julia was standing. Julia stood and watched for a while before her eyes filled with tears and anger. Todd looked hard at Julia then pushed Kim away. Julia ran from the garden in tears and up into one of the spare rooms to be alone. Joanne saw what was going on. She walked over to Kim and said, "I think you need cooling down."

Insultingly Kim said, "Well go on then, off you go. I'll have an iced beer."

"I think you've had enough to drink, but worry not, I know just what you need," said Joanne, smiling as she was planning something very crafty. 'Splash, splash, the dirty bitch needs a bath" she said, and she pushed Kim in the face, sending her flying into the swimming pool, dragging Todd along with her. Joanne's face lit up and the guests stood around looking astonished. Joanne looked down in the pool staring into Kim's face and said, "Mission accomplished!"

Julia rushed downstairs, stormed out the house towards Joanne and shouted angrily. "What was that in aid of? You have gone and spoilt the whole night! If you have a problem with Kim, deal with her in your own space and time. But don't drag Todd down with her. It's nothing to do with him!"

"Well sorry to drag your husband-to-be off his high horse, but if you weren't so busy entertaining your guests, this wouldn't have happened," said Joanne as Kim and Todd floated up to the surface.

"And what exactly is that meant to mean?"

"Well Julia, put it this way. While you're down here in the garden entertaining your guests, Kim was upstairs having her own private party with your husband-to-be."

"You bitch! How can you be so cruel?"

"You have picked on the wrong person love. If you need to take your anger out on anyone, take it out on Kim and your husband-to-be," Joanne said.

"That's it, Todd, get out. Let's get inside now! And what are you all looking at?" Julia shouted to some of the guests looking embarrassed. Todd climbed out of the pool drenched from head to toe, leaving Kim in the pool in shock and fuming.

Todd followed Julia upstairs into her bedroom. "So, explain to me what you and Kim were doing up here in the room?"

"It's not what you think, whatever Joanne told you, it is so far from the truth," Todd said.

Julia stared Todd in the face and said, "Well come on then, explain yourself."

Todd stuttered as he wiped dripping water off his face. "I... I... I..."

"Well? I what? You chose now to get back at me, tonight of all nights. I can't believe you're trying to get back at me because you thought something was going on with me and Curtis."

"No, it's not that way. I don't have a problem with you and Curtis. I know you're family and I wouldn't stoop that low," Todd said.

"So why did you make a fool out of me?" Julia asked.

"Sweetheart, Kim and I were both drunk. I went to put my head down and she followed me without my knowing. I don't think she knew what she was doing either. But I swear to you it didn't go any further than a kiss."

"For some reason, that doesn't sound very convincing, but I suppose you're telling the truth. Well, it's going to take a long time before I can trust you again."

Julia went back outside, kissed her three best friends and her boss and told them, "Thanks for being nice to me and thanks for coming, but the party is over." Her friends and boss kissed her and her boss said, "I have enjoyed myself and it's time I got home to my husband and my son."

Julia then announced to her guests. "Thank you all for coming, but sad to say the party is now over."

Detectives Hanson's brothers said goodnight to Julia and left. Curtis drove Joanne and her family home and saw them in before he got back home.

That night, Todd's brother Lance took him to his flat after he'd changed into some of Curtis' clothes.

All day Sunday, Julia refused to speak to Todd or see him. He phoned her constantly that day but she never answered or returned his calls. For the rest of the week they never saw each other or spoke on the phone. Having discovered that Todd had kissed Kim, Julia cried over Todd as she was so much in love with him. Todd was also thinking deeply about Julia in fear that they might never be together again.

Weeks had passed by and at work Julia thought about nothing else but Todd. She was getting lazy with her work and careless, leaving private documents containing important information on her untidy desk or anywhere in the office for anyone to read and most of the time she fell asleep on her desk after crying in silence. This was happening so often that her boss said to her, "Julia I've heard and watched you crying too often and yesterday I heard you sobbing and calling Todd's name and saying how much you loved him. I don't mean to pry, but for the past two weeks, I have noticed you've not been yourself. Julia, what's wrong?"

"I have come down with the flu or something," Julia said, but as her boss looked in her eyes, she said, "Truthfully, I'm not feeling well."

Her boss smiled as she knew Julia wasn't being truthful with her. She also knew it was a domestic problem between her and Todd. She then sent Julia home with a warning, "Get your act together and sort out what problem you may have. I'll give you a couple of weeks of sick leave."

Julia barely smiled before she drove home.

Her boss then rang Todd and had a good talk with him. He then told her he was thinking of asking for a transfer to Wales where one of his mates was working, as he thought Julia had finished with him.

A week later on Saturday evening Julia's boss called to see her. As Irene had just cooked supper, she asked Julia's boss to have supper with them. "Thanks," she said. Irene knew it must be of importance, so she set the table for Julia and Julia's boss in the dining room just for the two of them while she ate in the kitchen.

Over supper Julia's boss said to her, "Look Julia, I gave you sick leave because you told me you had the flu. But I know better. It isn't the flu is it?"

"No, it's not. It's Todd."

"Julia, there's a time when one has to swallow their pride, I could tell both you and Todd have not spoken for a while. Stop being so damn stubborn and call him. As I said, it's none of my business, but Todd loves you very much. You are both committing suicide slowly by widening the gap of mixing love and hate. Eventually you both will lose each other and what you two have going, including your jobs. I'm sorry to have to tell you this, I can't keep your position open for much longer. You have already had three weeks off and I'm missing you; you are a good friend and I'd hate to lose you. The quicker you sort out your problems with Todd the better and do control your jealousy. I mean that. The sooner you fall in Todd's arms the quicker your problems will be cured and you'll be back at work so we can pick at each other."

"But you didn't hear everything that went on on my engagement night," Julia said with tears in her eyes.

"Julia, I'm sorry to cross-examine you, but Todd's not a bad person. Deep down inside he loves you."

"I know. And deep down in me I love him too, but it's that damn Kim. She's like a bad disease over him," Julia said.

"Julia, you have to let Todd know you're still in love with him and please do this quickly as he told me he's going to ask for a transfer to Wales. It is hurting him not to see you or not being able to touch you. He thinks you no longer love him. I just had to let you know. However, I have to go now, and thanks for supper." But before Julia's boss left, she went and found Irene sitting in the kitchen. "Irene thank you very much for a lovely supper. Goodbye."

"Goodbye Mrs Goldwin."

"Julia saw her boss out to her car, watched her get in and drive away. That evening, Julia took her boss' advice and phoned Todd telling him she loved him and she missed him so much and she wanted to be with him. Todd came running to her. They talked, kissed and made up, then they both put on their engagement rings and he left mid-morning and went to his flat and stayed with his brother Lance.

The Sunday afternoon, Julia and Todd spent a loveable time together. Superintendent Peterson, Irene and Curtis were so happy to see Julia's face blossoming with happiness again.

On Monday morning, Julia phoned her boss saying, "Thanks for helping me seeing beyond my foolish jealous heart. I'm back in Todd's arms and there I will stay. I'll be back at work tomorrow if you'll take me back."

"Thank goodness you've seen sense. I look forward to seeing you next week Monday as I want you to spend some time with Todd."

"Thanks boss. I love you."

"I love you too Julia, and drop the boss. I'm your friend Lacy."

"OK. Lacy, will you let Joyce, Cathy and Sabrina know that I'll be in next Monday?"

"I will. Take care and give Todd a tight hug from me."

"I will," Julia said and her boss hung up first.

The following Monday, Julia's friends were so happy to see her that they took her to lunch.

Six weeks later, Todd and Julia sent out invitations to friends and family inviting them to their wedding in five months' time. At work Julia, her boss and friends were like five peas in a pod. They ate, drank, talked and laughed together. For five months they couldn't get any closer even if they had wanted to.

Five months later, the night before the wedding, Detective Todd, his brother Lance, Curtis, the detective's brothers Paul and Scott, friends Robin and Bruce, Officer Hodge, Cousin Kelly, Father-In-Law Superintendent Peterson, Todd's dad, his Uncle Eric, Julia's boss' husband Jamie and his brother and Cousin Colin and friend Bobby drank four bottles of champagne, two bottles of whiskey and three cases of twenty-four cans of beer. Irene cooked food for them and they spent the night at Todd's two-bedroomed flat playing dominos, chess, and poker and listening to music until mid-morning. Julia also had her nine friends at her home to have a drink and a meal. They too went home early morning. Julia broke down crying on Irene's shoulder saying, "Mum, I love you."

"I love you too honey. I wish your other mother were here to see you married. And I hope your father doesn't come home drunk."

"You love him don't you?"

"Yes Julia, I love him. Well honey, I've tidied the kitchen and I think it's time you went to bed as you have to be up early."

"You should go to bed too Mum, you've worked hard."

"I will soon honey. Goodnight," Irene said and Julia went to bed. Irene waited on the living room settee until Curtis and Superintendent Peterson got home before she went to bed.

At ten o'clock in the morning Julia and Irene went to the hairdressers and had their hair done and their nails manicured. By half past one the afternoon was very hot. At two fifteen, Julia and her ten bridesmaids left from Todd's sister's house to get to the church. At this time Superintendent Peterson saw Todd get out of a white Ford car then get into Detective Scott Hanson's car. The superintendent walked up to them and asked Todd, "Who was that woman?"

Todd smiled.

"Oh, she's a friend of my sister. Her name is Kerri Boyd. We were discussing the cost of the wedding drinks and food. Anything else you would like to know pops?"

"Well I'll be damned," the superintendent said smiling.

"Son, I can't help if I'm a little suspicious of you, I was young once and twice as handsome as you. Julia is my only daughter and I have to look out for her. I would be very hurt to know that my daughter is unhappy, so I would really like you to take the very best care of her. Well Todd, as you are going to be my son-in-law in about one hour, this is for you. Your wedding present and this cheque is to help you pay for the food and drinks. Thirty thousand pounds, and the other little gift, is just for you."

"Pops, you have already given Julia and me the best present ever, a big house that we can get lost in if Julia and I don't want to see each other for a while. However, thanks again for a lovely fully-furnished house and your most beautiful daughter who will be my wife in less than one hour," Todd said, looking his happiest ever.

"Todd, think nothing of the house. All I'm asking of you is to treat my daughter with respect and for her to return the same to you. I have to go to take her to the church, I'll see you there later. Oh, I think Curtis is interested in your flat if you decide to sell."

"My brother is living in my flat," Todd said.

"Oh, however, please treasure that small gift, I'm sure you will love it" said Superintendent Peterson smiling.

Todd opened the small brown envelope. Superintendent Peterson burst out laughing while Todd's face went serious. "Yes, son, the condom is for you. Happy wedding night!"

Todd stayed silent as the Hanson brothers looked on at him.

"Got you!" said Superintendent Peterson then burst into laughter again. Whilst Todd had not found it funny at first he burst into laughter too.

"Seriously son, I'm very happy that you're the one who's going to marry my daughter, I like you, Todd."

After Detective Scott had driven Todd away, Superintendent Peterson rang his friend John the housing agent. "John, I know this is a late time to invite you, but I'd like you and the Mrs to come to your goddaughter's wedding party and have a drink."

"Oh, Buddy, I don't know, the wife and I are eating out this evening."

"Please John, grant me this special favour and cancel eating out and come to my daughter and your Goddaughter's wedding reception please."

"Okay buddy, my wife and I would be delighted to. After all, you had invited us and I told you we mightn't be back for the wedding."

"Thank you John. I will also like you to help me find a nice three or four-bedroomed house for my son and his fiancée."

"Well old buddy, you leave everything to me. Where would you like to buy the house?"

"Well, I understand there are some nice three and four-bed houses in Erdington or the Selly Oak area. Preferably, I would like a detached house like Julia's. Just let me know when you have a nice one."

"Buddy, I had a four-bedroom in Selly Oak come up last week. It is valued at two hundred and thirty five thousand and it's a detached house. You can view it anytime next week."

"Thanks again old pal," said Superintendent Peterson and hung up.

John put the phone down and reported to his wife Ella that Superintendent Peterson had invited them to Julia and Todd's wedding reception. His wife was delighted, so she went to the hairdressers and had her hair washed and styled.

Meanwhile, everyone was very busy doing what they had to do. Julia and her bridesmaids set out to the Methodist Church in limousines, where she would be getting married in the next forty minutes. Petra was the chief bridesmaid. She looked very beautiful in her off the shoulder cream full-length satin and lace dress, high-heeled cream shoes and earrings to match her big hazel brown eyes. She looked like she was the one who was getting hitched. She was about five foot nine tall with a strikingly curvy size ten figure. She sat next to the bride-to-be in the rented limousine.

They arrived at the church. Petra walked into the church holding her hand with the ten bridesmaids paired up with pageboy partners walking behind two bridesmaids carrying the veil. The service was an hour and a half long and very exciting. Outside the church photos were taken before everyone went to the reception at the Falcon Club.

Officer Kelly eyed up Petra while she was sitting at the bride and groom's table, but she gave him a cold look and turned her face away to see Todd's brother watching her and smiling. She smiled back and then fixed her eyes on Detective Scott Hanson showing him an inviting smile. Todd's brother whispered to Detective Scott Hanson, "She's inviting you into her crotch mate, she's beautiful and I wish she had given me that smile."

Scott Hanson broke out smiling and looking intensively hard at Petra before he went mingling with his mates while still looking back at Petra.

Meanwhile, John and his wife were enjoying themselves so much that John made a nice speech before the table officially opened.

Superintendent Peterson opened the table with his late wife's favourite prayer she used to say to Julia before her bedtime. Julia cried as she remembered how much her mother had liked to say that prayer. "I miss her so much dad," Julia said as she rested her head on her dad's shoulder. Her husband took her in his arms and comforted her. Kim's face was green with envy and then she remarked, "There will be plenty more crying coming from her, but it won't be Todd's arms that will be comforting her."

Joanne heard Kim and pulled her over on her own, "I heard what you said. I want you to leave Julia and her husband alone from this moment on. You have been taking liberties for too long. Julia should be the one to say her husband was also a virgin. But she can't, because, you took that away from him. I'm so ashamed to be your sister. You go and fling yourself on some other whore of a man like yourself. If I ever see you as much as near to Todd again, I'll personally attend to you myself and I won't be pushing you in the pool."

"Joanne, Todd was mine from the time I set my eyes on him and when he hears what I have to tell him, he will be mine completely. Oh, he's my first," Kim said.

"Kim, I don't want to hurt you, but, if I have to break your leg, or your back to keep you away from him, then I will. You just remember what I said, leave Todd alone!"

Joanne returned sadly to her table and took her seat.

During the speeches Kim was looking at Joanne like a viper while everyone was paying attention and listening.

Superintendent Peterson faced Todd and said jokingly, "Todd, you take great care of my daughter, but never let her get the upper hand over you. A slap now and then will show her who the head of the house is."

The guests laughed and then gave a loud applause. Todd and the superintendent also laughed happily. In the presence of the guests, the groom's mother gave them a pair of white satin sheets and said, "I want to see red of love after your first night together." Some of the guest's eyes met in surprise, wanting to know what she was talking about. Julia was embarrassed as her boss and her work mates faced her smiling. Her husband kissed her. A black woman asked Mrs Todd, "Can you please tell us what you mean?"

Mrs Todd looked hard at the woman and said, "My son's wife has to be a virgin."

"What about your son, Aunt Dorothy? Doesn't he have to be a virgin too?" Kim spitefully asked.

Joanne knocked Kim down with a solid thump to her face, busting her lip. Then she dragged her outside the club and said, "I know you seduced Todd and you had to go and broadcast it. You took Julia's husband's dignity away. Kim, I'm going to slime you down into the ground like a worm. This the last time I'm going to tell you to keep well away from Julia and her husband."

Kim sucked her teeth, then spat blood out.

Joanne left her outside cleaning the blood out and off her mouth with a tissue and went back inside the club.

A handsome young mixed race man said, "Mrs Todd, I thought the sheets were a gift for your daughter-in-law and your son and not to display their sex lives. You should be happy Julia is your daughter-in-law. If your son rejects his beautiful wife, I would be happy to marry her."

Superintendent Peterson went to Allie and said, "If I had another daughter, I would want you to be my son-in-law, and thanks for your support." Allie smiled and as the superintendent looked at him, Allie said, "I was invited by Hanson my friend."

Then Superintendent Peterson went to Mrs Todd and smiled.

"Rodney, I hope you don't have any bad feelings against me, but I would want to know if my son's bride is a virgin. It's our tradition to examine the sheets our son's bride sleeps on, on their wedding night. I'm sure your daughter is a virgin but we, the mothers of our sons, must be completely sure our son's wife is a virgin. This is why it's so important for us mothers-in-law to give white sheets to see their wives virgin blood on the sheets after intercourse for their first time. Of course, I think your daughter's a virgin, but still it is in our interests to know our sons have married decent wives and shame will not be brought on the family. So I hope you will understand and won't be offended over what I said. It is vital, however, for me to know that my son has married a pure and decent wife and not a haggard."

"Dorothy, the truth is, if my daughter would listen to me, a coyote like you wouldn't get the chance to want to sniff her virgin blood. Dorothy, I think it's time you stop wiping your son's backside and attended to yours, don't you think so Dorothy? Well, as you mentioned, I hope no ill feelings come between us. My daughter is what you said, pure and decent, but can you say the same for your Todd? Well, Todd's a nice lad, I like him, but I know his virginity flew far away and left him behind; only my daughter doesn't know yet."

Mrs Somers, who was one of the guests, asked the groom's mother, "What if the bride refuses to sleep on the sheets?"

Mrs Todd replied, "It's our custom and if she refuses, then I would be disappointed and it would leave me believing my son's wife was not a virgin."

"Mrs Todd, I saw the virgin sign in the bride's face and I must admit she's pure and beautiful," Mrs Somers said.

Mrs Todd smiled before she took the microphone and said a nice speech concerning Julia.

Again there was an enormous applause from the guests. The party went on until early morning.

After the guests left, the superintendent drove his newly married daughter and son-in-law to their home. "Are you coming in, Dad?"

"No honey, this time is for you and your husband."

Julia's husband kissed her tearful eyes and carried her into their house. In the doorway he put her down gently on her feet. She kissed her father and Irene, waved goodbye and watched them drive away. Julia turned to Todd and smiled.

Todd hooked her around her shoulder and walked her into the dining room then into the pantry to show her at least a month of grocery shopping, then into the kitchen and showed her the cupboards with the utensils and dish sets and everything else. The double door fridge-freezer was packed with meat, chicken, fish, sausages, bacon, ham, cheese, milk and butter. Julia and Todd were very happy but surprised. They then retired to their bed after a glass of champagne.

When Todd was making love to her, she suddenly remembered what Petra had told her about pain for the first time of sexual intercourse. Julia felt deep pain, especially as Todd couldn't control his sexual movements when he was nearing ejaculation as he really went into her with full force.

She quivered as her husband's hands travelled over her body and especially when he injected his finger up her vagina while kissing her.

At one stage when he touched her vagina again, she pushed him away.

"What's the matter darling?"

"Oh nothing, it's just your cold hands made me shiver," she said trying her hardest to hold her crying back as she was feeling burning pain inside her.

"Oh, I'm sorry darling," he told her and kissed her as he saw on her face she was in pain.

She pressed her lips together and closed her eyes tightly as the pain rapidly went on in her. She left her husband in bed and went and had a warm scented bath. In the bath she patted her painful vagina and cried softly. After she took a long time in her bath, Todd went to her saying, "Are you going to sleep in your bath honey?"

She smiled looking up at him and said, "I'll be with you soon."

He smiled and went back to bed. She closed her eyes as she thought again over what Petra had said to her.

After she went to him, he kissed her and said, "Honey, thanks for saving yourself for me."

"Why do you say that?"

"I'm your first love and I would like to be your last and grow old with you. Julia I do love you."

"I know Todd. I love you too. Now let's get some sleep as I'm sure we will be having visitors tomorrow; your family."

"Julia honey, where would you like to go for your honeymoon?"

"Todd, anywhere, as long as I'm with you," Julia said and fixed her head in his arms and they went to sleep.

At eleven o'clock Sunday morning, there was a loud knock on the door. "Oh no, I'm still so tired," Julia said turning on her side facing Todd.

"I wonder who that can that be?" Todd asked getting out of bed naked. Julia laughed saying, "I dare you to go and open the door like that."

She pulled the cover over her head while Todd slipped into his pyjama trousers and went and opened the door to see his mother and the rest of his family standing behind her with smiles.

"Sorry son to be so early, but the suspense is killing me. Was she a virgin?"

"Mother, your sheet is in the washroom in the clothes basket. You go and have a look, then you let me know if my wife was a virgin or not," Todd said with a stiff upper lip.

His mother went to the washroom and took the sheet out of the basket and examined the sheet with extreme interest and seeing the patch of blood, she smiled nodding her head with contentment. She folded the sheet and shoved it under her arm and went to Todd saying, "Yes, she's my family now and you be gentle to her and treat her with respect always." She paused. "Julia's waited on you patiently for at least three years on and off. I would imagine one day you might be tempted to love some other woman, but always know Julia is the thorn in your heart and I love her as I love you. Oh, one other thing, when you and Julia fight, don't come running to me, for I won't be encouraging you to leave her or disrespect her. Son, there are not many young virgin women who would wait on their man for so long. Well, it's my job to take the sheet and have it returned to Julia spotless. See, I've even come prepared with my carrier bag to put the sheet in. Now, where's your lovely wife. I'm also here to cook breakfast for both of you and the family."

"Did you prepare the breakfast to cook too Mum?" Todd asked.

"Well, I expected you should have whatever's needed for breakfast."

"Well, mother, I hope you don't make this a habit. You'll find what you need in the kitchen. I will go and let Julia know you and the troops have come for breakfast." Todd went up to Julia but before he could say anything, Julia asked, "Has she gone?"

"Honey, there are eight of them downstairs. I could ask them to leave," Todd said.

"No, Todd, it's okay. Well who are the other seven?" Julia asked still looking tired.

"Well apart from mother hog, dad, my aunt and her husband, my sister, Joanne, Uncle Ural and the dynamite Kim," Todd said.

"Some of your family are missing," Julia said.

"Who?"

"Your half-brother Lance, your cousin Brandon and his wife and brother-in-law, not forgetting your sister's two children. I hoped they would come, then they could have all had a discussion with you about my virginity!"

"Honey, I should have put my mother in her place. I'm sorry."

"You should have invited your family into our bed last night for them to see how you were prancing up me. Luckily for me, your dick was limited, otherwise your mother would have had to chisel you out of me."

Todd laughed uncontrollably until his aunt and Kim rushed into their bedroom to find out what the joke was about.

Julia got out of bed and went to the bathroom. Kim looked at her then turned to Todd saying, "Did you enjoy yourself last night?"

"Kim, you're despicable. Let's get into the kitchen and help with the breakfast."

"Mum, there's more than enough help downstairs."

"Would you excuse me while I go and freshen up?" Julia said to Todd's aunt, then she gave Todd a funny look, as if she suspected he was having an affair with Kim.

Todd followed Julia into the bathroom and kissed her. "Are you not going down to your lovely family?"

"Julia, you're my family and I love you. As I said, if you're worried about that tart Kim, you have nothing to worry about."

Julia slipped out of her short silk pyjama pants and shirt. Todd smiled and kissed her nipples. "Get out of here before your woman comes looking for you."

"Julia, just what are you talking about? Kim and I have nothing in common. I don't even like her."

"I haven't said Kim's name. Why couldn't you call Joanne's?" Julia asked.

"Jul, I'm not naïve. Believe me honey, I'm not having affairs with Kim or anyone else. I just married the woman I'm in love with and who will soon be giving me a son or daughter. So honey you see, I can't afford to lose you. Anyway, I must go down to mother hog and family before she comes looking for me. Don't be too long honey." He went downstairs to his family.

"Todd, I really love Julia. And it isn't because she's beautiful, but because she's well mannered and always has a nice appearance as well as being honest. Yes, I'm happy you married her and I want you to keep it that way – I mean stay married to her," Todd's mother said looking at Kim smiling.

Breakfast was cooked by Todd's mother and his aunt. Julia went down to breakfast. Over breakfast, Todd's mother asked Todd, "Where are you taking your lovely wife to on her honeymoon?"

"Well, somewhere in the West Indies. Barbados I think, but Julia and I haven't decided yet. I know she wants to go to the West Indies as her friend told her she and her husband went on a Caribbean cruise and Barbados is beautiful. Well mother, Julia and I might take a cruise and see some of those beautiful countries."

Julia said nothing but smiled.

"Well lucky for some. I need a strong drink," Kim said and served herself with gin and lime. "Anyone care to join me?" she asked, smirking. No one answered. "What about you Todd, don't you want a drink?"

"No thank you. It's too early for me."

"Okay, I don't mind drinking alone," she said and she poured another drink, then took her seat next to Todd smiling. Todd's sister and his aunt looked at her perplexed and then they looked at Todd. Todd took Julia to one side and said, "Honey, Kim is not worth taking any notice of."

"Todd, I'm not worried about Kim. It's you I'm worried about. I can see through her that she wants me to know something, but she's giving it to me in small doses."

Todd looked at Julia and shook his head smiling.

After breakfast Todd's family said goodbye and left.

"Thank God. Seeing your family in two years from now would be a bonus," Julia said.

"Come here, you gorgeous married lady," Todd told Julia and he took her into his arms and kissed her. As Julia felt his erection, she pulled away from him.

"Honey, why do you pull away from me? I can't help my feelings towards you. You'll have to give in to me sometimes. I know it hurts for the first couple of times but after that you will enjoy me, as I will you. Please honey, I will be gentle with you. I need you now. Would you like us to go up to our bedroom or would you like us to make love on the floor here?"

"Oh Todd, I so want you, but you hurt me last night."

"Jul honey, that's how it would be with any virgin as they're so tight and we husbands have to penetrate to widen the inside. Honey, as I said, a few more times and I may have to run from you as I mightn't be able to give you enough of me."

Julia laughed and took Todd's hand into hers and led him upstairs into their bedroom and stripped herself naked. Todd stripped naked too, then had oral sex before making passionate love to her. This time she enjoyed him, even though she was hurt a little.

"I love you, Todd," she told him lying in his arms.

"I love you too, honey." He kissed her lips.

A while after they bathed together Julia was willing to give in to him again but he said, "We'll leave some for tonight."

"Todd honey, I hardly bled and I'm not throbbing inside as when you first made love to me. But I am feeling a little pain. I believe you're right that the more we have sex, the easier it will be for me. Well honey, I would like to cook us dinner. If you want to go to your mother or brother later, you can, but do keep away from that loudmouth Kim."

Todd smiled, had a whiskey and then went to his mother's, leaving Julia to open two full rooms of wedding gifts and hundreds of cards; some had money and cheques inside.

After Todd spent some time with his mother and family, he, his brother, cousin and brother–in–law went and had a drink in the pub. Todd went home and had his dinner of buttered corn-on-the-cob, roast chicken and roast potatoes covered in gravy, followed by apple crumble with custard and all washed down with red wine.

"Honey, I'd no idea you can cook so well. I must ask my friends and brother to come to dinner one day to let them know how well my wife can cook."

One week later on Monday morning, Todd went back to work as a Forensic Private Investigator detective. That same Monday morning Kim rang him at work and told him how much she loved him and that she wanted him to come to her eight o'clock that night. He told her it was impossible and that he loved his wife too much to further interfere with her or other women.

"I want you to meet me at the Pink Shell restaurant at eight and I won't take no for a fucking answer. You don't come, I will let Julia know about us and how you had me from behind and I sucked your cock."

Todd closed his phone, then closed his eyes in regret and then opened his eyes to see Detective Scott Hanson looking at him. Todd smiled.

Kim rang Todd again and said, "You put the phone down on me again, you will be a sorry arse."

Todd walked away from Detective Inspector Hanson and rang Kim. "Look Kim, what went on between us has now ended." And he closed his mobile phone again. Kim huffed in anger and then rang Julia telling her, "Todd belongs to me."

"Who is this?" Julia asked.

Kim blasted the phone down.

Julia pressed her palms over her ears, shrugged her shoulders, smiled and then went into her garden and was cutting flowers when Petra saw her.

"Morning Mrs Julia Todd," Petra addressed her with a charming smile.

"Good morning Petra." Julia greeted her back with a smile.

"Thanks for having me as your maid of honour. I really had a good time, thank you," Petra said. And she went on her way leaving Julia cutting flowers.

The next day Petra saw Julia getting into her car; Petra walked over to her.

"Mrs Todd," Petra smiled.

"Yes Petra?"

"Do you mind if I ask you a personal question?"

"Of course not Pet," Julia said, smiling.

"Do you love your husband?"

"Yes Petra. I do, very much. May I ask you why you ask me?"

"I just wanted to know."

"Petra, I know what you mean about raping and pain. My husband took me with such tender care but the pain was there and throbbing and burning inside me for at least five minutes. I can now understand why the rapists were punished and especially if these women were virgins," Julia said looking remorsefully at Petra.

"I'm glad you see it my way," said Petra and she walked away. Julia watched her as she went by. Petra looked back at Julia and waved goodbye. Julia waved back smiling then found herself wondering about Petra before driving away to meet her mother-in-law for lunch.

Over lunch, Mrs Todd said to Julia, "Now there are two Mrs Todds!"

Kim dropped a glass of wine on Julia's lap deliberately, then smiled. Joanne looked at Kim in disgust.

Kim left the table smiling and went to her room. Joanne followed her then closed the door. "Would you mind leaving my room?" Kim asked.

"Kim, do you like your life?"

"What the hell have you followed me for?"

"I told you before, leave Julia alone with her husband. But you just wouldn't. And to say, you deliberately ignored my warnings..."

"Joanne, why don't you get the fuck out of my room! You don't get it, do you? I love Todd and we had sex last week twice and long before. Joanne, he came back for more sex when everyone was upstairs sleeping. So I gladly gave it to him, as I love him. I even told him I'd let him marry that fool downstairs. So I'm not bad after all, but I'm jealous to see him smothering all over her."

Joanne slapped Kim's face so hard that Kim's lip bust and was bleeding. "If you make life difficult for Todd and Julia, I'll make your life a living hell. You just remember, I promised you a broken back if you ever hurt Julia in any way."

"Do you have to bust my lips every time you hit me?"

"Kim, I will do worse if you don't leave Julia alone."

Julia said goodbye and drove home to meet Todd sitting at the table eating a sandwich and drinking a can of beer. "What happened to your trousers?" he asked.

"Oh, I was at your mother's and Kim accidentally spilt some wine on me so I came home to get changed. Anyway, what are you doing home so early?"

"I finished early as I'm now my own boss and hardly had any work to do. Oh I've booked us a Caribbean cruise for our honeymoon leaving in two weeks on Tuesday," Todd said.

"I haven't cooked yet as I was at your mother's and she asked me to stay for lunch. Thanks for booking our honeymoon. I have everything in order such as my passport."

"Well, your dad and Irene want us to have dinner at his house," Todd said, feeling guilty about Kim.

"Okay, we'll go in the next couple of hours," Julia said. Two hours later, Todd and Julia went and had dinner at Julia's fathers. The next day Petra went to see Julia. Julia invited her in. In their conversation, Petra said jokingly, "Julia, I remember when I was fifteen and after one of my friends saw us, she asked if you were my sister."

Julia smiled then her eyes met Petra's. Petra smiled. Then Todd walked into the house.

"I came home to get my files," he said. Then he greeted Petra with a hello and a smile. Petra returned a hello. Todd got his files, kissed Julia on her cheek then left.

Petra again joked and asked Julia, "Were you a virgin?"

"Yes, I was, until... are you, Pet?" Julia asked her, laughing.

"Sure!" Petra answered sharply, feeling ashamed and cheated but she burst out laughing.

"What's so funny?" Julia asked smiling.

"Oh nothing, I was just thinking."

"Just wait until you get married, Petra Johnson."

"I don't think so. I would like to be in the police or a doctor, so that I could help people. I would really like to help those people in need," Petra said. "So you see Julia, I wouldn't have time to change nappies or scrub my husband's back."

"Oh Pet, it's not so bad being married, especially if you love your husband."

"Well Julia, I know you love your husband but as I said, I would want a career first before taking on a husband."

"Well, Todd is a good husband and I'm sure he would be a brilliant dad," Julia said smiling happily.

"That's good," Petra said.

After that conversation between Petra and Julia, they became good friends. Petra often went to visit Julia. But even so, Petra still had her very strong friendships with Stanley, Faith, Jenny, Elizabeth and Martin. As time passed by, Petra's friendship with Julia grew stronger and stronger. Nearly three years had passed and Petra became a policewoman. Kim went to live with a friend named U-nah on the outskirts of town with Todd's secret baby daughter Justine. Julia also had a five-month-old daughter named Candice. Todd didn't know that Kim's child was his.

Faith turned to nursing, Jenny went on to study to become a doctor, Elizabeth became a dentist, Stanley was in the last year of high school and Martin was studying at the University to be a pharmacist like his dad. Stanley was youngest of the six of them and decided that he wanted to become a doctor or a lawyer to help people. He was very bright and his teacher often told Mrs O'Neil that Stanley was at the top of the highest grade, following where his father Judge O'Neil had left off.

Mrs O'Neil smiled and said to Stanley's teacher Mrs Palmer, "I know my son is very bright, but he really wants to be a doctor or a lawyer and not a judge like his father."

Another two years had passed and Superintendent Peterson had married Irene, Julia had a second baby, a son named after her father Rodney Todd, but they called him Rod.

Stanley married Elizabeth and went to university to become a doctor. It took him almost two months after their marriage to make love to his wife. But as Elizabeth knew the circumstances they both got through it, she was very patient.

Stanley went on to become a doctor. During his working time, fourteen years young and black, Janet was admitted to the hospital after she'd been raped by her stepbrother with badly bruised and bloodied thighs and damage inside her cervix. Stanley was one of the three doctors who attended to her. As Stanley saw the extent of the damage within her, tears welled up in his eyes as her rape brought strong memories back to him of when he was raped by his stepfather.

Stanley left his colleagues to finish attending to Janet after seeing a nurse shaving her pubic hair. As he disappeared behind the screen he could hear her crying and groaning and complaining to the nurse that the pain inside her was unbearable. This was too distressing for

Stanley and he cried. After Janet had treatment and was comfortable in bed, he stood in the background behind the screen hearing her crying telling the two female doctors her insides was hurting so much. Stanley closed his eyes in disgust as he remembered the horrible pain he'd felt when his stepfather had raped him. He forced his eyes open, clenching his pearly white teeth in anger and frustration. Then as he heard Janet ask for him, he dried the tears from his face before he went to her.

He just about smiled saying, "Sorry, I had to go somewhere."

Janet cast her eyes on the blank television screen. "I'm hurting so much inside."

Stanley held her hand. "You'll be all right." Janet turned her back and he touched her shoulder then left.

On the last day of Janet's four days in the hospital, Stanley gave her one of his doctor's cards with his home address and telephone home and mobile numbers, saying to her, "If at any time you're in need of help or a friend to talk to, I would like you to come to our home or call me or my wife Elizabeth. No matter what time it is." Janet thanked Stanley while tears ran down her face and then went home with her mother.

Her mother opened the front door to see her stepson Barry standing with a broad smile.

"Hello Janet." She ignored him.

"Hello sis." He greeted her again, still smiling broadly. She still ignored him. He touched her arm and grinned in her face.

"Please Barry, leave her alone. I'm begging you please. She just came out of hospital from what you've done to her and she needs time and space to heal," her mother pleaded to Barry.

Barry went closer to Janet with a daring and conniving grin looking at her as she walked past him. She was halfway up the stairs when her mother called to her. She turned looking at her mother and waited on the stairs to hear what she had to say.

"Janet love, don't be angry with your brother. I asked him never to take you again."

Janet stood firmly on the stairs staring hard at her mother as she said, "Can you promise me your stepson will not rape me again mother?"

"Well well," her mother said. She seemed to be lost for words.

"Yes, well, mother! Your face pictures your ugly lies and false promises but the next time your fucking stepson of a bitch touches me, I'll kill him! And you take this from me mother as my promise is definite and solid. I guarantee you his death for you failing to speak out. One other thing, I will not tell you not to let him into your house because to you he is family, but he's not mine. But you tell him as long as I'm here, you best warn him to keep well away from me. I love you mother in spite of you upholding what he has done to me. But as I said, if he touches me ever again, I'll release my solid guarantee and kill him. And to add the final guarantee, there's no one I hate more than him. He's pure filth. Mother, when he leaves, please don't open your door to him again if I'm here."

"Janet love, I understand what you're saying but he's family and I can't not let him in."

"So mother, what are you telling me, that this bag of filth is welcome to come and fuck me whenever he wishes? And what for mother, a couple of fixes and few pounds he's giving you? You're my mother and I need your protection. He has raped me mother, and I told you as well as showing you proof. Oh, what the hell, I'm living here. Mother, we're supposed to be taking care of each other. Obviously I'm dead wrong. You let the bastard who is my so-called brother root his fucking big dick up me while you watch, high on your fix of cocaine. I pity you. Did you let him fuck you too without my knowing? "

"You dirty little bitch! How dare you speak to your mother disrespectfully, and who are you calling filth?" Barry climbed the stairs to Janet, shuffling his scruffy looking self with his eyes rolling as he'd just taken a fix of drugs in his arm and passed the needle to his stepmum.

"You, you grimy smelly fucker, you have the audacity to walk around the house like you are family. Well, your family values melted the minute you raped me," Janet said loud and brave.

Barry slapped her face. She pushed him down the stairs and walked down the stairs and stood in the hallway with her overnight bag holding what she'd brought from the hospital. He followed her. Her mother touched her face saying, "I'm sorry Barry slapped you."

She brushed her mother's hand away from her face. Barry stepped in between her and her mother and said, "I'll have you any time, I'm feeling horny." He laughed in a mocking fashion as he sprayed his saliva onto Janet's face and said, "Your mother agreed that I can bed you at any time I wish providing I bring money into the house and let her have her fix. The money I gave her is to support your arse and your dear mother. I'm only a son-in-law and without my money, you and your fucking mother would be on the scrap heap."

"Mother, did you tell this piece of shit he can have me when he wants?" Janet cried.

"Oh Janet, he's supporting us."

"Mother you're much filthier than that scumbag. I can't blame him for the way he is. I'm now blaming you."

"Janet, he is not a scumbag. I know he's not your flesh brother, but you should love and respect him for what he is giving us. There are so many people that are lone families. Besides, as I told you he's not a blood relative. So for my sake, please try and love him and also try and respect him for what he is."

"You respect him mother while I remain hating him. Well, remind me to go and look for my father so I can take him to bed and keep it in the family as you went to bed with yours for a fix of cocaine. So you know what mother, I respect my bastard father for leaving your dumb arse six years ago."

"Janet, that's enough! I know you're upset but it was only a couple of months ago that we lost your blood brother. Please, try and love Barry for my sake. It would traumatise me if I lost another son."

"You…" Janet screamed and pulled at her hair.

"Please, Janet," her mother said sympathetically.

"Get the fuck out of my face mother!"

"I will not have you talking to me or your brother like this, I will not! He will have you at any time. I swear he will." Her mother raised her voice, under the influence of drugs.

Janet looked hard at her mother with hate and said, "You're a nasty sore-minded bitch."

Her mother watched her as tears filled her eyes and as she stretched out her hand to touch Janet's face. Janet grimaced and clenched her fists saying to her, "I swear I hate you."

Her mother slapped her face again, and as hate and anger instantly built up within Janet, she punched her mother in her face and sent her flying. Barry caught his mother before she fell. Janet was looking hard at them as Barry put his mother down on a chair. Roughly, he grabbed Janet jerking her to face him and groping her firm breasts. "How dare you speak so disrespectfully to your mother?"

"Fuck you, arsehole!" said Janet, then spat in his face before kneeing him as hard as she could in his groin. He went down on his knees with his hands between his legs groaning with his face fixed to the floor. Janet watched him for a few minutes before she went to her father's toolbox that he'd left behind. From the box she took a mallet, rushed back into the hallway to meet Barry on his knees holding his crotch. "Fuck you," she bawled, then clubbed him with the mallet on his head. She then faced her mother with piercing eyes and set her face to look stone hard before she pulled her mother out of her seat and tossed her onto Barry. "Here's your bag of filth Mum, you stick him to your breast for his feed for I'm sure that's all he'll need from now on."

Her mother's tears streamed down her face while staring down at Barry as he lay curled up on the floor looking lifeless. Janet called the police and told them what happened. The police were very sympathetic but they had to involve Social Services. The next day the doctors told Janet's mum that the heavy blow to Barry's head had left him unconscious. Four days later and he was still unconscious. He spent two weeks in hospital and was stable, but he never fully recovered from the hit on his head. One week later, he was taken to a private home to help him recover, as he had no knowledge of the days and time. The doctors said he had lost fifty per cent of his memory.

Janet's Mum went to see him every day in the home, but he would only stare at her and growl like a puppy. Looking at him, she blamed herself for his condition.

A week later, on Wednesday morning, Janet woke up to find her mother dead on the living room floor with a needle stuck in her left arm. The coroner stated her mother's death was due to an overdose of cocaine. Janet also found a bag with cocaine tucked under the settee cushion.

At the inquest, Doctor Roach announced that her mother's death was an accidental overdose with cocaine. "I'm free," Janet said, but she cried, feeling upset over the death of her mother. As she was too young to live on her own, Social Services wanted to take her into care, but she rang Stanley and Elizabeth and told them what had happened. Stanley, his mother and Elizabeth took the case to court fighting for Janet with the backing of Superintendent Peterson supporting them to win custody of Janet. The court overturned the verdict and granted Stanley, his mother and Elizabeth custody of Janet, but Social Services insisted Janet should be put into care until she was eighteen and her mother's house should be rented out and the money be put in trust until that time.

Social Services appealed to the court, but Stanley and Elizabeth won. The court handed Janet over to Dr Stanley and his family when the court learnt Stanley was Judge O'Neil's son and Caroline his sister. Superintendent Peterson signed to be her guardian, as he knew Janet would be well cared for. The court also let Janet know she would remain with Stanley and his family for as long as she behaved until she turned eighteen – old enough to take care of herself.

Stanley and Elizabeth were very young of course, but the court was very happy to place Janet in their custody. They accepted the court's decision, but as time went on, Social Services would check up on the O'Neil family to check how Janet was getting on. After eleven months, they were extremely satisfied with Janet's progress. They told the O'Neil family and Superintendent Peterson that there was no need for them to continue visiting Janet.

"Well I'm pleased to hear that," Superintendent Peterson said to the welfare woman.

"Well Mr Peterson, we're not giving up on Janet just yet. It's just that she seems to be very happy and stable. We're very pleased with her school reports as well as with her work experience. I met Stanley's sister Caroline. We had a long chat and I know Janet will be well supported within the family."

"Yes Mrs Hall. Janet is one of the luckiest children."

"Mr Peterson, just for the record, is it true Stanley's sister is married to a shipping tycoon?"

"Yes Mrs Hall. What's this leading too?"

"Nowhere Mr Peterson, it's just that we have to get our facts right, just for the record. Will you please keep what I asked you between us?"

"Sure, of course Mrs Hall. I'll make sure I flush what you asked me down the toilet."

Mrs Hall laughed. "Well as I stated, I'm very satisfied that young Janet is well taken care of."

"Well, I'm sure young Janet is very happy Mrs Hall, as she came into a rich family that swore on oath to take care of her."

"Well thank you again Mr Peterson."

"Thank you also Mrs Hall."

They shook hands smiling before they parted.

Chapter 8

Four months later Mrs O'Neil had a stroke and her daughter-in-law Elizabeth and Janet helped care for her, along with a hired nurse and her stepdaughter Caroline. Elizabeth's mother and Caroline helped regularly doing the housework while Elizabeth and Stanley went to work as Janet was at university. Two months later, Mrs O'Neil was fully recovered, but the stroke had left her mouth slightly twisted. With regular therapy, she regained her nice looks within five months.

Meanwhile, it had been two years since Petra joined the police force. Another six months later she was working on Station Street in the City of Birmingham. Market Street was famous for prostitutes, druggies, alcoholics, tramps and layabouts.

Most of the time Petra and other officers would ignore such people. At times she looked at the youths puffing their rolled-up fix sending trails of smoke about their heads. She would smile seeing some of the lads with their jeans waists below their boxer shorts. She got to know most of the lad's faces by them calling her beautiful.

During Christmas week Petra was working on Carver Street. There were many other police officers working in different areas of the city as more fights than usual broke out at Christmas time.

That Saturday afternoon it was Christmas Eve. Petra was one of the officers working on Station Street when she heard someone screaming. She ran in the direction of the screaming, then stopped to listen, but the screaming stopped. "Some kids might be having a good time," she told herself. Smiling, she turned to get back on Station Street then she heard screaming again. "Help!"

She set out running in the direction of the screaming and nearing to the end of the road, the screaming sounded further away, then faded. After a few seconds, the screaming sounded again, taking Petra onto Carver Street, but as she heard nothing more she turned to get back to Station Street once again. She then heard the screaming repeatedly, "Help me! Help me!"

She was sure the screaming was coming from behind an almost deserted building on Station Street near to the bus station. She ran in the direction of the screaming and entered Market Street, where she saw a young mixed-race teenager running towards her screaming, "Help me!"

As the girl ran into Petra's arms, she pointed out two young black men and one white man who were chasing her. Trying to catch her breath, she held on tightly to Petra. The three youths stood at a near distance grinning.

"Hey, you monkeys," Petra called to them.

Craig faced her. "Who the fuck are you calling monkeys?"

"I saw no other monkeys chasing a poor frightened girl. Anyway, who let you three out of your cages and which zoo did you escape from?" Petra asked.

Blake flicked his penknife open, waving it backward and forward in Petra's face saying, "I'm going to carve your pretty face like pork skin."

Petra kicked the knife from his hand and knocked him down with a double punch to his head, then kicked him in the balls. His two mates flicked their penknives open. Petra aimed her gun to their heads in return. "I'll ask again, which damn fool let you monkeys loose?"

By this time the girl, whose name was Arlia, was standing behind Petra trembling.

Marlon put his knife in his jeans pocket saying, "Come on mates, let go."

"Not until I fuck the bitch," Drake said.

Petra hit him in his mouth with the gun butt and shoved the barrel in his mouth. "You foul mouthed son of a bitch. The next time you use such words to me, I swear, it would be the last word you say as I will empty every bullet down your throat flying your guts through your arse." Drake pissed himself and Petra pulled the gun out of his mouth and kicked him in the chest, sending him to the ground on his back. He held his chest as he got on his feet staggering. Marlon and Blake tried to help him to steady but he pushed them away. "Remember any of you monkeys cross my path ever, I'll make you watering cans," Petra said to them.

"Come on Drake, We'll get to fuck the bitch some other time," Blake said.

"Well monkeys, I think you should return to your cages before I take you in or blast you to hell."

"Come on Drake," Blake said as he took the lead walking slowly away. Arlia was still holding onto Petra's hand crying. "Help me please. I was on my way home from work."

"It's okay honey. I won't let them hurt you," Petra said.

"Lady, just give us the girl and pretend you haven't seen us," Marlon said.

Petra kicked him in the chest. He was staggering and would have fallen to the ground if Blake hadn't caught him. "I'm okay man, let me go."

"Marlon, I just prevented you from falling," Blake said.

"I'm okay man. The bitch caught me by surprise. I'll kill the fucking bitch."

"Marlon, let's go. We'll deal with this bitch another time," Drake persisted.

"Marlon, I think Drake's right," Craig said, "I think we should leave."

"Where the fuck did you get to when this bitch was giving us trouble?" Marlon asked.

"Man I went for a shit," Craig said.

"You drop in monkey. I think you should take your other three monkey friends and you lot get lost. I think also you four should go and have a bath before you are let loose on the street again," Petra said.

"You know what bitch? I think your mouth is too big for your size. Also, I think you need to be cut down," Craig said and backed away.

"Craig, for once I agree with you. I want you, Blake and Drake to watch me strip the bitch while I take her then one of you takes the little chick!" Marlon said with blood dripping from his lips. "Then I'll let you know if the big one was worth fucking," he went on to say.

"I know you're the mighty white and black monkey's assholes. You know what? I'm wasting time here with you four. One more word from any of you, I'll send a bullet into you. Now take your filthy asses off the street!"

Marlon wiped blood from his mouth and they walked away while Petra watched. Marlon turned and blew her a kiss. Then as Petra left with Arlia to go after them, they trotted off. Then Blake walked with a crowd of people and came up to Petra again and touched her on the back. Petra looked back and

Blake kissed her lips. As he tried to run, Petra grabbed him by his T-shirt and punched him on the side of head, then kneed him in the groin, sending him down on his knees, and then kicked him on the back of his leg. He fell to the ground face first, busting both his lips, then she shackled his hands behind his back and read him his rights. Craig faced Drake and said, "I like a fighting bitch! She don't look too bad either for a cop."

"Officer, we went too far. Please let my friend go then we'll be out of your face," Marlon said.

"You should have known that before now," Petra said.

Craig fired a hit at Petra's face and missed. She punched him; he stumbled and fell. She rushed into him and kicked him while he was down and Petra watched him trying to get up but kept him down with one foot on his throat.

"I think you should stay down. Any of you get close to me again I'll send a bullet in your arse."

Blake cried, "Officer, I'm sorry." Craig flicked his penknife open and was going after Petra but Arlia screamed out, "He has a knife." Petra turned to see him with the knife. She shot Craig in the arm. The knife dropped and she double-kicked him on the head. He fell. "Damn, I wish I had three more shackles," Petra said and put her gun in her holster. As she was radioing for an ambulance, Craig picked himself up staggering and bleeding. Petra pulled her gun out of her holster again and as Marlon and Craig went towards her, she aimed her gun at them. "I told you the next one of you to challenge me again I'll shoot." Craig raised his hands in the air and Blake said, "Officer, we're so sorry. Help us with our friend you shot."

"You stay here girl," Petra said to Arlia, then went with Marlon, Craig and Drake and stood over Blake. She said to them, "I know you lot don't value your idle lives, but it's best you four lazy nits take your arses home after you're patched up at the hospital. If I see you nuisance good-for-nothings near me again, I will end your lives."

"Look officer, my friends are sorry to chase the girl and make trouble for you," Craig said.

"Give us a chance lady," Drake said, trying to wriggle out of the cuffs. "Please beautiful officer, take these cuffs off and give us a chance before the ambulance comes."

Petra stared at him. "Like you four monkeys were giving that poor young girl a chance? I think you four had set out to take advantage of this girl. What if I wasn't present, what would you have done to her? Give her a bus ticket home after you had done what you wanted with her? Well, I think you four would have raped her and this makes you guilty of attempted rape." However, I will give you four a chance under one condition."

"Any condition officer," Craig said.

"What about you other three monkeys?"

"Yes anything," Drake replied smiling.

"Well I want you monkeys to help me find a Sydney Black."

"Sydney Black, are you crazy? Officer! Sydney Black is one of the most dangerous men in this town. You go and get help from someone else," Drake said.

"Well Drake, I'm sorry but I have to take you in since you're wearing the shackle and I haven't got the key. As for you other three, you can wipe the smiles off your faces as you're also charged with attempted rape."

"Come off it officer, we raped no one and you shot me in my arm. And the pain is killing me," Blake said.

Petra pushed Marlon and Blake forward, holding her gun on them. "Please officer. I don't want any of my friends to see me like this," Marlon said.

"Well, the sooner you help me with my enquiries, the sooner I'll let you get to hospital."

"Officer, I'm feeling uncomfortable with my hand cuffed behind my back. I will help you find Sydney Black but the rest is up to you as I don't want any other part in whatever else."

"Okay, Drake that's all I want you to do. Just lead me to the son-of-a-bitch," Petra said and took the shackles off Drake's hand. He rubbed his wrist. "Officer, you're a hard bitch but pretty." He smiled.

"I could always put you back in shackles," Petra said.

"No, no. I said I would help you. I'll take you to Sydney Black. You agree with me, friends?" Drake turned to his mates.

"Yes, we give our word." Drake, Marlon and Craig smiled.

"Look monkeys, here is my mobile number. Sorry I can't give you my home number as I can trust no one. Just give me a call. All I need from you is Sydney Black's address."

"Ok officer, we'll call after the ambulance has taken us to hospital to get stitched up," Marlon said pulling his T-shirt tight around his cut neck to slow the blood but his lips were still bleeding. Blake was groaning with pain and his arm was bleeding. Arlia went to Petra saying, "Officer, the ambulance should been here by now and can you trust them to help you with your enquiries?"

"Well girl, we'll soon find out. Are you hungry?"

"A little," Arlia said.

The ambulance arrived to take Blake and Marlon to hospital, but Craig and Drake got in the ambulance with them. Marlon called Petra from the hospital and said, "Officer ..."

"What now, Marlon?"

"Officer, believe me or not, I'm sorry and ashamed of what we did and said to you and the girl."

"Look Marlon, I'm sorry that I was a bit rough on you and your friends, but you brought it on yourselves. Look at it this way, the poor girl was really petrified. Imagine if it was your sister that three other monkeys were chasing intending to rape. Not to mention your other friend who came on the scene. What would any of you have done?" Petra asked.

"Officer, I get your point." Marlon wiped tears from his eyes.

"Look Marlon, I can tell you're not as tough as you make out to be. My name is Petra by the way."

"You're not a bad cop."

"Okay Marlon, I'm sorry I injured you and your friend but you deserved to be."

"Okay Petra, you'll find Sydney Black at his house at nine o'clock tonight. His address is 224 Richmond's Lane. His house is the biggest and it stands by itself at the end with white and yellow roses climbing the wall with the tallest arched black iron gate. You can't miss it."

"Thanks Marlon, you've been very helpful. Now take a little advice from me your friendly cop and keep out of trouble. About your busted neck and your friend's busted lips and arm, I'm sorry."

Marlon smiled. "You know what Petra, I wanted to be a police officer and to change direction instead of stocking shop shelves at night."

"Well, if you want to be a police officer, I would talk to you. You seem to be an intelligent lad. Marlon thanks again for your help and I will help you to be a policeman if you really want to be."

Marlon smiled. "Thanks officer."

Petra closed her phone, shook her head and walked with Arlia to the police station. "Wait here girl," she told Arlia while she went into her locker to get some money. She then left with Arlia and went back on duty patrolling Market Street. As the street was so busy with shoppers, she and Arlia went inside the market, but Arlia was careful not to be seen by friends.

As she and Petra were walking past the fruit and flower stalls, Arlia said, "The stalls look spectacular." She lowered her head and rushed away, seeing one of her school friends. Petra smiled, then caught up with her. "Why did you run?" she asked.

Arlia smiled. "I saw someone I didn't want to see. But I was enjoying looking at the scenery."

Petra looked at her, smiling. "Yes, everything looks so enchanting and inviting," Petra said as she and Arlia walked around from stall to stall. "Well everything seems to be okay."

Walking past a fruit stall, Arlia took two apples and a bunch of grapes while Petra was paying for some fruit. Petra gave her some of the apples and ate one herself. Walking out of the market, she met Julia and Joanne. She stopped to speak to Julia.

"How's married life treating you now?" she asked Julia.

"Well, as you can see, it's not that bad," Julia said smiling.

"Are you having a baby?"

"I'm sure I am Petra. It's been sometime since we met up. We should have lunch soon."

"I would like that."

Joanne watched Petra and smiled. "Well ladies, I'll have to go. I'll see you both some other time," Petra said and she touched Julia on her left hand.

"Well hello little one," Julia said to Arlia.

Arlia smiled.

"Well Julia, since you have been married, you've really developed into one of the most beautiful women."

"Oh Petra, I would understand if you said I looked well. Just look at you, you're beautiful."

"Julia, I meant what I said. You really are very beautiful, don't you agree with me, Joanne?"

Joanne smiled. "Yes, I have told her so many times," replied Joanne.

"Petra, I would like you to drop in for a visit at any time."

"Thanks, I will," Petra said. "Well goodbye both of you."

"Goodbye Petra," Julia said while Joanne smiled.

Petra and Arlia walked on while Julia and Joanne went shopping. Petra went back to patrolling Market Street.

"I'm really hungry," Arlia said.

"Me too," Petra said. As they were walking, Arlia almost fell as an empty bottle rolled under her foot. Petra caught her before she fell. "Are you okay?"

"Yes, I am."

"Bastards, they litter the streets with all sorts of rubbish. Just look at the empty bottles and cans all over the streets. Some people have no consideration at all," Petra said as she and Arlia walked into a cake shop. Inside the shop, Arlia noticed a crowd of people gathered on the other side. "I think there might have been an accident," she told Petra.

"Here, you buy us something to eat and a drink while I go and see what has happened," said Petra.

Arlia bought herself and Petra cream doughnuts and coke while Petra ran to the scene. A middle-aged woman said to her, "A fight broke out between two women and one has been stabbed. I understand they were fighting over a man who has run away with other women. Officer, tell me, why are some women so naïve?"

Petra smiled and radioed in for an ambulance. "Clear the area," she told onlookers. "The patient needs air."

"Arlia went over to Petra. Can I do anything?"

"No sweetheart, I don't think so. You stand aside."

"Look Petra, I can help. I had lessons in First Aid and I know how to slow down bleeding."

"So am I. Just keep out of the way. Hey, besides, the officers have done what they can," Petra said.

As the patient was bleeding too much, Petra and the other officers rolled her gently onto her tummy and fixed her head carefully for her to breathe easily. Arlia fixed her feather anorak under the patient's head. "She's getting weak," an officer said after feeling the patient's pulse. More police and the ambulance arrived. Onlookers moved. After paramedics put the patient in the ambulance they sped away. Meanwhile in the ambulance, they examined the patient's wounds to see if the belt was too tight and causing a blood clot, but the belt was supporting the wound and the blood was only seeping slowly. "Thanks for lending me your belt," Petra said to Arlia.

Two police cars came speeding to the location sounding their sirens with another ambulance following. Five police officers got out of their cars and rushed up to where the crime had taken place.

"Sorry officers, but you're fifteen minutes too late," Petra said looking at her watch. The young paramedic smiled. Then as he looked at the girl smiling, she said, "I'm here with my aunt. She is the police officer that actually saved the patient's life by using my belt." The young paramedic smiled. then said "Thank you."

Then a middle-aged white clean-shaven police officer with mixed black and greying hair on both sides asked onlookers, "Did anyone see what happened?" But they stayed silent. Constables Pitt and Jacobs asked the onlookers again, "Does anyone know what happened?"

An older black woman said, "I was told two women were fighting and one got stabbed. The woman who stabbed the other one, her name is Sky McCoy."

"She lives at 27 Fern Road, Great Barr," Petra told the constables Pitt and Jacob.

"So where's the woman that told you?" Constable Jacob asked.

"She left," Petra said.

"Have you taken the woman's name and address?" Constable Pitt asked.

"No, Constable Pitt. I did ask her but she walked away. Well as she told me on hearsay, I had no reason to pursue questioning her any further," Petra said.

Constable Pitt grinned, then radioed another constable to go to Miss McCoy's and told him to pick her up and arrest her. When the two constables got to Miss McCoy's home and asked to see her, her mother told them, "My daughter is not at home."

"Would you mind if we have a look ourselves?" one police officer asked.

"No officer, you can come in, but I'm sure you won't find her in here. Tell me officer, why are you looking for my daughter and what has she done?"

Mrs McCoy moved away from the door to let the police in. While one police officer went upstairs, the other one was looking downstairs in the rooms and outside the back of the house. As he came into the house he met his colleague and said, "She's nowhere here."

"Upstairs is clear," his colleague said. Then he said to Mrs McCoy, "As soon as your daughter gets home, will you let us know?"

"Officer, I would like to know what my daughter has done and why you're looking for her."

"Well, I take it that your daughter is not at home. However, we're sorry we cannot reveal any information to you until we speak to your daughter. If she turns up before we see her, would you please ask her to report to the nearest police station or please get in touch with us as we asked." He gave Mrs McCoy one of his cards with the telephone numbers. Mrs McCoy nodded and the officers said goodbye and left.

Ten minutes later, Belinda McCoy was picked up off the street near her home by Constable Jacob. He read her her rights and took her to the city police station for questioning. She denied stabbing Phoebe and as police couldn't find the knife, they questioned her.

"What have you done with the knife?"

"I didn't do anything to the woman. I saw her staggering and I went to help her," Belinda McCoy said.

"There was a witness that claimed they saw you arguing with Miss Phoebe Williams before she fell," Officer Pitt said.

"Yes, we were arguing, then I saw her fall, that is when I saw her bleeding and I got frightened and ran as we were arguing over the same man. I realized I should have called for help but I was frightened."

"Miss McCoy, we are charging you with grievous bodily harm to Miss Phoebe Williams until she can tell us what happened. In the meantime, we'll let you out on police bail. You will also report to the station at ten o'clock every morning until we're sure you had nothing to do with stabbing Miss Williams," Superintendent Peterson said.

At this time, an Officer Longford was just leaving as he'd received a phone call from Petra asking him to meet her at the crime scene. When he got to Petra, she told him, "Miss McCoy had nothing to do with stabbing Miss Williams. I understood Miss McCoy and Miss Williams were arguing over the same man before Miss Williams fell."

"Well Officer Jackson, do you know who stabbed Miss Williams?"

"No, not yet, but I know Miss McCoy didn't stab her."

"Did Miss Williams tell you this, Jackson?"

"No. Miss Williams was too weak to say anything at the time. But I should see her later and talk to her," Petra said.

"Officer Jackson, I think you should stay away from Miss Williams and let the other police officers deal with what happened to her."

"Well, thanks for the warning," Petra said angrily and walked away.

Sergeant March went to the crime scene searching for the used weapon but didn't find it. Within minutes the blood was washed away with a hosepipe. Petra and the girl ate their doughnuts before they went to the hospital to find out how the patient was doing.

Meanwhile Doctors Sean and Stevens had attended to her. Dr Sean said to Petra smiling, "This belt binding was a brilliant first class job."

Petra smiled.

"Who did this?" he asked.

"I did! I was only trying to help the women," Petra said.

Dr Sean looked up at Petra and said, "Please, I would like to speak to you as soon as we have tended to the patient."

"Doctor, I did what I could and there's no need for me to stay any longer as I have a child with me that needs to get home. Goodbye doctor," Petra said.

"Is she your daughter?" Dr Sean asked.

"No. Nevertheless, I have to go now." As Petra turned to leave, she faced Dr Sean and said, "Would you please put the belt in the bin."

Dr Sean stood upright and faced Petra. "Yes of course, but I didn't mean to offend you. Please, if I hurt your feelings in any way, I'm really sorry. I only asked because of the first class job that had been carried out on the patient. You have done a marvellous job by slowing down the bleeding."

"Yes doctor."

"May I ask your name?"

"Petra Jackson."

A bright smile came over his face. "Well thank you Mrs Jackson." He smiled.

"It's Miss."

Dr Sean smiled wider. Petra set out walking to meet the girl but stopped when she saw a police car drive into the car park and stop. Detective Mike Evans and Officer Kelly got out of the car and rushed over to Petra. "Officer Jackson, have you spoken to Miss Phoebe Williams?"

"No detective. I thought you were dealing with her."

"Hello Officer Jackson."

"Hello Kelly."

Kelly smiled. "We're here to take a statement from Miss Williams. Oh I guess you know Detective Evans."

"I've met him a couple of times," Petra said and went into the waiting room with the girl to have a drink.

Dr Sean showed himself. "Dr Sean, I was told you attended to Miss Phoebe Williams. Detective Evans and I would like to take a statement from her about what happened."

"No, you certainly can't at this moment as the patient is heavily sedated and now asleep."

"Well thank you doctor, we'll come back later," Detective Evans said and he and Officer Kelly walked into the waiting room to meet Petra and Arlia drinking coke and eating Mars bars. Detective Evans stared into Petra's face then said, "Oh it's you again Officer Jackson."

"And what's that supposed to mean?" Petra asked him.

He smiled and said," Anywhere you go, trouble seems to follow."

Petra looked him fully in the face. "Officer Kelly, will you move this lump of shit from under my shoes before I squash it."

Officer Kelly smiled widely then said to Detective Evans, "I think we should leave mate." Arlia laughed and Detective Evans raised his hand to hit Petra. "Hit me. You're at the right place for me to kick your arse into unconsciousness and into a bed."

Officer Kelly smiled with Petra and he and Detective Evans left Petra as the girl laughed. Outside the hospital Petra met Officer Karen Phillips. As they faced each other, Officer Karen giggled and said, "Officer Kelly told me what you said to Detective Evans. That man needs a good kicking up his arse."

"Believe me Karen, he's working towards getting that," Petra said. "Anyway, did you come to take a statement from Miss Williams?"

"No. I'm here to see my brother as he fell through the roof of a building he was working on this morning. I should have gone home to change but as it was getting late and I was near here, I just popped in."

"Well, I wish your brother a speedy recovery. I'll see you later," Petra said and she and Arlia left in her car. Dr Sean was on time to see her driving out of the hospital gate. "Petra, I forgot your shopping on the floor." the girl said. Petra looked at her and said, "Just as well we haven't got too far to go."

Petra turned her car around and drove into the hospital forecourt. Arlia got out and went and got the bag. Dr Sean saw Petra and he walked out of the hospital, went towards her smiling and knocked on her car window. Petra wound the window down. "Thanks again for helping the patient and making our job easier."

Petra smiled. "We forgot our bag, it's in the waiting room. Anyway, how is the patient doing?"

"Well, she's a little weak but that's to be expected after losing so much blood," he said.

Arlia got back with the carrier bag, opened the car door then sat next to Petra.

"Well I'm glad to hear she's okay," Petra said.

"You are so young to be a police officer," he said.

"Don't let your eyes deceive you Dr Sean. I'm eighteen. You look very young yourself."

"Miss Jackson, I'm twenty-three. May I take you and your sister to lunch one day?"

"Oh, she's not my sister," Petra said.

"Then may I invite you to dinner tomorrow evening?"

"If you give me your phone number I'll be happy to get in contact with you," Petra said.

"Sure," said Dr Sean reaching in his jacket pocket and taking out a card with his home and hospital numbers. As Petra was looking at the card he smiled, and then got into his car pulled out his briefcase, then walked back into the hospital.

Petra drove away. "So I see you found a doctor to love you," Arlia said smiling.

"Hey, you drop that saying. There are two kinds of men I don't want in my life and they are doctors and the police."

"You don't say?"

Meanwhile, Dr Sean went to Phoebe and examined her stab wound for further bleeding. "I remembered a lovely young police officer came to help me. She had a mole above the top of her right ear and she was very tall, slim and very beautiful too. I wish I could see her. I would really like to thank her for helping me."

"You sure gave me a good description of her. Her name is Petra Jackson. As a matter of fact, I asked her out to dinner tomorrow night. If she accepts my invitation, I'll be happy to thank her for you," Dr Sean said.

"Thank you doctor, I guess you are not married, I hope she accepts your invitation to dinner," Phoebe said.

"Yes. I hope so too," Dr Sean said. "Well you need plenty of rest. I will be back in the morning to see how you are doing."

"Thanks doctor."

Dr Sean left.

Later in the night while Dr Stanley and Nurse Randal attended to Phoebe, Stanley listened to her talking about how lovely Petra was.

"So do you know Petra?" Stanley asked Phoebe.

"Yes, but I only got to know her this afternoon. She helped saved my life after I was stabbed. I must say, she's a lovely young lady. Dr Sean asked her out to dinner. I think they would make a lovely couple."

"I'm sure," Dr Stanley said and smiled. After he examined Phoebe he said, "That's looks fine. Well, I'll check in on you tomorrow."

"Okay doctor," Phoebe said. Dr Stanley and Nurse Randall walked on to attend to other patients.

At eight thirty in the evening, Petra phoned Elizabeth telling her about Phoebe and that she met a Dr Sean and he asked her out to dinner.

"That's great Pet, I'm really happy for you. But honey, please be very careful," Elizabeth said.

"I will honey, but I haven't given him my answer yet," Petra said.

"Well, do you like him?"

"I think I do. But I don't see myself serious with him. Give my love to Janet. Well honey, goodbye," Petra said then she closed her mobile phone.

Ten minutes later that same evening Petra's phone rang. She thought it was Elizabeth as she had just spoken to her. Petra answered her phone. "Hello Elizabeth."

"Hey bitch! I heard you were looking for me," Sydney Black said.

"Who is this?" Petra asked.

"I have nine inches of a stiff weapon to put up your arse," he said and laughed.

"You sick bastard." Petra closed her phone.

"Who's that the girl asked?"

"You don't want to know. Look it's getting late and you should be home," Petra said as she was driving Arlia to the gate she claimed was hers. The girl got out and looked away in the distance. "Well, I'll be working around the same place tomorrow if you should be in town," Petra said.

Arlia smiled, but looked sad as Petra was looking at her. "Well you better go now Petra," she said. "Well maybe I'll see you as tomorrow is Sunday."

"Well, goodbye and I might see you tomorrow or some other time," Petra said. But before she drove away, she noticed the hesitance of Arlia opening the gate. Petra smiled with the thought that Arlia might not live at that address. After Arlia looked back waving, Petra drove herself home. After putting the shopping away she thought about Arlia as she had noticed signs of abuse in her eyes. "Damn! Why didn't I catch on that the girl was crying out for my help?"

Chapter 9

While Petra was putting the shopping away, a tin of tomatoes dropped.

"Petra, is that you?" called her mum.

"Yes Mum. Sorry I woke you."

"I wasn't sleeping. Pet, there's some supper in the oven if you want."

"Thanks Mum." Petra heated her supper and ate then showered. Lying in bed, she was thinking of the girl. She rolled over on her belly in frustration, then stabbed a pencil into her headboard breaking it. Poor girl, she hadn't even bothered to ask her name. Then Sydney Black came into her thoughts. She rolled over on her side looking at the wall clock and saw that the time was twenty past ten. She went down to the kitchen and made herself some tea and went back to bed, dropping off to sleep on top of her quilt.

Early the next morning she turned off the lights and went under the quilt. At seven she got up and had a shower before breakfast.

"Sit down," her mother told her.

She looked at her mother with a kind of funny smile.

"What's the matter Pet?"

"Why do you ask?"

"Couldn't you sleep last night? I heard every move you made."

"I'm sorry mother. I couldn't get settled."

"At least you don't have to go to work."

"I will be going to work mother, as I was asked to do a few hours and I accepted as I'm in need of some extra money. Besides, I have to be somewhere as I told my little friend if she wants to see me, I'll be working at a certain place."

"Why do you need extra money? Pet, you need rest."

"I know mother, but I had a phone call this morning asking me if I was available to work and I said yes."

"So when do you start working?"

"One-thirty until five-thirty."

"Well you should try and have a nap."

"Maybe after I finish breakfast. Oh mother, I will be having dinner with a friend tonight."

"Petra, you're now nineteen, I want you to be very careful about going out with men. I think you should protect yourself from getting pregnant until you're at least twenty-five and have a steady partner or are married."

"I thought you wanted grandchildren," Petra laughed.

"Yes Pet, I do, but I also want you to have a career first."

"Mother, I'm almost twenty and he's a doctor I met yesterday. I will be having dinner with him, without sex involved."

"Pet my dear, I still want you to be careful and you won't be twenty for five months. By the way, have you no other interest in any other men but doctors and policemen? Their month's never up as they spend their wages before they get it. You're beautiful. I don't like the idea of you working as a policewoman, but it is your choice. I'm sure most of your age group and friends are married or have steady boyfriends. I want at least a couple of grandchildren before I'm too old to help look after them. Your stepfather would have so wanted to see his grandchildren, but unfortunately his life was taken away."

"I wouldn't have wanted any children as I didn't want to tell them what happened and what I did. Most of all, I don't want to be reminded of that rotten bastard you married when you dumped my father. I'm sure you'll have enough grandchildren from Arden."

"Petra, that's not fair. Anyway, what are you talking about?"

"Nothing mother, I don't think I'm hungry after all. I'll have breakfast later. By the way, do you know a man called Sydney Black?"

"That man is trouble." Mrs Forbes faced Petra. "I want you to leave that man alone! You stay well away from him! Do you hear me? You stay well away from that man!"

"What do you know about Sydney Black, mother?"

"He's no good. He and his kind are famous for putting young girls and boys on the street and making them sell their bodies and drugs. When they do not turn up with enough money, they are lucky to be left alive. Sydney Black has a brother by the name of Ed Ryan. He's even worse than Sydney. I heard once, Ed, his cousin and two of his friends raped a fourteen-year-old girl named Monica, then Ed let one of the dogs have her while they watched and laughed. Then Ed ordered one of his men to throw her in the street after they pumped an overdose of drugs in her. Early the next morning she was found on the roadside stiff and dead."

"How do you know this?"

"Andrew Scrimshaw left a confession note before he shot himself in the head. That child was Madame Stall's granddaughter."

"This happened about five years ago didn't it?"

"Yes, I think so. She would have been the same age as you. So honey, don't you go looking for those good-for-nothing poison Black family as many powerful lawmen have failed to bring them to justice. I don't want you to end up dead like them. Sydney Black and his kind are happily doing what's evil and getting richer by the second up to this day! I don't want you chatting at work about what I've told you either. Sydney Black has many friends in the force."

"Like your husband? Anyway, thanks for the warning. I think I'll have some breakfast now. I feel like I could lift the world up since you spoke to me," Petra said with that mischievous grin.

Her mother smiled and put a plate with turkey drummers, eggs, tomatoes, waffles and a pot of black coffee in front of her.

"By the way Petra, Arden sends you his love. He's doing very well at university. He said he misses you very much and he's posted you a pair of gold earrings and matching chain for your birthday, you should get them in the next couple of days. I'm sure he has your birthday wrong."

"I do miss him too mother. By the way, is Grandma feeling any better?"

"Yes Pet, she's feeling much better."

"I think you should ask her to move in with us."

"I'll ask when I go to see her later, but I doubt if she will. When you finish breakfast will you please go and fetch what clothes you need washing."

Petra finished eating. She went to get her clothes and put them into her mother's hands.

"Mum, can I borrow fifty pounds?"

"What for?"

"I need to buy a dress. I might be having dinner with Dr Sean tonight, as I told you."

"You don't say."

"Mum, I'm only going to have dinner with him. That's all."

"And after dinner?"

"I'll be coming straight home to my bed."

Her mother smiled. "I was once young like you." She slapped Petra's bottom softly. Petra tickled her mother under her arms, making her laugh.

"Stop it Pet." Her mother was laughing hysterically. "Pet, stop it!"

Petra stopped tickling her mother when they both slid to the floor. "I think it's time to have a nap before I go to work."

"Pet, will fifty pounds be enough?"

"More than enough mother."

"I'll leave it under the bread bin."

That afternoon while Petra was working, she looked out for Arlia but didn't see her. After work, she went into a high street shop and bought a nice floral dress and a pair of white high-heeled shoes and matching handbag.

Much later in the afternoon her mother went to her room to speak with her but met her sleeping. Her mother woke her with a light slap on her bottom.

"Pet?"

Petra turned, facing her mother. "Do you want something Mum?"

"I'm going to see your grandma now."

"Tell her I will come and see her tomorrow after work."

"Oh Pet, if I'm not back by the time you go out, make sure you lock the doors, windows and don't forget to take your key with you as I might not be back in time to let you in."

"Are you planning to stay the night with Grandma?"

"I'm not sure yet Petra. Oh, your wallet is on the counter. I put one hundred pounds in it instead. I'm off now."

"You take care of yourself now mother."

"I will, you too Pet."

When Petra heard the door shut, she opened her window and shouted "Mum, you take care, give Grandma a hug from me."

"You take care as well. Don't forget to lock the windows and doors before you go out."

"Okay Mum," Petra said then went back to bed leaving her window open to let in fresh air.

Mrs Forbes was walking to the bus stop when two buses passed. "Oh no," she said then carried on walking to the next bus stop to meet a white woman waiting. "We must have missed the bus by few minutes," Mrs Forbes said.

"Yes, I saw two go past about five minutes before I got here."

"Well," said the woman, "I think we have ten minutes waiting before another one comes."

"Thanks for telling me. I think I will walk on to a shop to get some tissues then take the bus at the next stop."

The woman smiled and took her seat on the bench under the bus shelter watching Mrs Forbes as she went by.

Meanwhile, Mrs Forbes stopped at the small supermarket to buy mints and tissues, then she walked on to a children's playground passing a takeaway. Looking back for the bus, she carried on walking to the chemist where she stopped to buy some sweets, then walking on looking back for the bus, she passed a doctor's surgery, Sunshine Nursery, the Ladbroke betting shop and a newsagent before she got to the bus stop. Again as the bus took a long time to come, Mrs Forbes set out walking. When she came to a junior school and crèche her left high-heeled shoe got stuck in a pot hole and broke off.

"Damn! I knew I should have taken my car," she said but managed to walk to the bus stop. Just then a black Mercedes pulled up beside her and stopped.

Banjo wound down the window, popped his head out of the window and called, "Mrs Forbes, can I give you a lift?"

Mrs Forbes looked away ignoring him.

"Mrs Forbes, I'm talking to you," Banjo said looking annoyed.

Mrs Forbes walked away from the bus stop and carried on walking wearing her right shoe while holding the left shoe in her right hand. Banjo was driving slowly behind her. "Mrs Forbes, can I give you a lift to where you're going?"

Mrs Forbes stopped walking and went closer to his car. "Do I know you?"

"I don't think you do, but your husband was a good friend of me and my cousin," Banjo said. "And I know your daughter Petra very well."

"Are you a friend of my daughter?"

"Yes, and I really miss your husband. He was one of our best friends. Now do you want a lift, Mrs Anne Forbes?" Banjo asked again trickling out a husky laugh.

"I'm not too sure about you as I don't know you," Mrs Forbes said.

"Look, I won't bite you. I saw you limping and that's why I'm offering you a lift." Banjo flanged opens the car door.

"Okay," Mrs Forbes said and got in. "I thought you were alone."

"Oh, don't mind my two friends. They're harmless," Banjo smiled. Mrs Forbes looked hard at Aaron and Mark sitting at the back.

"Relax Mrs Forbes," Aaron said.

Mark and Banjo laughed, but Aaron kept silent and looked away looking sad.

"How's Petra?" Banjo asked.

"Do you know her very well?" Mrs Forbes asked.

"Oh yes, Mrs Forbes," Mark said. "Petra will be a very good friend to us after today."

"What do you mean? I don't understand, as for you Banjo, my Petra hasn't spoken about you."

"Come on Mrs Forbes. Young girls don't speak to their parents about men they have dated. Besides, parents are the last to find out the company their daughters keep, and also the last to know when they get pregnant."

"Are you trying to tell me that my Petra is pregnant?"

"Oh no, Mrs Forbes, I'm only stating facts. Petra is young, pretty and clever, I wouldn't want anything bad to happen to her. I like her," Banjo said smiling.

"Please, I would like to get out now, if you don't mind."

"Relax Mrs Forbes," Banjo laughed. "Mark is Sydney Black's brother. We heard your Petra was asking about his brother Sydney Black. He's my cousin. I also heard your Petra joined the force, so I hope she will be our friend like her stepfather was. My cousin doesn't like people asking about him. Especially cops he's not associated with. I heard your daughter is asking too many questions about my cousin. I don't think he would like to hear that at all, knowing she's a Babylon and maybe an enemy to him. Incidentally, Sydney has some good friends in the force. I hope your daughter will be one. You see

Mrs Forbes, my cousin is also my boss and believe me, he just wants to be left alone, selling his drugs and running his whorehouses. Do you get my meaning? My cousin Sydney is trying to make something of himself and at the same time, he's helped people like your husband. My cousin was born here, but his father took him to Jamaica after he split from his Trinidad-born wife. My cousin was just four years old when he experienced how poverty split his mother and father. He swore that he would never be poor. Well, his father took him to Jamaica where he spent seven years there before coming back here when he was seventeen. He became a big-timer and well respected selling drugs, women, music. He made it big. Now I think he deserves a great deal of respect and to be left alone to do what he's doing and that is to make plenty of money so that he can support both his parents in Jamaica and in Trinidad as living there is tough for them. Now his mother's well-off having her own business making and selling cakes, sweets and bread for every occasion. Well, as for my cousin Sydney, I personally don't see it's a big deal doing what he likes. Maybe if your daughter understands him, they might even become friends."

"You son of a bitch, let me out!" Mrs Forbes shouted.

"Take it easy, Annie Forbes," Banjo said.

Mrs Forbes tried to open the door to get out, but Mark pulled her back, pressing her down in her seat. "Sit your arse down and keep still," he shouted.

Mrs Forbes looked hard at him in anger. He felt her breast. She slapped his face. He punched her on her chest making her head flap onto Aaron's shoulder. "What the fuck have you done?" Aaron bawled.

"Shut your fucking gob and keep your eyes on the road."

Mark shoved his hand down Mrs Forbes' blouse. She scratched his face with her fingernails. He punched her hard on the side of her head, knocking her out for few seconds, then as he was going to rape her Aaron jerked his head backward, then punched him on the side of his head. He pulled a knife at Aaron. "If you believe you're bad, hit me again."

"Banjo, let's teach the pussycat soft man a lesson. He can't take on two of us," Mark said.

"Look, arseholes, I want no part in what you two want to do. What you were about to do was wicked and disrespectful."

"Shut your fucking trap Aaron."

"Would you like to shut it for me?"

Banjo grinned, then elbowed Aaron in the mouth busting his lips. Mark pushed Mrs Forbes backward to the seat and as he tried to force her legs open Aaron kicked him in his chest, sending him flying out the car. Mrs Forbes leaned forward to shut the door, but Mark yanked the door out of her hand and got in and cut Aaron on his leg with his penknife, then he and Banjo punched him on his face and body before Mark hit him with his gun butt to the side of his head so that he fell unconscious for a little time. "You interfere in anything I'm about to do again, I'll cap a bullet in your heart."

Banjo laughed and hit him again but Aaron was still flat out. Mark roughed up Mrs Forbes and forced her legs apart.

"No, no, please don't," Mrs Forbes cried." But Mark raped her. By then Aaron was coming awake but Banjo knocked him out again, then he raped Mrs Forbes. Aaron just about came to his senses to watch Banjo zipping his fly. "You thought you could a stop me having the bitch! I will get the daughter as well," Banjo said.

"Don't bother with the pussy arsehole. He's a wimp like a pussy," Mark said and laughed.

"It must be true they said. Old fowl makes tasty soup," Mark said.

"Man, what you have done is sickening," Aaron said.

"Fuck you man!" Banjo said then punched Aaron in his face out of anger. "I told you to shut your Pussyclart mouth. What is she to you to make you cry like a Pussyclart Pinckney?"

Mark laughed. "Do you think Lady Forbes here will let you court her bitch of a daughter? Well, when I catch up with the bitch and finish with her, you're welcome to her as you were out cold when we sampled the mother."

"I'm sorry for what they have done to you Mrs Forbes. I had no idea this would happen. Still, you're lucky they didn't rape you," Aaron said.

"But they did rape me. I'd rather be dead. Oh God! They could give me aids or venereal disease," Mrs Forbes cried. Aaron tried to put his arm around her to comfort her, but because she was crying so much, he didn't bother. He just punched the side of the car out of anger.

"Now look how you busted your knuckles over a woman because my cousin and I had a little fun with her. Tell me, is she worth the pain you're feeling?" Mark asked Aaron and laughed.

"You want to see to your leg Aaron. You should ask them to take you to a doctor," Mrs Forbes said.

"And what about you?" Aaron asked

"I'll be fine," Mrs Forbes said.

"You just sit tight and quiet," Aaron smiled. "I'll be okay."

Banjo drove down between a long and narrow stony road with high hedges on both sides before he came to an open wasteland and then onto a narrow stoned pathway passing a large old warehouse and a little further on to a massive estate saying, 'Private. Keep Out.' Banjo drove on for about fifteen yards and stopped on an enormous forecourt. Mrs Forbes stared at the four parked limousines and five Mercedes and other cars. "Just look at all those cars parked up."

"Don't worry Mrs Forbes. Every one of those cars will melt like butter against the sun. It's only a matter of time."

Mrs Forbes got out of the car then Mark said to Aaron, "You two get the fuck out." Banjo kicked Aaron out of the car on his face, then he laughed too. Mark got out and walked Mrs Forbes to the gate, then handed her over to two watchmen that were standing at the entrance.

"What is her business here?" the shorter one asked.

"She's that gal's mother who was asking question about my cousin Sydney. When she gets the news her mother is here, she would come and fall right into my cousin's hands," Banjo said. "You keep guard over her."

"Banjo, you bringing the mother here, do you think her daughter would be so stupid to walk in here?" the guard asked.

"Shut your black arse mouth. Just because you think you're smart, you think you can push me around, well, you can't, you are only a watchdog and me a cousin. Pussyclart boy, I'm family."

The guard escorted Mrs Forbes about thirty feet away and handed her over to another black guard who was standing in front of a heavy wooden door. As Mrs Forbes and the guard were walking towards a second door, she noticed a black guard was standing on a ledge overlooking the Sydney Black ten-bedroom mansion and another two guards were guarding the doorway, one black, one white. The guards were all big built and looked no more than twenty-five to thirty years old. The shortest of them was about five foot six and the tallest was over six foot, and all had striking features like models.

The guard took Mrs Forbes to Sydney Black's door and handed her over to Banjo as he was standing at the door. "Don't put your filthy hands on me!" she said to Banjo.

"Woman, you will always have me in you," Banjo said and ordered Aaron to take her into the mansion to meet his cousin Sydney Black.

As Aaron escorted Mrs Forbes into the mansion, her eyes were wide open as she saw the beauty of the hall. As she walked beside Aaron and entered into the spacious hall, her eyes lifted to the high ceiling to look at the exquisite four layers of multi-coloured pear-shaped crystal chandeliers. Then as they walked on, she lowered her eyes to look at the black carved dark mahogany wrapped African figurehead that sat on mahogany shelves on the wall. Aaron was looking at Mrs Forbes and smiling. Then walking on, they came to the centre of the wide corridor floor where there was a massive painted African man and woman in the nude kissing and sealed under about two square metres of unbreakable glass tiles. Further on, set in the same fashion, there was a beautifully painted Egyptian queen, which complemented the five feet long dark mahogany built-in glass wall unit that contained large expensive handmade crystal and gold rimmed vases from India, China and Africa. Mrs Forbes looked at everything with hate. As she and Aaron walked on, Aaron said, "Don't worry about what you've seen, they're just material and they are worth nothing as they were bought with drugs money."

"Why did you say that? Do you hate Sydney Black so much and yet you're working for him?"

"Yes, I do hate what they're doing Mrs Forbes, I just want to do my job."

"And what is your job Aaron, abducting youths and bringing them here to be forced into prostitution and onto the streets selling drugs?"

"Mrs Forbes, I'm not the person you think I am. But the time will come when you will thank me," Aaron said.

"So why were you with those two dirty lice? Aaron, they raped me." Tears welled up in Mrs Forbes' eyes.

"Mrs Forbes, they both had guns and knives that they were ready to use on me. I tried my best to protect you, but they knocked me unconscious. Do you think I like what they have done to you? No Mrs Forbes. I don't! But they were too much for me to handle. I promise you they both will pay for what they did to you and me."

Aaron walked her into a massive room and was almost coming to a halt when Mrs Forbes stepped onto a huge white furry cashmere rug. She noticed the four beautiful gold-plated side tables with large black gold double rings around their rims, and looked at Aaron and smiled. Aaron smiled back. Then as he walked her into a beautifully furnished pale blue room she stared intently and turned her head admiring everything in the room. She turned and faced Aaron, saying, "Much as I hate to be here, the brute has very expensive taste. Everything in this mansion is beautiful. It must have cost him millions. Just look at the length of the bar, with dozens of hanging crystal glasses and liquors. The ten-seater cream leather settees, how it is set out in the room with the plain white and gold-laced curtains in an exquisite design hanging from the ceiling to the floor to meet the cream and pale blue handmade tiles and rugs; this room itself is breathtaking. But the way he achieved it all is appalling and as you said, they're worth nothing."

"Yes Mrs Forbes, you just think of it that way and you'll get out of here soon."

"Aaron, I want to trust you. Anyway, if you're such good person, what are you doing here?"

Aaron smiled but didn't answer Mrs Forbes, as Sydney Black had walked into the room. He said to Aaron, "Hey you, I want you on watch early morning."

"Yes Boss," Aaron answered Sydney Black with his top lip screwed up.

"Why are you bleeding?" Sydney asked.

"I had an accident. Nothing to worry about."

Sydney Black left, and Aaron said to Mrs Forbes, "You try and show the ladies you're happy here, so that they will take less notice of you. I will find a way to help you to get away from here."

"I now realise you're not one of them," Mrs Forbes said.

"Well, I don't want you to broadcast what I told you," Aaron said.

Mrs Forbes smiled and stood in the middle of the room. Sydney Black entered the room and took his seat behind his piano and said to Aaron, "You're finished here."

Aaron left the room. Sydney Black twirled round in his white and leather gold-trimmed reclining chair and faced Mrs Forbes in his cream and white three-piece Armani suit. He looked Mrs Forbes up and down, then hissed through the gap in his front teeth. He then called Mark on his phone, but Banjo came running instead.

"I called for my brother," Sydney said.

"I know that boss, but your brother went to the toilet so I came instead," Banjo said.

"Tell me this, who is she?" Sydney asked in his mixed Trinidadian and Jamaican accent, but sounding more like a Rasta as he mixed so much with them.

"She's the mother of that bitch Petra. The same police gal that was asking questions about you," Banjo said.

"Banjo, who's the bitch Petra? I don't know her, so what does she want with me? Still, me like fee meet dis bitch," Sydney said. He then looked at Mrs Forbes and paused before he said, "You look sweet, and me thinks your daughter is worth me paying her a visit." He smiled then looked Mrs Forbes in her eyes again and said, "I would really like fee meet you daughter Petra. Even though I never met her, but I hear so much about her."

Mrs Forbes looked at Sydney with hate.

"Let me remind you, no one talks about me man, and me don't take action. Now that you are here in my den, your pretty daughter is sure to come looking for you."

"You leave my daughter alone. You touch her and I'll …"

"What will you do Mrs Forbes?"

"You rotten bastard, you touch my daughter and you'll know."

"Mrs Forbes, all I want is to take your daughter to bed and if she is to my taste, I will make her one of my call gals."

Mrs Forbes stared at him and said, "You dirty bastard! You touch my daughter and I'll kill you!"

Sydney burst out laughing. "So you'll kill me twice." He laughed happily again before his face turned seriously angry. Then he pounded on his piano, making Mrs Forbes jump then said, "Oh man, if this chick chats about me, so why must I not see her? After all, she has taken a shine to me."

Aaron walked into the room as the door was open and saw tears in Mrs Forbes' eyes. "What the hell do you want with this woman? Do you know Banjo and Mark raped her and then brought her here?"

"So tell me this Aaron, didn't you stop them? And tell me, is she too old for you?"

"You son of a bitch, I don't care if you shoot me dead right now. But the time will come when you and your kind will crumble. Why are you holding Mrs Forbes like she is a prisoner?"

"And what is she to you? You tink say me is one of dem fosse hole buoy you does run street wit? I want you shut your Pussyclart mouth when I big man a talk," Sydney said in his Patois accent, he then sarcastically tried to say in an English accent, "You gets me mate."

"Yes boss," Aaron replied quickly looking at Mrs Forbes with remorse.

"Now buoy me finish with you so you can go now." Aaron left leaving Banjo and Sydney facing Mrs Forbes.

"I heard this Petra is a tiger," Banjo said to Sydney. "Boss, maybe if we send a video or photo of the mother, the daughter might keep silent and leave us alone."

"I agree with Banjo," Mark was on time to say. "If we do just that, her daughter might back down like a lamb and leave us alone."

Suddenly Sydney's cousin Blakey entered the room without knocking and he raised his voice saying, "Watt de razz you a do in yah! And how many time I Mum must tell you bumberclart people you don't frigid in enter wit out me say cum in. So blood or no blood, you no start dem fuckries wit I Mum. Yaw must knock de bloodclart door before you enter, me warn you many times but you too hard a hearing. Now tek yaw bumberclart off fee me rug buoy." He then pulled out a gun from underneath his expensive cream suite and shot Blakey in his right arm. "De next time you enter dis room me a go kill you buoy, I hope dat shot will remind you no fee tests I man, even doe we have de same blood. Dat don't make us size. You enter by permission only!"

Blakey winced and put his hand over the shot wound.

"Now tek you razz out a yah, and stop out." Sydney told him.

Blakey sheepishly hopped away and went to the first aid room. He knocked on the hired doctor's door for attention. The doctor went to him immediately.

"What's the matter now Blakey?"

Blakey replied, "Dat crazy razz Sydney just put a bullet through me hand." The doctor looked at him and then said, "You mean your arm?"

"Don't it mean da same thing," Blakey said. "Hand or arm, what's the difference?"

Blakey was in a nasty mood. "I man does kill man fe joke. Him know dat I will shoot up him bumbaclart if him touch me again. I swear dat if the mudder fucker touch me again I will kill him."

"Blakey, he didn't touch you, he shot you," the doctor sarcastically said as she led him into her clinic. She helped him to take off his shirt before asking him to take a seat on the chair and then examined his shot wound and told him that she had to take the bullet out. He nodded as if to say yes, then turned his face away.

"Blakey, you'll have to have a jab to numb the wound so I can get the bullet out," the doctor said.

"Do what you have to do, woman," Blakey demanded.

"Okay," said the doctor. She then injected Blakey, putting him to sleep, then took the bullet out and bandaged his wound. When Blakey woke up and saw his bandaged arm, he thanked the doctor then left groaning. The doctor cleaned up her tools and put them away. She then put Blakey's bloodied shirt into a black bag and sent it to him with her assistant nurse. Aaron also had to have stitches in his leg.

Meanwhile, Sydney was looking at Mrs Forbes with a grin.

"Yaw sees how I man treat people who don't hear. Yaw see Mrs Lady Forbes, who can't hear must feel. But me does treat my workers dem good. Yaw husband use to wok fe me you did know dat? He was one a de best. He did bring muff young Pinckney come fe me including young buoy and he did even bring Madame Stall's daughter come fe me but me did not know she was Madame Stall granddaughter until me hear it on the news. Madame Stall's granddaughter was pretty she favour flower. If only she did do what I said, she would a here today. She was hard a hearing. So I had her cool dong by one my buoy. Yah know say your husband did lie dong wid your gel Petra?"

"Damn you! Damn you! My husband would never bed my daughter and I don't believe that he had anything to do with what you're accusing him of. My husband would never even look at you or dirty his hands on you unless he had to lock you up," Mrs Forbes said almost in tears.

"Mrs Forbes. Yah ever hear fisherman say den fish stink. You husband told me he was the first to score you gel. He also said he never love you?"

"You dirty bastard!" Mrs Forbes said interrupting Sydney while he was talking.

Sydney sucked his teeth, then grinned to show his gapped teeth before hitting Mrs Forbes in the face with the back of his hand saying, "Is a shame your husband dead, cur me would meck him tell you how him get him cash fe pay fe dat house you live in. Lady Forbes I pay fe dat house you live in! Drugs and whore money pay for dat! I did give him two hundred and seventy thousand pound as I think he did deserve it. My money he use Mrs Forbes! But a no me who did kill him, he did know him place wid me and he did know not to fuck wid I."

"Please let me go. I will never tell anyone about you," Mrs Forbes said.

"You knar go nowhere. You will be I man hostage until your data Petra woks fey me. Den I will see de flex from deer," Sydney said smiling.

A couple of minutes afterwards, Sydney walked away from his seat. He stood in front of Mrs Forbes and put his hand on her shoulder. As he was about to speak to her, Aaron entered into the room.

"You muss knock Buoy, even if my door is open," Sydney said angrily.

"I always enter this room without knocking," Aaron replied.

"Look pussy hole, me a go tell all you fey de last time u must knock my door den wait for me to tell you come in. Now tell I man what you want den tek you mudder skunt out a yaw."

"I came to ask the lady if she wanted something to eat or drink," Aaron said.

"If and when I decide she can eat I will call for someone to take her to eat. Now if you don't want to end up like Blakey, find an exit and hold it. Now you have been excused."

Aaron looked at Mrs Forbes like he was feeling sorry for her, then walked out of the room. Then Mark came charging into the room again without knocking. Sydney looked hard at him, then shot him in his left leg without saying one word.

"Why?" Mark asked.

He looked Mark straight in his eyes and said, "The next time you enter this room without me inviting you in, an undertaker will tek you out. Even though you're my brother I would not hesitate to kill you."

"For the love of Christ, do you have to shoot all your men?"

"Yes, if I have to. Anyway, wouldn't you want to see him dead after he raped you?"

Mrs Forbes gently took her seat and remained quiet. Sydney then took his seat facing her with a devious smirk on his face. After he looked at her for a few minutes, he went to sit in a single chair behind his highly-polished dark mahogany and gold trimmed desk with his left palm under his deeply dimpled chin. As Mrs Forbes' eyes clashed with his, he winked his left eye at her. Then in a teasing manner he began rubbing his right palm over the fly of his trousers and moving himself up in a slow motion, until his face was covered with sweat. He then went over to Mrs Forbes and felt her legs. She knocked his hand off and spat in his face. He smiled, took one of his white handkerchiefs and wiped the spit off his face, then slapped her face very hard, busting her lower lip. She covered it with her hands and began crying.

Sydney was thirty-five years old, heavily built and had a rough voice. He was five foot eleven inches tall and always very well dressed in a cream three-piece suit, with a heavy gold chain with a diamond scorpion pendant. He wore soft brown leather shoes, an expensive looking gold watch, diamond cufflinks surrounded with gold, and two thick gold and diamond rings on each of his third fingers. Sydney was also known to wear no other socks but silk. He also had a cheeky smile and had at least fifteen men working for him.

Later that evening Mrs Forbes was taken to the women's quarters, where she was so shocked to see at least fourteen black and white beautiful young girls working for him. Five of the girls told Mrs Forbes they had been kidnapped from their homes or off the streets and forced into prostitution. So where did that leave them but to making their living in prostitution?

"Mrs Forbes, I went to a policeman telling him that I had been abducted from my gate and taken to Sydney Black's residence, but he told me not to make any more complaints about Sydney Black. I was sixteen then."

Two hours after Mrs Forbes was escorted out of the mansion and taken to the women's residence she saw four beautiful youths standing in conversation; they looked no more than twenty years old. The darkest of them was looking very scared and shameful when she saw Mrs Forbes looking at her.

Mrs Forbes smiled and the four youths walked away, but Mrs Forbes had noticed the youth's white speckled face was in tears. As Mrs Forbes walked further up to the main arched door there were two other beautiful white teenage girls and further on three other young black girls that looked very attractive in their short skirts and cropped blouses, all getting into different cars. When they saw Mrs Forbes walking towards them, they giggled then looked at her scornfully. "Old lady what are you doing here?" A young, beautiful kid asked from her car window.

Actually, I was brought here by force like most of you were," Mrs Forbes said. "I was kidnapped."

"Shut your mouth," five foot eight broad-shouldered Ken said, as he pushed Mrs Forbes forward. "Shut up and move on." He walked her to a door labelled 'Women's Interview Room' where he met his mate Wilkins. "I'll take over from here," Wilkins said.

"Will you sign here to say that I delivered one old undamaged goods before you escort her to the WHQ?" Ken laughed. Wilkins looked at him strangely.

"I got you, you should see your face." Ken laughed again.

"Man, don't fuck." Wilkins burst out laughing, "Why can't you take her?" Wilkins said.

"I would if I had time, but there's somewhere I should be right now," Ken said.

"Okay," Wilkins said and gave Mrs Forbes a nice smile before he said, "Okay Mrs Forbes, I'm your guardian angel for now. It would be my pleasure to escort you to where you should be."

"Tell me," said Wilkins, "Why are you working for that louse Sydney Black?"

Wilkins smiled again, then escorted Mrs Forbes to the women's quarters and rang the doorbell for attention. A young woman answered the door. She looked at Mrs Forbes then smiled before she asked, "Are you the cleaner?"

"Just let us in," Wilkins said.

The young woman backed away from the door to let Wilkins and Mrs Forbes in. Again Mrs Forbes' eyes widened to see the beautifully furnished big room where Wilkins handed her over to a beautiful dark-skinned young woman and said, "I was told to bring this lady here."

"Thank you, I'll take over from here," the woman told Wilkins. Wilkins looked at her, smiling. The woman introduced herself to Mrs Forbes as Clara Bee. Mrs Forbes said nothing but looked her in the face, shaking her head.

"So you're the famous Mrs Forbes I have heard so much about. Well, please take a seat."

Mrs Forbes refused.

Clara Bee pushed her by her shoulders onto the chair. "Mrs Forbes, I'm not your enemy.

"How do I know that?"

"Mrs Forbes, all I'm asking from you is to work on the streets selling some drugs. That's all," said Clara.

"Never," replied Mrs Forbes with staring eyes.

Clara Bee turned looking at Wilkins then asked him, "Will you please leave us for a minute?"

Wilkins looked hard at Clara Bee before he walked outside and waited.

"Mrs Forbes, I'm only trying to help you. I haven't met your daughter yet, but from what I have heard about her, I'm sure she and I will become good friends. Look Mrs Forbes, sending you to work on the streets, doesn't it occur to you that I'm helping you to escape?"

"How do I know I can trust you?" Mrs Forbes asked.

"You don't. But you do as I ask and you'll be okay. Besides, I would like to get to know your daughter."

Just then, Wilkins pulled a half-smoked cigarette out of his mouth, tossed it on the ground, then pushed the door open and walked in, looking hard in Clara Bee.

"I asked you to wait outside," she said.

"I waited long enough," Wilkins said, looking at her in amazement. And just as he was about to speak again, Clara said, "I demand you to leave the room and don't come in again until I ask you in."

Wilkins refused to leave. "Would you like me to call Sydney Black?" she asked. He looked furiously at her, then left the room and stood outside the door waiting, smoking a cigarette.

Clara Bee closed the door and went back to Mrs Forbes smiling.

"Listen carefully Mrs Forbes, I'm a policewoman. Believe me. I want to wipe out the whole community of Sydney Blacks and his troupe." Mrs Forbes smiled, but her smile was showing doubt.

Wilkins became frustrated and entered the room again. "Sorry I had to enter but I think it's time I knew what you're going to do about the woman."

"Yes Wilkins, I think you're right. I was convincing Mrs Forbes what I want her to do, but she's a little stubborn. However, I was just about coming to ask you in," Clara said. Wilkins smiled. "Now Mrs Forbes, I need your answer now. Or would you rather I give you over to my friend Mr Wilkins?" She eyed Mrs Forbes in a friendly manner as Wilkins was admiring the spacious beautiful room with such an aggressive look on his face.

"Okay, I'll do what you ask. Just tell me what you want me to do," Mrs Forbes said sadly. She had caught on to what Clara was up to.

"I've already told you. All we want of you is to sell drugs, as no one would suspect you. Your payment will be fifteen per cent of the amount you sell and you will start tomorrow. You will be provided with a bodyguard until people get used to you. If and when we are satisfied with you and we trust you, you will earn the privilege of being allowed to go home daily after work."

Mrs Forbes nodded her head. Clara Bee smiled then said to Wilkins, "You may take Mrs Forbes to room 14 for the night. I would like you to treat her with respect. Please see that she gets whatever she needs. Tomorrow I'll decide what room to give her."

Wilkins smiled. "Yes, Miss Bee." Then as he was leaving with Mrs Forbes, Clara said, "Mrs Forbes, I expect no trouble from you."

Mrs Forbes walked with Wilson to her room. After he saw her settled in, he left then went to his boss Sydney Black and reported to him that Mrs Forbes was okay and settled in her room.

Ten minutes later there was a knock on Mrs Forbes' door. "Who is it?" Mrs Forbes asked.

"Clara Bee."

"What do you want?" Mrs Forbes asked in a dreary voice.

"I would just like to speak to you. Please open the door."

"I want to be left alone. Why don't you go and speak to your boss and tell him what he's doing to the youths is wrong," Mrs Forbes said.

"Mrs Forbes, I want to help you."

"Why don't you help those young kids to escape from this wretched place and leave me alone?"

"Look Anne, I knew your husband but I'm still puzzled about what made him work for Sydney Black. Mrs Forbes, your husband wasn't what you think he was. I learnt a lot about him that I would like to tell you, so would you please open the door."

Mrs Forbes took her time to get up from off her bed to open the door.

"You sure took your time to open the door. Look, whatever you may think of me, I'm your friend. Do you mind if I call you Anne?"

"Of course not, Anne is my name," Mrs Forbes said harshly.

Clara smiled. "Anyway Anne, I don't want you to speak to anyone, especially any of the girls, about me or your daughter Petra. I also want you to be extremely careful about what you say to any of the girls if you get the chance to speak to them. The reason is, some of the older girls are prostitutes by trade but some are here by force. So at this moment, I don't want anyone here to find out who I am, at least not yet. Mrs Forbes, I'm a policewoman. I would like to know that I can trust you as I can trust a friend here. You and that friend are the only two know who I am, that friend will not tell; I could trust him with my life. I would like to think the same of you. So Mrs Anne Forbes, if you fuck us up by telling anyone that I am a policewoman, we will both be killed. Anne, your husband was really working for that bastard Sydney Black. I wanted to see that bastard husband of yours locked up behind bars more than anyone else for what he'd done, but he's dead and I can't say I'm sorry because I'm not. I was told your husband watched Sydney Black's brother murder my cousin Stella after she refused to have oral sex with a lesbian. Mrs Forbes, your husband was a bastard! I can't do anything to him but I have waited for this chance to get even with Sydney Black and his kind. I am here of my own free will on the pretence of working as a beauty consultant."

"Can I ask you, how did you know my husband was working for Sydney Black?"

"Anne, I know a lot about what goes on here and which police officers were and are now working for those bastard Black brothers. I want to be the one to nail those bastards in their coffins. I'm sorry I have to speak so disrespectfully about your husband, but what I told you is true. Mrs Forbes, I feel no pity for your husband. If I had had the chance to kill him, I'm sure I would have. Some youths were fifteen years old and my cousin was just a little more than a baby at fourteen and in school. Youths were afraid to be on the street after school as many were kidnapped and taken here. I was told the screaming of the youths was horrifying when the bastards ripped into them. However, three days after my cousin was held captive here a friend helped her to get away. That night she left a letter telling her mother what had happened. Then that same night while catching a train to go and live with other relatives, she was murdered. Shot in the head by one of Sydney's associates. You know what hurts me most, I heard that she asked your husband for help hiding in his car and he threw her out. This is when my friend found out he was one of the police officers that worked for Sydney. Anne, three men raped her that night. Also a girl called Monica was stripped naked and raped by those bastard Black brothers and cousin and then they spread her feet apart and set one of their dogs on her. The poor child pulled one of the men's guns from their holster and shot herself in her head. I found out she was Madame Stall's fourteen-year-old granddaughter." Clara Bee then broke down crying.

"Oh Clara, I'm so sorry," Mrs Forbes said sympathetically, then tears welled up in her eyes.

"By the way Anne, tomorrow evening I will try and help you to escape. If you should get away, please be very careful not to go to the police as I've told you some police are working for the bastard Sydney Black and his brothers. At this moment, the only two people I can trust are Aaron and Hans. I will send your supper with Hans later. Although he can be trusted, please be careful what you say to him. You will know him because he has one hand as he lost his other one to his boss Sydney Black brother's Mark who ordered one of his men to chop it off, after he found out Hans was trying to help a fifteen-year-old girl to escape. Hans also told me that Sydney Black has a half-brother called Johnny Blimps, carrying out the same work at the Crescent House. These two bastard brothers are evil and should be put down like aggressive dogs. Well, I'll see you later. And remember, if you get out of here, please do not mention my name to anyone. Sydney Black has many friends on the side of the law who come here for regular sex. Even the late Judge O'Neil used to come here for his regular pleasure, mostly with young men. Hans told me and it took me a while to believe. So, you see Anne, even powerful judges worked for Sydney Black. All these bastards take advantage by having sex with the youths that are kidnapped and brought here. When I heard your husband and Judge O'Neil were murdered, it filled my heart."

"Clara, this has hurt me too, what you have told me about the youths. I think I'm sensible enough to treat what you have said seriously. So please don't worry, you can trust me. Now go," Mrs Forbes said.

Clara Bee looked at Mrs Forbes and then smiled before she left.

Mrs Forbes was on her way to the kitchen when she bumped into three beautiful mixed-race girls, Tanya, Shi-Ann, and Precious. Shi-Ann and Precious stood and watched her hard, but Mrs Forbes recognised Tanya, who turned her face away with her eyes fixed to the floor.

"Tanya, that's you?" Mrs Forbes asked.

"No, I'm not who you think," Tanya said.

"Mrs Forbes smiled then went and stood facing Tanya saying, "I understand if you don't want me to know about you. But I could never forget your beautiful face and hairstyle like you have it now."

"Lady, I don't know who you are and I don't see any harm wearing my hair short above the nape of my neck."

"Tanya, I could never forget your beautiful looks and I know some of you are not here by your own will."

Tanya turned her face away. Mrs Forbes walked on. Shi-Ann and Precious burst out laughing, but Tanya covered her lips with the palm of her hand trying to choke back her crying.

"Tanya, what's the matter with you? When the old lady speaks to you, you seem to want to lie down and roll in your vomit," Precious said.

"Shut your fucking mouth! That old woman is my godmother and her daughter is my friend. I have to escape from this place."

"And where would you go?"

"Anywhere but here. I lied to my parents that I'm working in a children's home. Shi-Ann, my life is fucked now that Mrs Forbes has seen me here," Tanya said tearfully.

"Tanya, I'm sure the old bitch is not too sure she knows you. She hardly paid any attention to any of us," Precious said.

"I'm absolutely sure she knows me. I wonder why she's here."

"Tanya, we're pros. We're paid good money and get the best medical attendance. Even if she saw you, what can she do?"

"Her daughter is my friend. I came here because my stepfather wanted to have sex with me when my mother was confined to her bed with sickle-cell," Tanya said.

"So what if you sleep with him. At least he's not your blood relative. I slept with my stepfather countless number of times for money to buy a fix," Precious said.

"You're a fucking dirty slag. Have you no feelings or shame for your mother?" Shi-Ann asked.

"Shi-Ann, she had none for me either. I watched her in bed with my boyfriend after she'd fix off him. And when I lashed out at her, she told me my boyfriend said she fucked better than me," Precious laughed.

"So, you fucked my boyfriend and I fucked your husband, that's how it should be hey? Precious, you're talking about your mother's partner, that's as good as your father. You know what my friend, I don't think I want to be in your company anymore," Tanya said.

"Well fuck you too Tanya," Precious said.

"Hey, you two cool it mates. It took an old woman to rip us apart," Shi-Ann said and hugged Tanya and Precious saying, "Come on friends, we've been friends for seven weeks. I don't like it here either, but we're better off here than on the streets, we play by the rules and we'll be okay. Since I came here I have saved seven thousand pounds. Where else would we be paid one thousand a week, plus tips, clothes, food and board? Not to mention first-class check-ups. We're call girls and even if we change our jobs, call girls will be our first name. So let's stick together."

"I know what you're saying Shi-Ann, but I still have to get away from here and soon as that Mrs Forbes saw me."

"Well Tanya, if you really have to go, I wouldn't blame you. But it won't be easy for you to get away from here. Look, you could have what money I have to set up a place outside Birmingham."

"Thanks, but I'll be okay Shi-Ann."

"Well good luck Tanya. And I meant what I said about the money," Shi-Ann said.

"You can have what I have too Tanya, and I'm sorry to get under your skin," Precious said. "Now girls, let's go and have supper."

Mrs Forbes knocked on the 'Information' door and a middle-aged woman opened it. "Come in Mrs Forbes. I was waiting for you. I'm Winey." Mrs Forbes walked into the room. "Please take a seat."

Mrs Forbes smiled then sat down.

"Mrs Forbes, I have been told there's a change of plan. You will be looking after the girls instead of working outside. From this room you will book each girl's name as they go out and come in; the girls will be you're responsibility. Tomorrow I will teach you how to set and turn off the alarm as well as showing you the girls' room. All you have to do is to see no man enters any of their rooms except by invitation cards. Each customer has to pay you five hundred pounds to one thousand before seeing the girls or young men and you should make sure our girls and men wear protectives to avoid disease. I'll teach you how to spot the super-rich so you can charge them up to a grand. Any trouble from any one of them, ring this bell here under your desk. "

Mrs Forbes nodded her head. Winey smiled. Hans knocked on the door. "Come in," Winey said.

Hans entered the room. "I'm here to take Mrs Forbes back to her room."

Mrs Forbes left with Hans. "What were you doing in that room?" Hans asked her.

"I was told to be here," she replied.

"Hans, where can I find a toilet?"

"There is a toilet next door to your room, and please, don't lie to me. I would like you to trust me as I will you. I'm going to get you some supper now," said Hans. He left after seeing Mrs Forbes to her room. Shortly he returned with her supper saying, "It's roast beef." He smiled then took the cover off the food. "It smells good too," he said.

"Hans, why couldn't I eat with the others?"

"You're not one of them," Hans said.

Mrs Forbes smiled and began eating, but as her eyes caught Hans' amputated arm she said, "Oh Hans I'm sorry you lost your arm."

Hans wiped sweat off his eyebrows. "Sydney Black has at least thirty young girls and at least fifteen young men working for him. Most of these young girls and boys were brought here by crooked police officers, especially when they had been caught shoplifting."

"So all of them are shoplifters?"

"No Mrs Forbes, some were already on the game. Only the attractive ones were brought here. As far as I remember, nearly all these youths were virgins. Most of the men who come here for sex are very wealthy. Even studs would be sent out to rich women to have sex with them as well as homosexuals. Most of these wealthy folks would fork out from five hundred a time upwards. I saw one of the girls suck a man until he ejaculated in her mouth and made her swallow. I thought that was gross but I couldn't interfere. He then gave her two grand and paid five thousand to Sydney Black. When I asked the man why he made the girl swallow his semen, he said he paid for what he wanted. I felt disgusted for the rest of the day.

"Within one year, Sydney and his brothers made millions pushing drugs and selling women and young men. Anyway, one day he asked this girl called Miranda on the streets to sell drugs. When she refused his brother Mark and cousin Banjo raped her before beating her badly, then they knifed her to death. They told the police that they picked her up off the street with stab wounds but she was dead before they could get her to a hospital. I cried, as I couldn't do one thing to help the girl or tell the truth about what had happened. I want to see all those bastards get what's coming to them and then sent to hell. Sydney Black would have the girls beaten if they showed their clients they didn't like them. They had to do what he wanted and then they might get a smile out of him and his evil family. He bought the crooked police he has working for him nice homes. If you get out of here, please be very careful not to speak to any police."

"Hans, thank for the warning. A friend has told me the same, to be very careful," Mrs Forbes said.

Hans smiled.

"Hans, why have you told me this?" Mrs Forbes asked.

"I have three teenage sisters and two cousins and I'm so afraid for them," Hans said as tears built up in his eyes.

"Why do you work for this man?"

"I was only a messenger and he was not like he is now. Mrs Forbes, I have tried to get away from this place. But his brothers Redd and Mark threatened me that if I leave they will kill my whole family, then me. Mark also told me he would give both my sisters to his dogs and make me watch before he killed them and I know he would. He had my hand chopped off even though I pleaded with him to be merciful," Hans said.

"I know he gave you a choice to have your penis or your hand and you've done right to give your hand. I'm so sorry Hans, but do you believe he would kill your family and get away with it?"

"Yes Mrs Forbes, I saw and know what those Black brothers and family have done and got away with. They are ruthless people; they are not to be played with. They're worse than the devil. They chopped my hand off and I know they wouldn't hesitate to kill my family if I escape."

After Mrs Forbes had eaten, Hans took the plate and was ready to leave when Mrs Forbes said to him, "I believe you Hans. You're a good lad and I'm very sorry about what you have been through. Go before someone comes looking for you and sees us getting too friendly."

Hans smiled and left, but he returned when it was very dark and raining heavily. He was very careful not to be seen and instead of knocking, he opened her door with a nail file. "Hans is that you?" "Yes, it's me," Hans whispered. "I have come to help you get away from here."

"Just give me a minute," Mrs Forbes said.

"Hurry, we haven't time to lose. Now is your best chance as it's dark and raining and everyone is indoors."

"Okay Hans I'm ready and thanks, I will never forget you," said Mrs Forbes, but before they left Hans turned on the bedroom lights saying, "No one will bother you if they see your lights on." Mrs Forbes hugged Hans. "No time for that either, every second is precious to you. Look even if a nail should pierce your foot, I want you to be brave and keep quiet."

"I understand you perfectly Hans," Mrs Forbes said walking behind Hans through rubble, bushes piled up, worn car tyres and rubbish. "We're well away from the building. Are you okay? Sorry I had to bring you this way but I had no choice. Do you think you will be okay walking from here? It's about ten minutes from here to call a taxi as I haven't got my phone with me. Here is some money."

"Hans..."

"It's okay Mrs Forbes, you'll need this money. Take it and hurry away before the rain stops." Mrs Forbes took the money and thanked Hans. "Remember not to go to the police or to your home tonight."

She hugged Hans. "Thanks."

"You be careful."

"Thanks Hans, I will." Hans watched her hurrying down the long bushy stony pathway before he ran all the way back to his room, showered, and climbed into bed. Mrs Forbes took Hans' advice and booked a room in a hotel and phoned Petra.

But Petra had already left to visit her Grandma and afterwards she went and had dinner with Dr Sean. "Well Sean, thanks for a nice evening and dinner," she said. As he was going to kiss her, she dived in her bag for her ringing phone. He smiled. "Thank you but I have to rush," she said.

Then on her way home, she stopped at Lambert's liquor shop and bought a bottle of brandy. She left the liquor shop and got into her car. As she turned the key in the ignition, Mark fired a bullet that hit the side of her car. She ducked her head and drove away, picking up speed before turning onto Pilgrim Road. Following, Mark made such a sharp U-turn that his car screeched and almost overturned but he was still following close behind. He fired another bullet at Petra as he drove closely behind her and then he rammed her car. She looked back but couldn't see who was driving. He rammed her again and then catapulted a stone with a note glued onto the back of her car window then drove past her at full speed.

"Shit!" Petra said then stopped at the side of the road and picked the stone up, took the note from it and read. 'Bitch, I'm going to fuck you upside down like I did your mama.' Petra grinned, then brushed most of the pieces of glass with her handbag off the seat and onto the floor. She looked back at her broken window. "Shit-shit-shit!" She read the other part of the note. 'And my brother wants to meet you, bitch!'

Petra smiled and drove onto Coleman Street, where she noticed the same car was following her. She turned off onto Richmond Street still being followed. She fixed her side mirror to see Mark grinning with Banjo sitting next to him smiling. She then turned onto Fern Avenue and waited in a cul-de-sac.

Mark drove into the cul-de-sac and stopped, hung his head out of his window and shouted out, "Hey bitch! We had your mama yesterday and she's a hot bitch!" He and Banjo laughed loudly. Petra smiled as she rested her head on the steering wheel. In desperation she clambered out of her car. "I'm going to rip you two and your kind to fucking pieces," she said.

"Not until we take you to my brother Sydney. But before we do, I want to know if you fuck better than your mama," Mark said.

"Man, what the hell are you two talking about?" Cliff got out of his car. Mark and Banjo got out. Mark faced Cliff saying, "Banjo and I had the bitch mama yesterday."

"Man, you two are fucking sick in the head."

"Shut your bumbaclart mouth Cliff!" Mark elbowed him in his mouth making him bleed.

"Mark, Banjo, I want to take no part in your world to want to rape anyone." Cliff turned to Petra. "You find your mother and learn the truth." He caught his dripping blood in his handkerchief.

"Look here, you look like a nice lad. You get back to your brother and tell him I said to come and get me himself," Petra said.

"Look bitch, I told you we fucked your mama yesterday so which part of that you don't understand? I repeat, my cousin Banjo here and I fucked your mama yesterday and she is a prisoner at my cousin's place until we decide to give her to our dogs."

Petra kneed Mark in his testicles and banged his head against her car and said, "You and that son of a bitch smashed my car window. I need you to fix it and fast."

"I didn't. Look, I didn't throw the stone at your car. I was woken by their loud talking," Cliff said.

"I don't care. You're as guilty as these stinking bastards." Petra roughed up Mark against her car and searched his pocket and she pulled out a see-through bag of drugs and a bag with full of ten, twenty and fifty pound notes. She took two hundred pounds from the money and threw the remainder to the ground saying, "This is to fix my car and I won't arrest you just yet as I would kill you with no questions asked. You and your ugly family follow me again I will kill both of you." She kicked Mark twice in his left side and one to his mouth busting his lips and then she turned and kicked Banjo, knocking him down. "I will ask my mother about what you told me and if you harmed her in any way, I will kill you both." Petra kicked Mark and Banjo in their balls again and watched them go down on their knees. "Tell your boss or brother I'll kill him." Petra smashed all their car windows with her gun butt, took their drugs, got into her car and drove away, leaving Cliff smiling.

"Mark, we are no match for that bitch. She kneed me in my balls and I'm in pain. If Sydney wants that bitch, he can get her himself," Banjo said.

Cliff laughed. "As I said Banjo, you and Mark are no match for the tiger Petra. That bitch got you two looking like plucked chickens!"

"Shut your pussy mouth man, you go and get the bitch next time," Mark said.

"Mark, there won't be a next time or any other time as the chick would kick you to death. She's something. Woo!" said Cliff. Mark boxed Cliff in the mouth. Cliff kicked him away from the car "Pussyclart!" he said. Then Banjo kicked Cliff to the ground. Cliff got up, brushed the dirt off his trousers and kicked the side of the car then said, "You use your foot on me again I'll fucking break it off." He then made a fist with his left hand to punch Banjo.

"Me razz, he seems to be left-handed," Mark said and laughed. "You go and bring the bitch to me," Mark said and they got in their car and threw the broken glass out. Cliff, let's go get the bitch," Mark said.

"You fuck off and if you want the bitch, you go and get her."

Mark punched Cliff in the face and they both began fighting so badly that they used knives on each other. Banjo joined in and cut Cliff on his right arm. Cliff pulled his gun on him and then cut Banjo on his leg. The three of them ended up having several cuts to their bodies but nothing life-threatening.

Cliff grinned. "Man, let's go. We'll tell the boss that we can't find the girl. She's a tiger. She's one bitch I wouldn't want to meet again. She's tough and smart." Cliff tightened the bandage on his arm to slow the bleeding.

Mark looked hard at Cliff and shook his head then tore his shirt to have a look at the wound on his belly.

"Come on mates, let's go," Cliff begged. Just then Ira drove up, stopped his car in front of them and got out. Banjo left his car staggering to him. I saw Petra and you two look like she gave you whooping." He left Banjo and he went to Mark and Cliff. He smiled. "I saw you boys were playing a bad game carving each other. Was it over the beautiful dove Petra?" Ira joked.

"The boss asked me to find you three and tell you he wants to see you," Ira told them."

"Look Ira, about the bitch, we don't want my brother to know we had her and let her go," Mark said.

"And how would he know? Would you tell him you had her cage but she flew away because you left the door open and let her go?" Ira said.

"Look Ira, get the fuck out of my face and go get the bitch," Mark insisted.

"You want her, you go and get her and I hope you have a good reason to let him know how his car windows got smashed up. I'm here only to let you know your boss brother wants you. I'm sick down to my arse seeing people like you harassing people; I have a young sister fifteen years old man. And what Petra's doing is only because she cares. You two had your way with her mother. Isn't that enough?" Ira looked mad.

Mark hissed through his teeth and drove on, looking for Petra. They met her sitting in her car outside her gate.

"Why are you following me?" she asked him.

"I came to take you to my boss and I want no trouble from you."

"Fuck! Haven't you two had enough? Now, you double pieces of shit, why don't you piss off back to your fucked-face boss and tell him I said to take his muzzle off his face and come to get me."

"Look Petra, let's take you to my boss," Cliff said.

"You ugly monkey-faced son of a bitches. I thought you were different. It's now four of you so you think your strength has bobbled," Petra laughed. "Your mother must have had you while climbing a tree and dropped you face down on your daddy's prick!"

Ira laughed loudly and looked deeply into Cliff's face. "That is true mate. You really are one ugly son of a bitch!" Ira again burst into laughter and as Cliff stood facing him said, "Man, take your ugly face out of mine."

Cliff's lips seemed to expand three times the size, as he was feeling ashamed and vexed. He punched Ira hard in his face, splitting his lips with the lion signet ring he was wearing. Ira rocked unbalanced and Cliff rushed into him and punched him cutting him on his chin. Blood spouted from him like a burst tap. As he was catching blood in his handkerchief, Cliff pushed him off balance and he fell. He got up quickly saying, "You son of a bitch."

Cliff punched him again and they fought. Cliff had a knife. Petra leaned against her car looking at them. Mark aimed to shoot Ira but Petra kicked the gun from his hand and landed a kick to his chest sending him flying to the ground. She then saw Ira staggering towards his car with blood seeping through his shirt from his tummy. She went to help him. She opened his car door and he got in the driver's seat. "You better get out of here. And Ira, get a different job."

"Petra, thanks." He drove off.

Petra turned to walk back, but Mark kicked her in her back, pitching her forward. She turned looking at Mark but he ran to his car and locked the doors. "Look prick face, I got no time playing with you." Mark and Banjo pushed Cliff out of the car and sped off.

Ira drove back to Petra. "You don't look good," she told him. "I'll radio in for help. By the way, why were you following me?"

"I wasn't. I came to give those jerks a message from their brother but I can't tell you anything else at the moment."

"However, you don't look so good and you are losing plenty of blood."

Ira grinned. Petra watched Cliff fall sideways and he was bleeding. "Shit," Petra said and went to get Cliff into her car to take him to hospital. But then Mark came back driving at full speed and nearly hitting Petra. He slowed down and pulled Cliff into his car and sped off down the road. "You two pussies, run like rats from one woman," Cliff teased them.

"No man, I can't let that bitch think she beat me," Mark said and he turned the car around, drove back to Petra and got out. "Hey bitch! I'm ready for you." He walked up to Petra holding a penknife.

Petra took a knife out of her right knee-length boot. Mark charged into her with his knife, giving her a small gash on her arm. Madly, she sliced him across his chest then kicked him flying onto his back. Before he could get up, she went for him again and yanked his head up holding her knife to his throat. "No. Don't do it lady!" Ira cried. Petra drew back the knife and jammed her boot on his hand. He let the knife drop. "The next time I see you, I'll waste your arse!"

He looked up at her, his eyes looked pitiful.

"You keep out of my way. I'm going to help your friends until an ambulance comes and if you interfere, I'll kill you!"

"Help me, please, my eye," Cliff begged as he stretched out his hand to Petra dragging himself on his belly towards her. She looked at him, then at Ira. "Damn!" she said. She hit the side of her car before leaning against it while waiting for the ambulance. Thoughtfully she looked on the three of them in turn, then went to Ira and felt his pulse. "You'll live," she told him. "As for those three arseholes I couldn't care if they live or die. You hang on. An ambulance will soon be here," she told Ira and walked away groaning in pain as she was wounded.

As the ambulance was taking a long time to get to them, she bandaged her wounded arm with a red bandolier, then said to Mark and Banjo, "You sons of bitches don't deserve my help, but I will as I will kill you two rotten asses as soon as I've talked to my mother."

After waiting for more than twenty minutes for the ambulance, which never arrived, she struggled to help them into Ira's car and told them, "I'll be back as quickly as I can." She then left them and went to her Godfather Slim Parker's garage, which was about five minutes' drive away. When Mr Parker saw her, he rushed to her. She got out her car. "You're bleeding," he said. Petra smiled. "It's not that bad. Can you please keep an eye on my car until I return and I would be happy if you'd fix my window?"

"With pleasure," Mr Parker replied. "I certainly will, my Petra."

Petra smiled and asked Mr Parker if one of his men could take her to where she left the wounded men."

"Sure," Mr Parker said then turned to Ricky. "I want you to take my goddaughter to where she wants."

"Yes boss." Ricky opened his car door and Petra got in, buckled up and he drove Petra to the wounded men. "What happened?" he asked looking at Petra and when he recognised Mark and Banjo he said, "I don't know why you bother. You should be concerned about yourself as you're bleeding."

"It's just a flesh wound. I'll be fine."

"Petra, you pick up your car in the next two hours," Ricky said helping Ira into his car, and then he drove back to the garage.

Before Petra got into Ira's car, she took one good look at the four of them then shook her head and got into the driver's seat with Ira sitting next to her. Even though she was in pain, she smiled to see Mark, Banjo and Cliff leaning on each other like limp plants. As she turned the key in the ignition, she had one last look at them, closed her eyes in a moment of thought and faced the steering wheel. She then noticed that Ira was losing a lot of blood and seemed to be slipping into unconsciousness. Cliff took his T-shirt off and tied it around his forehead, stopping blood dripping down his face. And as for Mark, he was looking like a rat struggling to get free out of a trap. His groaning sounded horrifying and his clothes were saturated with blood.

Banjo remained still with his eyes closed and his head on Cliff's shoulder. After Petra had one last look at them, she drove them to Accident and Emergency at the hospital and delivered them to doctors and nurses; she waited to hear how Ira was doing.

After they had been stitched up and were safely in their beds for the night Ira asked for Petra. Nurse Baker went to her. "You're bleeding. Would you mind me taking a look at your arm?" she asked.

Petra held her arm out to the nurse and she moved the tie. "I think you'll need a few stitches. Would you like to come with me?"

Petra walked with her to the dressing room and she cleaned the blood before stitching her arm. "You have seven stitches. They will dissolve when you have a bath, but please try not to get the spot wet for about ten days." Petra smiled and thanked Nurse Baker. As the nurse was walking Petra back, she told Petra that Ira had asked to see her. Petra went to Ira.

Then as Petra was standing by Ira's bed, Stanley walked up to her. They greeted each other, then she asked Ira to excuse her while she walked away with Stanley and chatted about old times.

"You know what Petra my friend, you could pass as a doctor. You look so beautiful in that white dress," Stanley complimented her.

"Thanks. I had an accident and I remembered that I had this dress in my car. How's Liz?"

"She's very well. She's expecting."

"Well Stanley, that's great. What would you like to have, a daughter or a son?"

"Pet my dear friend, it doesn't matter as long as the baby is alive and in good health."

Petra laughed, so did Stanley.

"Stanley, considering what you've been through, you really have done well for yourself."

"I could say the same for you my dear friend," Stanley said.

"Oh, I joined the police force. My brother is now in Canada studying. He told Mum he's not sure whether he wants to be a crime lawyer or a doctor."

"I'm glad to know both you and my good friend Arden are doing well. Anyway, what brings you here?" he asked.

"My arm. Three rats almost killed each other by fighting after chasing after me and hoping to take me to their boss."

"Are you talking about Sydney Black?" Stanley asked.

"Yes, that same one that has youths prostituting. I don't know why I helped these bleeders laying wounded in your hospital. Still, I suppose I had to so I can kill them when they get well again," Petra said and laughed softly.

Stanley smiled and said to Petra, "How would you like to have dinner with Elizabeth and me tomorrow evening?"

"Oh Stanley, I'd love to, but I have already promised to have dinner with a friend tomorrow at the same time. I'm sorry. But we have to get together again," Petra said.

"That's okay, there's always other nights. I meant another time. And yes, we five must get together again and more often."

"I would really like that," Petra said. "Oh by the way, the patient fourth from the left said that he would like something to ease his pain."

"I'll see to him at once. He took you for a nurse," Stanley said.

Petra touched Stanley on his shoulder and said, "Well my friend, goodbye for now." Stanley smiled and went to see to the patient while Petra went back to see Ira. She pulled up a chair by his bed and sat.

"Thanks for helping me. I guess I might have come off worse or been killed if you hadn't stepped in. However, I'm really glad to be alive. Thanks to you. I owe you one," Ira said.

"You owe me nothing. The next time you cross my path I'll kill you without hesitation," said Petra as she got up.

"Please sit down. I only wanted to help you. Hans is a good friend of mine and he told me all about Sydney Black and his kind. He also helped your mother to escape from Black's place. Banjo and Mark raped your mother. If they had caught on that I know you, I would now be boxed up in a dead house. I'm a detective. My real name is Holt Ira Chambers, but I use Ira. I'm an enemy of the Black brothers, Sydney, Redd, Johnny and Mark. Banjo is a cousin. Sydney doesn't know I am a detective. My brother Aaron is working undercover as well. Those Blacks are very devious and dangerous men. They are the founders for drugs, prostitution, money launderers, murders and anything that links to nasty doings. I want to see the son-of-the-bitches behind bars for life. The Black brothers have crooked police working for them. I want you to be very careful, and the two that raped your mother are Banjo and Mark; those two rats you brought here. I understand my brother tried to stop them but was beaten up."

"Thanks for the information about my mother. I don't suppose you know where she escaped to?"

"No, I'm sorry," Ira replied.

"Well, I have to go and search for her," Petra said and got up.

"Will I see you again?" he asked.

"I don't think so," Petra replied and left. She phoned for a taxi from the hospital and gave Nurse Payne the car keys asking her to give them to Ira and to tell him that his car was parked in the hospital car park.

Chapter 10

At the garage, Petra spoke to Mr Parker. "Thank you for looking after my car and thanks for fixing it. How much do I owe you?"

"A drink, my goddaughter, when we meet on the dance floor on your wedding day."

Petra laughed. "Thanks again, godfather." She took her car and went to visit her grandma.

"Your mother promised me she would come and cook dinner."

"Mother is not very well. That is why I'm here to cook my favourite grandma the best supper you will ever taste," Petra said.

"Oh, will you dear?" She smiled.

"You just relax, granny." Petra went into the kitchen and cooked a tasty fish, vegetable and mashed potato supper. She had white wine while her Grandma had a glass of cold beer.

"Thanks for a well cooked and tasty meal my dear granddaughter. You should come and cook my meals more often, so I can have a proper meal. My body needs good food now as my time on earth is limited."

"Please grandma, spare me the heartache as you still have many years left in you."

"Pet, please don't make a fool of your old grandma."

"Gran, I have to go now, but I'll be back tomorrow. By the way, mother and I want you to move in with us."

"What did you say dear?"

"I said, mother and I would like you to move in with us. You have a serious think about that. Please make sure you lock and chain the door after I leave."

"You're really thinking about me."

"Shouldn't I gran?"

"Oh yes of course my dear Pet, I love you so much."

"I love you too. I must leave you as it's nearly time for you to go to bed, but I'll be back tomorrow."

"Okay," her grandma said sadly. Petra kissed her goodnight before she went home. She checked the answer machine for her mother's calls, but there were none. She sat in waiting by the telephone in case her mother called.

Two hours later, at ten past nine, the phone rang.

"Hello."

"Petra, it's me."

"Mother, where are you?"

"I'm calling from a hotel." Her mother burst out crying saying, "Pet, please get out of there fast and meet me at the hotel, I'm in room seventeen."

"Okay mother, which hotel?" Petra asked.

"The one we always eat in." Her mother was very cautious not to name the hotel.

"Ok mother, I'll be with you very soon. But I'm not running and hiding from those germs. I know what they've done to you and they'll pay."

"Just get yourself out of there quickly honey."

"Okay Mum." Petra put the phone down, had a shower, put on a pair of black trousers and a long-sleeved pale blue satin shirt, black two-and-a-half inch high-heeled shoes then drove to the hotel and parked. Hurriedly she got out of her car and walked into the hotel. Heads turned looking at her with widened eyes, so much so that a wife splashed wine in her husband's face when he looked at the beautiful Petra smiling.

"What the hell did you do that for?" her husband asked, wiping his face.

"Your eyes should be on me and not some chick that just walked into this hotel."

"Honey, my eyes are always on you, but let's face it, you can't ignore that chick. She's beautiful and a little above my class," he said with a quiet smile.

"Cheeky," said his wife and she and her husband laughed softly. Meanwhile, a middle-aged diner began to inhale the scent of Petra's perfume as she was walking amongst the diners looking for her mother. Many diners were inhaling the perfume odour. Petra smiled, but her eyes were searching for her mother.

As she noticed some diners were inhaling with their eyes fixed on her, she stood in the middle of the room looking at them in turn. One young diner left her seat and went to her and had such a good sniffing that her lips almost met Petra's. "I have no interest in women," Petra said. The woman moved her face and asked, "Where did you buy your perfume?"

"I mixed three types together," Petra told her.

"You're kidding me," the young white woman said.

"You do the same and you'll find that I'm right," Petra told her. The woman smiled and went back to her seat to be with her companions. Then a middle-aged white woman left her table, went to Petra and touched her on her shoulder. Petra faced her.

"I had to come over to say that I simply love the smell of your perfume. It has made the place so alive. I haven't smelt such a nice fragrance in a long time. What is it?"

"I brewed it myself," Petra joked.

"Please miss beautiful. You're too attractive to be wearing such perfume. You really don't need it to attract men," said the smiling woman.

Petra smiled, took the perfume out of her handbag and gave it to the woman.

"Thank you my beautiful one, my name is Gloria Small."

"Well, it's a pleasure to meet you Mrs Small. I do hope you enjoy wearing your perfume," Petra said.

"Thanks, I will," the woman said. Petra smiled then continued up the stairs and stopped at room seventeen whistling a tune. As her mother heard her whistling, she opened the door to let her in.

Her mother hugged her tightly. "Thank heavens you are all right."

"Mother, I'm so sorry those bastards hurt you."

"Never mind me Pet. I'm old enough to overcome what they did to me. It's you I'm most frightened and worried for. I love you and Arden so much. I lost my husband; I don't want anything bad happening to you or Arden."

"Mother your husband was a liar, a big crook and a rapist!"

"Don't say that honey. He was a good husband and your dad."

"Mother, your husband raped me three times," Petra said.

"You're a liar!" said her mother as she flung a hard slap on Petra's face.

Petra looked hard at her mother before she walked towards the door. With her back turned to her mother she said, "Mother, I don't expect you to believe me as he poisoned you against me and had you beat me badly before, but then I grew up. Please don't ever hit me again for telling the truth."

"Pet, I'm so sorry I hit you and before."

Petra was still facing the door when her mother got up off her bed and walked up behind her and attempted a few times to touch her, but each time she tried, her shaking hands dropped at her sides.

Petra turned facing her mother. "Mother, I love you very much, but I couldn't let your husband rape me again. Mother, he did rape me three times. First is when you and Arden went to Grandma and I cut my hair to avoid smelling his horrible scent he'd left on me."

Petra's mother hugged her crying. "Oh Petra love, I'm so sorry I didn't believe you."

"Well mother, I decided I wouldn't let him rape me again. I'd tried to tell you but you beat me away from you, then left the door wide open for him to have me as one of his whores. Mother, I was fifteen and a virgin and you helped him to take that away from me," Petra said, then closed her eyes as tears welled up. "Mother, I did what I had to do. If it was possible to kill that bastard again, I would do it in the worst way! Trust me mother, your husband wasn't a man but a creature from the pit of hell!"

"Oh God. Why didn't I catch on to what he was doing to you?"

"You're five years too late mother."

"Honey, if only you'd told me I would have killed him myself and saved you from dirtying your hands."

"Don't worry mother, now he's out of my life, I'll take good care of you," Petra said.

"I know you will honey. If the police find out that you killed the rat of my husband, I would take the blame. So don't say a word to anyone."

"Mother, I wouldn't want you to take any blame for me. He raped me, he hurt me and he is where he should be!"

Just then there was a knock on the door. "Who's that?" Mrs Forbes asked.

"The waiter, you ordered food." Petra opened the door with her gun ready to use. The young waiter rolled in a silver food trolley.

Petra looked at her mother, "I knew you would come so I ordered for both of us."

"Thanks," Petra said and tipped the waiter ten pounds. "Thank you," he said then left.

When Petra and her mother had eaten, Petra got up. "Mother, I'm going now and I don't want you to answer the door to any one or answer the phone. If you need me, call me immediately on my mobile. I will leave after the waiter collects the trolley. Please lock the door after I have gone."

Sometime later, the waiter collected the trolley. Ten minutes later Petra hugged her mother before she left. While walking to her car, she saw Ira walking towards her. "What now?" she asked him.

"I was just about to go for a meal when I saw your car parked."

"I thought you were badly hurt and lying in bed in hospital," Petra said.

"I wasn't as bad as you thought. I'm okay."

"You never saw my car, you followed me here. Why? Besides, you look as if you could collapse at any time. Look Ira, I don't need a bodyguard. I can take care of myself."

"I know you can Petra, as I told you, my wounds are just minor and I'm okay."

"Well I'm glad to hear that Ira. Now will you get off my back, I only have enough strength to carry myself."

"Petra…"

"What now Ira? I told you to get off my back."

Petra drove out of the hotel gate smiling. "Damn woman," he said and got into his car, but before he drove out of the hotel forecourt, Redd Black spotted him and drove at full speed, hitting his car from behind. He then passed him, made a U-turn and drove at him again, smashing Ira's car bonnet and lights. Debris from the lights fell to the ground. Redd laughed and rammed Ira's car again.

Ira's head jerked backward and forward as his eyes dimmed lazily, then in a flash he shook his head and seeing blood coming from his forehead he dazed at Black. "Why don't you fucking look where you're going?" Redd Black said laughing.

In a trance, Ira could see two of Redd Black's men grinning as he shook his head with half-closed eyes. Barely coming to his senses, he opened his car door and slid out. He shook his head vigorously before getting up and staggering into someone's car, triggering off the alarm. Just before the owner of the car hurried out of the hotel, Ira came to his senses wiping blood off his face then went to Redd Black and his mate Gus and asked, "What's the reason you rammed my car and almost broke my neck?"

"You bastard, I found out you're a cop and you're working with that bitch," Redd Black said.

"Look Redd, I'm not a cop. I'm working for your brother. But Petra and I were good friends way back and not seeing her in a long time I couldn't ignore her. She doesn't even know I'm working for your brother," Ira said.

"Shut your fucking mouth, you lying bastard," Gus said and pulled out of his trouser waist a black handle that looked like a kitchen knife and held it under Ira's throat saying, "Boy, you had better look back all the time. You don't know when you'll get this knife stuck in your neck!"

Redd laughed heartily. "Let the damn fool boy go but the next time I see him with the bitch, he's mine. I'll show him I'm not like Mark or Banjo."

Redd laughed again and Ira got into his car and leaned his forehead against his car window, groaning as he nursed his wounded forehead. Touching the cut on his forehead, Gus threw the knife on his car window, smashing it. Ira looked hard at him. Redd pointed his gun at him smiling. As Ira's blood ran from his forehead into his mouth, he spat it out and went up to Redd and Gus and said, "You draw a knife or a gun on me again, I'll make you swallow it, handle as well."

The man looked at Ira, Gus and Redd then said, "I'm going back in the hotel to my wife and I would like the three of you to keep away from my car."

There was silence and the man went back into the hotel to his wife. Ira turned to get back into his car. Gus fisted him on the back of his head. He quickly faced Gus asking, "Why did you hit me?"

"So why don't you hit me back?" Gus said laughing, then ranging his gun at Ira's head. Ira gave him a double punch to his face, knocking him down. He kicked the gun out of his hand and kicked him in his groin, face and body, then watched him fold up in pain.

Redd fired a missed punch at Ira, then watched Gus lying hopelessly on the ground. He then charged into Ira with an opened penknife, but Ira shunted away from the knife and gave him a heavy punch, knocking him down. "Look Redd, I don't want to fight you or Gus. But if you two come after me again, I'll have to kill you both," Ira said as he was getting into his car again. But Redd kicked him in the back and said," I'll kill you boy."

"Go home Redd," Ira told him.

"Pussyclart boy. Me going to kill you," Redd said.

Petra was sitting in her parked car about fifteen yards from the hotel. As she hadn't seen Ira following her, she had the gut feeling that he might be having a hard time with Redd and Gus as she saw them drive into the hotel.

"Shit!" Petra said and drove into the hotel to see Gus and Redd fighting Ira with knives. She drove near to Redd and flung her car door open, knocking him over. Then she got out leaving her engine running and charged into both Redd and Gus giving them a wicked beating and kicking them in their groins leaving them on the ground bleeding from their mouths and faces.

"I knew I shouldn't have left you alone."

"I'm okay Petra."

"You're not okay. I came to help you and to take you home but it looks like I will have to take you back to the hospital to see about your wound again."

"Believe me, I'm really okay," he said.

A few minutes later a man drove in and went into the hotel telling the diners it looked like a fight had broken out outside. Within seconds dozens of onlookers flocked outside.

"Okay, I understand you said you're okay, but I would still like to take you to the hospital as you're bleeding badly."

"Okay Pet. But I think I will be okay going to the hospital alone," Ira said.

Petra smiled. "At least let me help you to your car and you make sure you go to the hospital," she said as she put her arm around his waist supporting him while walking him to his car. As she saw him into his car she closed the door and leaned forward over the wound down window. "You should really go to the hospital now."

Ira smiled and as Petra turned to walk away, Redd sneaked a knife out of his trouser waist and cut her on her arm below the cut she received from Mark. "You bitch, I'll kill you," Redd said. Petra smeared her blood over the front of her blouse and went after Redd. He drew his knife on her again but missed cutting her as she quickly twisted away. As he went for her again with his gun, she kicked the gun out of his hand and landed a hard kick on the left side of his head, sending him flying to the ground. Ira got out of his car and even though he was wounded, he fought Redd and Gus bare fisted and kicked both of them onto their car. He and Petra left Redd and Gus lying lifelessly on the ground. Petra said to Ira, "When I watched you whop those two faggots and forced them to drop their knives, my pain disappeared. I must admit, you were so cool about it all."

"I had the best teacher on knife controlling. I think her name was Petra Jackson," Ira joked.

Petra laughed. "Really Ira, you were in control all the time."

With Petra and Ira's backs turned, Gus struggled up and staggered into their car bleeding from his mouth and over his right eye leaving Redd stretched out on his back on the ground.

"I'll be right back," Petra said to Ira before she went and kicked Redd hard in the groin. "Get your arse up creep. I'll kill you when I'm ready," she said.

Gus started his car. Redd struggled up, holding his crotch, then crawled into the back of the car. As they were driving out of the hotel gate, Ira threw Gus' knife at their windscreen smashing it. "I'm not done with you two lizards yet!" Ira shouted.

Redd shoved his head through the wound down car window to shout out, "Fuck you!" Then Gus drove off at full speed.

"Well done mate," Petra told Ira. "But your wound seems to be bleeding heavily. Would you like me to take you to the hospital?" she asked him.

"I'll be fine," he said. "What about you? I think you're famous for getting cut on your arm."

Petra smiled, "Don't worry about me. It's no more than a plaster cut."

By now the onlookers were moving back into the hotel. "You can all get back to you meals now the show is over," Petra told them and displayed her badge saying, "I'm a police officer."

An old woman shouted, "Well done police lady. I watched you fight well and send those two cowered rats to their knees. I'm sure their balls will be painful for months the way you stamped and kicked them both."

"I didn't enjoy hurting them," Petra said.

But a few minutes later Gus and Redd drove back, got out of their car and went after Petra with knives. She managed to kick Gus in the chest, sending him onto Redd and they both fell. Redd pushed Gus off him and staggered up then went after Petra again, waving his knife in her face. Petra kicked it out of his hand. He drew a second knife at her saying, "Me a go carve you bloodclart face gel." As he charged into her, she elbowed him with a hard blow to his throat, knocking him down, then stamped her right shoe on his chest, cutting him. She picked his knife up, but when she raised the knife to stab him in his face, Ira cried out. "No Petra. Don't do it!" Petra looked at him crossly then rose up off Redd and kicked him in his left side then said. "You're a lucky bastard this time to have my foolish friend stop me piercing out your fucking eyes. But the next time I won't hesitate."

She then went after Gus, but he ran away and got into his car and started the engine, but the engine failed to start. Ira burst out laughing, leaned against his car and shook his head.

Petra went back to Redd. "The next time we meet, I'll poke your filthy eyes out of your head before I kill you."

Ira looked at her smiling before he got into her car. She looked hard at him. "Why did you stop me from killing those two bastards when they raped my mother?"

"I know what they did and they will pay. But it's not those two," Ira said then looked away squinting from his pain.

"Ira, there's only one way those bastards will pay and stop them doing wicked things and that is to cut them up into pieces and scatter their filthy parts into the depths of hell! I've no pity for bastards such as them. To me they are all rapists and murderers and that makes them guilty."

"I do agree with you Pet, but as I said they will pay for what they have done and heavily."

Petra looked hard at Ira and drove up to Gus and Redd's car. In vexation she rammed their car, shackled their hands to the steering wheel and radioed for the police telling them where to pick up Redd and Gus.

"On what charge?" an Officer Charles asked.

"Rape," Petra told the officer then said to Ira, "Let me take you to the hospital."

The police and the ambulance came almost together as Petra was about to drive away. As she and Officer Charles' eyes met, she got out her car and told him and his fellow officer, "Redd Black and Gus threatened to rape me and Redd's brother Mark and his cousin Banjo raped my mother yesterday in their car. I want them arrested, charged and without bail."

"Have you proof of what you said about your mother, Officer Jackson?"

"My mother's word is proof," Petra said.

"I'm Officer Melbourne."

"I know who you are. You let these bastards go free and you will both pay for what they did to my mother."

"Are you threatening me?"

"You take it whichever way you want, Officer Melbourne," Petra said.

Then Ira tumbled out of the car bleeding and said, "Officer Jackson is telling the truth."

Melbourne grinned before reading Gus and Redd Black their rights and told them on what charges they had been arrested. Gus denied raping Mrs Forbes or having anything to do with her in any unlawful way, while Redd laughed looking proud.

"Petra made a fist to hit him but Officer Charles said, "They're in our hands now."

Superintendent Peterson arrived. He walked over to Petra and said, "Jackson, can you tell me what happened to those two jerks the ambulance just took away in shackles?"

"They tried to rape me, wounded me and boasted that their brothers fucked my mother. They will pay heavily. You go to the hospital and ask them," Petra said.

An old white woman eyed Petra and touched her on the shoulder showing her her thumbs up, and then smiled before saying, "Congratulations sweetheart. You're beautiful as well as being a great fighter."

Petra hugged her and said, "Thanks, but this was not what I wanted."

"I understand you had to defend yourself."

Petra smiled at her as she was getting into her car. Superintendent Peterson turned to the old woman. "Can you tell me what happened?"

"No officer, I saw nothing except that those two lice the ambulance took away were extremely out of order."

"Hmm," said the Superintendent, then he walked over to Petra and stared into her eyes.

"What now Superintendent?" Petra asked him.

"I'll trap you one of these days," he said.

"Superintendent Peterson, a maggot has already done that when I was fifteen and I slimed it into the ground. Believe me Super, I've no intention to let anyone trap me again against my will. I shall see you one of these days too. However, will you see that my friend's car is sent to the police garage to be fixed as those two rats smashed his car in the line of duty; he'll collect it after it's fixed. Here are the keys. He is an undercover detective and he's the only honest officer I can trust so far. If you'll excuse me, I have to take him to the hospital." She got into her car and buckled up before taking Ira to the hospital.

Superintendent Peterson smiled as he looked at the keys then went back to Officer Hodge and said, "Don't ask me what she said, but my advice to you is to avoid beautiful women like that one!"

Officer Hodge smiled. Petra drove away with Ira sitting next to her. As she drove out of the hotel gate she said to Ira, "You have a habit of stopping me killing those dirty bastards. Why don't you let me do my job and save the taxpayers the trouble of bringing a case against them? However, I have enjoyed kicking their asses every time."

"Redd Black and his kind will go down as I told you. But I know Gus and Redd took no part in the rape of your mother," Ira said.

"Why are you defending them? Were you there?" Petra asked.

"I'm not defending them. The two that raped your mother were Mark and Banjo. Redd Black is also guilty of raping other women. As for his brother Sydney and their disciples, we'll get them. But I have to be careful because my brother Aaron is working undercover at his place."

Petra frowned.

"Pet don't you worry, I will get them and they'll choke to death on their own blood before I kill them!" Ira said.

"I have a better plan for them, I assure you. Those rotten bastards will suffer before they crumble under my law!" Petra said in anger.

Ira smiled but his face showed he was feeling pain. "Here's my house."

"Nice black gate," Petra said to him. "Did some of the Black's money buy you this home?"

"Pet, don't make jokes like that." Ira's white face instantly changed to bright red.

"Only testing you my friend, I was only testing you. Anyway, don't you want me to take you to the hospital?" she asked him smiling.

"I'll be okay," he said.

"Okay." Petra watched him hard. "Petra, I'll be fine. Just help me inside."

"Okay Ira." Petra got out of the car. Then as Ira slowly got out, she circled her right arm around his waist to support him. His dark skinned girlfriend saw them walking up the yard, and she opened the door and let them in.

"What happened to him?" his girlfriend asked.

"He will tell you himself," Petra said.

"Is this another one of your whore fights? Who the hell is this woman that you have brought into my house?" she asked furiously.

"Ellie, this is my house. This woman who you address so disrespectfully is Petra Jackson and she is a police officer. She saved my life. Incidentally, she isn't one of you. Even if you were born again and wanted to be like her, you'll never be! As of now you will address her as Officer Jackson or a friend," Ira said. His girlfriend looked at Petra smiling and her face wriggled with shame.

"He is in need of a doctor right now, but he refused to let me take him to the hospital. May I use your phone?" Petra asked his girlfriend.

"Please do," she replied with her eyes glued to the floor.

"Thanks," Petra said then called her friend Dr Stanley saying, "Hello my friend. It's Petra."

"Oh hello my dear Petra, what can I do for you?"

"Stan, I've a very special friend who's badly in need of your help right now. He's been badly hurt during a fight but he refused to let me take him to the hospital. Will you be so kind as to come and see what you can do for him? I'm calling from his home in Bromsgrove."

"What's the address?" Stanley asked.

"I'll put his girlfriend on so that she can tell you," said Petra then passed the phone to Ira's girlfriend.

"It's 134 Governor Road."

"Ok, I know where," Stanley said. "I'll be there as quick as I can."

Stanley put his phone down, gathered what he needed and told his wife Elizabeth that Petra needed him to have a look at a friend.

"Well, you better be off to our dear friend. Will you give her my love and tell her to call me sometime."

"I will my precious, I will," Stanley said and left in his car.

While he was driving to Ira's, he was admiring some of the beautiful houses on both sides of the street that were for sale. To every unsold house he liked, he nodded his head smiling. As he drove further on, he saw a beautiful detached four-bedroomed house for sale. He drove slowly just to have a good look at it. After he passed the house he looked back looking at the house again, then sped on to Ira's house. He stopped by the gate, got out, walked up to the door and rang the bell.

Ira's girlfriend answered the door, let him in then took him to the living room where Ira was lying on the sofa. When Dr Stanley and Petra's eyes met they smiled. Stanley washed his hands and had a look at Ira's wound. "You're in a pretty bad state," Stanley said looking up at Petra.

"Please Stan, do what you can for him," Petra said.

Stanley nodded and took off his jacket, rested it on a single chair and began tending to Ira's wounds.bAfter he had done what he could, he said to Ira, "I will want you to come to the hospital for a check-up in a week. Apart from anything else, I think you'll be okay. I'll see you in two days to see how you're doing, change your bandage and check that the stitches are holding."

"Thanks doc. How much do I owe you?" Ira asked.

"Nothing," said Stanley.

"Nothing?" Ira asked surprised.

"That's right my friend. Anyone who is a friend of Pet's is a friend of mine. You take care and I will come to change your bandage in two days. After that I would like to see you at the hospital," Stanley reminded Ira then turned to Petra and asked, "Would you mind me taking a look at your bleeding arm?"

"I'm okay," replied Petra smiling then asked, "How's Liz?"

"Oh, very well. It won't be long now before our baby is born. By the way my friend, she told me to ask you to phone her sometime."

"Yes, of course. I shall do one better. Tell her I'll be there this Sunday for dinner if it's okay with both of you."

"Petra, we would be delighted to have you at our home anytime and to have many dinners. Besides, I think it's time we spent some time together like the old times, the five of us."

"That would be nice," Petra said. "The five of us will have to get together and have a drink."

"I'd like that," Stanley said. "Yes, I would really like that." He paused for a second before he attended to Petra's wounded arm. "You'll be fine my dear. I have put in a few butterfly stitches but the cut is not too bad." Petra and

Stanley embraced giggling while Ira and his girlfriend Elli watched them. After Petra and Stanley parted, she kissed his cheek. "Give that to my good friend Elizabeth. Don't forget to tell her I will be there Sunday for dinner."

"My dearest friend Petra, I won't." Stanley washed his hands then left.

"You must be very special to each other."

"Yes Ira, we've been friends since school days. Now we are like family," Petra said.

"Oh, please fill me in with the details later," Elli said rudely as she was jealous.

Petra looked at her hard.

"Petra, I'm very sorry about the way I spoke to you," Elli said.

"Don't worry about that. You just take care of my friend, or I'll deal with you. However, I have to go now but I'll see you both soon."

Ira saw Elli flash her eyes at Petra. "Thanks mate for your help," Ira told Petra then said to Elli, "You want to grow up."

"You both take care and I'll see you soon." Petra left and went to the police station.

"Officer Jackson, I would like a statement from you," Superintendent Peterson said.

"I will give you all the statements you need when I am satisfied. And that will be the time when I toss the Black brothers at your feet, dead. Now if you'll excuse me, I've my own business to attend to." Petra walked away leaving Superintendent Peterson rubbing his chin in wonder. Detective Todd smiled.

The following morning Petra signed in at work and Officer Hodge told her there was a meeting in the conference room at ten o'clock. Petra said nothing but left him standing in the entrance. As she walked into the information room, the receptionist said, "Superintendent Peterson wants you in the conference room at ten."

"Thanks," Petra said.

"Petra, don't say anything yet, but I think one day you'll be your own boss," the receptionist said. "Don't forget you're wanted in the conference room."

"They can wait for me for another couple of minutes," Petra said to the young dark receptionist, then she went to have a cup of coffee from the machine. On her way back, the receptionist said, "Petra, you have such a beautiful figure. Your legs are long and attractive with those firm nipples pointing straight at me."

Petra looked hard at her. "My nipples are telling you to mind your own business and get on with your work."

The receptionist smiled, and Petra walked past her. She went to the conference room drinking her coffee. Before she took her seat she looked at everyone to see smiles on their faces. Officer Bradley pointed out a seat next to her. His smile was friendly. Just before the meeting started, most of them began to laugh. Officer Bradley looked at Petra then took time to look at those that were laughing. "How come you're not laughing?" Petra asked Officer Bradley. Petra looked serious.

"Oh Petra, I hate being here, especially with this bunch of turkeys," said Officer Bradley.

Just then, Officer Marian Stevens got up out of her seat laughing loudly then went and turned the blackboard round revealing a drawing of a cow with a face that looked like Petra's with a red bull sucking her right nipple and the bull saying, "Pet honey, cock your legs, I'm coming." The laughing was extremely loud especially from Officer Marian Stevens and Detective Scott Hanson. "If you bunch of idiots had brains you'd be as dangerous as hell fire," said Officer Joan Bradley. Petra looked at her and smiled before getting up out of her seat and facing her colleges. As they were still laughing, her eyes were travelling on each of them in turn. Then her eyes met Detective Inspector Hanson. Still he and Officer Marian Stevens carried on laughing, the tilt of their voices penetrating the ceiling enough to blast the roof away.

"Detective Inspector Hanson, you're such a jerk," Officer Bradley said.

Petra slipped off her trousers and peeled her shirt off, leaving her black heart-patterned knickers and bra, and said to her colleagues, "Take a good look at my cow-shaped body you bunch of sick-minded fucked maggots."

Detective Scott Hanson and Officer Stevens were still laughing at the top of their voices. Petra slid into her trousers then took time unbuckling the sides of her knickers. She slid them out of her trousers, walked over to Detective Inspector Hanson and shoved her knickers in his mouth. Then she slapped Officer Stevens. All eyes widened. Marian Stevens suddenly stopped laughing and looked at Petra in shock with staring eyes.

"I thank you turkeys for your silence. Especially you, you pale-faced bitch," Officer Bradley said, although she was white as well.

Shamefully, Detective Inspector Hanson took the knickers out of his mouth and shoved them in his jacket pocket, then wiped his lips with his handkerchief. Petra smiled at him, then walked over to the blackboard, wiped it clean and said, "Let me show all of you bastards how to draw a picture." She then drew Detective Inspector Hanson's face on a donkey's body with a long and big dick fixed in Officer Marian Steven's mouth with words saying, "Don't push no further, you're choking me Scott Hanson." There was loud laughing. Detective Inspector Hanson looked at his mates and his brother Paul. They stopped laughing, but Joan Bradley and Petra were laughing hysterically. Tears came into Officer Bradley's eyes as she was laughing so much.

After a while, Petra said to them, "You bunch of sick-minded bastards. You all had a good laugh at me and now I return the joke by drawing Mr Smart Arse and his fool. Mr Smart Arse only had to look at you and your laughter stopped instantly. Well, my laughing hasn't."

Petra then went to Detective Inspector Hanson and laughed in his face and said, "As for you Mr Smart Arse, has your laughing run out? Always remember the trick you play on someone might turn on you." She slapped the back of his neck and he coughed few times.

Petra held Officer Bradley's hand and said, "Let's get out for some fresh air." Before she and Officer Bradley left, she went back to Detective Inspector Hanson and whispered in his ears. "I wish you had choked on my knickers and it doesn't matter the women you have had, the taste of my pussy will always be in you."

He smiled. As Petra and Officer Bradley were about to walk out of the conference room, Officer Hodge, Superintendent Peterson and Detective Todd walked in and saw the drawings on the blackboard. Superintendent Peterson looked Detective Todd in his eyes, then they burst out laughing while Officer Hodge kept a straight face.

"Who's responsible for this?" Superintendent Peterson asked.

"I am," Petra proudly said. "Your dummies forced me to do so."

Then Officer Baxter said, "Super, I haven't seen such a slim and curvy body as PC Jackson's. What I wouldn't give to rest my head between her lovely breasts."

"Come on Petra, let's get out of here," Officer Bradley said.

"Petra, I know what you did was self-defence and I'm proud of you," Officer Hodge said.

Petra smiled and said, "Thanks." Then before she and Officer Bradley left, Superintendent Peterson said, "I'm sorry that this meeting hasn't taken place but I want to see all of you here in two days at the same time and nothing like this should ever happen again. Officer Jackson, I would like to see you in my office in twenty minutes."

"Yes Super," Petra said. The Superintendent and Detective Todd left the conference room laughing. They walked outside to the courtyard to see Petra sitting talking on her mobile phone. They were about to go to her when Detective Inspector Hanson walked up to them and asked, "Who is she?"

"Detective Inspector Hanson, you don't want to know, but she is the best I've come across," Superintendent Peterson said. Detective Todd smiled broadly and Hanson walked away.

Petra and Officer Bradley went to the ladies. Petra took a pair of light blue lace knickers out of her bag and said to Officer Bradley, "Luckily for me I bought a set of three knickers and left them in my handbag."

"What about the ones you shoved in Detective Inspector Hanson's mouth?"

"He can keep it and choke on it for all I care."

"Pet, call me stupid if you want but I saw in Hanson's eyes, he fancies you."

"Joan, I wouldn't give him a second look. He belongs with that bitch Officer Stevens. And don't say another word."

"Petra, my lips are sealed."

Petra smiled and later that day, Petra and Detective Inspector Hanson were called out to a murder scene along with other police and forensic officers. When they got there, a woman said, "Mrs Ryan has been shot dead."

Petra asked onlookers to tell her what they saw, but no one said anything. As she was about to walk out of the crowd, A Mr Benjamin said to her, "Her son Ed Black shot her. He is related to Sydney Black I think."

"Yes I saw him too," a nineteen-year-old told Petra, then everyone seemed to be moving away in case Ed showed up again.

"What's your name my young friend?" Petra asked the young lad.

"My name is Ravel."

"And did you actually see Ed shoot his mother?"

"No, officer lady."

"Well thank you Ravel. I think it would be best if you went home," Petra told him. Ravel smiled, then left.

Petra radioed in for an ambulance then reported to the station that a Mrs Ryan had been shot dead by her son.

"I've already done so. My name is Claudia Hynes."

"Thank you Claudia."

"But you're so young and beautiful. Couldn't you pick a safer job?"

"Thanks for your concern Claudia, but I chose this job because I want to help people."

Claudia smiled, "I'm seventy-two years old and I just witnessed Ed gun down his mother. That boy's useless and wicked. I know of many times he went to his mother asking for money to supply him with drugs and I know of a few times he beat his mother when she didn't give him money. Ach, I knew he would kill her sooner or later. He put his father into hospital two weeks ago with a broken leg and broken ribs and he raped his girlfriend's thirteen-year-old daughter, but she claimed her daughter had lied. Now he's killed his mother. He and his father are two of a kind as his father used to beat his mother as well if she refused him money. But poor Mrs Ryan, she suffered so much at the hands of her wicked son and husband, who are both related to Sydney Black."

The ambulance came. After Petra saw the porters zip up Mrs Ryan's body and carry it to the ambulance, she and Detective Inspector Hanson drove to the station in their own cars once forensics had secured tape around the crime scene.

Superintendent Peterson scratched behind his right ear as a habit and sighed. "Hmm" he said, staring into Petra's face. Detective Inspector Hanson walked away and stood his distance, looking worried as he looked at Petra.

"Well, the truth is, I'm sure with you tracking the bad guys, they will tumble out of the box like a clown."

"Tell me Superintendent, what the hell is going on between you, corrupted cops and the Black organisation?"

"I don't know what you mean Jackson. Be careful what you say."

Petra lashed out. "Even though the police knew Ed Ryan murdered his mother, they still didn't question him or arrest him. What the hell is going on between these bastard Blacks and the police? Anyway Superintendent Peterson, what did you want to see me about?"

"Oh it's okay, I got what I wanted," Superintendent Peterson said and Petra left.

Detective Inspector Hanson left with Petra and asked her, "What the hell are you implying?"

"I'm not implying anything, but I'm sure I will be the one to bring these scum down," Petra told Hanson and she hurried walking away from him.

"Petra, you really are difficult, but I might be the one to keep you in line," Hanson shouted out to her. Superintendent Peterson walked out of the station to hear that and he said, "Good luck with that one Hanson."

Petra walked into her house and had such a shock seeing the furniture was out of place. "Mother what have you done?" She put the furniture as it was, then she sat and waited for her mother to come home.

Four-thirty that Friday morning, she was woken by the ringing telephone. She lazily opened her eyes and stretched picking up the phone. "Yes?" she answered, half asleep.

"Hello Petra, its Ira. Sorry to wake you."

"Ira, have you any idea what time it is?"

"I'm sorry Pet, but I can't get to sleep."

"Why don't you call your girlfriend?"

"Pet, she's sleeping next to me but you're so different and understanding. Pet, I…" He paused. "Anyway thanks again for helping me out." Tears welled up in his eyes.

"That's all right Ira. But don't make a habit of getting beaten up," Petra said jokingly and giggled. Ira laughed then whispered, "I love you Pet." Elli woke and asked, "Who are you talking to at this time in the morning?"

"Go back to sleep."

"Is she one of your women?"

"No Elli, I'm talking to Petra."

Elli grabbed the phone from Ira and said to Petra, "Thanks for looking after my man."

"Don't worry about it. You take good care of him," Petra said.

"Petra, Ira and I owe you a drink. Would you like to come and have dinner with us next Saturday evening?"

"I would love to, but I've already said yes to having dinner with a friend."

"Well, what about the following Saturday?"

"Okay Elli, I'll be there."

"Thanks Petra and you can bring a friend if you like."

"Okay Elli, I'll see what I can do."

"Petra thanks again for looking out for Ira. And I'll see you in two weeks."

"Goodbye Elli," said Petra and put the phone down then turned her pillow over. When she saw her gun, she smiled then put it in her bedside drawer, dimmed her bedside lights and turned on her back. A good while after she still couldn't get back to sleep so she had a shower then poured herself a glass of orange juice and a glass of red wine then went back to bed. She only drank the wine then fell asleep leaving the juice on the side cabinet.

The next day she was off work so she spent the day with her Grandma as her mother was there.

It was Saturday morning and she took her mother and Grandma shopping, treated them to new clothes and lunch, then spent the rest of the day with them both. In the evening she had dinner with her dear friends Stanley and Elizabeth.

On Monday morning Petra reported to work and joined her comrades in the conference room once again. She took her seat behind Detective Inspector Hanson and pinched his neck. Hanson screamed and looked back at Petra and smiled.

"This meeting is about the Blacks' organisation," Detective Superintendent Harrogate said. "I agree strongly with Officer Jackson and it's time we got off our asses and stopped that evil Black organisation killing, raping, kidnapping and abusing people. We'll track down from the frailest of the Black gang to the strongest and any corrupt cop who is dealing with them. We'll search from tomorrow from eight o'clock till we get everyone, including bad cops. I expect honesty by giving up those you're sure of working with Sydney Black and Co. As for me, I would give up any corrupt member of my family to protect decent people. Thank you for being here and this meeting is closed." He went to Petra and shook her hand, saying, "Thank you." Then he left the room.

That evening Officer Haley Devine went to Ed Ryan and told him what was said in the meeting. She went on to say, "I didn't give any clues that I'm your woman and no one knows about us."

"Good, you keep it that way. You report everything you hear about my family and me. Go now," Ed Ryan said.

The next morning at work in the tea room Petra said, "Those Blacks bastards, I would like to crush them under my feet." Officer Haley sucked her teeth and her and Petra's eyes met.

After breakfast Petra got up to leave. Officer Haley rushed towards her almost knocking her down.

"What's the matter with you Officer Haley? You almost knocked me down," Petra said.

"Have you got a fucking problem with that?" said Haley.

"Well, not until just now. But let me warn you, if I offend you in any way, you let me know without touching me again. If you do, I'll split your arse in two," Petra told her.

Haley slapped Petra's face and Petra thumped her in her stomach and she fell to the floor. Detective Inspector Hanson looked hard at Petra and shook his head. Petra walked past him. He caught her going to the coffee machine. She looked at him and he smiled. She took her coffee and walked away. He followed her and touched her on her shoulder. She looked back at him. "Petra, you should take it easy. Would you like to tell me what's bothering you?"

"I'm okay. Now I want to be left alone."

"Okay, but if I see you lay into anyone again like that, I will report you."

"Get the hell out of my face and stay away."

"Just remember what I told you, Petra."

Petra just looked at him and walked away. Hanson smiled and went to get a cup of black coffee, and then joining his colleagues in the office sat down still thinking about Petra. Sipping his coffee, he put his hand in his pocket, feeling her knickers, then smiled.

"What are you smiling about, mate?" Detective Todd asked him.

"Nothing," he said.

"Have you given her her knickers back?"

"Todd, what are you talking about?"

"Hanson. I know what she did to you, and you have her knickers."

Detective Inspector Hanson smiled broadly. Detective Todd smiled, then sat at his desk, leaving Hanson smiling.

That night Officer Haley drove to Sydney Black's house, where she met her man Ed Ryan and told him what was being said again. As she was leaving she saw Officer Clara Bee having supper with Sydney Black.

Clara Bee kept her head down as she saw Officer Haley was walking over to them. Officer Haley stood facing Clara, took a piece of her steak and looked at her before putting it in her mouth. "Sydney, I think you should be careful with women and who you're eating with. Especially, some police."

Sydney looked up at Officer Haley and smiled as he caught on to what she said. Clara Bee stopped eating.

"Finish your supper honey," Sydney said.

"I'm not hungry any more," she said.

"It's such a shame to see good food go to waste. May I?" Officer Haley asked.

Clara Bee shrugged. Officer Haley sat and ate Clara Bee's food and drank her wine.

That Thursday night Sydney Black ordered one of his men by the nickname of Pilot to take Clara Bee away from his estate and shoot her. Pilot was tall, handsome and white. He was clever in convincing Clara Bee that he was going to take her on a night out. She liked that and agreed to go. That night Pilot took her miles away from the estate and shot her in the head, then put her body in a black bin bag and tossed her body in front of the police station gate.

Early next morning police officers saw the bag and called in forensics. They were shocked and disgusted, as they had no idea who'd murdered the officer. They didn't even know she was working at the Blacks' residence as an undercover cop.

Later that morning, Officer Bradley said to Petra, "I watched Officer Haley absorbing everything that was said at the conference. Did you know she's Ed Ryan's woman?"

"No," Petra said.

"Well, she is and I know she has reported everything that has been said to the Black brothers. Petra, I know she knew about Clara Bee's death."

Petra closed her eyes tightly then opened them saying, "You keep what you told me between us."

Officer Bradley smiled then her tears dropped.

The police failed to charge Sydney Black or any member of his associates with Officer Clara Bee's murder. This left Petra feeling angry and disappointed.

Two days later Petra went to the chemist to buy cough medicine for her grandma, as she had the flu and was coughing too much. Mrs Dean waited outside the chemist until Petra got back into her car. Mrs Dean knocked on the car window. Petra wound down the window.

"Could I speak to you Miss Petra?"

"Sure."

"Not here, someone might see us and I have to be very careful not to be seen talking to you."

"You sound very serious Mrs Dean."

"Yes, it's about that Black family. This is why I have to be careful not to be seen talking to you with my husband working for Sydney, especially as you're a police officer. I'm also worried about my two granddaughters. They are seventeen and fourteen years old. I'm so frightened for them both," Mrs Dean said.

"Yes, I can imagine how you feel."

"Well, about the Black people. My husband can tell you more than I can as he's working in their garage and he has seen many bad things happen. He said nothing to the police after he saw Sydney and his brother give two police envelopes filled with money. Both the police and the Black brothers threatened my husband. If he talked he would put our granddaughters in danger. I knew what they meant. Petra I can't trust anyone else but you. My husband and I are very afraid for our grandchildren."

"I understand, Mrs Dean. But if you tell me what you know I'll take you, your husband and grandchildren to a safe place until we get the whole community of Black's, as well as the corrupt police officers, and put all of them six foot in the ground or in prison for a long time where they belong," Petra said.

"Oh Miss Petra Jackson, I wish it was that easy. Those good-for-nothing brutes are very dangerous and very well protected by the bad police. So you see, my husband and I have to be very careful as we've other family. Well, if you show up by the post office tomorrow morning at ten o'clock you will see my husband waiting for you. He will be wearing a pale green shirt, black trousers and a black cap. My husband is very grey and he is about six foot tall and has an old body," Mrs Dean joked to make Petra laugh. "Well, goodbye Petra," Mrs Dean said then left. Petra put her seatbelt on and drove away to her Grandma's to give her the cough medicine.

At ten o'clock the following morning, Petra drove to the post office and waited in her car for Mr Dean. She looked at everyone that came her way but didn't see Mr Dean. After a while she looked at her watch; twenty-five minutes past ten. Still waiting in her car and looking in vain for Mr Dean, she looked at her wristwatch again and saw the time was five to eleven. She breathed out deeply before starting her car but didn't drive away.

"Well Mr Dean, I don't think I can wait for you any longer," Petra said to herself. But her eyes were still searching for him. "Come on Petra, pull yourself together and get away from here," she muttered. Then as she saw people running down the road, she put her dark glasses on as it was very sunny and got out of her car, pressed the fob to lock it and went to look at what the people were running to see. About twenty-five yards from the post office, a large crowd of people had gathered in the street and were flocking in front Mr Green's paper shop. "What's going on and why are you people gathered here?" Petra asked.

"An old man's been shot," a woman said.

"We don't know who he is," another woman said.

Petra looked amongst the crowd for anyone who looked suspicious and she saw Officer Haley and Redd Black. Officer Haley saw her and whispered in Redd's ears and they hurried away, got in their car and drove off. Officer Hodge and Superintendent Peterson called the ambulance.

Petra left the crowd to go after Redd Black and Officer Haley but met Mark standing by her car. "Bitch!" he said. She kicked him in the mouth and pointed her gun at his head. "I ought to blow your brains out of your fucking dumb head," Petra said.

"Take it easy Pet," Ira said.

"Where did you come from? And is it a habit to stop me from killing these maggots?" Petra asked.

"Look my friend, they aren't worth you dirtying your hands for. So leave them to me," Ira said. He shot Mark in the leg and told him, "The next time I see you, I'll send a bullet straight into your wicked heart."

"You shot me in my fucking leg! I'm in pain and I need a doctor," Mark said.

"Hop your arse to the hospital of your choice," Ira told him and he saw Petra get into her car and drive off. But Petra stopped her car when she saw Drake, Blake and Craig.

"What are you boys doing here?" Petra asked them.

"We came to help you," Drake said.

"Why do you think I'm in need of your help?"

"Because Redd's police bitch and a couple of his men are looking for you saying they're going kill you," Blake said.

"Thanks for the warning. But I think you boys better make yourself scarce," Petra said and as they saw Mark hopping and bleeding, they asked Petra, "What happened to him?"

"He got in the way of my friend's gun and it went off and shot him in the leg. The lucky bastard only ended up with a flesh wound."

"Pretty face, you're one dangerous lady," Drake said.

"Look boys, I don't want any one of you to get hurt. I appreciate your kindness in wanting to help me, but I think I can manage as I have found these maggots are no match for me," Petra said. "Anyway, let me introduce you boys to my good friend. Then get lost."

"Don't worry about us. We'll be okay as long as we stay behind you," Blake said.

Petra smiled and introduced them to Ira saying, "Boys, this is my friend Ira. He's a detective. Ira, meet Blake, Craig and Drake my three friends and you'll get to meet another, Marlon."

"I guess you know by now Haley is Ed Ryan's woman," Blake said. "And she's one of the biggest crooks and an informer for them."

Suddenly Mark drove away passing Petra and the lads and shouted from his car window, "Fuck you lot." He then picked up speed, driving to the hospital.

"Wait a minute, you boys are the ones I stopped from chasing a young girl, am I right? And where's the other one?" Petra asked.

"You're right. But there's not much time for any of us to read a book now. Anyway, I have a brother who is a cop and I don't want him to find out about what I was going to do with that young girl," Craig said. "Petra we heard about your mother, so we left Marlon with her at her house. Your mum will be all right with him."

"Boys, I thank you. But I still don't like the idea of you being here," Petra said.

"No! Oh no," Petra's tears dropped.

"He is dead, Petra," Blake said, touching Petra's shoulder. Petra looked up at him. "Pretty face, he's dead." Blake held her hand and helped her up off her knees.

"I met his wife. He had information for me."

A black woman walked up to Petra and said, "I saw a young woman shoot the old man and run away. I know you. You're a good police officer," the woman said.

"I'm trying to be."

"I know you're a good one. My name is Florence Matthew. I saw what happened as I had just walked out of the chemist. I saw the young and pretty woman shoot the poor old man right in his chest. I think the woman may be wearing a pillow under clothes to look pregnant."

"Why do you think that, Mrs Matthew?" Petra asked her.

"Her tummy was too high and looked unusual. I haven't seen anyone that pregnant and their tummy spread like hers was." Mrs Matthew looked confused. "Then again, I saw her put a gun in her pocket before running off with a black young man."

"Thank you for the information, Mrs Matthew," said Petra.

"Oh," said Mrs Matthew, "I think the shopkeeper was the one that called for an ambulance."

"Thank you again," Petra said to Mrs Matthew and covered Mr Dean's face with her jacket.

Chapter 11

Fifteen minutes later three police cars sped to the crime scene with the ambulance following. Onlookers gave way for Mrs Dean to identify her husband's body. Police and the coroner moved the jacket off the dead person's face and Mrs Dean said, "Yes, he's my husband." She had a good look at him then the police put the body in a body bag.

"Thanks for covering his face," Mrs Dean said. Petra nodded. Mrs Dean wiped tears from her eyes and said, "I had expected this would happen."

"I'm so sorry Mrs Dean."

"Miss Petra, I've got this for you. It's from my husband's safe. I think he wanted you to have it. You'll find something there that might help you with your enquiries."

"Thanks," Petra said. Mrs Dean walked away from the crowd leaving Petra looking at a list of names. One name was listed that Petra didn't recognise. She repeated the name 'Peats' in a whisper as she looked hard at the name before putting it in her pocket when she saw Superintendent Peterson and Detective Inspector Hanson walking towards her. She had one last look at Mr Dean's body before the paramedics zipped up the bag to carry him to the ambulance.

"Are we done here mate?" the driver asked. Superintendent Peterson smiled. "You can take him mate." The paramedics drove away. Police secured more tape around the area where the crime had happened.

As most of the onlookers left, Mrs Dean appeared again and told Petra that her husband had threatened the Black brothers if they didn't stop turning young girls into prostitutes. "He said he would go to the newspapers, as he didn't know which police to trust and who were working for the brothers. But he didn't tell me."

Ironically, Petra had known about the Black organisation since she was thirteen years old. And now she was nearing twenty and the Blacks brothers were still carrying on with their evil doings.

Petra went to Judge Clews with information concerning the Black brothers, but was told by the judge not to interfere with them and that her information was purely fabrication.

When the judge saw the angry look on Petra's face, he said, "Officer Jackson, I want no trouble from you. I want you to stay well clear of Mr Sydney Black and his brothers."

Petra looked Judge Clews in his eyes. "I mean it Officer Jackson. You keep well away from the Black brothers," the judge said, raising his voice in anger.

Petra stared Judge Clews in the eye. "From when I was thirteen, I knew you lot were protecting those bastards in exchange for having sex with teenagers, money and drugs. Well, I'm much older and wiser now, and there's only one way to stop me getting to the Black brothers and that is to kill me. Believe me Judge Clews, while I'm alive, I'll bring those bastards down and whoever with them. I know the ones that are paid well by the Black brothers, and I call that fucking stinking blood money!"

"Officer Jackson, I'm warning you not to interfere with the Black brothers. If you do, I will have you arrested."

"Kiss my ass, Judge," Petra said, walking away. Judge Clews said to Officer Hodge, "Arrest Officer Jackson."

"Why? Because she wants you to kiss her ass?" Officer Hodge said rudely. "She has the right to tell you, as you're hindering her doing her job."

Hanson said, "Judge, you're one lucky man to get invited by her to kiss her ass."

Everyone burst out laughing.

Judge Clews laughed too and said to Detective Inspector Hanson, "I wouldn't like to get in her way even though I'm a judge. Still, I would very much like to get to know her." He then rested his head back on his chair, looking relaxed and smiling.

Detective Inspector Hanson had the feeling that Petra might be going to the Blacks' residence. So he asked to be excused and followed behind her, but kept his distance for a while until he saw her turn onto Moor Croft Street, then he blew his car horn to let her know he was following her.

When she realised it was Detective Inspector Hanson, she pulled over to the kerb and waited, looking into her side mirror and watching him walking towards her car. She smiled. He knocked on the car window twice before she wound down the window.

"What the hell do you want from me detective?"

"You've been warned by Judge Clews to keep away from the Blacks."

"You and Judge Clews can go straight to hell so that I wouldn't see any of you ever again! And you know what Hanson, I'm sick of you always sniffing my arse."

"Petra, you could end up dead."

"Have you finished?"

"You just cannot keep your nose clean," he said.

"What is that supposed to mean?" Petra asked him.

"Look Pet, honest police officers might have been murdered by the Blacks and nothing has been said or done as we can't prove they've done it. I don't want you to play God. I really don't want you to get hurt. We will get those bastards," he said.

"When will that be, when they rape your mother and sisters? Hanson, I would not want anything to happen to me either, but I'd rather die trying to bring those guilty bastards down for the crimes they've committed and are still committing. Now get the fuck out of my face and stay out!" Petra said. As she started her car to drive off Detective Inspector Hanson banged against her car window saying, "I care about you Petra." She looked hard in his face then drove away, almost dragging him down to the ground as he was leaning against her car.

As he balanced on his feet he said, "Shit! Blasted women!" He shook his head and got into his car and went after her, but as he couldn't see her car he drove home.

Petra went to the Zanzibar Club to have a drink. While she was sitting alone in the corner drinking orange juice, Ed and Banjo walked into the bar and stood in front of the bar. When Banjo saw Petra, he touched Ed on his shoulder and pointed. Ed grinned and he and Banjo walked over to Petra and sat either side of her. Banjo picked up her orange juice and drank some. She looked at both of them and called a dark waitress. "Would you like another orange juice?" she asked Petra.

"Yes please, and a bottle of vodka," Banjo said.

The waitress looked hard at Petra. Petra smiled. The waitress left and returned with a glass of orange juice and a bottle of vodka. She put the orange juice in front of Petra and put the vodka in front of Banjo. Banjo took a drink from her juice again. Ed laughed. By this time, the waitress and the manager were watching them, but were afraid to do anything.

Petra got up and was moving to another table when Banjo held her hand and forced her to sit down by pressing down on her shoulders. The manager saw, but he remained still as he was scared. Still, he went over to them and looked hard at them.

"What do you want?" Banjo asked him.

"Please leave the lady alone. Can't you see she's not interested in you?" he said.

Banjo pushed him away.

"Please, I want no trouble."

"Get back behind your bar, wash the dirty glass and keep your eyes and mouth to yourself like the rest of the customers," Banjo told him.

"Please Mr Black, I don't want any trouble. I don't want to lose my licence."

"You'll lose more than your licence if you don't get back behind the counter where you belong and wash the dirty glasses," Banjo said and laughed.

Ed Ryan laughed. He also drank some of the orange juice and lifted the glass to Petra's mouth, saying, "Finish it." Petra took the orange juice and threw it in his face and punched him on his wounded leg saying, "You killed your mother and still the fucking bent cop left you to run free."

As Banjo raised his hand to hit her, she hit him with the bottle of vodka on his forehead. Blood poured down his face and Banjo drew a knife at her. She cocked her gun, aimed it at his head, then forced his hand to stab his right shoulder, leaving the knife in. Ed pulled a knife out of his jacket pocket and she pulled Banjo's knife out of his shoulder and rammed it into Ed's arm. Ed dropped his knife. The customers left their seats and gathered around Petra. She showed her badge. "I'm a police officer."

"They both deserved what they got," the manager said.

Petra then called in the police to come and arrest Ed Ryan for killing his mother and Banjo for assaulting her.

The manager thanked Petra after Banjo and Ed dropped on the floor and she shackled them together. While waiting for the police to arrive Banjo cried out, "My shoulder!"

"You should have thought about your shoulder before you made trouble," a woman said.

"Someone that knows about first aid should help him," a second woman said.

"Let him bleed to death," the manager said angrily.

A swarm of police then arrived. Superintendent Peterson went to Petra, looked her in the eyes, smiled and shook his head. "Officer Jackson what happened this time?"

The manager spoke out, telling the Superintendent and his fellow police officers what had happened. Just then Detective Inspector Hanson walked into the bar, took Petra on her own and said, "I asked you not to go looking for trouble."

A third woman who was on her way out heard the detective. She turned saying, "This is not so detective, the lady was on her own drinking orange juice when these two good-for-nothings walked in and walked over to her. I have to say, I'm very proud of her for defending herself. Detective, we need people like her."

Petra walked away. Hanson smiled and followed Petra, saying to her, "You can't fight Sydney Black and his men by yourself. I understand you were protecting yourself. But believe me Pet, we want to have all the Blacks including the bad cops, but we have to be very careful about how we go about it. I suspect a few police officers and a judge but I have no proof and I can't afford to mess things up after working for so long and hard to let the bad lads get off free after doing wicked acts. Petra, I want you to trust me. I'm asking you to please keep away from Sydney Black and his brothers."

"Okay Hanson, but I'll be watching you. You have one month and if I don't see those bastards behind bars, I'll do what you arses failed to do - kill or make sure they are tucked away for a very long time," Petra said. "By the way, I thought Ed Ryan was Sydney Black's cousin."

"No, Ryan is his half-brother."

"Well, I don't care if he is his whole brother. All I want to do is eliminate the son of a bitches from this world for good!" Petra said, looking as mad as ever.

"Petra Hanson, please just don't cross my path and make things worse," said Detective Inspector Hanson.

Petra stared at him. "My name's Jackson and you could move your fucking name Hanson from Petra and that goes two ways! Detective Scott Brett Hanson. You don't cross my path either!" Petra walked away. Detective Inspector Hanson laughed as he realised that he had called Petra by his own name. He went after her.

"Petra!" he bellowed.

"Fuck you!" Petra told him and rushed away smiling to the counter to pay for her drinks.

"I'm talking to you, Officer Jackson."

"We've nothing to say to each other. Remember you told me to stay away from you. So I'm doing just that. Mr Hanson, I suggest you do the same," Petra said, giving the manager a twenty pound note.

"Please officer, you owe me nothing. Please come again as often as you can."

"Thanks," Petra said and gave the waitress the twenty pounds instead. Then she walked outside with Detective Inspector Hanson following. She stopped by her car and asked him, "Have you got nothing else to do but follow me around sniffing my ass?"

"Woman, can't you tell that I'm falling in love with you?"

"Well, you're wasting your time as I have no interest in you or any other man."

"Petra, I love you. Damn it woman, I want to be with you." He touched her, and she backed away showing him her palms as a warning to keep back.

He smiled. "Petra, I love you. Damn you!"

"Too bad. I don't even like you," she told him. Then his detective brother Paul Hanson got out of his car and walked up to him and Petra saying, "Why don't you two go and cool off in the swimming pool?"

Petra frowned. "Just tell your brother to keep clear of me."

Paul smiled and said, "Banjo and Ed Black filed a complaint about you Petra. But I warned both of them off. Both of them are tucked tightly in their cell."

Just then, Redd Black drove past at full speed and fired a bullet that caught Detective Paul Hanson in his right shoulder. He then screeched away.

Detective Inspector Hanson and Petra grabbed Paul. Petra tore his shirt open and Detective Inspector Hanson looked at his arm.

"Shit!" Petra said and stamped her right foot. "How bad is he hurt?" she asked Hanson.

"He will live. As from now, I want you to back down and leave the Blacks to me," said Detective Scott Hanson. His face was angry.

"So it's my fault your brother got shot. Is that what you're trying to say? Is it? Well fuck you! Only I'm sorry it wasn't you that got shot instead of your brother. For some weeks, you've been riding on my back. I'm warning you, if you don't get off, I will take your ass to the ground!" Petra started walking to her car. Paul said to Hanson "Go after her."

"No! How did she know my name is also Brett?" Hanson asked.

"I can't answer that brother, but she's the best I have seen. I wish I'd met her before you. She's too good to let slip away. I can tell you're both attracted to each other."

"What if she really doesn't like me?" Detective Inspector Hanson asked.

"Trust me brother, I'm older than you and I've enough experience to know when someone loves someone. Have you told her how you feel? Have you ever wondered why she stuffed her knickers in your mouth, I think she's hungry for you to ask her out."

Detective Inspector Hanson smiled and asked, "Do you think so?"

"Why don't you go after her and see if I'm right."

"I'll go after her after I've taken you to the hospital," Detective Inspector Hanson said.

"By then it might be too late," Detective Paul said quivering from his pain. "Go after her brother."

"Paul, she will not go with anyone else if you're right about her loving me." And as Detective Inspector Hanson was getting into his car to take his brother to the hospital, the ambulance siren sounded and within few minutes the ambulance arrived and Detective Paul Hanson climbed in. As Detective Inspector Hanson was getting into the ambulance, Paul said, "Oh no brother, you go and find Petra. I'll be okay."

On Petra's way to the hospital to see Paul, she saw Lucas, one of Sydney Black's cousins. Lucas rammed into the side of her car then disappeared, then was back and rammed her car again. He fired a bullet missing her but smashing the back window and sped off. She chased him and he crashed into a wooden fence cutting his forehead and chin and a piece of wood broke off in his leg.

"Help me bitch!" he groaned loudly.

"Yes, you wicked bastard, I'll help you go to jail," said Petra and stamped the wood further into his leg. "You will pay for what you have done to those youths. I ought to put a bullet straight through your heart, but I'd rather you go to jail and be a bitch till your arse is rotten and then they kill you!" She kicked him in his mouth knocking three of his front teeth out. "The trouble with you creeps is you're nothing but bad smells. The youths you and your kind rape and then kill are no more than sixteen years old," Petra said furiously.

Lucas laughed, even though he was in pain and bleeding. Petra held her gun to his head saying, "I should blow your fucking eyes and brains across the street, but as I said, you'll serve some sons of bitches well while you're in jail." She then read him his rights and called the police and ambulance as he was groaning with pain and losing blood. Then he said to her, "When I get better, I'll give you a bad fucking bitch but in your ass busting you wide open." His laughing was so irritating that Petra shouted, "Shut up!" but the more she told him to shut up the more he laughed.

He stopped laughing when he heard the ambulance siren and said, "You lose, bitch! But I'll tell you this, they will take me to hospital, patch me up, give me three false teeth then pat me on my shoulder saying, son, you're lucky to be alive. Then in a week or two, I'm free to catch up with you and fuck you inside out!" He laughed so loudly that it sounded fierce.

"Oh no, you're going to jail for at least ten years for selling drugs," Petra told him.

"You're really stupid! We own the police force," he said.

"Well if that's the case, fuck you!" Then she shot him in the chest. He groaned in pain. "You don't even want the Black brothers,' he said. 'The man you want is my Uncle Johnny Blimps. He's the master, leader and genius and he has most of your bitches tied around him while he kicks their asses." He laughed. "Bitch, you want to clean out your police force and praise my uncle for his smartness." Then his head sagged and he died with his eyes wide open.

Within minutes the street was crowded with onlookers. Superintendent Peterson and Detective Todd, Officer Hodge and Detective Inspector Hanson rushed through the crowds.

"How did this happen, Officer Jackson?" Superintendent Peterson asked.

"Why don't you ask him?" Petra bawled out in anger.

"How the hell do you expect me ask a dead man if he's dead?" The people laughed, as did Officer Hodge and Detective Inspector Hanson.

"Officer Jackson, I want some answers and now!" Superintendent Peterson said, outraged.

"With the information I have found out, I'll deal with it. Your dirty asses sit back and relax sipping tea and coffee. You don't give a damn about who's been raped, sold as a sex slave or been murdered. Do we have to wait until any of your family are chained and sold for sex, raped and murdered before you stop those wicked and festered bastards from killing and raping people? Now if you will all excuse me I have a Johnny Blimps to go and see," Petra said.

"You still have not answered my question, Jackson."

"Superintendent, I don't want to disrespect you. I have nothing to tell you at this time, except he keeled over and died staring at me; as you can see his eyes are open. Also I will not stand aside and let your crooked cops encourage those criminal bastards to feed on the weak and scared people. You can now get out of my way and stay the hell away from me," Petra said then got into her car and rested her forehead on the steering wheel sinking into deep thought over what the Black family had done to her mother. She lifted her head up to see Superintendent Peterson walking towards her car. She drove away.

"Officer Jackson," Superintendent Peterson shouted. She ignored him. "Officer Hodge, go after Officer Jackson and arrest her."

"On what charge Super?"

"Prostitution, murder, attempted burglary, and harassing an officer of a higher rank, me! I don't care on what charge, just go and arrest her so that I can keep her under my control until she gives me some answers."

"If you want her so badly, you go and arrest her. Each time she spits the truth out, you're ready to have her arrested," Officer Hodge said.

Superintendent Peterson looked shamefully at Detectives Hanson and Todd. Hanson and Todd looked at each other and burst out laughing then got into their cars and drove away.

"You arseholes! You will both answer to me!" Superintendent Peterson shouted then spat on the ground before he got into his car and looked hard at Officer Hodge to see him smiling. "You can wipe that smile off your face then take me home to get something before we go the station."

"Ok Super," Officer Hodge said and he took the Superintendent to his home and waited in the car. A few minutes later, the Superintendent returned eating a slice of cake and carrying a small wrapped parcel. He got in the car.

"Where do you want me to take you now?" Officer Hodge asked.

"To the station, Officer Hodge."

Meanwhile, as Petra was going into Nichols Superdrug store, she met Lucas' girlfriend coming out. "I'm Lucas' woman," she said with a straight face.

"So?" Petra asked.

"I'm glad the bastard's dead. He forced me into prostitution. Did you make him beg for his life before you killed him?"

"Look here woman, I don't care whose woman you are. Just keep out of my way and leave me alone. If you want to know if I enjoyed killing him, the answer is no, I didn't. But I am not sorry either. Now will you get out of my face and take yourself off somewhere?"

"Look Petra, I heard a lot about you, and I think you're doing a good job, helping us people. It means a lot. You care about people and I respect you. You're not like the other police officers that have failed to protect us. We need you Petra and us folks like you… I mean Officer Jackson. You make us feel safe. About the Black family, they have raped and murdered folks, sold young girls as sex slaves and sold drugs with help from the crooked police for too long. I think it's time the Black organisation got crumbled and blown to hell. Petra, you might not believe me, but oh my, how I wished for my bastard man to be dead. Whichever way, I couldn't care a damn. Just take a look at my neck where the bastard cut me when I refused to go to bed with Judge O'Neil. I'm Susie," Susie said and she lifted her hair off her neck to show Petra the long proud flesh scar. "However, the bastard is going six feet in the ground and I don't think I need a man in my life just yet. My God, when he was alive, he had so many men grab me with their filthy hands forcing my lips on their rank smelly crotches. Anyway, thanks for doing a great job," Susie said.

"Well Susie, I think it's time I left," Petra said, but before she left she asked Susie, "Why didn't you go to the police about Judge O'Neil?"

"Are you out of your mind? If I'd gone to the police, I might have got killed, leaving my four-year-old son motherless. He would have been put in a home as my mother didn't want to know my son or me. He's seven now."

"Surely there were some good police officers that would have protected you?"

"Petra, I'm sorry, but I found it hard to trust any police at that time, as most of them were working for the Blacks. Even judges, superintendents, detectives, doctors and officers are on the Black's payroll. So what chance do you think I would have had? Petra, you must be the only cop who cares about us. However, I got a house out of the bastard Lucas and a million pounds. Pet, you give us girls hope. I'm sure they would agree with me. You're the best amongst the rest. Look at me. I'm so ashamed to even face my family."

"Don't worry Susie. In time your family will find you and your son. Just give them time," Petra said.

Susie smiled nodding her head and said, "I hope my family get in touch with me, I have felt lost without them. Now that the bastard's are out of my son and my lives for good I can live a decent life."

"Look Susie, I have to go and fix my car for a second time then go to the hospital to see a friend. You give your family time and they will come running to you and your son. You'll see I'm right," Petra said.

"Officer Jackson, thanks for listening, and remember you're our hero and the best. And good luck in bringing down those bastard Black brothers and their kind. I'll pray for you at all times."

Petra smiled and left. Susie smiled and tears dropped on to her bosom. Then she drove home.

Petra went to Mr Parker's garage to have her car fixed and new windows put in. "Well, your car is damaged badly this time. It seems you're unlucky. What if I bought this and sell you another?"

Petra smiled.

"I'll give you a good deal."

"Well, what the heck, Godfather, can you show me around?"

"Sure."

Mr Parker showed some cars to Petra. She stopped at the black Mercedes and smiled. "You like that one?"

"Yes I do. But I couldn't afford the payment."

"Come with me Petra. I'll take your car and you owe me four Gs. Here are the keys, it's brand new."

"Godfather, why would you treat me this special with the car?"

"I'll tell you one day, but it's not because I'm your Godfather," he said. He didn't tell Petra that he had been dating her mother for eight months before she got married to her dad.

Petra drove to the hospital to see Detective Paul Hanson. "How are you now?" she asked.

"I'm getting better by the minute, but I'm still in a considerable amount of pain. Mind you, I could have been killed."

"Then you wouldn't be complaining about your pain," said Petra. He laughed, so did Petra.

"Seriously Petra, my brother loves you."

"I'm here to see you. I must go and see another friend in the other ward."

"I can tell you're in love with my brother too."

Petra kissed him on his forehead, smiled and left to see Ira in the other ward. "I heard you were admitted last night."

"Yes, my wound has opened up and I was bleeding."

"I'm sorry."

Ira smiled broadly and said, "I would like you to go to my house, here's my key. In my wardrobe you will find a disc in my plain grey suit jacket pocket. Take it home and have a look."

"What would I be looking for?"

"You see for yourself," he said as Nurse Williams walked towards them. "Hello Mr Handsome, I need to take your temperature before changing your bandages."

Petra smiled and kissed Ira on his forehead and left. On her way downstairs, she met Officer Phillips and Detective Bryan. "How is he?" Detective Bryan asked.

"How is who?" Petra asked.

"Ira. We are on our way to see him; we're good friends. Anyway, I've heard so much about you and I'd like to meet you again," Detective Bryan said.

"Well detective, I don't think that's going to be possible," Petra said. Detective Bryan gave her an inviting smile and walked away. Petra smiled saying to herself, "Detective Bryan, you're not looking too bad, but I have my eyes on the man I love." She was going to the machine for coffee when she bumped into her dearest friend Dr Stanley. They were so happy to see each other that they embraced. After they parted, Stanley said, "Petra my dearest friend, I'm feeling so happy to see you once again."

"Oh Stanley, I'm glad to see you too. How's Elizabeth?"

"She's fine and she's nearly ready to give birth," he replied looking joyous.

"That's marvellous. I must visit her soon."

"Oh, she's still seven weeks away. Why don't you come over? I'm sure Liz would like to have you for dinner again. We'll be having a dance for doctors and nurses. Why don't you come and have some fun?"

"I would love to, but I don't think I can make it. Anyway, thanks for the invitation. Tell Elizabeth I will come and see her soon."

"There's an invitation for two if you change your mind. Elizabeth and I will be there," he said.

Petra took the invitation and said, "I'll try."

Stanley smiled. Petra turned to leave then Stanley said, "Pet my dear friend, I'll take very good care of your friend Ira. Anyway, I do hope that you'll come to the dance. Our two friends Jenny and Faith will be there."

"Okay Stan, I'll try, but I see Jenny and Faith often."

Just then Dr Stanley was called on his bleeper to ward eight. He asked Petra to excuse him. Petra smiled. Before he left Petra thanked him and said, "I'll see you again soon, my faithful true friend."

Stanley smiled and walked away quickly. Petra watched him disappear behind the entrance door, then she left the hospital. On her way home, she went to the Black Pearl Casino to look for her friend Amelia. Turning to go to the fifth gambling casino table, she saw a young black Pete roughly handling eighty-year-old Madame Stall and trying to take her handbag. Petra went to him. "Oi ... you take your hands off her."

"And what if I don't?"

"I'll kick your ass to kingdom come."

"Tell the old bitch to pay up and take her with you after she pays me the eight hundred pounds she owes me from a gambling debt. If she can't pay the amount, the old bitch must hand over her house to me."

"She must hand over her house to you because of a lousy eight hundred pounds? Anyway, who are you calling old bitch?"

"Look bitch! Just tell the vintage to pay up then both of you get the fuck out of here and don't come back."

"Madame is there any truth in what that smelly armpit bulldog said," Petra asked Madame Stall.

"No," she replied looking frightened. "I was cheated out of ten thousand pounds less than ten minutes ago. I tried to win back some from what he cheated me out of, but he kept my winnings. So, how could I owe him money?"

"Look old women, I want my eight hundred pounds or your house keys," Pete said and pushed forward his broad chest. His mate David went to him. "Dave, will you tell that old bitch to give me my money?"

Dave looked hard at him and shook his head as he saw Petra. He asked Pete to go with him but Pete pushed him away and turned to Petra and Madame Stall, saying, "You bitches." Petra boxed him in his mouth and blood came running out. "You foul-mouthed stinking sweaty armpit. This old bitch as you called her is my godmother and she owes you fuck all. She claims that you cheated her out of ten thousand pounds and I believe her. So, I'm asking you nicely to pay her the ten thousand pounds so that we can get out of here as you asked."

"Bitch, you're talking through your pussy. You tell your old godmother to pay up or her house is mine. Or better still, you can give all my nine employees one year's supply of free fucks." He spat blood out on his T-shirt. Petra thumped him in the mouth again and his blood was now dripping on the floor. The players stopped playing and watched. Some shook their heads. Dave rushed to Pete saying, "I want to speak to you."

"After these bitches pay up," Pete said.

"Pete I saw her hit you. She is…" Pete pushed Dave away. "Look Dave, you can get back to your table and let me take care of these bitches." Pete faced Petra saying, "Bitch, I'm going to shove my dick up your ass right here so everyone can watch."

"Pete…"

"Dave, I told you to get back to your table and leave the bitch to me. Anyway, how come you know the bitch?"

"Pete, she's Petra, Officer Forbes' daughter. I believe she's a cop," Dave said.

"What the fuck do I care," Pete said.

Dave stood before Petra and she said, "Dave, as your friend said, you better get back to your table."

Pete drew a knife on Petra and she shot him in the hand. He dropped the knife and then she shot him in his right foot.

"Now you bags of shit! You owe my godmother ten thousand pounds and she wants to be paid now with eight hundred pounds interest, so all together she wants ten thousand eight hundred pounds and now," Petra demanded. Then she said, "And for every minute that goes by, one hundred will be added."

Dave rushed back to them and saying to Petra, "I don't know what all this is about but you are scaring my customers."

"You should have asked your foul-mouthed friend to tell you what all this is about before I scared your customers. However, your friend stole the twelve thousand pounds my godmother won."

Dave gave her a card for twelve thousand pounds saying, "Take it to the checkout, get your money and both of you get out please. And I'm sorry it had to come to this."

Petra pulled the card from his hand and gave it to Madame Stall, then Pete said, "The money you gave those bitches was mine."

Dave sent him to the floor with a punch. "Get the fuck out of here before I finish you off with a bullet you thieving bastard. I've only been proved what I've heard about you."

Petra walked with Madame Stall to cash her money. "I'm Mrs Woods," she told Petra, not letting her know that she was actually Madame Stall.

Petra left Madame Stall to cash her money and went nosing around. After Curtsy gave Madame Stall her money, she said,: "Well, nice to see you again and do be careful carrying that money. Would you like me to call you a taxi?"

"No thanks Curtsy, my goddaughter is with me. She's walking my way now." Petra got to Madame Stall and smiled.

"Well my dear, I think you should take care of this money until we get home," Madame Stall said and she passed the money to Petra. Then as she and Petra turned to leave, a well-built six-foot white man who looked about twenty-nine barred Petra from passing. "I believe you and the old turkey have our money under false pretences," he said. Petra smiled and pointed her gun at his knee. "I heard you have a habit of capping people's knees," he said.

"Rue, let them go. Madame is a regular customer and she's lost a lot of money in the past."

The man moved, letting Petra and Madame Stall go.

Outside the casino Petra laughed. She asked Madame Stall, "Will you be okay to go home by yourself?"

"I think so."

"Did you tell those snakes where you lived?"

"No my dear, I don't think I did," she said, looking scared and worried.

"Do you have a car?"

"No Petra. But I'd be grateful if you would call me a taxi. With so much money, you never know. Besides, I can't be sure if any of them will not follow me. Oh Petra, let me give you half of this money."

"Oh no. You have earned every penny of that money, I really don't need your money. But I'll be happy if you let me take you home."

"Petra, I'll let you take me home if you say you'll stay and have a drink with me."

"Okay. I'm a police officer by the way," Petra said and opened the car door for Madame Stall to get in. Petra drove her home, walked her to her door, watched her take her door key from a hanging flower basket, open her door and walk in. She switched on the lights and invited Petra in. "I live alone."

"Yes, I've noticed."

"You noticed dear?"

"Yes Mrs Woods, everything in this room is so in its place and very tidy," Petra said.

Madame Stall smiled putting down a silver tray with two china cups filled with tea on it and asked Petra, "Would you like something to eat?"

"I wouldn't say no to a sandwich," Petra said.

"Well Petra, if you wash your hands, you could make us both a sandwich. I'll go up to my room to put this money in a safe place until Monday morning when I can put it into my bank account."

Petra smiled and washed and dried her hands. She took ham from the fridge and made two sandwiches, then took them into the large dining room. A few minutes later, Madame Stall came into the dining room and they ate and drank.

Petra got up. "Well Mrs Woods, thanks for the sandwich and tea but I've got to go now."

"So soon?" Madame Stall asked looking very pitiful.

"Mrs Woods, I've got to go as I'm on early morning shift. But I could pay you a visit tomorrow lunchtime if it's okay with you."

"I would like you to come and visit me tomorrow at any time you like. I will even give you a key to let yourself in."

"Mrs Woods you have only known me for about ten minutes. I might be a thief or a killer and have lied to you about being a police officer."

"Petra, I've been around too long to know when someone is a criminal and I'm certain that you are not one. But from what I saw about you, you stand for no nonsense. Well, I'll see you tomorrow?"

"Goodbye Mrs Woods and thank you for supper," Petra said.

Madame Stall showed Petra out.

"Mrs Woods, please make sure you lock the doors and windows, and don't answer the door to anyone. If you need me, call me. This is my phone number." Petra gave her a hug then left smiling and got into her car, waved goodbye and drove home. As her mother heard the door shut she called, "Pet, is that you love?"

"Yes Mum."

"Your supper is on the cooker."

"Okay Mum, but all I need now is a bath then some sleep."

"Pet, you can tell me, your mother, about your boyfriend?"

"Mother I don't have a boyfriend. Now, go back to bed. I'll see you in the morning."

"Well if you don't want your supper put it in the fridge. Oh and your Grandma will be coming to live with us soon."

"That's good news mother."

"Oh, and there were two phone calls for you from Dr Sean and Julia. Julia said to call her at her place tomorrow afternoon at two 'o clock and Dr Sean said to call him as soon as you get home. No matter what time it is."

"Oh no," said Petra.

"He said it's urgent."

Petra rang Dr Sean.

"Yes who's this?" he asked.

"Petra."

Dr Sean sat up in his bed. "Pet, I would really like you to accompany me on a trip to New York in two weeks. I will be going to one of my best friend's wedding. I would really like you to come with me as company."

"Sean, can I get back to you tomorrow and let you know?"

"Like you did a couple of weeks ago?"

"I'm very sorry about that, but I had some troubles on my hands and I totally forgot to call you."

"Petra, I really would like to get to know you. I would also like you to come with me to New York. This would give us time to get to know each other. You don't have to worry about money."

"I'll call you tomorrow." Petra smiled.

"Afternoon or evening?"

"Sometime tomorrow I'll call you. Goodnight Sean." Petra put the phone down. Dr Sean put his down smiling. He lay back in bed thinking of Petra and found that he couldn't settle. He got out of bed and slipped off his pyjama top, had a cold glass of grapefruit juice with little whiskey in and eventually he fell asleep.

Chapter 12

The following morning at ten o'clock Petra called to see Julia. Her husband answered the door.

"I came to see Julia."

"I'm sorry Petra, Julia left a few minutes ago to see her father. I will tell her you called."

"Please do and I will give her a call."

"Would you like a drink?"

"No thanks."

"Would you like to come in and wait? I'm sure she won't be long," Todd said.

"No, no thank you. Just let her know I called and I'll call tomorrow at about two o'clock. Goodbye Todd."

"Petra, I'm glad you're here. Do you mind if I speak to you about your father's death?"

"That man has been dead six years now. He wasn't my father and I do mind speaking to you about such a dog as him. I do hope you'll never ask me about him again," Petra said.

Not long after Petra had left, Julia let herself into her house to find the children beating each other with toys. "Todd!" She heard the lawnmower going and looked out the back to see him cutting the lawn. She went to him. "I didn't expect you to mow the lawn now."

"Well, if I don't do it today, it wouldn't have got done for another two months as I wouldn't have the time."

"Todd honey, I appreciate you doing the lawn but leaving the children in the living room on their own, they could have had an accident."

"Jul honey, I wouldn't have left them if I knew they were not safe. Besides, they're playing with soft toys and I have looked in on them often. By the way, Petra came to see you, but as you were out she said she would call you."

As Todd looked at Julia and saw sadness written all over her face he asked, "What's wrong honey?"

"Why do you ask? Do I look like there's something wrong with me?"

"Well, I saw that look before when you got pregnant with our son."

"Well Todd, I can't hide my looks or pretend I'm happy that I'm pregnant again."

"Are you sure?" he asked her smiling.

"No, but I've got morning sickness the same as when I was carrying P.T.," she said.

Todd hugged her and they walked inside to their children.

Later that day, Kim took her and Todd's daughter Justine to see Todd's mother but they only found Joanne there. Julia also went to see Joanne, but when she spoke to Joanne she seemed distant and hardly wanted to speak.

"What's the matter Joanne?" Julia asked her.

"Oh nothing," Joanne replied. But as Julia looked at her, she said, "I have a toothache."

Julia smiled as she didn't believe her.

As Kim and her six-year-old daughter walked into the house, little Justine walked to Julia and held her hand. Joanne smiled. Julia lowered her eyes on Justine looking at her then asked, "What's your name honey?"

"Justine. My mummy's in the other room talking on the phone. Would you like to see my mummy?"

"Yes honey, but another time as I have to leave now," Julia said.

Joanne smiled. "Family can look so much alike but her mother hasn't said who her dad is."

Kim walked into the room. "Hello Julia."

"Hello Kim."

Joanne said nothing, but smiled and went upstairs then returned shortly to see Julia's hand on her forehead. "What are you thinking Julia?"

"I forgot I had to be somewhere right now and I'm late," Julia said.

"I was hoping you would spend more time with me," Joanne said.

"I wish I could, but really, I have to go. I will see you soon, take care."

Julia went home and phoned her brother Curtis asking him to come over to her house. Curtis went to see her. "Curtis, have you seen Kim's little girl yet?"

"Yes Julia. Why do you ask me?"

"Well, there's no point in me beating around the bush. I was with Joanne earlier when Kim and her little girl walked into the house. Believe me Curtis, she looked so much like my little girl Candice."

"Julia, Kim and Todd are family," Curtis said smiling.

"Curtis, the child has a likeness to mine and looking at her, I could see Todd's face in hers."

"Julia, I think you're being paranoid over nothing. Todd loves you and I think he's faithful to you. So sis, I don't think you have to worry about it."

"Well thanks for putting my mind at rest brother, but, I think I'm pregnant again and I really didn't want another child so soon."

"How does Todd feel about you having another baby?" Curtis asked.

"I don't really know. I told him I thought I was pregnant and he kissed me."

"There you go, that means he's happy," Curtis said.

"Curtis, I don't want to be breeding like a rabbit. Todd and I have been married for six years and already I have two children with a third on its way. With two children, I can hardly have a decent bath. I can't even go anywhere without having to rush back. Curtis, I'm not sure that I want to have this child."

"Look sis, you know dad and I wouldn't let you go without. We share minding the kids so you can have some time for yourself."

"I know that, but it's not that that's bothering me. I just can't cope with three babies dangling around my feet crying and I don't know what to do."

"Sis, Irene is like a grandma to your children. If you should have this one, you could prevent having any more children, even though they're very precious. So many folks would go to great lengths to have one. Just have this one for us and especially for you and Todd."

"Okay Curt," said Julia.

"Julia, I love you."

"I love you too."

"Now, where are my favourite niece and nephew? Oh, and by the way, what can you tell me about Joanne?"

"Curt, I don't follow you. What do you mean?" Julia asked.

"Is she a nice girl?" Curtis asked interestedly.

"Yes, I believe she is. Why?"

"I love her. I'm going to ask her to be my wife, with your and dad's blessing of course."

"Well Curtis, if you want to marry Joanne, you have my blessing. She is a lovely person and I honestly think she's the one for you. How long have you been seeing her?" asked Julia

"The truth is, I've never asked her out. I hardly see her, but I love her and I would like to marry her very soon if she will have me," Curtis said.

"Well, why don't you go and tell her how you feel about her and if she feels the same, then you can talk about marriage. I'm sure dad would love a couple more grandchildren."

"Yes, I would like a couple of my own some day. I tried to buy myself a home, but our dad told me to live with him and Irene and save my money. Irene is like a mother to you and me. She gave me seven thousand pounds and told me to buy myself a car."

"That's because you're using dad's too often," Julia said with a giggle.

"Was dad complaining?"

"No Curtis, I heard him tell Irene that you needed your own car. He was going to buy you one. Well, at least you got your own car and a new one at that. As for Irene, she is like a mother to us."

"Yes, she is," Curtis agreed.

"I'm glad dad married her. The children love her so much and she spoils them rotten. They call her nanny," Julia said.

"Well, I'm going to see Joanne now. If she accepts me, we'll have a little get-together next Saturday. I will ask Irene to prepare the food and I'll buy the drinks if that's okay with you."

"Curtis, that would be lovely," said Julia

"Then I'll let you know."

"Okay Curtis, you had better go and see Joanne now, then come back to me with a yes. She'll marry you," Julia said.

Curtis smiled then left in his car to see Joanne. That same night Curtis rang Julia telling her that Joanne was very pleased when he asked her to marry him. Without thinking, she said yes. As soon as he got home he told Irene and his dad the good news; they were very happy.

"What about the family getting together to celebrate your and Joanne's engagement?" Julia asked.

Curtis giggled. "The get-together will be this Saturday as I will be working the following weekend. Julia, do you mind getting some drinks in? I'll ask Irene to cook some food. Just our families are welcome to accept Joanne as my fiancée and my future wife. Here is four hundred pounds for the food and drinks."

"Don't worry my big brother. You keep your money, everything is on me."

"Oh Julia, bring Todd and the children," said Curtis and they both hung up.

As Soon as Todd walked into the house, Julia told him that Curtis asked Joanne to marry him and she accepted. So he's having a little celebration with the family and would like us to come over to take part in the celebration this Saturday.

"Oh," Todd said with hardly any breath.

"What's the matter with you Todd?"

"Does it look as if something is the matter with me?" Todd snapped at her thinking she knew about Kim's daughter being his.

Julia said nothing more to Todd but went to bathe her two children then put them to bed. She went to bed shortly afterwards leaving him in the living room drinking whiskey.

The following morning, Julia went into the living room and saw Todd sleeping on the settee. She woke him, "Hello honey," he said. "I fell asleep after I had eaten and had a couple of shots of scotch. Why didn't you wake me?"

"I did try but you were deep in dreamland. Todd, I'm taking the children to see Mum."

"Okay."

Julia drove her and her kids to see her mother-in-law and let them in. "Irene," she called. "Your dad is at work."

"Good," Julia said. "It's you I've come to see."

"What's wrong Jul, don't tell me you and Todd are having problems."

"Oh no, it's nothing like that. Irene, I think I'm pregnant again and since I've told Todd, he seems to be so distant. I don't know if I should have an abortion or not?"

"Julia, you'll do no such thing. I'm always here for you and Curtis and the grandchildren. Did you know that I was never married until your father married me," Irene said.

"But you said your husband was dead."

"Julia, I lied because I was ashamed that I wasn't married. I was pregnant because of my father. He raped me when my mother was in the hospital dying from a tumour." Tears welled up in Irene's eyes. "My father used to come into my room on Friday and Saturday nights when he came back from the pub and rape me. I told my Aunt Helen and she called me a liar. She then went to my father with what I told her. He said I was a liar and beat me in front of my aunt. My aunt slapped me and stopped me from going to her house. She said I was a bad influence on her daughter Iona. I didn't complain to anyone else because I'd no one to complain to. My father liked that. He started coming into my room three nights a week to rape me. After he got me pregnant, he got a Miss Johnston to give me a backstreet abortion. She almost killed me. Two weeks later he raped me twice in one week but this time he was wearing condoms. Then when my mother died, he came into my room and wanted to rape me. I ran away.

"Three days later my Aunt Helen was searching for me. I decided that I had to go home on the fourth day, but as I was getting close to home, I saw about four policemen. Then as I got to our gate, I saw Miss Johnston in handcuffs in a police car. As I looked at her, she said she had killed the son of a bitch, my dad, when she found out the truth about him. I asked her how she found out. She said my dad confessed to her when he was tipsy. So she stabbed him with a knife straight through his heart. I cried feeling sorry for Miss Johnston, but she told me not to worry. Two days after she had been locked up, however, one of her cell companions found her dead in bed. They found out she had had a massive heart attack; she had a pacemaker. I didn't want to have anything else to do with my Aunt Helen even though she cried and asked me to forgive her. So I left home in search of work at the age of sixteen. I didn't stop working or running until now. Julia I'm forty-eight years old. I've some money of my own that you are very welcome to anytime you need it. You, Curtis, the children and your father are my family now. I was so happy when you and Curtis accepted me."

"Oh Irene, I'm glad dad married you. I love you."

"Thanks Julia. Now, do you want some breakfast?"

"I wouldn't say no, but I have to be home soon to release Todd from the kitchen. He's helping me to cook dinner before he goes to work for two o'clock and Petra is coming to see me."

Irene made breakfast for her and Julia. After they had eaten, Julia insisted that she would put the plates in the dishwasher.

"Have you any money of your own sweetheart?"

"Yes Irene, I have some."

When Irene saw the hesitance on Julia's face she said, "I don't want you or the children go without."

"Irene, I'm okay, I really am. Todd's looking after us very well. So far, he has never let us want for anything. If I should really need something and can't afford it, of course I'll come to you or dad. But really, Todd's treating us first class."

"Julia, I'm glad to hear that," Irene said. "Anyway this is for you; it's your wedding gift. I know it's nearly six years late, but you're my daughter now. Here take it."

"Take what Irene?"

"Just a little something, it's nothing much. You could put it away for when you most need it and don't want to bother Todd. Julia, I'm really happy to be part of the family. I know that I can never take your mother's place, but I would like to be as near as a mother to you and Curtis, a Grandma to the children and also a good wife to your dad. I don't want you to say anything. I'm spoiling you a little." Irene laughed.

Julia looked at the cheque. When she saw it was for twelve thousand pounds, her eyes popped wide open. The surprised look on her face brought a cheerful smile to Irene's face. Julia stared at Irene saying, "Thanks Irene, but this must be all your savings. No, it's too much for me to accept."

"Well Julia," said Irene. "I've twice this amount, and with no other family but you, the children and Curtis, I thought giving it to you now would ease some pressure off my forgetful brain. Your father doesn't need it. You're young with two babies and with another one on the way. Since you can't share the home with us any more, Curtis and Joanne will be living here with your father and me for the time being. So you take that money and put it away for when you need it. I also have some money tied up which both you and Curtis' children will inherit. Oh, your father told me that he would be putting some money in a trust fund for the grandchildren too."

"Oh Irene, can I call you Mum? I've got to go now before you make me cry my eyes out and before Todd comes looking for us. Thanks for this amount of money," Julia said with tears in her eyes.

"Julia you can bring the children over every Saturday as I have nowhere to go. Starting this Saturday, I would like to take you and the children shopping then have a meal. I want to treat the children."

"Okay Mum." Julia hugged Irene telling her, "Thank you, I love you." Irene smiled then walked Julia and the children to the gate then watched them drive away. When Irene got back in her house she said to herself, "Julia honey, I love you and the kids," then a bright smile came on her face.

On Julia's way home she saw Kim and her little daughter going into the Paradise fish and chip shop on Clover Street. Julia reduced her speed to look at them. She looked hard at Kim's child; she shook her head then looked back at her daughter Candice. "Todd, what have you done, Kim's child looks so much like mine," Julia whispered. She dried tears from her eyes as flashbacks of Kim when she'd kissed Todd and made a pass at him went through her mind. She pulled over to the kerb, looked hard at her four-year-old daughter Candice again and was certain that Kim's daughter and hers looked so much alike. After looking at her daughter one more time she faced the steering wheel and closed her eyes, trying to hold her tears back.

"Mummy, why are you crying?" her little girl asked.

"I'm not crying honey. I poked my finger in my eye, that's why it's watering."

The shock Julia had experienced almost caused her to crash into the back of another car as she drove off too fast and was unable to stop when the driver stopped at the crossing to give way to passers-by. As she slightly touched the back of the driver's car, she realised how close she was behind him. The driver got out of his car and walked up to her. He knocked on her car window. She wound down the window halfway and looked at him.

"Woman, what's the matter with you? Are you on drugs, or are you half asleep?" he asked.

"Oh no sir, my thoughts were so far away, and thanks for being so polite and understanding."

"Lady, I was only polite to you because you don't look like a road hog. So please pay attention to your driving and don't let your thoughts get the better of you, especially when you have kids in your car."

"Yes, of course, thank you very much sir," Julia said.

"You have lovely kids," the driver said giving little Candice a nice smile. Then he got back into his car and went about his business while Julia went home to meet Kim and her daughter sitting in her living room.

"Todd saw us and picked us up just as we came out the fish and chip shop."

Todd looked at Julia with a guilty look as Julia was looking very shocked knowing that she had just seen Kim with her daughter going into the fish and chip shop.

Candice held her father's hand saying, "I saw my other uncle."

"What's the matter darling and what is Candice talking about?" Todd asked.

"Oh, I was speaking to a driver. As he's white she thought he was your brother."

Todd laughed then lifted up Candice and kissed her. Then Candice saw Kim's little girl Justine and jumped down from her father's arms and went to be with Justine. Julia walked into the kitchen.

Todd followed behind. "Why are you looking so upset Jul?" Todd asked.

"Why is Kim here?"

"Jul, I picked her up on my way to see my mother, but I came here first to find out if you were back before I went to work."

"Todd, I almost bumped into the back of the driver's car that Candice thought was your brother."

"What made you almost bump into the back of his car?" Todd asked.

Julia had a really good look at Kim's daughter and Todd. She could see the resemblance clearly but she said nothing, smiled, then went upstairs and sat on her bed crying. When she heard footsteps coming up the stairs, she dried her eyes quickly and took her son to the bathroom to bathe him as he had messed himself. While she was soaping him, Todd walked in.

"Julia, I'm taking Kim and her daughter home."

Julia didn't answer. He held her by her shoulders, twirled her to face him and kissed her. She pulled away from him. "What's the matter with you Jul?"

"When you want to bring your woman in our home, would you let me know?"

"Jul, Kim meant nothing to me. She's here because we're family. Look Jul, I'm taking the day off. I'm taking Kim and her daughter home then I'll be back."

"Yes," Julia's voice croaked.

An hour later, Julia and the children took a taxi to Todd's mother's house.

"You just missed your husband," Joanne said.

"I wasn't looking for my husband. My children and I are here to visit their grandparents if it's all right with you."

"Sure Julia, whatever your husband's doing, it won't trouble me," Joanne said.

"Joanne, I shouldn't talk to you that way and I apologise."

"That's okay Julia. By the way, your brother asked me to marry him and I said yes. Julia, I thought he wasn't that interested in me."

"Joanne, Curtis adores you. Do you love him?"

"If I didn't, I wouldn't have accepted his proposal. Yes Julia I love him."

"I'm so happy for you Joanne."

"Thanks, anyway, why don't you, Todd, Curtis and I have dinner out tonight to celebrate my engagement to your brother? My treat," Joanne said smiling as she was looking happy.

While Joanne was speaking to Julia, Julia looked so distant. "Julia, I'm speaking to you."

Julia raised her eyebrows smiling. "What were you saying?"

"Julia, I'm asking you and Todd to have dinner with Curtis and I tonight at the Bamboo Shay Restaurant. Would you and Todd like to come to celebrate with Curtis and me?"

"Sure, oh yes, Joanne. Todd and I would be very happy to have dinner with you and Curtis."

"Are you sure Julia?"

"Of course I would love to, but the truth is, I don't know if Todd has anything planned as he took today off."

"Well, we won't be going to dinner until seven."

"Joanne, we'd be happy to."

"Julia, Kim's child is..."

But Joanne said nothing more, because then Mrs Todd walked into the room with biscuits and pop for her two grandchildren. "Julia, are you okay? Todd told me you're expecting again."

"Yes. I am. After this one, I don't think I will want to have any more though." Julia forced a smiled.

Mrs Todd smiled. "I wanted at least four children. Two of each, but I ended up with two sons and a daughter. Still, I should be very thankful as many people can't have any."

"Anyone like some coffee," Joanne asked.

"Yes please," Mrs Todd said.

Julia sat looking downhearted.

"Look Julia, cheer up sweetie, I'll be here to help you. Having three kids, it's not really that much. I'm sure both grandparents will help you look after them. Julia, I'm glad I'll be your sister-in-law soon. I would like to have at least four children, two of each. Jul, what would you like to have this time a boy or a girl?"

"I really don't mind. I just want him or her to be healthy."

"Well, whatever you have, I'm sure Todd will be happy," Joanne said.

"By the way Julia, your friend Petra, have you known her very long?" Joanne asked interestedly.

"Well, I have known her for at least six years. I think she's a nice person. She's Candice's godmother. Anyway, yes, I like her, I really do. She's straightforward and honest. That's why I asked her to be Candice's godmother," Julia said.

"Yes, she seems like a nice person," Joanne said.

Julia smiled. "Well I have to get home before Todd comes looking for us."

Just then the front door opened. Todd, Kim and her daughter walked into the living room. Todd came to a halt when he saw Julia. He swallowed deeply like something had got stuck in his throat.

"Todd, Julia and the children have been here for at least two hours. I think you should take them home as they came in a taxi," his mother told him. He smiled then went to Julia telling her, "Get the children ready and I'll take you home." Julia looked at him then said, "We came by taxi and we'll get a taxi home when I'm ready."

Todd lifted up his son then headed towards the front door. He said, "Julia, we'll be waiting in the car for you. Don't be too long."

"Jul, I think you should let Todd take you and the children home as it is raining heavily," Mrs Todd said.

"Yes," Julia said as she took her daughter's hand then she gave Joanne a smile before going out to the car. Todd looked at her smiling. "Julia, I love you you know." He put his hands on her knee; she gave him a dirty look. He smiled. "Julia, there's nothing going on with me and Kim so you mustn't worry. I will never leave you and my children to be with any other woman. You and my children are all I want."

"Are you sure Todd?" Julia broke her silence. "Why have you taken the day off work? I should have known you had intended to spend the day with Kim. Tell me this Todd, is Kim's child yours? How long have you been deceiving me? Todd, I saved myself until the day we were married to prove to you that I loved you so much and I thought you had been faithful throughout all that time."

"Honey, you're wrong. There's no one else in this world that I would put before you and my kids," Todd said.

Julia said nothing more. Eventually they arrived home. Todd carried his son into the house and laid him on the settee as he was sleeping.

"You can go back to your girlfriend as she might be waiting for you. My children and I will be all right now."

"Julia, what are you talking about? Kim's not my girlfriend. I'm only being nice to her because she's my cousin."

"What fucking cousin are you talking about? Don't you think I can't tell the difference when my husband's carrying on with another woman! Todd, I'm warning you, if I find out that you're sleeping with Kim I will throw you out and make sure you never see the children ever and I will divorce you."

Todd stood frozen looking at her. "What the hell are you waiting for? Why don't you go back to Kim?"

"Julia, if you don't want me to sleep with you, I'll sleep in another room."

"Todd, am I the only woman you have made love to?"

"What's brought this on honey?"

"You can't answer me, because I'm not the only one. I'm sure Kim is laughing behind my back calling me a fool. Todd, I saw the resemblance of you in Kim's child. All I have is memories and heartache that you have both left me with."

"Julia, you and my children are the ones I love. Please don't make this a newspaper headline. I was foolish to be around Kim. I'll never see her again; I'm with you. As for her child, we're family." Todd sounded shameful. "Jul..."

She stared at him and was about to speak when the telephone started ringing. He picked up the phone. "Hello."

"Hello Todd, it's me. Curtis."

"What can I do for you Curtis? Do you want to speak to your sister?"

"Has she told you that Joanne and I have invited you both out for a celebration dinner?"

"What's the occasion?" Todd asked in surprise.

"Joanne and I will be getting married three months from now. So we would like you and my sister to have dinner with us at the North Star restaurant tomorrow at seven o'clock. Irene will look after the children as I have already asked her. What do you say?"

"Curtis, it will be our pleasure," said Todd then hung up.

Curtis then called Irene to remind her that Julia would be bringing the children over the following evening. Irene was very happy to look after the children. She said, "Curtis, your father and I are always happy to babysit our grandchildren."

Meanwhile, Todd asked Julia. "Why didn't you tell me that your brother and Joanne had invited us to dinner tomorrow night?"

"I didn't think you would be interested," Julia replied.

"Well are you going to dinner?" Todd asked.

"Do you want to take Kim?"

"Julia, I don't want to hear any more about Kim; you're my wife. You and I are going to have dinner with your brother and his fiancée to celebrate their engagement, so get yourself ready tomorrow," Todd said.

Just then the phone started ringing. Julia answered.

"Hello."

"Julia, can I speak to Todd," Kim asked.

"It's Mrs Todd for you," said Julia harshly. Kim smiled then put the phone down. Julia ran into Todd's arms. "Todd you know I love you."

"I know," Todd said. "I love you very much too."

Julia left Todd to finish cooking the dinner.

After they'd eaten, she bathed the children then put them to bed, and at ten thirty they went bed. Todd dived under the covers kissing her toes up to her lips. She grabbed hold of him and took him between her legs. He slipped her pyjamas off and as he was naked and erect, he went into her and they enjoyed intimate and romantic love-making.

The following evening as it was still raining, Superintendent Peterson and Irene went to Julia's house instead and let themselves in with the key Julia had given to them.

Julia was in the bathroom putting her make up on. "Julia," Irene shouted up to her.

"I'm in the bathroom Mum." Then she stood on the landing looking down at Irene saying, "Come right up Mum."

"Mum?" Todd said teasing, but more surprised. "Todd I love her as I would love my mother. She's so good to the children. She treats dad, Curtis and me so nicely. You should call her Mum too out of respect as I am. I know she's not my blood mother, but she's the second best mother I'll ever have." As Irene was still downstairs, Julia shouted over the landing to her saying again, "Come right up Mum." Irene went upstairs to look at the children. Then she said to Julia, "Your father and I came over to stay with the children because it's raining so much."

"Oh Mum, Todd and I were going to bring the children over."

"The children are too young to be taken out in this weather at this time. You and Todd go and have that dinner with your brother and his fiancée. Julia, it's time you had a break. By the way, here's a little change for you to take."

"Don't you think you have already given me enough?" Julia said but happy.

"Honey, it's only fifty pounds. It's nice to be independent," Irene said.

"With you always giving money to me, I don't think I would be able to prove to myself that I could be independent!" Julia said.

Irene smiled, "Jul, remember you're not working any more." Irene went downstairs. Shortly after, Julia and Todd went downstairs.

"Mum, I put the children to bed. I don't think you will get any trouble from them. Candice is sleeping and P.T. is on the edge of dropping off to sleep."

"Well, you both have a good time and don't worry about the children," Irene said."

"I won't," replied Julia then she kissed Irene and her father on their cheeks before she left in the car with Todd to pick up her brother Curtis and his fiancée Joanne.

Julia let Todd and herself into her father's house with her key. Todd helped himself to a drink of brandy while Julia went upstairs to call Joanne. A few minutes later Joanne and Julia came from upstairs to join Todd and Curtis for a small brandy.

After Julia had a couple sips of brandy, Todd took the glass from her and said, "I think you've had enough." Joanne looked at Todd and he said, "I think she has had enough as she's not a lover of alcohol." And he drank the remainder.

"I haven't said a word," Joanne replied smiling. Then she glanced into Todd eyes saying, "I would like to get married in December but Curtis wants us to get married sooner."

"Well, congratulations to both you and Curtis," Todd said.

Julia hugged Joanne saying, "Oh where's my sense of humour. Congratulations honey to both you and Curtis."

Curtis hugged Julia. "Thanks sis," he said then turned to Joanne and slipped a beautiful diamond ring on her finger then blessed it with a long kiss. As he took his lips from the ring, he faced Todd and asked, "Who's ready to go?"

Todd swallowed his last drop of brandy. "Well, I'm ready. He put his arm around Julia's shoulder walking her to the door. Outside, he said to Joanne, "Curtis is a good bloke."

"Thanks, I know," Joanne said. Curtis made sure that the door was locked.

"Shall we take my car or yours Todd?" Curtis asked.

"We'll take mine," Todd said.

So they got into Todd's car. Julia and Joanne sat in the back while Curtis and Todd sat in the front. As they were approaching the restaurant, Julia said, "I hope the children are still sleeping."

"Relax Jul," Todd said.

"I was only thinking of dad and Mum."

"Here we are, one of the best restaurants in town," Curtis said. Todd parked his car under the spotlight by the side of the restaurant door then locked his car before the four of them walked in. When they walked into the diners' room, a beautiful mixed-race waitress walked up to them and escorted them to their table. Todd and Curtis pulled Julia and Joanne's chairs out for them so they could sit down.

"Would you like something to drink?" the waitress asked, smiling. "We'll have a bottle of your best champagne." The waitress smiled then left and returned shortly with the bottle of chilled champagne. "Please enjoy your champagne," she smiled. Todd looked at her with a warm smile. Then as he lowered his eyes to Julia's, she looked seriously cross with him. "Someone is in for a beating tonight when they get home," Joanne joked.

Todd and Curtis giggled then Curtis said, "I'm not guilty."

Todd giggled again as he said, "Julia knows she is and will be the only woman in my life." Joanne attempted to laugh, but as she had champagne in her mouth some squirted over Curtis' face and jacket. She swallowed. "I'm sorry honey," she said wiping his face with her handkerchief but Curtis held her hand, kissed her then said, "I'm okay honey." He dried his face with his handkerchief.

The waitress returned to take the food order. "I'm Linda," she said warmly, even though her name was displayed on her badge. "Are you sitting comfortably?" She smiled.

"Yes. Thank you," Curtis said.

"I'm happy to hear so. Well, I hope you enjoy your meals as I have enjoyed your company," she said then left.

When they began eating, the manager brought another bottle of chilled champagne to them saying, "Congratulations on your engagement Curtis and Joanne."

"Thank you," Joanne and Curtis said. The manager popped the champagne open and filled the four glasses saying, "I hope you enjoy your meals and the rest of the evening." He then rested the champagne in the bucket beside the first one to keep it chilled. He smiled then left.

As they tucked into their meals, an attractive young white woman went on stage and introduced a very tall and handsome young black man, saying, "Please welcome Duncan, ladies and gentlemen. He has the most charming and smooth voice that would charm even the most aggressive animal. Ladies and gentlemen, I give you Duncan."

Duncan trotted on stage and as he began to sing Lady In Red heads turned to watch him, especially the women's. As Julia turned to look at him, Todd held her hand. She turned and looked at him and smiled showing him how much she loved him. Curtis wiped his lips and kissed Joanne telling her, "I love you so much." Then as she put food in her mouth, Curtis began eating again.

While Julia was eating, she happened to cast her eyes on Petra on the other side of the room. Petra rose her glass to her with a smile. At this time the singer was singing and he was walking towards Petra with his eyes firmly on her.

"Petra, who's the lovely lady waving to us? She's beautiful," Madame Stall asked.

"She is a close friend of mine and her name is Julia. Her husband Todd is wearing the brown suit and her brother Curtis and fiancée Joanne are the other couple."

As Petra and Joanne's eyes met, Petra waved to her; Joanne and Julia waved back.

As the singer finished his song, loud applause echoed through the room. The singer then took Petra's hand, kissed it and winked at her then asked her, "Would you like a drink?"

"No thank you," Petra said but giving him a friendly smile.

"I hope I will see you again," he said.

Petra smiled but didn't reply. He went away smiling then walked up the aisle. A loud applause came rattling again until he disappeared out of sight.

Just then the waitress Linda went to Petra and Madame Stall to take their order for food. At this time Sydney Black and company were sitting at table number ten.

Sydney beckoned one of the waitresses to come to him. "Yes sir, what would you like?"

Sydney smiled. "I want you to take a bottle of your best frosted and chilled champagne to table seven and give it to the most beautiful young lady with my love. Charge it to my bill."

The waitress smiled and left to go get the champagne then she took it to Petra with his compliments.

Petra looked up at the waitress, smiled, then looked over at Sydney Black. He rose his glass smiling.

"You're very beautiful," the waitress said.

Petra took the champagne. "Thank you," she said. The waitress smiled then turned to leave. "Please wait a sec," Petra said then went into her handbag, took out a pen, and wrote 'Fuck you' on a compliment slip. "Now would you please return this to the dog that sent it." The waitress looked hard at Petra before taking the bottle back to Sydney. She stayed stood in one spot looking into Petra eyes. "Please, take the champagne to the dog that sent it." As the waitress knew the character of Sydney and his kind, she looked nervous. "Don't worry," Petra said.

"I don't think he would like that," the waitress said.

"Well, I'll take it over myself Susan," Petra said, seeing her name on her badge.

Madame Stall placed her right hand over Petra's saying, "Do you think that would be wise?"

"Yes!" Petra replied promptly. "I'm doing the decent thing to return the dog's champagne. That dog is pure shit! He and his men raped my mother. Now, tell me if returning his champagne to him isn't the right thing to do."

"I suppose so Petra," Madame Stall said, pausing nervously.

Petra took the bottle of champagne off the table and said to the waitress, "Thanks for your kindness and I admire you for keeping away from that dog."

Petra took the champagne to Sydney and banged it down on his table. He looked at her with a fake smile.

"You dirty son of a bitch! You take your bottle of champagne and shove it up your ass!"

Banjo jumped quickly onto his feet and slapped Petra's face, then said, "Bitch, you belong to us." Petra dived forward and pulled Banjo over the table, knocking off the plates and bottles of drinks. As Banjo dropped to the floor, she kicked him in his balls and in the mouth. Then as she turned to walk away, Banjo got to his feet, pulled his knife out of his jacket pocket and rushed up behind her saying, "You fucking bitch!" Petra twisted round and punched him in his left eye, then double-kicked him to his body and head, sending him flying to the other side of the room. Some of the diners were watching in horror while others were looking happy, smiling or laughing, as most of them knew the vicious and cruel acts the Blacks had carried out. Of course, they had not dared to speak against any of the Blacks, as they were petrified of what they would do to them and their family.

Sydney stood watching his cousin Banjo take a bad beating from Petra.

Then he pushed a few chairs out of his way, walked up to Petra and took a wasted punch, missing her face. "You want to do better than that," Petra said and kneed him in his groin, sending him down on his knees. She twisted his right arm behind his back, then rammed her right knee into his spine, pinning him to the floor with his face down. Banjo was on the floor curled up with pain.

"I'm not well," Sydney Black said coughing repeatedly loudly and sounding as if he was choking on the blood seeping out of his mouth.

Petra lifted her foot off his back and stamped down hard on his neck, pressing his face to the floor. Banjo gathered a little strength and went pitching forward with a knife swinging. Petra kicked the knife from his hand before kicking him in the neck and the throat. As Sydney struggled and got up, she kicked him in the throat as well, knocking him down backward and then she spat on his face.

Constable Brooks and his wife had just walked in to see Petra kick Sydney in the chest while he was down on the floor. He left his wife standing and went to Sydney. "I'm a police officer. Would you like to press charges and have this woman arrested?"

"No my friend, I can handle her. Thanks all the same," Sydney said and wiped blood off his busted lips.

"You should really have me arrest that woman. I wonder if she has a licence to fight," the constable said. He walked up to Petra. "Have you a licence for karate fighting?"

"Are you talking to me?" Petra asked him.

He stepped backward as Petra stepped forward and pulled her ID badge out of her trouser suit pocket and pushed it in his face telling him, "If I was your wife, I wouldn't bother to dine with you. You're a disgrace leaving her standing to take care of a maggot."

"I'm sorry. I had no idea you were one of us," Constable Brooks said.

"Well now you know," Petra told him.

Constable Brooks went back to his wife feeling ashamed. His wife went to Petra and said, "You were good." She smiled then went and sat with her husband.

Banjo and Sydney left the hotel without paying their bills, but the hotel manager was happy to see the back of them. "I don't mind that they left without paying as they are serious troublemakers and often come here demanding food and drink, and upsetting the customers. Thank you so much officer. I think they will stay away for a while now."

Petra looked hard at the manager before bursting into laughter. The manager laughed too. "I think I should reward you with a special dinner if you come tomorrow any time after six or whatever day of your choice."

"I'm sorry sir, but I'm only here as it's my grandma's birthday," Petra replied.

"I'll pay you very well to come here and keep people such as Sydney Black and his kind out of my restaurant."

Petra smiled and went and sat at her table. Todd asked to be excused by his family before he went over to Petra.

"You're very good, I saw what you are capable of. Tell me Petra, do you enjoy using your power against the weak?"

"Why don't you get back to your lovely wife and her family before I take the privilege of kicking your ass to your table and tell your wife about your deceitful little child you have with Kim. If I'm not mistaken, I think Kim's supposed to be your family. I also believe that makes you an incest buck, which means you have the instinct of rabbits to breed your own. I do hope you understand what I'm saying. Oh, I'm sure you met Julia as a pure and innocent virgin when you married her. But could she say the same for you Todd? No, I'm sure she has no idea that Kim took your virginity. I don't want to tell her to ruin her precious memory; Julia is a lovely lady. I hope you or that cheap bitch Kim doesn't breathe a word to anyone that you two had sex. I wouldn't want anyone to laugh behind Julia's back or in her face. So tread carefully Todd and warn your whore to keep her trap shut about you and her."

Todd looked hard into Petra's eyes. She said to him, "You know what Todd, I won't sink so low to tell Julia about how dishonest, despicable and unfaithful you have been to her. But brother, don't you shit in your underpants as Julia would want to know why. I care too much about her to hurt her over maggots like you and Kim. I'll leave it to you to tell her about the bitch that took your virginity. That is if you're honest enough. On the other hand, please don't."

Petra really sunk her words into Todd and he just stood looking at her, smiling out of shame and giving the impression to Julia that he was getting on so well with Petra.

As Todd's smile widened, Petra asked Madame Stall, "Do you smell anything rotten?" Todd's smile faded then he went back to sit at his table. "She's like a firecracker."

Curtis smiled.

"I like her," said Julia.

"You like who?" Todd asked.

"Petra. I think she's lovely."

"I like her too," Joanne said.

"Yes," Todd said in a dull voice as he forced a sad looking smile.

"She's very beautiful," Curtis said looking strongly at Petra and only stopped looking at her when Joanne said to him, "You may look, but you can't touch." He then faced Joanne with a smile saying, "I'm in love with you sweetheart."

"I really think she's beautiful," Curtis said again.

"But she's a tiger. You'll find me less aggressive," Joanne said.

"Still, what she did was absolutely right. I wish I could defend myself the way she did."

"God help the man that takes her on," Todd said.

Julia looked hard at him.

"I'm going to invite her to our wedding," Joanne said.

"And why not?" Curtis said. "Now shall we finish our food?"

"Sure," said Todd and they began eating again. Meanwhile, Petra and Madame Stall had finished eating. Petra beckoned one of the waitresses to come to her. As the waitress stood silently at their table, Madame Stall looked up at her badge. "Your name is as pretty as you, Cassis. I simply love that name."

"Well, thank you Madame," Cassis said.

"We'll be happy to settle our bills," Madame Stall said.

The waitress added up the amount and put the bill on the table in front of Madame Stall. Petra took the bill had a looked at it. Smiling, she paid the amount adding a ten-pound tip, plus a twenty-pound tip from Madame Stall.

"Well thank you both," the waitress said smiling then left with the money to go and pay it to the cashier. Before Madame Stall and Petra left, they went to Julia and her family bidding them goodnight.

Chapter 13

Outside the restaurant Madame Stall said to Petra, "The singer is so handsome. I'm sure he chose to sing that song because you were wearing a red top and earrings. Oh, and I have to collect something that's very important from the store I work at." She then gave Petra directions. As they got to the store, Madame Stall said, "Stop here, Petra."

Petra pulled in near to the doorway and stopped. She looked hard at Madame Stall before opening the car door for her to get out. "Are you not coming with me?" Madame Stall asked her. "You go and get what you want; I'll wait in the car."

Madame Stall looked in Petra's eyes, "Please come with me," she asked Petra again.

"No," Petra said.

"And why not?" she asked Petra smirking.

"Because it doesn't feel right and I wouldn't want to be arrested."

"Petra, we will be okay. I can be here when I please. Please come with me."

"Okay," Petra said. "But I'm still not too sure we're doing the right thing by being here."

"Petra my dear, don't worry. If I wasn't sure we would be okay, I would not ask you to come here."

"Ok," Petra smiled and got out of her car. Madame Stall walked to the door and turned back to face the car. "Come on Petra," Madame Stall said, taking Petra's hand in hers.

"Okay," Petra said. "But if anything goes wrong, I will take the pleasure in locking you up myself," Petra said.

Madame Stall kissed Petra on her cheek then she took the key out of her handbag and opened the door setting the alarm off. "Oh dear," she said quickly turning off the alarm. Then she turned on the lights and walked in with Petra behind her. "Mrs Woods, are you sure we should be here?"

"Yes my dear Petra. Take a deep breath to make yourself feel better, then let me show you around."

She looked at Petra. "This is the Hot Legs Store. I'm sure you have heard of it. It belongs to my boss." Petra smiled then said, "You have committed a crime by breaking into someone's property."

"Don't worry about it. Let me show you the rest of the departments, then we'll have a little refreshment, then you can take me home."

"I think we ought to get out of here before someone calls the police."

"Pet, you are the police and no one will find out about us being here. So, just relax."

"Why do you have a key?"

"Oh, I used to be an inspector here you know."

As they walked into the cosmetic department, Petra stopped to look at the displayed perfumes. "Take the perfume you like; they're test samples."

"I don't need any perfume," Petra said as she walked on to look at the jewellery counter.

"Would you like me to buy you something tomorrow?"

"No thank you." Petra carried on walking along the isle looking at the beautiful jewellery in the glass cabinet. She came to a halt, staring at a most exquisite matching necklace, earrings and diamond bracelet.

Madame Stall walked up to her and looked at the matching set, then looked Petra in her eyes smiling. "Don't bother asking," Petra said then walked on into each department viewing everything. After they left the store and were getting into the car, the night watchman shone his torchlight in their faces holding his gun up ready to use it.

"Madame Stall, what are you doing here at this time? I almost shot you," he said, still holding his gun in position. Madame Stall looked at Petra and her face went suddenly pale. "Why didn't I follow my instinct and go straight home?" Petra fumed.

"Please Petra."

"Don't even bother to explain anything to me. You're so dangerous and untruthful."

Madame Stall fixed her eyes on the night watchman.

"Madame Stall! Why have you lied to me by telling me your name was Mrs Woods when you're Madame Stall?"

The night watchman looked hard at Petra, then turned to look at Madame Stall and said, "I'm sorry for interfering."

"No you did not. Thanks to you I know, the truth about Madame Stall. The famous wealthy Madame Stall and not Mrs Woods as she'd told me her name was. I can never trust you again Madame Stall, or Mrs Woods."

"Oh dear Mr Jordan, you had to come and spoil our fun. Some people just can't keep their mouths shut! Petra, I didn't lie to you about my name, my maiden name was Woods before I was married."

Petra looked hard at her. "You should have told me the truth."

Madame Stall faced Petra. "Pet, you're my only friend. If I had told you who I was, you wouldn't have stuck around me. I like you so much. Pet, my only granddaughter I had was brutally murdered about six years ago."

"You didn't expect me to fill your granddaughter's shoes, did you?"

"Petra, I love you. You're the only good thing that has walked into my life since the death of my granddaughter. The rest of my family have died. I'm asking you, begging you, to not forsake me now." Tears came in her eyes. Petra turned her face away, then stepped a couple of paces forward, and then turned towards Madame smiling. Madame Stall returned a lovely smile back dropping tears and said, "You're absolutely right. I shouldn't have strung you along with my pretences. Are you still angry with me?"

"You almost had us killed and I could have killed someone in the casino over a lousy twelve thousand pounds when you have millions!"

"I'm sorry Petra, but I'd really won that money and they wanted to cheat me out of it. Petra, I didn't keep the money. I donated it to the orphan's home after you refused to have it. Pet, don't give me your answer now but I would like you to come and live with me and be my heir."

"I'm sorry Madame Stall, or whatever your name is. Living with you would be impossible because I wouldn't be able to trust you. I think I should take you home now," Petra said.

"Yes, I think you should Petra, after I have had a word with Mr Jordan," Madame Stall said. Then she said, "Mr Jordan, can I have a word?"

"Sure Madame Stall," the night watchman said.

Petra went to sit in her car leaving Madame Stall and the night watchman talking.

"Mr Jordan, I could have been a burglar. And the time my friend and I have been in here, we could have escaped with half of the contents."

"I'm so sorry, I must have gone to the gents after taking some medicine for my cold. I'm really sorry."

"Well, I suppose I can forgive you after working for me for nearly twenty years, but I'm dissatisfied with tonight. Why didn't you call in sick? Still, you're an honest and kind man."

"Thank you Madame Stall. I assure you, it won't happen again."

"I believe you, Mr Jordan."

Madame Stall joined Petra in her car. Petra looked seriously at her then smiled and drove away. On her way to Madame Stall's home, they saw a crowd of people. Petra could just about hear someone screaming and it was raining hard. Then driving on a little further, she could hear clearly a woman crying out, "Help me!" People were coming out of their houses with coats or umbrellas over their heads.

"What the hell's going on?" Petra asked. Then driving near to the kerb to stop, she saw a beautiful brown-skinned young woman running in the street crying out, "Help me!" The street lights were extremely bright. The young woman was running from person to person but they seemed to be running away from her. Petra didn't understand why. Then as she saw a mixed-raced man chasing the woman with a long wooden-handled knife, she got out of the car and said to Madame Stall, "You sit tight until I get back."

"Poor girl," Madame Stall said. "No one wants to help her."

Petra shut the car door then went running towards the crying woman.

"Murder, help me!" the woman was screaming out repeatedly, but none of the onlookers helped her. "Murder!" the poor defenceless woman screamed out. "Help me!" The onlookers were moving away as she was running to them crying for help. One woman spoke, "Go to the police, we're too afraid to help you. If we did, your man and Sydney Black would hurt us."

Madame Stall was thinking to herself, "Maybe a robbery had happened and the police had been called out." She was peering through the rear window looking for Petra but the rain was hindering her and she couldn't see Petra or what was happening. She wound her window up and sat relaxing. Then as the rain eased, she wiped her window to see a tall young good looking brown-skinned woman running and came to a halt when Petra stopped her and showed her police badge. "Protect me!" she screamed fiercely.

"Protect you from whom?" Petra asked.

"My husband, he's going to kill me."

"Where's your husband?"

"He must be somewhere in the crowd hiding. He must have seen you displaying your badge."

"What's your name?" Petra asked her.

"Loretta."

"Loretta, why does your husband want to kill you?"

"I refused to go to bed with his mates in exchange for clearing his drug debts."

"Did he beat you up?"

"Yes, he said he's going to kill me." He beats me up all the time when I refuse to let the men have sex with me. I will no longer be a whore to support his drug habits."

"Here's my husband now. Help me," Loretta cried shaking like a leaf against the wind and wearing only a white net vest and black knickers. Petra walked her to her car to get her out of the cold and rain. But Loretta's husband rushed up to her and tried to grab her. Petra pushed Loretta behind her and showed her husband her police badge.

"What the fuck!"

"Hey sourmouth, mind your language," Petra told him. "I think you should go home; your wife is afraid of you. She will come home later."

"Move the fuck out of my way and let me get to my wife."

"I'm not going home to him ever again," Loretta said.

"Well, you heard what your wife said," Petra said.

He punched Petra on her chest. Petra punched him to the ground and the knife dropped from his hand. Loretta quickly picked the knife up and held it behind her back. Petra then grabbed him and jammed him against her car. She bound his hands behind his back with her leather belt, then she read him his rights and was about to bundle him into her car to take him to the police station when she saw a police car pull up and stop. Then as she turned and asked Madame Stall, "You okay?" Loretta plunged the knife into her husband's groin. He screamed. Petra watched Loretta in horror.

"He has done worse to me," Loretta said, staring madly at Petra.

Madame Stall covered her eyes with her hand as she saw blood coming from Loretta's husband.

"Loretta, what the hell have you done?" Petra asked her. "Shit!" Petra then handed Loretta's husband over to Officers Kelly and Hodge as they walked up to her.

"What's he charged with?" asked Officer Kelly.

"Living off immoral earnings and selling his wife for sex without her consent," said Petra.

"What's a knife doing in his balls?" asked Officer Evans who'd just arrived.

"I put it there. It's up to you to get the bastard to a hospital and then into a cell where he belongs. The fucking moron makes me feel sick to the pit of my stomach," Loretta said boldly.

"Get him the hell out of my way," Petra said to Officers Hodge, Kelly and Detective Evans.

When Loretta saw Officer Kelly put handcuffs on her husband and shove him into their police car, she looked at her husband crying then asked Officer Kelly, "Can I have a word with my husband?" Detective Evans thought for a moment, then moved out of the way. She smiled and then quickly kicked the knife further into him. Her husband screamed out in agony. She then spat on his face before she went and sat in Petra's car.

"Loretta, your husband will be after you. I think you should go home, get yourself some clothes then find somewhere to stay for a while just in case he gets out on bail," said Petra.

"Well he shouldn't be out on bail," said Loretta.

"Loretta, it's your word against his. If it were up to me he wouldn't see outside ever again. But the law is so fucked up nowadays and especially when it comes to one of the Black organisation, there's no guarantees he'll be locked up."

"But I have nowhere else to stay," Loretta cried. "I have no money, no friends and my family don't want to know me because of him."

"You can stay with me until you find somewhere," Madame Stall said.

"Oh no," Petra said, "She will not!"

"Well, whatever you say dear, I will obey."

"Well thank you, I hope I can trust you on this one," Petra replied and took her jacket off, giving it to Loretta. After Loretta swung the jacket over her shoulders, Petra told her, "You will need to go home and get some clothes. I will find somewhere for you to stay tonight."

"Petra dear, your top is only thin. You'll need to cover your chest so as not to catch a cold," Madame Stall said with concern.

"I'll be okay," Petra said. "I'm wearing my trousers and bra as well."

Petra drove into Madame Stall's gateway and parked. Madame Stall and Loretta got out of the car. While Loretta waited for Petra to get out of the car, Madame Stall opened her door and turned the lights on. Petra and Loretta walked into the house. Petra turned to Loretta saying, "I'll need my jacket before I go home."

"Are you going now?" Loretta asked.

"After I've seen my old friend settle down, I'm going to take you back home to get some clothes, then bring you back here again for the time being. But, do not take my friend for a ride or abuse her in any way, otherwise you will be out on your arse faster than you got in. I do not want you to phone anyone while you're at this address. She's too old to play hide and seek. Now if you give me my jacket, I'm sure my friend will find you something to wear," said Petra

"Sure," replied Madame Stall, then right away she trotted upstairs to her bedroom, brought four dresses and put them into Loretta's hand.

"I hope one of them will suit you."

Loretta looked at Madame Stall smiling, and then said, "Thanks."

"The bathroom is on the left, the shower room is on the right. If you should care for a swim, you'll see 'swimming' written on the end door. The water is just like the sea with gently foaming waves. I used to use it often when I was much younger. Now I would be so happy to share it with any of you. I have it maintained four times a year."

"Thanks," Loretta again said to Madame Stall as they were walking shoulder to shoulder up the dark patterned and gold-coloured mahogany staircase. Petra walked behind them and as Loretta went to the bathroom Petra took Madame Stall aside saying to her, "I don't want you to tell Loretta that you're Madame Stall. You're Mrs Woods and this house was left to you by your parents and all you have is this house. Nothing else. Do you understand me?"

"But Petra, she looks like a nice person."

"Granny Stall, I'm only being concerned for your safety. You lied to me about your name, I suggest that you lie to her too until we're sure we can trust her, as right now we don't know if we can."

"I get your point Pet, but my name is also Woods as I've explained to you."

"Good! I'm glad you do and I now believe you. Now, I'm going to take Loretta home so that she can get some clothes. Will you be okay until we get back?"

"Sure Pet, I'll be all right. Now be off with that poor young lady and when you get back, you will find me waiting for the both of you. However Petra, please call me Andrea."

Petra smiled, kissed her on her forehead then left with Loretta. When they got to Loretta's house she said, "Loretta, you go and pack what clothes you want and let's get out of here."

"How much do you think I should take?" Loretta asked.

"Well, I think you should take a suitcase full as I think it's best for you to find somewhere else to live," Petra said.

"Yes, I should do that," Loretta said and she packed most of her clothes, shoes, jewellery, make-up and struggled down the stairs with them.

"Let's get out of here now," Petra said helping her carry the suitcase to the car. But as Loretta remembered she had few bottles of alcohol, she rushed into the house again and took two bottles of whiskey and a bottle of gin and brandy then got into the car. "Take us home Petra," she said.

"I beg your pardon?" Petra said looking hard at her.

"Well, you know what I mean," she said smiling and Petra took her to Madame Stall's house.

"Oh dear, I can see you are here to stay for a while," Madame Stall said to Loretta.

"I hope not for long," Loretta said.

"But you have eight pairs of shoes, two pairs of slippers and a suitcase of clothes. She has the right to ask. Well, I'll have to go now, but I will be back in the morning," Petra said. But before she left she touched Madame Stall's shoulder and whispered in her ears, "The less talking you do, the better. Remember you're Mrs Woods."

"Petra, I haven't forgotten what you asked me to do. Besides, I'm going to have a bath and then I'm getting into bed with some hot milk. I'll see you in the morning then."

"Yes," Petra replied then left to see her mother at the hotel. She knocked at the door softly and her mother let her in.

"I have just opened a carton of orange juice. Would you like some?"

"Yes, give me a minute to catch my breath though," Petra said.

"Thank God you're all right,"

"And why shouldn't I be all right mother?" Petra asked her.

"Well I've already heard that you beat up a Loretta's husband. Pet, I'm really worried and afraid for you."

"Mother, please don't. I can take care of myself."

"Pet, I know you can, but sometimes you don't see what's coming to you until it's too late. Besides, you're up against too many bad ones," her mother said looking worried.

"Mother, I'll be okay. I'm more worried about you. I brought an overnight bag for us, as I will be sleeping with you. I have settled up with the manager," Petra said.

"Have you eaten? If you want anything, I will order."

"I had dinner at a restaurant. What about you, have you eaten?"

"I had supper and I'm really full. Thank you for staying with me."

At eleven o'clock the following morning Petra asked her mother to check out of the hotel. But her mother said, "Honey, I don't want to leave just yet as I'm feeling safe here."

"Mother, I don't feel too happy leaving you here. This is a public place and someone could easily spot you, then the bad boys would come looking for you. So, please come home with me."

"I'm so afraid to go home Pet."

After some persuasion, her mother agreed to go home with her. Petra thanked the manager for letting her stay the night and they checked out and went home.

Nervously her mother opened the windows to let fresh air in, then they cleaned the whole house from top to bottom. After that they both sat down to a ham salad lunch, ice cream and coffee, then they went to spend the afternoon with Petra's Grandma.

Petra kissed her Grandma and asked her, "How are you Grandma?"

"I am feeling good now that you are both here. I was so worried. I haven't seen either of you for four days."

"Gran, we're okay. How would you like to come and live with Mum and me?"

"I don't know. I'm so comfortable living here. This has been my home for more than forty years. Although I would like to live with you and your mother very much I'm really not sure."

"Then what if we move in with you," Petra asked her Grandma.

"Well I would like that, but why the sudden decision?"

"Grandma, we have to think about each other."

"What will your mother do about her houses, if you decide to live here?"

"Mother can rent hers," Petra said.

"Mother, have you eaten yet?" Mrs Forbes asked her mother to stop Petra talking.

"Yes Anne. I had a bowl of soup and a cheese sandwich. I really don't care much for cheese, but it was quicker than cooking."

"Well, you're in luck gran. I'm going to nip out to the butchers and get us some lamb chops for dinner," Petra said.

"I get my meat from Morrison's supermarket on Coventry Road."

"Okay, I will go there," Petra said and she went shopping. From the meat section, she brought two trays of lamb chops, chicken portions, pork steaks, and a rolled piece of beef, two packs of bacon, sausages and ham. Her other groceries included, a dozen eggs, fresh fruit and vegetables, a bottle of red wine, brandy and a case of stout for her Grandma.

At the checkout the assistant looked hard at her. After the assistant checked the amount she said, "Forty seven, eighty four please." Petra paid and received change from fifty pounds. Just as Petra was leaving, the assistant smiled saying, "I think I know you from somewhere."

Petra smiled but didn't encourage the assistant, as she had known him from Heartlands High School but from a class higher. Petra walked away, but she looked back to see the assistant watching her. Petra smiled and went to put her shopping in her car boot. While doing so, the assistant walked up to her. "Petra Jackson."

"Yes?"

"You really don't remember me do you?"

"Should I?"

"I'm Ti-Shay Marsh," he said.

Petra closed her car boot after putting her shopping away.

"Can I see you sometime?" he asked. "Petra, I really would like to see you."

"Maybe," Petra said and got in her car and drove to her Grandma's. When she carried the shopping into the house, her mother looked surprised to see how much she had bought.

"Did you buy all the meat that was there?"

"I almost did," she laughed. "Well at least Grandma will have a few weeks' supply of meat and groceries." She called Stanley on her mobile, but neither Stanley nor his wife Elizabeth were at home. Petra then asked her mother to look after her Grandma until she got back.

"Where are you off too now, Pet? I wanted the three of us to spend some time together."

"I won't be too long mother," Petra said and left in her car to take the bottle of brandy for Madame Stall.

"I could do with some now, I don't keep that sort of drink in the house," Madame Stall said. Petra opened the brandy and poured some in a glass and gave it to her. She swallowed it all in one go then said calmly, "I'm so happy to have you and Loretta staying here with me."

Petra smiled. "Don't build up your hopes too much. Loretta and I have our own lives to live."

"I know that Petra, I know."

Meanwhile, Mrs Forbes had started cooking dinner.

At half past three Petra phoned and asked her mother if she and her grandma were all right.

"Yes Pet honey, I've started dinner."

"Mother, I don't think I will be with you and Grandma until tomorrow. If you need me, call me."

"Okay honey. Take care, goodbye and I'll see you soon."

"Sure Mum, look after Grandma for me."

"Pet, are you all right?"

"Yes mother, my friend Loretta and I are sitting on our friend Granny

Stall's veranda in the warm breeze drinking Malibu and coke. So please don't worry about me."

"I'll see you tomorrow then."

"Sure Mum. Goodbye."

Madame Stall took her family photo albums and showed them to Loretta and Petra. They took at least an hour to finish looking at the photos then Petra packed them away in the small suitcase and handed it to Madame Stall. Petra didn't notice that the photo of Madame Stall's granddaughter had dropped on the floor under her seat until Loretta picked it up and said, "Isn't she a pretty girl?"

"Who are you talking about?" Petra asked.

"The nice looking girl in this photo," Loretta said.

"Let me see this?" Petra asked.

Loretta handed the photo to Petra. Petra had a good look at the photo and realised she was Madame Stall's granddaughter as her name was written on the back. Petra dried her tears and put the photo in her handbag.

"What are you going to do with that photo and why all of a sudden do you look stone cold?" Loretta asked.

"I'm going to get those bastards that cut her young life short. Loretta, they not only raped her, they gave her to their dog." Petra's tears flowed down her face.

"And did the dogs have sex with her?" Loretta asked.

"What do you think Loretta?" Petra asked.

"Oh no, that's so cruel and horrible," said Loretta then tears welled up in her eyes.

"The worst of it all was that she was only fifteen years old. Oh God! She was only a defenceless child," Petra cried.

"What happened to her really hurts you doesn't it Petra?"

"Yes Loretta, it damn well does! Loretta, I'm going to send those rotten bastards to hell!" Petra fumed.

"Pet, have you ever been raped?" Loretta asked her.

Petra thought deeply before she answered. "Yes, I've been raped by my stepfather and I killed the bastard in the worst way as he deserved!"

"I'm sorry Pet," Loretta said.

"Don't be, a bug crawled into me and I killed it."

"About your stepfather, how could he be so cruel to you?" Loretta asked and dried her tears.

"Well he can't give you any answers now, so let's leave it there. All I want is to deal with the rapists who are living," Petra said.

"Pet, you should seriously think about getting married one day and put everything behind you."

Petra looked hard at Loretta and smiled.

"Pet, I'm very serious about what I said," Loretta said.

"Sure, I will one day when I find the right man. However, when I do, you'll be the first to know," Petra said.

Madame Stall walked over to them with three cups of Milo. "Well girls, I hope you like Milo. Here, get this down you," Madame Stall said as she put the silver tray on the table. Loretta and Petra took their Milo leaving one for Madame Stall as she went to get the deserts.

"Girls, I think you should move inside. It looks as if it's going to rain," Madame Stall said.

"Rain, but the breeze feels so refreshing," Loretta said.

Just then the rain poured down heavily, spraying on the veranda.

"I told you it was going to rain," Madame Stall said.

"Well girls, I'm going to the bathroom and then to bed once I've finished my Milo. So I'll see you two in the morning. Oh, you sleep in any room. Loretta thanks for a lovely dinner."

"Goodnight granny," Loretta said to Madame Stall.

"That goes for me too," said Petra,

Madame Stall eyed Petra then went to bed.

"I'll be off soon," said Petra.

"Oh Pet, please stay here with me tonight," Loretta said.

"Loretta, even if I wanted to, I couldn't. I've nothing to sleep in," said Petra.

"You can borrow one of my nighties," Loretta said.

"Okay," said Petra. "I can stay as I have already phoned and told mother I won't be coming home until tomorrow."

"So that means you'll stay?"

"Don't push your luck Loretta. Yes, I'll stay but only for tonight. As for you, don't get too comfortable here as I will be helping you to find somewhere tomorrow."

Loretta grinned. "Madame Stall has some of my favourite CDs. Let's play a few," Loretta said.

Petra went to the toilet and returned to find Loretta playing one of Madame Stall's CDs. Petra listened to the words of the love song, 'you'll never know how much I love.' Her thoughts immediately focused on Detective Scott Hanson. "Ah, I can tell you're in love Pet, I saw it in your eyes. Are you going to deny it?" Loretta smiled.

"It's none of your business."

"Petra, I can tell when someone is in love and you are. Would you like the CD changed?"

"No, no. I don't know," replied Petra. "Anyway, it's much too sentimental for me but I guess it is nearly finished.'"

"You're a good pretender. I was watching you shuddering through the playing of the disc and it tells me you're in love."

"Loretta, there is someone I like very much, but I doubt if anything will come of it. What I mean is, I wouldn't know how to deal with a relationship. I'm so scared of getting involved with men."

"Pet, if you're in love with your man, nature will take its course when the time is right. I was so much in love with my husband until he forced me into prostitution just to keep him in drugs and gambling."

"Why didn't you leave him?"

"He would have killed me."

"Well Loretta, I'm going to take a warm shower then go to my bed and hug my pillows. Goodnight."

"Goodnight Petra. As soon as this CD stops playing I'll be up. Well, I'll see you in the morning," Loretta said.

Petra smiled and went to the bathroom, then had a shower. As she was getting into bed Loretta entered her room with a bottle of brandy, a bottle of tomato juice and two glasses.

"Let's have a drink," she said.

"Loretta, I've got to go to work tomorrow and I've got to get up with a clear head. So I'll see you tomorrow before I go to work."

"Please Pet, just a small one to begin our friendship," said Loretta.

"Our friendship began when I rescued you from your husband. Now take that brandy and put it back from where you got it," Petra told Loretta.

Loretta poured some brandy, mixed it with the juice and gave it to Petra. "Here honey, drink this," she said.

"No Loretta! I really shouldn't, I don't want a drink now. Please go. I'm really tired and I have to go to work in the morning."

"Please Pet. It will relax you and you'll have a good night's sleep."

"Okay, but after I drink it will you let me sleep?"

"I promise," replied Loretta:

Petra took the drink and drank it in one go then she handed the empty glass back to Loretta.

"Oh Pet, this house is so big that it makes me feel so scared to sleep on my own. Can I share your bed?"

Petra looked hard at Loretta.

"Please Petra."

"No Loretta, you have at least five minutes to get out of this room. There are three bedrooms to choose from. You only have to choose the cheerful one. I think your five minutes is up. Goodnight Loretta." Petra then switched off the headboard lights.

Loretta got up off Petra's bed, walked to the door and said, "Goodnight." Petra didn't reply.

Loretta walked out the room, closed the door quietly and went to her chosen room.

The following morning, Loretta was the first to get up. She went to Petra's room and gave her a light slap on her bottom to wake her. Petra turned facing her yawning.

"What time is it?" Petra asked her.

"Twenty-two minutes past five."

"Look Loretta, I must get at least two more hours of sleep."

"Do you mind if I sit on your bed for the next two hours?" Loretta asked.

"So long as you let me sleep, then I really don't care," Petra said.

Just then the phone rang and Loretta answered it.

"It was your mother. She said a Detective Inspector Hanson had phoned her to tell you to meet him in the police canteen as soon as you arrive at work. Isn't he the handsome detective you can't make up your mind about?"

"Well yes, but I also like Dr Sean," Petra said.

"I think Detective Inspector Hanson is the man for you. By the way, why is it that you beautiful bitches always get the most handsome son of a bitches to pick and choose from?" Loretta asked.

"I think you got married too young, my friend," Petra said.

"I think so too," Loretta admitted. "But that's now behind me. The future is now forward for me and I would very much like to meet your friend Dr Sean," Loretta said giggling. "Anyway, it appears to me that your mother couldn't sleep either. As for Detective Inspector Hanson, I think he's in love with you as well."

Loretta climbed into bed beside Petra and they both fell asleep.

By ten past six Loretta was awake again. She woke Petra at six thirty. They went for a swim in the indoor swimming pool, got dressed, then went for a drive to Cannon Hill Park. After they parked the car, they went jogging around the park for at least fifteen minutes then dropped sitting on the grass puffing and trying to catch their breath. As Petra lay on her tummy and she plucked a piece of straw and held it between her teeth thinking about Detective Inspector Hanson. "Pet. your face looks distant. Are you thinking about Detective Inspector Hanson?"

Petra rolled on her side facing Loretta and smiled.

"Petra, I'm going to divorce Phil."

"Hey!"

"I was referring to my husband Phil. I'm going to divorce him."

"Yes, I think that's for the best."

"Pet?"

"Yes, Loretta."

"Have you ever been in love, really in love?"

"No, not really," Petra answered, thinking about Detective Inspector Hanson. "Come on Loretta, I'll race you back to the car."

They began jogging down the hill to get to the car but as Loretta slowed to walking Petra did the same. When they got to the car Loretta leaned her back against it. Petra pressed the fob to open the door. "Let me catch my breath before I get in," Loretta puffed out strongly.

Petra got in the driver's seat, buckled up and waited for Loretta to get in.

Loretta got in and sat next to Petra. "Will you buckle up?"

"Oh yes Petra."

Petra drove to Madame Stall's and after she and Loretta showered they had breakfast. "Well, I have to go to work soon so I will see you later," Petra said.

"Pet, my husband is a cousin of Sydney, Redd, Johnny and Mark Black. Those brothers really are bastards. I believe they murdered your friend's granddaughter, but the police haven't prosecuted anyone. That makes me feel sick and disgusted. Petra, I knew a lovely bloke by the name Hans. He told me that he saw Redd and Mark take a young girl and pump drugs into her before they fucked her senseless then left her lying naked on a cold tiled floor with blood coming from her and one of their dogs was sniffing her. Hans told me that he knifed the dog to death when Mark came back and saw him. Mark gave him a choice of losing a hand or his dick for killing their dog. So he told them to take his hand. It must have been so awful for the girl and Hans." Tears were flooding down Loretta's face then she closed her eyes saying, "Pet, I'm still feeling bitter and it's worse now that I know the poor little thing was Madame Stall's granddaughter."

"Loretta, I don't want you to breathe a word about any of what you have said to Madame Stall or anyone else."

"Petra, why did she tell you her name is Mrs Woods?"

"Well she had her reasons. Woods is really her maiden name, but it had nothing to do with what you have told me."

"Pet, you think what happened to her granddaughter made her change her name?"

"No Loretta, she hid her name Madame Stall from me because she had wanted me to help her get her winnings from the Black's casino and she also didn't want me to know that she was the wealthy Madame Stall. I guess like you, I didn't know her," Petra said.

"However, I don't think she has ever found out the full truth about her granddaughter. Pet, I could never live with my husband again. Although, I think he had nothing to do with her granddaughter or any of the youths who have been murdered, I know if I don't leave him, it would only be a matter of time before he hurt me badly or even killed me. I've even got a list of police names who are presently working for the Black brothers."

"Loretta, do you mind if I ask you to give me the list with those names?"

"Pet, you may have those bastard names with pleasure. I'll get it for you for when you come home from work. The list is in my china teapot in my kitchen wall unit. I hope every one of those bastards gets what's coming to them. It must have been awful for those youths to suffer in their hands. Oh my God." Loretta cried again emotionally. Petra's tears came too. Then after Petra dried her eyes she said, "Loretta, I don't think it's wise for you to go back to your home. I'll get a warrant and pick the list up myself when I finish work."

"Petra there's no need for you to get a warrant. I'll be okay going back into my own home. Besides, my husband is in the hospital licking his balls, I'm sure of that."

"Loretta, I wasn't referring to your husband. Any one of your husband's family or friends could hurt or have you killed."

"I agree with you Pet. You'll find the note in a gold china teapot with eight names on it. Judge O'Neil, Officer Forbes; those two bastards are now dead. The other six names, I'm not sure. I didn't get the chance to have a good look at the other names because my husband was coming towards me so I dropped it in the teapot. I, I think an Officer Delta's name was on the list," said Loretta in thought:

"Thanks Loretta, it's time the weeds are plucked out from amongst the good vines," Petra said.

At twelve-thirty that day, Petra met Detective Inspector Hanson in the canteen where they had lunch together. Over lunch they had a disagreement over Sydney Black when she told him she would take Sydney and his gang down. Hanson watched her hard.

"Look Hanson, give me one good reason why I shouldn't go after those four bastard brothers. I know some of you are on the Blacks' payroll."

"Pet, please mind what you say," Detective Inspector Hanson said. "Anyway, why do you hate the Blacks so much?"

"Because they're murderers and rapists."

"Petra, you're no match for any of those Blacks," said Detective Inspector Hanson.

"Hanson, since I was fourteen years old, those sickening, stinking Black bastards have been paying most of you with a few shiny pence for taking defenceless youths to them to abuse in the most horrible way. Well, I've grown up now and I'm wide awake to see those bastards hands' saturated with youths blood after they rape them and leave them for their dogs. I'm talking of boys and girls from thirteen years old to twenty and none of you so-called good lawmen have tried to raise a finger to stop them. My stepfather was a police officer and an informer for those bastards, and he raped me. So I did what I had to do to the dirty maggot."

"Petra, what are you talking about?" Hanson asked.

"Put it this way, I don't need any help to bring these other bastards down, not even help from the law. As for you, I certainly don't need any help or advice. I think you should crawl back into your shithole and stay there. I will succeed where you sleeping bastards failed. Scott Hanson, you cross my path and you'll never live to cross it again. By the way, I never want you to phone me or my mother again!"

"Pet, I don't want you to get hurt," he said then closed his eyes.

"I've already been hurt by my stepfather. From now on, you address me as Superintendent Jackson as I will to you as Detective Inspector Hanson. Don't you ever forget," said Petra angrily.

"Petra, all I'm asking you to do is to keep out of trouble."

Petra tossed her glass of coke into Detective Inspector Hanson's face and left. He dried his face with one of his handkerchiefs and followed behind her. But as he saw his two detective mates Robin and Bruce laughing, he called out angrily to Petra saying, "I'll get you for this!"

Petra stopped walking and faced him saying, "Keep the hell out of my way."

"I'll never let you, or any other woman speak to me like you just did!" Detective Inspector Hanson said.

"Hanson, why don't you crawl back to your clown friends before I really give them something to laugh about?"

"Why are you so difficult and hard of hearing?"

"I want you to stay away from me." Petra turned to leave, but Hanson grabbed her hand, turned her to face him and slapped her face. She slapped him back, then kneed him in the groin, sending him to his knees. She then pulled her gun out of her waist belt, cocked it and aimed it at his forehead. "The next time you put your hands on me, I'll make sure you'll never use them again!"

Detective Inspector Hanson took his hands from his crotch and looked up at her in shock. Detectives Robin and Bruce kept silent while the other officers were outside laughing so loudly that they alarmed the others to come out of the canteen to look at Detective Inspector Hanson on his knees.

Petra stared at them then went about her business leaving Detectives Todd, Bruce and Robin to help Detective Inspector Hanson up.

A couple of minutes later, Detectives Robin and Bruce found it so funny that they burst into laughter. Detective Inspector Hanson looked hard at them grinning and looking exasperated.

"I'm sorry pal," said Detective Todd, "But that lady is dynamite and she's also in love with you. Hanson, you just have to learn how to control her and love that temper she has for you."

Detective Inspector Hanson smiled.

Two days later, Judge Lewis summoned Petra to his office. She met Corporal Roberts, Detectives Todd, Paul Hanson, Superintendent Peterson, Lieutenant Gladstone and Chief Inspector Tyson sitting around the table drinking coffee. Petra stood watching them.

"Officer Jackson," I summoned you here as I understand that you're putting your head where you might get it blown off. In other words, you're interfering with the Blacks. I'm warning you to butt out, stay out and leave the Blacks to us," Sergeant Roberts said.

"When will that be, Sergeant Roberts?"

"We'll get the Blacks in our own time without you, Officer Jackson," Sergeant Roberts flared up with squinting eyes.

"Well Sergeant Roberts, I'm going on twenty-two years old. Since I was fifteen years old, those Black brothers and associates have been raping, killing and turning youths into prostitutes and you lot gave them the power to do so. So, don't pretend any of you care, for I know none of you give a damn or have feelings about what happened to the defenceless. And I wouldn't put it past any of you to be getting well paid by those bastards, plus a guarantee that your family will be safe providing you leave them alone to carry on their wicked doings!" Petra brawled furiously as she was gutted. "By the way all of you, when I'm sure you're straight, I will give you my respect. Right now all I can see is five lumps of stale shit that sicken my stomach. Detective Inspector Hanson, I hope you have a strong stomach. As for me, I'm getting out in the fresh air."

"Officer Jackson, I want your gun and badge on this table by tomorrow morning," Sergeant Roberts said.

"Why not have them now? I'm going to bring down those evil Black bastards where your asses failed without my gun and badge." Petra was very angry and she slammed the gun and badge on the table and walked away.

"Officer Jackson!" Sergeant Roberts shouted.

Petra shouted to him, "Kiss my arse, all five of you." She walked outside smiling. As she opened her car door to get in, Detective Todd ran towards her.

"Petra!"

"What the hell do you want from me, Todd?"

"Petra, I believe in what you're doing. But you can't fight the Black organisation alone. I also think you're going about it the wrong way!"

"Look Todd, I didn't ask for your opinion. In fact, why don't you get back under Kim's skirt and go play with your secret daughter. You shitheads are nothing but a pile of shit. Now get out of my way."

Todd smiled and stepped aside to let her get into her car.

Petra drove to her friend Faith's, then Jenny's, where she spent some time with them before going to visit her Grandma. She parked up at her Grandma's gate and hit the seat of her car in temper. She eventually got out of the car and let herself into the house with her keys. She met her mother in the kitchen.

Her mother noticed the aggression on her face. "What's the matter honey?"

"I just quit my job."

"Honey, would you like to tell me why?"

"Okay, I didn't quit. I was sacked and I don't want to hear any more about the stinking job. Where's Grandma?"

"She's upstairs having a rest," her mother said.

As Petra was going upstairs, her mother called to her, "Petra."

"Yes mother," she answered with her back turned.

"Where's your badge?" her mother asked her.

"Mother, I'm no longer a police officer. I just told you I was sacked from the force."

"I thought you were joking honey?"

"Mother, I would really appreciate it if you wouldn't question me

307

anymore. I'm really very tired. All I need now is a hot bath and then to go to sleep," Petra said.

"Pet, you told me before not to take any messages from Detective Inspector Hanson. He phoned to tell you that he wanted to see you. I told him you didn't want any contact with him, but he said to tell you it's very urgent and please call at his home about six o'clock this evening. His address is on the television. Honey, I couldn't help but take the message."

"That's okay mother, I will see him," said Petra smiling and she went to have her foam bath.

In the bath she rested her head on a waterproof cushion and spread her feet apart with a flannel covering her face. She moved the flannel off her face to see two big bubbles floating on each sides of her legs and she named them Sean and Scott. "Now," she said, "Scott Hanson, you're on the left because you're a bad lad. Sean Bailey, you're very nice, but I'm not in love with you. Well, whichever one of you lasts the longest will be my date tonight."

After she watched bubble Sean fading slowly and meeting the other tiny bubbles, she smiled and popped bubble Scott Hanson with her fingers saying, "You had to fucking win didn't you?" After running more hot water, she closed her eyes with Hanson on her mind before dozing off. She only woke up when her Grandma knocked on the bathroom door saying, "Petra dear, don't drown yourself. I think you've been in the bath long enough!"

Petra stood up and washed the foam off her bottom and legs before getting out, drying off and getting dressed. In the living room she nervously watched her Grandma's old grandfather clock ticking away. She gulped down about a quarter of a pint of cold milk.

"Pet, your dinner was cooked an hour ago."

"Mother, it's ten to five. I've got to go and see that Detective Inspector Hanson. Afterwards, I will be going to see an old friend and will eat there. I will call you to make sure that you and Grandma are all right. If I don't see you tonight, I'll see you both in the morning," Petra said.

"Are you planning on sleeping with Detective Inspector Hanson?" her mother joked.

"Mother!" Petra smiled and rested her overnight bag on the settee. "Well, I'll see both of you tomorrow." She kissed them on their cheeks and said, "Goodbye."

"You be careful honey," her mother said.

"Don't worry about me. Just look after yourself and Grandma until I get home." Petra then picked up her bag, kissed her mother again and left in her car. She got to Detective Inspector Hanson's house just before six o'clock. Before she got out of her car, she took her bag from off the front seat and put it on the floor under the seat. She got out, walked up to Detective Inspector Hanson's front door and rang the doorbell. Hanson's mother answered the door. When she saw Petra she smiled and escorted her into the living room to meet Hanson then left the room.

"Please take a seat?" Hanson asked her.

Before she sat down, she asked him, "Why have you asked me here?"

"Please sit," he asked her again. She looked into his face and sat on the settee.

"Would you like a drink of any kind?"

"No thank you," she replied.

"Then you won't mind if I have some brandy?"

"Hanson, I don't really care what you have. I only want to know why you have summoned me here."

"Look Petra, Chief Inspector Roberts and his sergeant brother rang and told me that you resigned from the police force this afternoon and that he wants me to follow every move you make then report back to them."

"So that is why you asked me here?"

"Well not exactly. Pet, in spite of what you've done to me, I love you. I don't want to see you get hurt." Hanson kneeled down at her feet, held her left hand and closed his eyes. "Petra honey, I'm in love with you."

"Hanson, I quit the police force to bring those rotten Black bastards down and to toss them flat on their stinking arses for the world to see. I hate to say this, but if I catch you blocking my way, I'll send your balls flying out through your mouth like a football being kicked across a football pitch."

"Okay Pet, you've made it very clear. I will not even try to follow you. But the only thing I would like from you is for you to have dinner with me please," Hanson begged smiling.

"Okay, I'm hungry I admit," said Petra and smiled.

"Now?" asked Hanson still smiling.

"Well all right. Where shall we go?"

"Here, I've cooked dinner for two, us two."

"What about your mother and your brother Paul?"

"Mother will be going to spend the night with her sister and Paul has already left for his night shift."

"Oh, I see," replied Petra.

"Anyway, my brother told me that you were sensational telling Sergeant Roberts what you think," Detective Inspector Hanson said.

On Hanson's mother's way out, she stopped and kissed Petra on her forehead. "Well Petra, Hanson has done all of the cooking; I hope you enjoy your meal. I've got to go now to see my sister Paulette. I'll see you soon I hope. Goodbye Petra."

"Goodbye Mrs Hanson."

Mrs Hanson left. Petra and Detective Inspector Hanson heard the door shut.

"Out of all my lady friends, you know you're the only woman my mother has taken to."

"Hanson, I'm not one of your lady friends, I think I'd better leave."

"Please Pet, I promise I won't touch you. Let's go into the dining room and eat," said Hanson. He took her hand into his, helping her out of her seat then went to kiss her, but she stepped away. He smiled and led her into the dining room.

"Your mother has a nice home," Petra told him.

"Yes she has," he said directing her to the seat facing him. As she sat, she looked up at him smiling.

"I hope you like roast beef," he said and went to wash his hands. He then took the roast beef out of the oven and placed it on the table. Carving the beef, he gave her a nice smile then said again, "I do hope you really like roast beef."

"Only when it looks so tasty and tender like this."

"Just wait until you taste it," he said looking into her eyes.

As his look softened her, she quickly cast her eyes onto her plate until he'd finished serving, then smiling she looked at him as he was pouring red wine into her glass. After he'd served himself, she looked at him again; he winked his left eye and put on a Louis Armstrong CD: We Have All the Time in the World.

"Shall we eat?" he asked.

"Well, I'm starving," she said.

"I'm glad you are here," he said. Then they began to eat. Over dinner, he said to her, "I think my mother really likes you."

"I think your mother was pretending to be polite to me," she said.

"You're so wrong about my mother, she would really like us to get married. I think my mother would like to be Grandma to our children," he said smiling while looking at her in such a sentimental way. She looked at her wristwatch; his head tilted and he looked at her romantically and with a smile on his face.

When she saw him looking at her, she got up and went and admired the photo of him and his brother Paul in their police uniforms. "I was eighteen then and my brother was twenty-two."

As she hadn't drunk her wine, he took it from the table and gave it to her. She smiled looking into his eyes.

"Finish your drink, honey," he said. She took a sip, then another sip, then sip after sip as they talked until her glass was emptied. As he was going to fill her glass again, she said, "No thank you. I should be on my way now. Thanks for dinner and the wine."

"Must you go so soon?" he asked.

"Yes Hanson, you did not invite me to spend the night, did you?"

Smiling, he replied, "No, but I would be happy if you did."

"Let's both remember this time how close we were and… well, who knows where it will take us? Well, thanks again for a wonderful dinner. I'll see you some other time," she said and walked to the door. He followed behind her. As they both stood face to face gazing into each other's eyes and smiling, a beautiful little grey and white kitten walked over to Petra rubbing itself against her ankle. She picked up the kitten and said, "Oh, she's very beautiful. Isn't she Hanson?"

"She's a handsome he, like me," Hanson joked then took the kitten, put him down and opened the front door. As Petra walked out, he held her hand walking her to her car. She opened the door and got in. As she was going to start the car he said, "Petra, I love you."

"I know," she said smiling.

"Well, are you not even going to give me a goodnight kiss?" he asked.

"How are your balls?" she asked laughing.

He laughed. "Oh one of these days they will tell you personally how they are and I'll even let you examine them. You can tell me how they feel against your soft legs then you can judge them for yourself." They both laughed.

"See you then," she said. "I like a man that holds on to hope."

He smiled.

"Well I'll see you soon," she told him and as she drove away with the window wound down, he shouted, "Petra I love you." She smiled. "I love you too my love," she whispered.

Chapter 14

On Petra's way to see Madame Stall, she laughed heartily about Hanson telling her he would let her examine his balls. She stopped laughing and seriously began thinking about him as she felt love for him. As she was driving past the chemist she saw her friend Martin. She stopped near the kerb and blew her car horn to attract him.

When she realised Martin wasn't taking any notice she popped her head out of her car window and shouted, "Martin!"

Martin heard his name called. He turned looking to see Petra sitting in her car waving. He started walking towards her. She got out of her car and was walking to meet him when Sydney's brother Mark appeared and spitefully bounced her, almost tossing her to the ground.

"Hello sweet bitch! Ever since I had your mama, I've been wondering if you're as sweet as her!" He roared with laughter.

"Look pussy mouth, I will deal with you some other time," Petra said and walked off to go to Martin where he was waiting.

Mark rushed up behind her and grabbed her breasts. She turned and pushed him away. "You do that again and I'll kill you," she said. She continued walking towards Martin but Mark hit her on the back of the neck. She fell.

"Now bitch, I'll do what I set out to do, then I'll let you know out of you and your mama, which one I enjoyed the most." As Petra was getting up, he tried to put his hand up her skirt but as she was so dizzy, she only stared at him.

"I'm going to fuck you here in front of all these people." He laughed in an arrogant way and said again, "I'm going to shove my dick right up you," as he pulled her by her hair into him. Martin punched him, but he put a knife to Martin's chest. "Me a go kill you pussy claret boy." Martin backed away.

An old black woman saw Mark pressing his lips against Petra's crotch and beat him off with her walking stick, then screamed, "Will someone help this young girl and call the police?" But everyone was moving away. The woman was wondering why no one was taking any notice of the situation. Looking at the onlookers, she could see fear in some of their eyes. Petra was coming out of her dizziness. She shook her head vigorously and popped her eyes open to see Mark holding his penis in his hand, rolling his head with drugged-up looking eyes.

Petra took a can of beans from the woman's shopping bag, pulled the ring open and emptied it over Mark's penis. Then she saw two dogs running towards them. She kicked him towards the dogs and one dog bit the penis off. Blood spouted and Mark stood frozen for an instant before he screamed out, fainted and fell flat on his back. As she lifted her foot to his face to stab his jaw with her high-heeled shoe, the old woman said, "He isn't worth your shoes touching him. Besides, the dogs have done justice for you."

After the old woman left, Petra was still so furious that she kicked Mark in the side and the mouth, then said to him, "I hope the dogs fuck you." She then spat on his face before driving away leaving him bleeding.

While all this was happening, Martin was already in his father's chemist, as he didn't want anyone to catch on that he knew Petra. As Petra didn't want anyone to know she knew Martin either, she didn't bother going to him. Instead, she left to go to Madame Stall's, but as she turned into Madame Stall's gateway she changed her mind. She turned the car around and began driving to her Grandma's. A police car spotted her and the siren sounded to tell her to stop. She smiled then slowed down as they caught up with her. She pulled over to the side of the road, stopped her car and got out. Officers Hodge, Philips and WPC Rogers stopped their car behind hers. They got out and went to her. "Officer Jackson."

"What now, Officer Philips? Don't you know that I was sacked?" Petra said.

"Officer Jackson, you are a good officer, one of the best. I agree with your methods, but please do be careful and be very discreet about what you intend to do. I was asked to bring you in, but I can't as my hands are hurting me. So, can you please do me a favour and turn yourself in?" Officer Hodge asked.

"Okay," Pet replied.

"Well, thanks Officer Jackson," Officer Hodge said.

"Wait just a minute, what am I charged with?"

"Officer Jackson, I'm taking you in for grievous bodily harm to a Mr Mark Black," said Philips.

"Leave her, officer. Officer Jackson will turn herself in. Our job is finished here," Officer Hodge said as he winked at Petra and got in his car.

Officer Philips and WPC Roberts got in the car. "What hold does Miss Jackson have on you, Officer Hodge?"

"Just mind what you say Officer Philips."

"Mate, I would like to know why you're favouring Miss Jackson when we were supposed to read her her rights and take her in," WPC Rogers said.

"Take her in my arse," Officer Hodge said.

"Officer Hodge, you give me the impression that you like what Miss Jackson's doing."

"And what if I do Officer Philips?" said Officer Hodge.

"Please you two, give me time to concentrate will you?" WPC Roberts said. Silence was then restored between them and Officer Hodge smiled.

Petra drove to the police station and gave herself up. She rang Loretta, telling her that she had been arrested for emptying a can of beans over Mark Black's penis and letting a dog bite it off. "Please don't say anything to Granny Stall." Loretta laughed so heartily that Madame Stall went to her asking her, "What's the joke?"

Loretta said to Madame Stall, "My friend phoned to say she had a crush on someone, but it has turned out to be her half-brother!"

Madame Stall laughed before she went to sit in the living room.

Loretta promised Petra that she would never breathe a word about it to Madame Stall.

"Thank you Loretta," Petra said then put the phone down.

Two hours later, Loretta took the chance of going to her home to get the list of names. But the teapot had been moved from the wall unit and was on a tray with stale tea in it. "Shit!" Loretta said looking confused. "Where will I find that list of names," she asked herself looking in the trash basket.

"Shit shit shit!" she said again in frustration. She spent at least twenty minutes searching everywhere in the kitchen for the list of names. Then she gave up and sat on the chair. She flapped her folded arms underneath her breasts and thought deeply as to where the list could be. She got up after deciding to leave when she spotted the piece of paper on the floor under the table. She picked it up and saw it was the list of eight names. She smiled in relief and looked up to the ceiling saying, "Thank you God." She smiled cheerfully, then took the list to the police station and gave it to Petra. Petra studied the names, then put the paper in her bra for safety.

After she had been held for more than three hours, WPC Collins released her and escorted her into a private room where she met Chief Inspector Lemoore and his uncle Commissioner Frank, Superintendents Lewis, Peterson and Detective Todd. They were all in conversation around a table, drinking cold sodas and coffee.

WPC Collins ordered Officer Jackson to stand before them in a private trial. Judge Lewis rushed into the room breathing heavily with sweat pouring off his face. He took his seat next to Superintendent Peterson saying, "I'm sorry for being late." He looked at Petra before saying, "Officer Jackson, you have been warned never to go looking for trouble, especially with those Black brothers." He paused for a brief moment then went on talking. "Officer Jackson, you deliberately disobeyed orders. Have you anything to say?" he asked looking pleased, then he swallowed a tablet.

Petra belted out, "This is the second time I have had to stand before you asses. I was fourteen years old when I learnt that those criminal bastards own you lot. All you bastards have done is sit on your asses sipping coffee, brandy and champagne while the Black brothers, cousins and companions are raping and kidnapping youths and you have done nothing to help them. Of course you won't, because these youths mean nothing to any of you! Well, I have been on the same road as those youths. I know how loud their screams sound and I feel the agony of their pain as those bastards penetrate their dirty dicks into them. Not to mention how dirty they feel and I know this from experience. Those bastard Blacks have raped my mother. You really want to know why I threw baked beans on Mark Black's penis? Because I knew the dog would bite it off. The bastard will never rape anyone again. Oh, and before he lost his manhood, he grabbed me round the neck, groped my breasts, put his hand up my skirt, took his dirty penis into his hand and broadcast to everyone watching that he was going to fuck me like he fucked my mother. Well, the dogs did me a favour and saved me from dirtying my hands. Now tell me, what would you have done to protect yourself if you were me, or, if they had done the same to your daughters or wives and they had protected themselves in the same manner as I did? Would you lock them up like you did me as if I'm the animal?" Petra questioned her accusers. "I can see the four of your mouths gaped open and none of you answer my questions."

The room was left in silence and they all looked shocked by what Petra had told them. Superintendent Peterson swallowed deeply and his eyes grew moist as he thought about his daughter Julia. Chief Inspector Roberts got up out of his seat, looked at Judge Lewis and shook his head, then looked hard into Superintendent Peterson and Detective Todd's eyes. He did not say another word but sat down. Judge Lewis dragged his hand across his lips as his eyes became moistened with tears. He shook his head repeatedly then looking up at Petra he said, "I must wet my throat before I say anything." He took a drink of water then said, "On this day, you Officer Jackson have woken up my lazy brain. You're so damn right about what you have said. I have been studying your work, and to my surprise, you've succeeded where we son of a bitches have failed. As of now, my brother Superintendent Lewis will reinstate you as Superintendent Jackson. You should wear your badge proudly as you've earned it. I want you to go out to the Black brothers, cousins, mothers, fathers and whoever else is connected with them. You bring them to me alive or dead, whichever, I couldn't give a damn. You go with my blessing and stake out those bastards and toss them into the pit of hell or in my cell."

Superintendent Lewis paused, breathed in and out deeply then said, "Dead or alive as my brother said. Will you need any backup?"

"No sir. I prefer to work alone. If I should need any backup I will get my own. Straight and honest like me. One other thing sir, there are too many crooked animals around here and I think it's time they should be found and tossed into the depths of hell where they belong with the Blacks. Judge Lewis, I intend to bring down the crooked cops too!"

"Superintendent Jackson, Chief Inspector Roberts here will supply you with your badge along with your gun. Use them wisely; you have earned them. Thank you for your honesty, wear your badge proudly and go forth with my blessing. Gentlemen and WPC Collins I thank each of you for being here. Superintendent Jackson has no case to answer to. This case is now closed," Judge Lewis said. Petra smiled then tears of joy rolled down her face. Judge

Lewis, his Superintendent brother, Chief Inspector Roberts and his sergeant brother Hilton smiled.

"Oh by the way Officer Jackson, your salary will be made known to you in due course as you've been promoted to a higher rank. My colleagues and I know you deserve it for what you have achieved. Don't you agree with us Superintendent Jackson?"

"But Superintendent Lewis, I've never complained. All I wanted was to be a good honest cop."

"I know that, you have worked damn hard to earn your promotion and a good salary. Now, anyone here who thinks that Superintendent Jackson shouldn't be offered her promotion should speak out now," Judge Lewis said.

Superintendent Peterson went forward to Petra and asked, "May I kiss you?"

"Sure," said Petra. He kissed her on her cheek then said, "You're brilliant. God Bless."

"That goes for me too," said Detective Todd.

Superintendent Lewis smiled and his brother Judge Lewis said, "Well, I'm sure we all have unfinished business to get on with. Good day to you."

Petra and WPC Collins left the room. On Petra's way to her car she smiled as she met Detective Scott Hanson. He stopped her, "I heard what happened so I came to bail you out."

Petra smiled. "You're one hour late. You've missed all the fun. Besides, I don't think that I'll need a lawyer, any lawyer."

"Pet, if you should need a lawyer you can always count on me, your future husband," said Detective Inspector Hanson and smiled.

"Are you a lawyer for real?" Petra asked him teasing.

"Yes. I'm a lawyer by profession. I'm also a private detective. Hey, and what is this I have heard that you're a Superintendent?" Detective Inspector Hanson asked.

"Chief Inspector Roberts and Judge Lewis think I deserve that promotion."

"Pet, I don't want you to get hurt. Do you understand what I'm saying to you, I don't want you to get hurt or killed," said Detective Inspector Hanson seriously.

"Why do you think I'll get hurt or killed? Have you no faith in your future wife?"

"Damn you Petra! I love you," Detective Inspector Hanson told her.

"Hanson, if you love me as you said, you'll support me with what I'm doing and let me do my work."

"What work? Pet, you're playing with fire and you'll get burned, very badly. I might not be there to pour water over you," Detective Inspector Hanson said as if he was ready to cry.

"I think you've got your facts back to front. Right now the fire's blazing and I'm the water to put it out! However, if it happens to be me on fire, fan me well and let me blaze to hell. Now would you please stop pestering me and keep the hell out of my way?"

Detective Inspector Hanson smiled then asked, "Apart from everything, how would you like to have dinner with me again tonight?"

"I've things to do tonight. Sorry."

"What about tomorrow night?"

"I will be busy as usual."

"I see, there's no love lost as usual!" said Detective Inspector Hanson.

Petra blew him a mock kiss then walked past him. He walked into the room to be with Chief Inspectors Roberts, Saunders, Superintendent Peterson and Detective Todd. Again they were talking of the great work that Petra was doing when Judge Lewis left to get a drink. Chief Inspector Robert's brother knocked on the door and walked in. He took his seat next to Detective Inspector Hanson. A few minutes later, Judge Lewis, and his detective son Shane Lewis joined them. Superintendent Baldwin came rushing in saying, "I hope I haven't missed much."

"You're just in time. We were just about finishing discussing Officer Petra Jackson's excellent work. I've promoted her to Superintendent, as she deserves," Judge Lewis said.

"Have I heard you right, that you have promoted Officer Jackson? Have you gone mad? How long has she been in the force? If I remember rightly, she's been here four years. It took me half my life to get where I am. That's about fifteen years to reach my goal as superintendent," Baldwin said and fisted the table in anger. As all eyes looked on him, he went on saying, "Officer Jackson heisted from being a simple street playing cop to a highly paid superintendent; I think the lot of you have gone mad."

"Not mad Superintendent Baldwin, I recognise quality and Officer

Jackson as you addressed her, has that naturally by birth. Now, anyone else that thinks the same as our colleague, Superintendent Baldwin, feel free to clear your conscience and speak out. But whatever you think or say, it won't make any difference because I've already put right what should have been put right."

Superintendent Roberts nodded and smiled. "We need young, strong and brave officers like Miss Jackson."

"I'm not wasting any more time here listening to this rubbish," Baldwin said, getting to his feet.

"We weren't mad to accept her as a street playing cop to root out the filth we left unturned, but now she has done what we failed to do, we're mad to promote her to superintendent? Well here's my opinion Superintendent Baldwin; she is one of the best and most honest police officers in the entire force. I have made my decision and it will remain solid. Now Superintendent Baldwin, don't let me stop you leaving and thanks for coming."

Superintendent Roberts smiled. "Judge Lewis, I couldn't agree with you more. Our new Superintendent Jackson is one of the damn best police officers to join this force. She's bright, smart, intelligent and smooth."

Judge Lewis smiled as he faced Superintendent Baldwin.

"Well, as for me, I think Officer Jackson has worked hard and has earned her promotion," replied Detective Todd.

"I agree with that," Superintendent Peterson said.

"And good luck to her with her promotion and everything that goes with it. The force needs officers like her," said Detective Inspector Hanson. "She's the woman I'm going to tame and make her my wife."

They all laughed.

"I think she is too young to be a superintendent," said Superintendent Baldwin.

"I'm glad you brought that up," said Detective Inspector Hanson. "Miss Jackson has earned her position by working very hard. Yes, I agree that she is young, but not too young to exceed where all of us have failed. Superintendent Baldwin, I believe you either have a grudge against Miss Jackson or you are in favour with the Blacks."

"What are you trying to imply?"

"I'm not implying anything, I'm just stating facts."

"Baldwin, although you are my brother-in-law, I agree with Detective

Inspector Hanson. Why are you so against Miss Jackson? I gave her a promotion because she deserves to be of a higher rank. Gentlemen, I've heard enough! Superintendent Jackson is young and a powerful force on her own. If we're not careful, we won't be needed in the force providing Miss Jackson is doing our jobs. I know she's one of the best and will get better. Now gentlemen, ladies, if you will excuse me, I have to take my wife to dinner in the next hour. I'm sorry to invite you all here at this time, but I thought it was an urgent matter and well worth it. Goodnight to each of you," Judge Lewis said.

"I second that. My wife and I have to be somewhere in the next two hours," said Chief Inspector Saunders.

"This discussion is now over," said Judge Lewis and he left the building.

By this time Petra was in her Grandma's house. Some hours later she drove herself to Madame Stall's house and rang the doorbell. Loretta answered the door.

"You really had me worried. I rang the station and they told me you were released about three hours ago. Where were you Pet? Why didn't you phone to let me know you had been released and that you're okay? Mrs Woods kept on asking for you. Even though I told her you were spending time with your mother, I could see the downhearted look on her face. Pet, she didn't even touch her dinner. She was so worried that something bad must have happened to you. I didn't tell her that you had been arrested."

"Thanks for not telling her Loretta, but why you two think so little of me. Didn't you two have confidence or faith in my returning?" Petra asked.

"Yes of course Petra. But still, I was worried," Loretta said.

"Where's Granny Stall?" Petra asked.

"She's having a nap I believe," Loretta said.

"Okay my friend. I saw Hanson less than three hours ago and he invited me to have dinner with him at his home again tomorrow night, but I turned him down. I've also been promoted to superintendent with a good salary and I will know soon what my salary will be. I might be getting at least twice the amount of what I was getting as a street cop. By the way, I hope you're not lying to me about not saying anything to the old lady."

"Pet, you have not only become my best friend, you're like a sister to me. I would never lie to you or betray you. I didn't tell her anything... and Pet,

I'm so happy for you. Now that you're a highly ranked police officer, will you drop me because I'm no one special?"

"Loretta, everyone is special in some way. I've come to like you a lot and as you said, you have become like a sister to me."

"Pet, I think Hanson is so much in love with you," said Loretta.

"Loretta, you're one of my good friends. I've other good friends of course, but they're all special in other ways. These friends stretch back some years. One day I might tell you about them and me. Even if I become prime minister, you'll still be my good friend. I'll never forsake you Loretta. Speaking of sisters, your case will be heard soon, won't it?" Petra asked.

"No Pet, there will be no case. No trial," Loretta said.

"You mean you won't be bringing a case against that rat of a husband?" Petra asked.

"Exactly," Loretta said.

"Loretta, give me a chance to catch my breath, I don't understand why you don't want to take that rat to court."

"He's willing to give me a quick divorce, providing I don't take him to court. So I agreed. After he sells the house, he will give me half."

"Oh that is excellent news, but can you trust him?"

"I think I can trust him this time. His cousin Sydney Black bought the house cash for us."

"Loretta, I still think that you should take him to court for what he has done to you," Petra told her.

"You know what Pet, let's drop this subject. Besides, I might end up getting the house and I could sell it. We could be partners buying a different house, or move in together. What do you say Pet?"

"Well, it's a good idea, but I really don't know if we might be doing the wrong thing. We are both young and there might come a time when we both would like something different, like having a family, kids, a husband and a house of my own."

"Okay Pet, I've got the message loud and clear," Loretta said.

"Suppose I invite Dr Sean and Hanson to dinner and make arrangements for Madame Stall to have dinner with my Mum and Grandma?" Petra asked.

"Would you do that Pet?" Loretta asked.

"Yes. I want to see the sparkle in Hanson's eyes when he looks at my beautiful body," said Petra, smiling happily.

"This Dr Sean, hasn't he got a girlfriend?" Loretta asked.

"Well, I don't think he has or he wouldn't be inviting me out. If you go along with my idea, he just might have a girlfriend. Then after you get divorced, maybe, you might be inviting me to be maid of honour at your wedding."

"Oh Pet, you've made everything seem so pretty and easy. Let's invite them to dinner sometime next week," Loretta said.

The following day at work, Petra asked Detective Inspector Hanson if he would like to have dinner with her and a couple of friends on Sunday afternoon at four o'clock.

"Yes please," Detective Inspector Hanson replied happily.

Petra gave him the address and directions to Mrs Wood's house. Later on she rang Dr Sean asking him the same.

"Yes, I would like to very much," he said gladly.

On the Friday night Petra asked Madame Stall if she would like to have dinner with her mother and Grandma and to spend the night with them.

"I'd love that very much," Madame Stall said.

On Saturday morning Petra told Madame Stall the reason why she wanted her to have dinner at her mother's house and to spend the night there.

"I understand," Madame Stall said. "I do hope one day this house will be blossoming with children," she smiled.

"I wasn't planning on having children," Petra said and smiled back.

"I didn't say that dear, but it would be nice for a baby to run around the rooms. Oh, how I long for a grandchild, but as my only granddaughter was murdered, I guess it won't be possible to see a baby born in this house."

"Don't count on that. I was thinking of moving in with you … that is if you want me to. By the way, I've been promoted from a street cop to superintendent. Now that I will be getting a good salary, I will be able to afford to pay rent."

"Pet, I don't need your money. I've over two billion pounds plus other things and no one to leave it to. I nearly left it all to the government, but now I will have someone to leave it to."

"Mrs Woods, I really don't need your money," Petra said.

"Well Pet, when I leave it to you, I don't care what you do with it because I know you'll do what you believe is right. Your friend Loretta is a nice girl. I am going to give her the interest that I haven't touched for about fourteen years. Would that be all right with you dear?" Madame Stall asked.

"Is what all right with me?" Petra asked thinking about Detective Inspector Hanson.

"To give your friend Loretta the interest from my account I haven't touched."

"Sure, of course it's all right with me. It's your money and you do whatever you like with it," Petra said.

"Pet, from the time I set my eyes upon you and you came to my rescue, I have been magically drawn to you. There's no one in this world I think I could love as I love you. I'm so very happy these days. All I have will be yours. I will call my lawyer first thing on Monday morning and make a fresh will. I'm seventy-seven years old on the fourteenth of next month. I'm so happy you're here. When you came to my rescue in the casino, I thought that you were sent from heaven above. You leave me now and my world will be dark again," Madame Stall said with saddened eyes.

Petra led Madame Stall into the dining room, where they had supper. After supper Madame Stall freshened up before going to bed.

"Petra, I would like to know for sure. Is Mrs Woods really Madame Stall?" "Yes Loretta, Mrs Woods is Madame Stall, the same very wealthy Madame; her maiden name was Woods."

Loretta stared into Petra's face as the news sunk in.

"Petra, I have to find a home now as I can never let Madame Stall know I was married to one of the family that murdered her granddaughter."

"Don't be silly Loretta. This is our home until we decide that we really want to leave. The truth is, if she saw how your husband treated you she would be happy you're here, as I am. We're like her children. Don't you see, us two belong here with her. Loretta, let's not upset her feelings of happiness. She will be seventy-seven next month. I want her to be very happy and feel confident about us, so I don't want you to say anything to her. I don't want her to know about your husband or come to remember what has happened! So please do us a favour and let's leave the past in the past. She told me that she's going to give you some money and I'm talking of maybe millions," Petra said.

"What? Me? Ah, pull my other leg! Still, if you're not having me on, I could deposit the money she gives me on a house," Loretta said.

"Loretta, I'm serious," Petra said.

Loretta was gobsmacked like it was all too much for her to believe. Loretta reached for the bottle of whiskey and filled up her glass half way. Out of excitement she gulped all the whiskey down her throat and threw herself on the sofa laughing happily.

Petra looked seriously hard in her face.

"I will be rich! I will be rich! And Petra I love you!" she said loudly spreading her legs over the chair arms smiling from ear to ear and showing her red knickers. Petra dropped and sat next to her and said, "I hope you keep your legs closed when our diners are here."

Loretta laughed louder.

"Well Loretta I don't know about you, but I'm going to freshen up, then get to bed as I'm very tired."

"Pet honey, I want to hear more about Dr Sean."

"Loretta, I think it's time we went to bed. I'll go and shower and then I'm going to bed," Petra said.

"Pet, don't you think we should decorate and lighten up the whole place since we'll be living here?" Loretta asked.

"Yes, we'll speak about it tomorrow," Petra said.

As Loretta opened her mouth to speak again, Petra said to her, "I have to go to work in the morning and make a good impression that I love and care about my new job. Don't forget to turn off the lights on your way up."

"But Petra, it's only ten o'clock," Loretta said.

"Loretta, for the past four days I've hardly had any sleep. I've got to go to my bed now because I'm very tired and I don't want to be late for work in the morning."

"Please Petra, stay with me just for half an hour more?" Loretta asked.

"No Loretta. My shower is waiting on me and my bed is calling me. Besides, when I have to get up at six, you will still be in bed. Goodnight!" said Petra and she went to have a shower then went straight to bed.

Loretta had a quick swim then went to her bed.

At four o'clock the following morning Loretta went to Petra's room, as she couldn't get back to sleep. She switched on Petra's headboard lights, sat on her bed, poked her on the back and asked, "Are you sleeping?"

Petra woke up, but she didn't answer. "Petra," she shook her until she answered.

"What's the matter Loretta? By the way what time is it?"

Loretta replied, "Four minutes past four. Pet, this Dr Sean, is he as handsome and tall as Detective Inspector Hanson?"

"Oh Loretta, you woke me up just to ask me about Dr Sean?"

"I'm so nervous about meeting him," Loretta said.

"It's Saturday morning and I'm still tired. We have another day left before our dates. If you think that you're not ready to have dinner with them I could always tell them we've changed our minds," Petra said. "And yes Loretta, Sean's tall and very handsome."

"Pet, I'm only feeling nervous because I don't know if he will like me."

"What makes you think that he wouldn't?" Petra asked her.

"Well, apart from that, I don't want him to get hurt."

"And what makes you think he will get hurt Loretta?"

"You know. One dinner might lead to another and to going out with him. My husband might find out and then he might come looking for a fight."

"Loretta, I thought you told me that your husband is willing to give you a divorce."

"Yes, he's very willing providing we split everything and I don't take him to court. Pet, the money that Granny Stall is going to give me, I really think I would appreciate you keeping it for me until after my divorce."

"Okay, that's not a problem," Petra said.

As soon as Petra got to work her secretary, Fern Elliot, gave her her key. As they sat drinking coffee, Fern said, "Super, I know we're the same age, twenty-two, and I think we'll get on well even though I'm a secretary."

"We sure will Fern. Well, you can call me Petra outside work," Petra told her and they both laughed. That morning, her colleagues welcomed Petra and wished her well in her new job. Detective Inspector Hanson presented her with a gold chain as a sign of friendship, which she accepted happily and he hooked it around her neck.

As time went by, Petra and Loretta made Madame Stall very happy by staying with her. The three of them appeared like mother and daughters. Madame Stall told them she would pine if they ever left her.

"Honestly," Petra said to Madame Stall. "I was thinking seriously of moving in with you altogether."

"Nothing I would like better, with Christmas just a few months away. I would be so happy to smell fresh baking, roast turkey, the cooking of fresh vegetables and many more mouth-watering meals."

"Granny Stall, I was thinking that the whole house could do with decorating to bring the place alive. I'm being cheeky aren't I?" Petra asked.

"No! You're not cheeky. I totally agree with you. I'll call a decorator tomorrow and we'll have this house nicely decorated from top to bottom. I'll let you choose the paints and whatever else you fancy," Madame Stall said then she went on saying, "Pet, I've done something very silly. I should have told you before, but I couldn't bring myself to tell you."

"What is it?" Petra asked.

"Pet, I'm extremely wealthy. The store that I took you in, I own it. I'm so happy to have you and Loretta sharing this enormous house. Petra, I own other businesses without even a mouse to share it with. Since I have got to know you and what you stand for, I wouldn't want you to leave me. But, I also wouldn't want you to do me any favours either by staying here with a frail old woman if you didn't want to. However, nothing would make me happier than if you move in with me or even just visit me regularly."

"You old brute," said Petra laughing. "Just you try and stop me from moving in with you. I think I had better start calling you granny from now on," Petra said.

Tears came into Madame Stall's eyes. She laughed then hugged Petra and said, "I really love you like my very own. I'm really very lucky to have gained two lovely granddaughters."

"We're very lucky too, both Loretta and I."

"Pet, I'm really happy that you and Loretta are here with me," Madame Stall smiled.

"Granny, I'm so happy too," Loretta said.

"Well Loretta, I have this for you." Madame Stall gave Loretta a cheque for fifty million pounds. "We'll see the bank manager tomorrow morning," said Madame Stall. "And Petra, this is yours." She gave Petra a bankbook with over two billion pounds in it and said, "I'll put everything else in your name." When Petra had a look at the amount, she was so flabbergasted that she drank a glass of wine. Loretta was so lost for words she couldn't even manage to say thank you. Madame Stall knew that the gigantic gifts of money were a drop in the deep ocean for her, so she took her lips to Petra's and Loretta's so they would give her a kiss, which they did.

The next morning Madame Stall called in an interior designer and told Petra to tell him how she would like the rooms to look.

Mr Foley, the designer, showed Petra, Loretta and Madame Stall the designs and colours. Petra decided how she would like the rooms, but before she had the rooms decorated, she had them re-modernised so that more sunlight would come in by replacing the wooden windows and doors with plain glass.

Three weeks later Madame Stall's house was renovated and decorated and was looking very beautiful inside and out. Madame Stall paid eleven and a half thousand pounds. When Petra offered to pay her back, Madame Stall said, "You didn't think I'd give you all of the money, did you?"

"But you gave me so much," Petra said.

"Pet, I still have at least two and quarter of a million pounds to buy what I need. I will make you my next of kin so you will have what I leave when I pass away anyway."

"You know, I may even give you the couple of grandchildren that you so long for," Petra smiled.

"Petra, you'll have to first find a nice husband to have children with."

"Don't worry granny, I already have one sealed in a block of ice and when that ice has melted, I will introduce you to him."

Madame Stall laughed heartily.

"Don't worry granny, I intend to give you a couple," Loretta said.

Madame Stall chuckled away in laughter until tears came into her eyes.

On Sunday afternoon, Madame Stall went to have dinner with Petra's mother and Grandma, leaving Petra and Loretta cooking dinner. At five thirty Dr Sean arrived, shortly followed by Detective Inspector Hanson. Dr Sean brought a bottle of red wine and Detective Inspector Hanson brought a bottle of champagne and flowers. Loretta put on Stand By Your Man while they were having dinner and Dr Sean and Detective Inspector Hanson's eyes met. Petra smiled and changed the disc to A Man Without Love by Engelbert. Detective Inspector Hanson gazed into Petra's eyes smiling then served the four of them wine. After dinner, Loretta and Petra showed them around the estate, then they went back into the house for a bottle of champagne and a dance. Loretta put on So Many Ways by Brook Benton. That will be our wedding song," Hanson whispered in Petra's ears.

Dr Sean and Detective Inspector Hanson behaved themselves so well that when they were ready to leave, Petra and Loretta rewarded them both with a kiss on their cheeks. It's now ten o'clock and I'm ready for bed," Petra said.

"The night is still young Petra. We should have asked them to stay longer as you're not working until Tuesday. I think I'm in love with Sean. I must admit he's not as handsome as Hanson, but he's good looking and I love him," Loretta said.

Petra looked at her and smiled. "And thanks for keeping your legs closed."

"Don't worry Pet, the time will come when I will sling my feet around Sean's neck," Petra smiled.

On Monday morning, Petra's mother took Madame Stall home.

"How were your guests?" Madame Stall asked.

"They left at ten o'clock." Madame Stall looked surprised.

"Don't look so surprised, it's only our first date with them and we must not let them think we're easy droppers between their crotches." Petra grinned. Madame Stall laughed happily and said, "I haven't heard words like those in a long time."

Loretta laughed and then called for a taxi. Some hours later Loretta returned home and said, "I went to see Dr Sean."

Chapter 15

One week later Detective Inspector Hanson rang Petra and asked her out to dinner. "Will you ask me some other time?" Petra said and put the phone down.

"Pet, you have money, looks and a shallow head with little brains if you let him go that easily. That young man might not accept your invitation to the next dinner or ask you out again," Madame Stall said.

"Don't worry granny, he will. Oh and by the way, I'm on night shift and after lunch I'm going to sleep so please don't wake me. Where's Loretta?" Petra asked.

"She's gone shopping to spend some of her money and I don't blame her. Oh and she's filing for her divorce she said. I hope she marries a much nicer husband in the future," Madame Stall said.

"I think she will," Petra said.

Four hours later Loretta drove into the yard in a brand new car filled with new clothes and shoes. Petra helped her to carry the clothes and shoes into the house. She then hooked a pretty heart gold chain around Petra's neck and a beautiful silk scarf around Madame Stall's shoulders.

"You're more than a friend to me," Loretta told Petra and kissed her face. "As for you Madame Stall, you're the mother I never knew. I love you both so much."

Three days later Loretta asked Petra to accompany her to see a lawyer and to sign over the house to her husband, in order to be free of him. She was even willing to pay for a quick divorce. Petra took her to Detective Inspector Hanson, as he was a qualified lawyer, a defendant and a witness to see her ex-husband sign the divorce papers.

Two days later Loretta received a phone call from her husband asking her to come home and that he would make it up to her, but Loretta told him never.

One week later Loretta's ex-husband was shot dead outside his gate by his cousin Banjo before the house was doused with petrol and set alight. He then called Loretta a whore after he found out she was with Petra.

The following morning Petra broke the bad news to Loretta that her husband had been killed by Banjo. Loretta grinned. "But I have just told you your husband has been murdered?" said Petra.

"What do you want me to do Petra but to see the brute deep in the ground, then to have a two week holiday away! My first choice would be Florida and then I would like to go to Africa next year," Loretta said.

"Well, try and not develop a taste for travelling as your Dr Sean wouldn't have time."

"Well Petra, I would like to go on a Caribbean cruise as well but with Sean or you Petra."

"I would love to but I have just started my new job."

"Well, will I see Sean again?" she asked.

"I think I could arrange that, and after you get married, will you leave me alone?"

"What are you up to, and who will you marry?"

"Leave it to me, your favourite sister. You'd like us to be sisters wouldn't you?"

"Pet I would really like us to be that," Loretta said, hugging Petra.

"Well we have seven weeks left before Christmas. You could get married at any time because money is now no object, but it wouldn't be fair on other people to invite them at such short notice. Loretta, what if Sean asks you to marry him?"

"He won't ask me."

"But how can you be so sure, don't you like him?" Petra asked.

"Yes, I loved him the first time I met him," Loretta said smiling.

"Well that's what I wanted to hear," Petra said.

"Pet what are you really up to?" Loretta asked anxiously.

"Nothing much Loretta. You shall marry your prince in January."

"Pet, I let him take me," Loretta said looking ashamed.

"When?" Petra asked.

"Two weeks ago. I went to see him and we made love. He was so gentle and loving. Pet I want to be with him always. Oh Pet, I'm so selfish talking about myself, what about you and Hanson?"

"What about us? Okay, I like the bloke very much, but I don't think that I want to be serious with him, or anyone, at least not yet," Petra said.

"Why not Petra, is it because you've been raped?"

"Yes Loretta, I've been raped. I was only fifteen years old. It was my stepfather."

"Oh Pet, I should not have said that, I'm so sorry."

"That's okay Loretta. I expect a slap in my face from time to time to remind me I wasn't strong enough to stop my evil stepfather from raping me!"

"Oh Pet, please forgive me," Loretta begged.

"Don't be sorry, we're fighting like real sisters," said Petra.

"Yes," said Loretta, "But I wish I hadn't said what I said. I'm still sorry for reminding you about that wicked bastard," Loretta said then tears came in her eyes.

"Hey, it's okay, dry your eyes. Say, we could invite our two friends to dinner again," Petra said.

"That would be so cool Petra. What about if you have dinner with Hanson at his house and me at Sean's?"

"Loretta, you really are doing your homework. Still, it's not a bad idea. Well, I'll speak to Hanson and you speak to lover boy," Petra said happily.

"Okay, but let me bury my rat of a husband first," Loretta said.

The following Friday Loretta buried her husband at the Witton cemetery and the refreshments were at the Bamboo Shoot Club. Superintendent Peterson, Chief Inspector Saunders, Chief Inspector Lewis, Detective Todd, his wife Julia, his brother Lance, Joanne and fiancé Curtis, Kim, Officer Hodge, Kelly, Detective Inspector Hanson and his brother Paul, Ira and fiancé, his brother Aaron, Petra's mother, Madame Stall, Stanley, Jenny, Elizabeth, Faith, Petra's four new detective friends, Marlon, Drake, Craig, Blake and so many others were there. As for Sydney Black and his brothers, they made sure no one had to buy drinks. All the mourners knew that they were showing off by putting four bottles of sprit on every table, plus juices, bottles, cans as well as endless pints of beer at the free bar. Even the Black gang were treated with respect that day. As time passed by, more mourners showed up to pay their respects, mostly on behalf of Loretta. Both sides of the hall were full with mourners and Sydney Black seemed glad for the opportunity to speak to Petra. He pinned Petra into a tight corner.

"Look arsehole, I can drop you right here, but I will respect this day even though your cousin deserves to die like a vicious animal," Petra said.

"Look man, Petra. Me no u no likes me but dots okay. Still, deer could be a lickle sumthing develops between us. Listen yah, promise me dat you'll leave me brooders alone and I will give you a whole heap of names that bring Pinckney to me fey money. Mi nat vex with you for what you do to me fool brooder Mark. I hear what he done to u. Now he without a dick. Still, he is very lucky to be alive," Sydney said.

"You evil bastard brothers raped my mother and you will all pay. No deal. I'm going to cut you and your brothers' balls off and shove them down your fucking throats and then leave you to choke on them. Then, I'll whip your arses till you're nearly dead. Now let's save this until another day," said Petra and pushed Sydney out of her way. As she got back to help serve the mourners with food, Detective Inspector Hanson took her to one side.

"Where have you been for the last ten minutes?"

"Are you watching every move I make?" Petra asked him.

"No, not every move, but that Sydney Black, I don't like you talking to him. You keep away from him," Detective Inspector Hanson said towering over Petra.

"Are you asking me or telling me?" Petra asked.

"Both," replied Detective Inspector Hanson.

"Well Mr Detective or Lawyer Hanson, I can take care of myself."

"Pet, I know you can, but I still don't want you to have anything to do with him or anyone connected to him."

"Why do you want to protect me so much?"

"You little fool, because I love you. Pet, will you marry me?"

"Couldn't you ask one of your other women? Or that bitch Marian you had laughing at me before I stuffed my knickers in your mouth to shut you up?" Petra asked.

"I don't want any other woman! I only want you," Hanson said.

"Well sorry Detective Inspector Hanson, I'm not for sale, hire or to give away. You see those four nice people standing and talking to each other?" Petra said, pointing them out.

"I can see many people in groups of fours," said Detective Inspector Hanson.

"Okay, those four standing by the table, those three ladies and gentleman."

"Oh yes, what about them?" Detective Inspector Hanson asked.

"Well, they're my dearest and best friends from school days. We were no more than fifteen when we first met as friends. Apart from that, we're carrying the biggest secret for one another," Petra said.

"That must be some secret," replied Detective Inspector Hanson.

"One of the greatest," replied Petra. "Would you like a drink?" she asked him.

"A cold beer please," he said smiling.

From the fridge she took a cold can of beer and put it in his hand. He squeezed her hand around the can and smiled as he looked at her. She smiled and took her hand away. He pulled the ring open and drank deeply.

"Petra, can I see you again?" His blue eyes showed love.

"Sure you can see me every day and anytime at work," she told him.

"I meant alone for dinner," he said.

"You know what? I think you're in luck. Loretta would like you and Dr Sean to come to dinner. I'll give you the time tomorrow when I get to work." Petra then went up to his brother Paul and said, "Hello Paul. How are you and can I get you anything?"

Paul replied smiling. "I'm very well thank you and thanks for asking but I'm okay for now."

"Well you take care," said Petra and left him eating a plate of food and drinking scotch.

As Petra turned to walk away, Paul said, "Petra would you please do me a favour?"

"Yes of course Paul. What would you like me to do?" she asked him smiling.

"Marry my brother as I asked you before and put him out of his misery," Paul said.

Petra made no reply but smiled and crossed the room to be with her friends Stanley, Elizabeth, Faith, Jenny, Martin and Loretta.

As they stood together talking, laughing and hugging each other, Paul and Hanson were watching them and smiling. Meanwhile, as the room was noisy with music playing and all the talking, Julia went outside and phoned her stepmother Irene and asked her what the children were doing.

"Well, Candice is sleeping and the little master's having his supper. Don't worry about them; they're not worrying about you. As a matter of fact, I don't even think they missed you. Anyway, how's your father behaving?"

"Oh very good. He has to behave himself, especially because he has a beautiful wife like you," Julia said.

Irene laughed. "You take care and don't worry about the children."

"I won't. And Mum, I love you."

Julia walked into the club just in time to see her husband kissing Kim. She said nothing to either of them, but she was very upset and when he touched her she walked away. When it was time for her to go home, he took her and Kim in the same car. She sat beside him without saying a word. As he knew what he'd done, he said nothing to her either except that his face was riddled with guilt. He dropped Kim off at his mother's gate then took his wife home so that she could change her clothes before collecting their children.

Just before they left to get the children, he tried to kiss her, but she slapped his face telling him, "You keep away from me." On their way over to Irene's he put his arm around her shoulders. She flung his arm off her and slapped him again.

"Don't touch me!"

"Why are you doing this to me?" he had the nerve to ask her.

"I saw you kissing that bitch!" Tears welled up in Julia's eyes.

"Oh," he said shamefully. "She tried to kiss me but I pushed her away."

"Todd, you're such a damn liar. I watched you kissing her. I wouldn't be at all surprised if her child turns out to be yours."

"Look, I've two children and another on the way. So don't you try and give me another one," he said.

"Todd, I liked pleasing your parents by proving to them that I was a virgin when we got married. You had no idea how embarrassed I was. I thought our sex life was our business. I had no idea that your parents would interfere. They just had to know when we first made love."

"It could have been worse," Todd joked. "Dad could have sampled you first to check that you were," he laughed tickling her.

And that made her laugh as well.

"This means I can touch?"

"No Todd. If I ever find out that Kim's child is yours, I'll leave you. I don't want to see you anywhere near to Kim again if you want our marriage to last."

"Our marriage will last till death do us part. We're a family, you, me and our kids," Todd said, touching Julia's belly. "And this one inside you."

Julia smiled and put her hand over his. Todd drove into Superintendent Peterson's driveway and turned the engine off. Julia got out and opened the door with her key and let both her and Todd into the house to meet Irene sitting in the living room watching television.

"Mum, we've come to take the children home."

"But they're sleeping. Besides, I think it's too draughty to take them out. Why don't you come back for them tomorrow?"

"But Mum, they might be too much for you to look after. Since we're here we might as well take them home," Julia said.

"Please Julia, I can manage with the children, I really can," Irene said.

"Okay, I'll be over early in the morning to help you bathe them," Julia said then she and Todd went to have a peep at the kids.

"Julia, you know Candice will miss you," Todd said.

"I know, but it would hurt Mum's feelings if I take the children home. Todd, she is so grandmotherly to them."

"I know that Jul, but think about how the children might react when they wake up tomorrow morning and don't see either of us. Especially Candice, you know how miserable she can be when she doesn't see you."

Julia went and told her stepmother Irene that she was going to take the children home. Smiling, Irene said, "I understand, but please bring them over at the weekend."

"Yes, of course," said Julia then she woke the children up and wrapped them in warm sheets. Her husband carried Candice while she carried her son to the car. Irene saw them drive away then closed the door. On their way home, Julia was deep in thought as she sat in the back with her sleeping children. As Julia kept silent, Todd looked back at her saying, "Honey, why are you giving me the silent treatment?"

Julia smiled and lowered her eyes on the children.

"What's the matter darling?" he asked her.

"Nothing," she replied and cuddled her children closer to her.

Todd tried to make Julia laugh by saying, "It would be nice if we could have a unisex child this time."

Julia sounded a little giggle then she went back to being silent.

When they got home, ten minutes had passed before the phone started ringing. Julia picked the phone up.

"Hello," she said but there was no answer, just a dead ring tone.

Five minutes later the phone rang again, but this time Todd answered.

"It's Kim, where were you?" she asked crossly.

"Why?" Todd asked.

"I've been trying to reach you for the past twenty minutes. I want you to come over right now," she said.

"Why?" he asked and turned his back on Julia.

"It's Justine," she said.

"What about her?" He asked.

"She has a fever, I think. I want you to come over right now," she demanded.

"Why don't you call a doctor in?" he asked then turned to look at Julia making coffee. He hung up, went upstairs and rang Kim back. "Why have you called me?"

"I'm calling her father. If you don't want your wife to know about our first child, I suggest you come over right now," she said.

"You..."

She put the phone down, cutting him off.

"Damn!" he said in vexation and went down to Julia. "Honey, I've got to go and get your father home."

"I'm sure Curtis will take him," Julia said.

"I'm not sure about Curtis. I'll be back soon," he told her and rushed out of the house.

When he walked into his mother's house, Kim hooked her arms around his neck and led him upstairs to her room.

"What's this about my child? You didn't tell me Justine is my child."

"Do I ever see you to tell you anything, and can't you see that Justine is yours?"

"Look Kim, I don't want Julia to find out. I'll give you enough money to keep the child until she no longer needs support."

"And don't you think she is entitled to know who her father is?"

"Kim, you gave yourself to me willingly and most of the time you encouraged me. I told you that I didn't love you then or now! You accept the money or nothing and then I'll have to tell Julia the truth myself," Todd warned Kim.

"And what then? Do you think she will welcome you with open arms and pat you on your back for being a good husband. I really don't think she will!" Kim said smirking.

"Even if my wife kicks me out, I know that I don't want a little tramp like you. Take what I'm offering you or nothing! Whichever way, I won't give a damn. And I want you out of my mother's house by the end of next month. You have six weeks!" Todd fumed.

"Okay, I can be as reckless as you. You want to play? I can play a better game than you," Kim shouted.

"What do you mean by that?" Todd asked.

"Well, since you don't want me to tell your wife about our daughter then let's hear what your father and mother will have to say," Kim said.

"Kim, you say anything about us to my parents and I'll kill you!" He dragged her by her hair, tossed her on the floor and fucked her hard from behind, making her groan till he'd finished. He then wrote a cheque for one hundred and fifty thousand pounds, flung the cheque into her face and threw a five pence coin on the floor at her feet.

"That cheque is for the child, the five pence is for the fuck and to remind you never to tell anyone about us. No one! Not even our daughter you said is mine! Don't ever phone my house again. If you do, I'll force my wife to sue you for harassing her and then I'll kill you!"

"Fuck you!" Kim screamed. "Get out! Get out!"

"You have six weeks to find somewhere and get out," Todd told her.

Just then Todd's mother knocked on Kim's door.

"Come in," Kim said drying her eyes.

Mrs Todd entered Kim's room to see her son Todd. "I thought I heard your voice."

"Yes, you did. I was just telling Kim about a flat I saw to rent."

"But I thought Kim was happy here with little Justine? Sometimes Justine reminds me of you. If you and Kim weren't cousins I would swear Justine was yours. She resembles you so much! There's cold meat in the fridge if you want to make yourself a sandwich."

"Thanks Mum, but I've got to get back to my wife."

"Oh, tell her that I want to see her tomorrow."

"Why do you want to see her?"

"Todd, this is between Julia and me. Just give her my message please."

"Sure." Todd looked hard at Kim.

Kim turned her face away and Todd left.

"Well young lady, you get yourself some rest. You look so tired."

"Aunt Dorothy,"

"Yes Kim."

"I've been thinking about getting a place of my own for some time."

"What brought this on?"

"Oh nothing, I just want to see if I can make it on my own. I really would like to try to be independent."

"Well, if that's what you want, I'm happy for you, but if you are in any need of my help, please don't hesitate to ask me for it. Anyway, when do you think you will be leaving?"

"As soon as I find a place of my own," said Kim.

"Why don't you ask Todd to help you look for somewhere since it was his idea?" Mrs Todd's smile was letting Kim know that she knew about her and Todd.

"Sure aunt, I think I will do just that," said Kim

"Well goodnight Kim."

"Goodnight Aunt Dorothy."

The next morning Kim put the cheque into her bank account and then went looking for a house when she happened to meet Officer Hodge.

"Hello Kim, what's brought you around this area?"

"Oh, I'm looking for a place for me and my daughter to live."

"If you don't find what you're looking for I've a couple of rooms you could rent," Officer Hodge told her.

"Do you mind if I have a look at the rooms?" she asked.

"I thought you might like to search around first, then if you don't find anything you like, you can have a look at the rooms. My mother is living with me but she's as quiet as a lamb. I think you will like her," Officer Hodge said.

"Are you proposing to me?" Kim asked him.

"If that's how it sounds to you, I apologise," Officer Hodge said.

"That's okay, but I would really like to see the rooms," Kim said.

"Would tomorrow afternoon suit you?" Officer Hodge asked.

"Tomorrow afternoon would be fine," said Kim and Officer Hodge wrote the address down and gave it to her.

"Thanks," she said.

"I'll be at home because my mother has arthritis and cannot move around too quickly," he said.

Kim smiled and walked away.

The following afternoon Kim went to Officer Hodge's house to look at the rooms. He showed her around and she was extremely pleased with them. She told him that she would take the two rooms and asked him how much he wanted.

"We'll discuss the amount when you move in. We'll share the kitchen and bathroom," he said.

"Well can I move in sometime next week?" Kim asked anxiously. "And I won't mind sharing."

"Sure, you can move in whenever you please. Just let me know when you would like to move in and I'll give you a key."

"Okay."

"Would you like to come with me and have a drink?" Officer Hodge asked her.

Kim got into his car and had a drink with him in the local pub. After they had had a few drinks, he took her home. Later that night, Kim told her Aunt Dorothy that she had found a place and that she'd be moving out the following weekend. Her aunt wasn't too pleased, but she accepted and respected Kim's decision.

"Kim dear, I do hope you know what you're doing. If you really want to move out I won't stand in your way."

"Aunt Dorothy thanks, but I really do need my own space, especially as I have a child and Curtis is sometimes here with Joanne."

"Kim, are you sure that's the only reason you want to move out?"

"There's no other reason Aunt Dorothy. Justine and I will visit you often."

Mrs Todd smiled and went into the kitchen to make lunch.

Meanwhile, Todd's conscience was getting to him so much so that he hardly touched his lunch. When Julia told him that she wanted him to take the children to his mother's house so that she could go to the clinic, he told her to take the children herself.

"What's the matter with you?" Julia asked.

"Nothing," he replied and he took the children to Irene's instead.

The next morning Julia decided to some clothes that they wore to the dry cleaners. Searching through the pockets before taking them she found Todd's chequebook in his jacket pocket. She couldn't resist looking to see how and on what he spent his money. Suddenly her face turned to stone when she saw that he had written out a cheque for one hundred and fifty thousand pounds. She said nothing to him, but put his chequebook on her dressing table so that he would know she had seen the amount withdrawn.

That morning he didn't look Julia in her face, but when she looked at him, he walked away as he knew that she knew about the money.

Two weeks later, as Todd's conscience was choking him, he lied to Julia and told her that he lent his dad the money. By that time, however, Kim had told Joanne about the money and Joanne had told Petra. Neither Petra nor Joanne said anything to Julia, but Petra made it her business and said to Todd, "It's best you tell Julia about Kim's child." Petra further said, "Julia is a very understanding woman." Todd didn't like what Petra said, so he got angry and slapped her in the face and told her to mind her own damn business. Petra slapped him back and said to him, "I'm woman enough to take care of my own business. Your wife chose me as her friend and I'm godmother to your daughter Candice and I've the right to tell her what she's up against. I don't want to see my goddaughter ending up hurt and without her father and with another man that might abuse her. Use your head Todd. Tell your wife about Kim's child before someone else tells her. It won't be easy, but I know Julia will understand and forgive you. Todd, Julia loves you very much; you might possibly save your marriage now. But next week it might be too late, especially if she hears it from Kim or your mother. You think about what I've said," Petra told him.

Soon after, Petra went to the police canteen to have lunch. While she was eating, Todd took his lunch over.

"Can I sit with you?" he asked her.

"Why?"

"I was thinking about what you said to me. May I sit down now?" he asked politely and smiling.

"Sure," Petra said with her mouth full with food.

Todd took his seat. "Can I buy you a drink?" he asked her.

"Thanks, a coke would be fine," she said.

He asked Petra to excuse him while he went to buy the drinks. He then bought two large glasses of iced coke and returned to their table. He put one in front of Petra and one in front of him. He then took his seat and began to eat. Over lunch he said to Petra, "One day you'll make a man very happy. That's if and when you find a husband," he smiled.

"Well thank you," Petra said.

"I really meant what I said Pet, what you said, you're absolutely right, but I really don't know where to start to tell Julia about Kim's child."

"How about starting with the fact that you were drinking too much the night before your wedding and Kim took advantage of you," Petra advised Todd.

"Pet, I gave Kim one hundred and fifty thousand pounds to keep quiet as a one-off payment to support the child."

"Todd, that's the worst thing you could have done. Does Julia know about the money?"

"I think she does, but she doesn't know I gave the money to Kim. I suspect she saw the chequebook and I lied by telling her that I lent the money to my dad."

"Look Todd, suppose I gave you the money to put back." Petra said.

"Really? Could you do that?" Todd asked as he was looking at Petra in wonder.

"Now Todd, I'm doing this because I wouldn't want to see you and Julia's marriage fall apart," said Petra as she wrote a cheque out for one hundred and fifty thousand pounds and handed it to Todd.

Todd looked hard at the cheque then at Petra seriously and in disbelief.

"It's genuine. I'm a very serious woman. What I do is for real. Todd, I'm doing this to save your marriage," Petra said.

"Sure," replied Detective Todd. "But can you afford this amount?" he asked Petra.

"If I couldn't, I wouldn't have given you the money," Petra said.

"Thanks and I'll see you get every penny of it back," said Detective Todd.

"Give it to Julia and she doesn't have to know about this," Petra told him.

"But can you afford this much, can you really Petra?"

"Todd, I'll let you on in a secret, I have inherited a large amount of money."

"You're joking?"

"No it's true. As a matter of fact, I've already invested ten million in Candice's name. The money must not be touched until she's eighteen. I think that is the right age for her to have access to it, as she will know the value of money by that time. Well, I think eighteen is a mature age anyway; I want her to spend some while she is young."

"You gave my daughter ten million pounds!"

"She's my godchild and I swore to take some responsibility for her upbringing and future. I also hope that I'll get the chance of helping to counsel her while she grows into a young lady. I would like her to have a much better life than I did."

"What are you saying Petra. My daughter's parents aren't capable enough to take care of her?" Todd asked.

"No! I'm not saying that at all. Todd I was raped twice by my stepfather at the age of fifteen and almost a third time. That is why I don't want you and Julia to split up. From when I got to know Julia, I got to like her very much; she's a lovely person. She didn't have to invite me to her wedding, but she did."

"Yes," said Todd, but as he knew that it was him that invited Petra, he said nothing more.

Their lunchtime was over and they went back to work.

Two days later, Petra went to the Blue Moon casino. She went to the counter and called for an iced coke. While waiting for her drink, she turned and faced the players on table ten. As her eyes met Sydney Black's, she turned and faced the proprietor's daughter. As she put her drink on the counter Sydney walked over to her. She took her drink then went to her table and sat down. Sydney picked her drink up and drank some, then smiled in her face.

"So watts up, de mighty and loveable Pet? The more I see you, the more beautiful you look."

"That's me," Petra said.

"You want me fee buy you another drink?" he asked Petra.

"Why not, seeing as you've put your mouth on mine," replied Petra smoothly.

He called the pretty waitress over to Petra's table. The waitress went to him immediately.

"I want a double whiskey and gee de lady what she wants."

"Just a coke please," Petra said.

"Why coke, you nu want brandy and coke knar champagne? I man want you to feel happy and have the best," Sydney said.

"No, just a coke will do," Petra said to the waitress.

The waitress returned and put the glass of coke down in front of Petra. Petra thanked her. She smiled and said to Petra, "It's a pleasure serving you." She then put the glass of whiskey on the table in front of Sydney, barely smiled and left. Petra took a sip of her coke.

"Yah crises you know gel," Sydney said.

"And you're really a bastard," Petra told him.

"Yu sit really high, me must admit mi envy you."

"Why should you envy me? You're a very rich and powerful man. You can do what you want and get away with it. Even the police seem to fear you. You can also buy any woman you want. That's if they are blind and stupid enough to fall for a rotten bastard like you," Petra said.

"Yes man, yah right, me have de money and me have de power. But me no got de gal dat I want. You get me? I want you, you pretty."

Petra's friend Amelia was sitting at table eight when she saw Petra and Sydney. She went to Petra and asked, "Can I see you?"

"Yes of course," Petra said and got up and walked away with her. They stood some distance away from Sydney and stood talking.

"Petra my friend, I'm so disgusted seeing you and Sydney Black sitting together and drinking."

Petra smiled broadly then said, "Amelia, you have nothing to worry about. I know what I'm doing. By bringing down that evil bastard and dangling him under my shoe heel, his other followers will be nothing for me to crush. Are you on your own?"

"Yes, I'm fresh out of money. I just lost my last two hundred quid on the machine and I could do with a stiff whiskey without ice."

"Then let's get back to the bastard and milk him to our hearts content," Petra said then she and Amelia went and sat with Sydney. "This is my friend," Petra told him.

"Good to meet you. You want a drink?" he asked her.

"Yes please, thank you," Amelia said then looked at Petra smiling.

"Waiter," Sydney called.

The waiter went to him. "Serve the lady," he said.

"A rum and coke please," Amelia said. "And another bottle of your best champagne," Sydney said.

The waiter returned with Amelia's rum and coke and the champagne. "Well ladies, nothing but the best for you."

Then Petra and Amelia asked Sydney to excuse them before going to the ladies.

"Petra I really don't like that man. He's evil. He's the spider and you might end up like the fly. Let's say goodbye to him and leave."

"Amelia, I really know what I'm doing. If I have to marry him in order to kill him, I will do so. His men raped my mother."

"What!" Amelia said shocked then asked, "Did he ask you to marry him?"

"No not yet, but he will and I would accept just to crush the bastard and his men. I want you to keep this to yourself. You tell anyone and it gets back to him, you might be coming to my funeral as you suggested. Now let's go back and drink him dry. I feel like a stiff brandy this time," Petra said in high spirits and in a mocking way.

They both left the toilets and returned to their seats to sit with Sydney.

"A what u two want to drink dis time?" he asked.

"Well I'll have a brandy this time," said Petra.

"The same for me please," said Amelia

"Yu hear dat waiter. Two brandies and a rum and coke fey me." Sydney popped the bottle of champagne, filled the glasses and said, "Drink up beautiful ladies."

Within minutes their drinks were on the table. Petra ended up with three brandies and her friend had four rum and cokes, two brandies and champagne. At closing time, Sydney gave Petra a kiss on the back of her hand, his telephone number and told her to call him anytime, day or night. He also invited her to a day out viewing his estate and to the horse racing at Newbury. Petra loved that and she ended up kissing him on his face in pretence. She then rushed away quickly to the toilet to wash her face and then rushed home to scrub her face with soap and water.

Chapter 16

The next day at work, Detective Inspector Hanson took Petra to one side and asked her, "Were you with Sydney Black last night?"

"Why do you ask?"

"Petra, what the hell do you think you were doing?"

"I don't know what you mean," Petra said.

"I'm referring to last night in his casino!"

"Oh that!" Petra said.

"Yes! Oh that! Pet, I warned you to keep away from trouble."

"Yes, you did but I know what I'm doing."

"Pet, have you any idea what you're getting yourself into?"

"Yes Hanson I do! Anyway what do you care?"

"I do care, I ... I ... Oh, never mind," he said angrily.

Before Petra turned to walk away, Detective Inspector Hanson gently twirled her around and kissed her hurriedly. She pulled herself away and slapped his face.

"The next time you want to kiss me, ask me first!" she said and walked off quickly.

"Is my kiss telling you anything?" he shouted to her.

"No," Petra shouted back, "But I bet my slap told you never to kiss me again."

Smiling continually she walked away. Detective Inspector Hanson then felt the spot where she slapped him and smiled. "Oh Petra, you'll never know how much I love you."

At tea break Detective Inspector Hanson went to sit with Detective Todd.

Detective Todd watched him fold a piece of paper, tear it making a pattern, then stretch it open to reveal shapes of a man, woman, a boy and a girl holding hands. Detective Todd smiled then said to Detective Inspector Hanson, "What's the matter with you mate, you're looking so lost. Are you thinking about Petra by any chance?"

Detective Inspector Hanson answered. "Yes, but she can be so damn stubborn."

"I like her. She's great, one of the best," said Detective Todd.

"I love her," Detective Inspector Hanson said bluntly.

"Well, why don't you tell her how you feel?"

"I've told her. I even kissed her and she slapped my face. Frankly I think she dislikes me."

"It's more likely that she disapproved of you kissing her by surprise. But I do think she's madly in love with you. Shoving her panties in your mouth, she's telling you she's in love with you. She's yours mate. It's a matter of time before she invites you to her crotch," Todd laughed.

Hanson's eyes stretched open then a big smile spread over his face.

Todd looked at him and smiled.

"Hanson, what I'm going to tell you, I don't want you to ever speak about it to anyone, especially her."

"I promise," said Detective Inspector Hanson.

"Firstly, she is godmother to one of my daughters. Secondly, she is a very wealthy woman with at least two billion pounds wrapped around her plus the Hot Leg Store. The money and the store is inheritance from someone I don't know. Thirdly, she has just helped me to save my marriage by giving me one hundred and fifty thousand pounds that I had to give to Kim as a payoff for a child she claims is mine. Hanson, I was so stupid to fall for a little tramp like Kim and that almost cost me my marriage, not to mention some details I wouldn't want to go into. Petra even gave my daughter ten million pounds, but most importantly, she told me her reasons for trying to be a good cop, and why she wants to achieve so much: her stepfather raped her twice at the age of fifteen. So now you know why she slapped your face."

"Oh my God," Detective Inspector Hanson said then tears welled up in his eyes. "Todd, I didn't know. Neither had I any idea what she went through. I'm so sorry. How can I face her? I really love her Todd, I really do."

"Well if I were you, I would be really careful about how you handle her, especially when she's just been promoted to superintendent and is so very wealthy and beautiful. Of course, also not forgetting that she can take care of herself. Any man would snap her up, including me if I wasn't married."

"Thanks for telling me mate." Hanson dried his tears.

"That's the least I can do mate. But you tell her how you feel."

After work Petra went home to speak to Loretta.

"Loretta, when I got in last night you were sleeping so I didn't wake you. You won't believe this, I was drinking with the devil himself last night, Sydney Black!"

"Pet, are you going mad? After that bastard let his men rape your mother? Petra are you going out of your mind drinking with that animal?"

"Loretta, I can handle him."

"Pet, I hope so."

"Don't worry about me, I'll be okay."

"What if he decides he wants to have sex with you?"

"Trust me sis, that will never happen. All I want to do is to wipe out all those bastards. And if I have to marry the bastard to kill him, then so be it. My intention is to take everything that he owns and give it all to the orphans. Then I'll send his sorry arse to the depths of hell, him and his kind."

"Petra for your own sake, I only hope you know what you're doing."

"Sure I know what I'm doing Loretta. Anyway, I owe this much to the youths, my mother and especially to Madame Stall's granddaughter. So the only way for me to end the chapter of Sydney and his kind is to wipe them off the face of this earth. Madame Stall has paid me very well to destroy the beasts that were responsible for raping and killing her granddaughter. Loretta, there's no one else trying to protect people from those brutes and killers; not even the police. So it's down to me to try and stop the brutal bastards and that includes the crooked police. Oh I'm so angry I will blast them all to hell with the Black's bunch. Loretta, all I want you to do is to have faith in me. The rest is up to me to restore justice and that I will do," Petra said.

"Petra, what about Hanson. Do you love him?"

"Yes Loretta, I love him. But I can't afford to get involved with him until I finish what I have set out to do." Petra said.

"Pet, I love you very much, you're like a sister to me and I am feeling so scared for you," Loretta said.

"I'll be okay Loretta. Once I have power over Sydney, I will have the others squashed under my shoes like lumps of shit."

"Pet, you and whose army are going to take the Blacks down?" Loretta asked sarcastically.

"Loretta, if you're trying to be funny, please doesn't bother going there," Petra said.

"Pet, what if Sydney invites you to his estate to trap you?" Loretta asked but her face showed fear.

Petra laughed, then kissed Loretta on her forehead.

"Pet, I'm very serious. Sydney and his kind are not to be taken lightly. I mean Sydney might really love you, but at the same time he might hate you for busting them."

"Well Loretta, I realise the anxiety you're feeling, but I will be okay," Petra said.

"Still I don't like the idea, but it's your life Pet. Promise me though, if you should go to that Sydney Black's place and anything should happen to you, let me know so that I can send the police; I mean Hanson."

"Okay, you're right. I promise you if I need help I will get word to you, then, just call Hanson or his brother Paul. But I doubt if I will need them. Hey, do you want to go to a party on Saturday night?" Petra asked Loretta.

"Sure." Loretta's voice sounded sad.

Later that night Petra went to see her mother and Grandma. After she left them she went to Julia's and spent some time with her and the kids. Before she left she gave Candice her four-year-old Goddaughter the proof of her ten million pounds she'd put in the bank, made out to Mrs Julia and Mr Vincent Todd. "It is for the children's future," Petra explained. When Julia saw the amount of money she almost had a fit; she thought Petra was playing a prank on her.

"But... but..." said Julia, lost for words.

"Julia, I really can afford it. When I told you about the money, I saw the doubtful look on your face. However, I want my Goddaughter and the rest of your kids to be independent when they become adults. I love Candice like my own child and little Todd too."

"Well, I don't know what to say but thank you." She hugged Petra then tears welled up in her eyes. "Petra, I really don't know what to say."

"Say nothing and dry those pretty glittering eyes."

"Petra, I know you're ready to leave, but I'm hungry. Would you like a turkey or salmon sandwich and some homemade ginger beer?"

"I would love a turkey sandwich please Julia."

When they had finished eating, Petra gave Candice a hug then said to Julia, "Thanks for the sandwich and beer but I'm afraid I have to leave."

"Well goodbye Petra and our home will always be open to you."

Petra kissed little Candice on her face before she left.

Two days later Sydney Black invited Petra to his estate; she accepted. He escorted her inside and showed her around his mansion, then took her horse riding around his fifty-acre estate. As they rode side by side he said to her, "I and I man sorry for what me brooder done to you mudder."

Petra smiled and mumbled an inaudible response.

"One day all of this might be yours if you marry me," he said.

Petra smiled without giving him an answer. As they were exploring his enormous estate, he asked Petra to be his wife.

Petra replied, "I will need time to think."

"I agree," he said. "Tek all de time you need. But you have fey remember I man time is limited. De pain is running deep in me like burning fire. And most time it feels like me blowing me last breath like me feeling pain dis minute. So be quick wid de answer," he said.

"What's the matter with you and what about your girlfriend?" Petra asked him.

He replied solemnly, "I man is very sick and de hole heap of deem woman I man had nasty. When I want pleasure, I explore in deem like the world. None of deem I would or could make special. It's you me love, I man got more love for you than I love me self. I done many wrongs, I know it would be very hard for you to forgive me. Especially what me brooder and cousin done to your mudder, but believe I was under a great rock and in a lot of pain. Pet, I beg you straight from the heart... find a lickle soft spot for me no?"

"Maybe I can, but why did you ask me to marry you?"

"Cause me love you and me know you here to destroy me. But we can't let dat happen. Me no want fight you. I love you. Come on now, we have to get back in because me have to take my medication."

"You know that I'm out to destroy you and you still want to marry me?" Petra said.

"Yeah, that's why I man want to marry you. 'Cause I know when you lick two bullets in me backside, it won't look as bad as the people out deer know I am a bad man. And plus me no want no stranger fey kill me. Love hurts but I will eventually establish dat."

Petra faced him saying, "How dare you say that! You, you don't feel anything. You're heartless. What do you know about love and feeling hurt?"

He turned his back on Petra as tears ran from his eyes and said, "I man dying from a very rare sickness but I only told you. When I die, my wickedness will die wid me." He then faced Petra and said, "I'll give you the name of judges, lawyers, detectives, police officers and others that used to bring the young pickiness to me, white and black for a fee. But promise me dis, you'll look after me brooder Redd and you drive him away from harm. Don't let him get lock up or end up dead. And one more ting, if you have to shoot me by your hand send the bullet right in my heart so I'll die quick. Listen carefully, me know want no one to find out me a die from a sickness. Pet, me have about fourteen weeks left and my sight is now deteriorating wid muff sores brook out 'all over me body and half de time me can't even bear the pain. But wid you here now, the pain is much more less. It was only last week me have me blood clean, my mudder die from the same disease five mont ago. As I man told you before, I'm constantly in pain, real pain. I want to give back to deem people what me taken; I know I am an evil rotten bastard. But even the devil needs a friend at some time. Petra, I am begging you only if you marry me, everything that is mine will be yours to give to charity as you had state to help the youths. I'll be soon gone but I hope I'll never be forgotten and you will be de hero that capture me."

Then he put a loaded gun into Petra's hand and kneeled at her feet saying, "Shoot me Pet. Shoot me straight in my heart." Petra backed away saying, "If you so want to die, why you don't commit suicide?"

"No! In my eyes suicide wouldn't be justified, it will only make me a coward. But if I die under your hand you will be classed as a hero and will be rewarded to a higher rank and you could have my fortune go to charity or even build home for the mothers. So, me beg you kill me now to end my pain. You fey tell police you kill me in the line of duty. About my fortune nobody fey interferes when I leave it all to orphans in your care."

"I don't like your deal, but I'd go along with what you've decided and only for the sake of what you said," Petra said.

"Then come gal, marry me in two weeks. Don't keep me waiting," Sydney pleaded.

"Before I do, I want you to make the will out and give it to Sister Hanley to build homes for abused mothers and kids. All your money and what you have I want you to give up. Tomorrow morning when you have done so, I'll marry you. But remember this is only out of pity and not love. I shouldn't even feel pity for you, but I do. I'm also doing this for the people who need it."

"Okay that's sweet, whatever you say. All understood," said Sydney. "But I man will want you to have few millions to remember me that I'm not all bad. One more thing my sweet, after I man hear that two of my workers raped Madame Stall's granddaughter and then give she to me dog, I man shoot them. Me begging you to forgive me for the bad I did. Gal, I man love you so much it is unbelievable."

Two days later Sydney made out his will and sent for Sister Hanley and gave more than half of his wealth to her in the presence of Petra and his and Sister Hanley's lawyers. Petra also sent out invitations to her friends stating that she was going to marry Sydney Black.

When Sydney's family and workers heard that he was going to marry Petra they began to demand money and leave his estate. But his lawyer Larry Herbert and Banjo challenged Petra to a fight. Larry aimed his gun at Petra, but she kicked it out of his hand and Sydney shot him in the chest, killing him instantly. Banjo fled for his life. Sydney gave the gun to Petra and pressed his palms together and closed his eyes saying, "Trust I, it was self-defence."

Petra called in the police and told them what had happened, but as some of them had received money from Sydney, they dismissed Herbert as an intruder and stated his death was an accident. That same Thursday morning Petra reminded Sydney that marrying him was purely a deal so that all his assets would be shared amongst charities.

Later that evening Petra went to tell Detective Inspector Todd. She told him her reasons for marrying Sydney.

"Well the truth is Pet, as a friend, I don't approve. I respect your decision, but please do be very careful my friend. My blessings are with you." He then hugged Petra and kissed her on the cheek. Petra smiled and left with a clear conscience.

The following week at two o'clock Petra and Sydney were married at his mansion by a middle-aged parish priest. As the priest knew Sydney's character he took Petra to one side and told her, "I understand you are a police officer. Still, be very careful with your husband." Then his eyes dropped on Petra's one and a half million pound sapphire, ruby and diamond wedding ring. "Good Lord, he must be really in love with you. And to add to that, you're a very beautiful young lady."

"This is for the church." Petra gave the priest a cheque for a quarter of a million pounds.

"Thank you." The priest's eyes instantly became clouded with tears.

After the marriage the party began. Petra's childhood friends and family stood by her in support. They were her brother Arden, Stanley, his wife Elizabeth, Faith, Jenny and Martin. They called themselves 'The Bitter Desires'. Stanley saw Sydney sitting on his own but didn't realise he was in pain. He went to him and spoke softly in his ears, "You hurt my friend in any way and I'll send you straight to hell with the deadliest poison."

Sydney smiled, "I could never hurt what I mon deeply love and treasure."

Stanley saw Detective Inspector Hanson standing with Detective Todd and he went and asked him to make a speech on behalf of Petra, but because he was so in love with Petra, he shed some tears and walked away. Detective Todd went on stage and made a speech instead. As the guests applauded him he walked to Petra and said, "Hanson was here but he left."

When Superintendent Peterson went on stage to make his speech the noise in the hall reduced to complete silence; you could have heard a pin drop. When Petra caught a glimpse of Hanson standing alone outside, she knew then how much he loved her. She went to him but he rushed away, got into his car and drove off.

A few days later Petra rang Chief Inspector Saunders, Superintendent Lewis, Judge Peters, Officers Clews, Hatchet and Baldwin to let them know that she knew that they were responsible for many youths' kidnapping and murders.

The following week, Superintendent Lewis committed suicide.

Two days later, Chief Inspector Saunders was fished out of his swimming pool dead. His wife told police the barking of their dog woke her and as she turned on the lights she saw her husband lying face down in the swimming pool. She also told the police that her husband was drinking heavily that night.

Judge Peters was also found dead by his son Danny in his library sitting in his chair with a bullet hole in the side of his head.

Five days later, Officers Chambers and Hatchet turned themselves in, saying they were guilty of kidnapping teenagers and taking them to Sydney Black for money. Two other officers also confessed to selling youths to the Black brothers. They were all tried, found guilty and sent to prison for eight years each.

Another week later and Blacky went to Sydney and asked him, "What this me hear about you married that police bitch?"

"Yes, me love her, so what u want to do about it?" Sydney asked.

"Me bin working for you since me a boy and now u want to drive me away without nothing? Well since you only want the police bitch to finish you off, you give me four hundred thousand let me fuck out of your life."

"Blacky, I have nothing now. I man give all me had away," Sydney said harshly.

"You fucked up man, me a go cut you bloodclart trout if I don't get watt me ask you for." Blacky flicked his knife open. Sydney grabbed his gun and fired. Click – the gun was empty. Sydney stumbled to his piano leaning against it as he was in pain, clenching both hands around his chest.

Blacky rushed towards him. "You tink dis the time when you shot me, boy, I man a go swipe you bumbaclart trout! Then I man will deal with you bitch after me kill you."

Sydney stared at Blacky in surprise, but groaning heavily in pain.

"I man did had you ask me cousin but no more," Blacky said and he took the chair up, beating it against Sydney's piano. He did not stop until the chair and piano fell to pieces. He then kicked Sydney backwards to the floor and cruelly dragged his knife across Sydney's throat. "Fuck you," he brawled when he saw blood spouting. "Who fucked now?"

Blacky walked over Sydney and began smashing up the bedroom searching for money. From the safe he got seven thousand pounds. He left in his car like a wild deer.

As Petra didn't care about Sydney, she didn't bother contacting him to see if he was all right.

Then one Sunday morning, a woman was walking her dog and discovered Sydney's brother Mark and his cousin Banjo's bodies in a car by the roadside with bullet wounds in their foreheads.

On the Monday morning at work, Superintendent Brooks and Judge Evans partly blamed Petra for their colleagues' murders, but they hadn't the guts to tell her to her face. Even so, they honoured her with a solid gold wristwatch engraved with the word 'Exceed' on the back.

That Monday night, Petra left her mother and went to Sydney's to discover his body on the guest room floor with his throat slit. She called in the police and the ambulance. The police checked Petra's story and found out she was telling the truth and that Sydney had not been dead for more than twenty-four hours.

Petra didn't bother to find out who had murdered Sydney. The next day she learned that he had left nearly a billion pounds to her. Hundreds of packages of drugs, as well as sacks of money, were discovered in his warehouse. "Well bastard Sydney, you lived a powerful life, but it was worth nothing in the end," Petra fumed.

Two days later Petra handed over more of Sydney's fortune to the Sisters Hanley and Helen to distribute amongst orphan homes and to schools across the country. She also kept fifteen million pounds to compensate those who had helped her. The police destroyed the drugs. Petra compensated Mrs Dean with two and half a million pounds because her husband had been killed while helping the police. She also gave Craig, Blake, Marlon and Drake jobs as informers as their work was as good as private investigators and she compensated them by giving them one million pounds each and sent the same to all for helping. The chief of police also signed them up to the force.

Petra was happy for the four of them. They each in turn kissed Petra on her cheek and Marlon said, "Petra, God bless the day when we met you, but we're really sorry for what we set out to do."

"Well, it's behind us now. And I'm truly grateful for your magnificent work with me."

Petra went to see Sister Hanley. "Mrs Black, these amounts of money you've given to charities, are you sure about this? My marriage to Sydney was purely business as I knew he was dying from an illness. If that wasn't so, I would have killed him. I also married him so his wealth and whatever he owned would go to charities."

"Petra, whatever the reason you married Sydney Black, we thank you for your generous gifts. I will let Sister Helen know and I'm truly grateful and thanks again."

"Sister Hanley, I will get my lawyer to make out everything else to you and Sister Helen, including his mansion, for you to do whatever is best."

"I don't know what to say, except I wasn't expecting this great wealth. Thank you once more; we'll never forget you," Sister Hanley said.

Petra smiled. Sister Hanley gave Petra a hug. "Please come at any time to see us." Petra nodded and left. Outside the gate she met Detective Inspector Hanson standing and waiting. She stared hard at him.

He smiled. "I'm sorry to hear your husband was murdered," he said.

"Well, I'm not. And he wasn't my husband, nor could ever be. Anyway, why are you here? How did you know I was here?"

"To tell you the truth, I heard you tell Officer Bradley, so I'm here to take you home. Pet, it's only a matter of time. All who took part in the youths' kidnapping and murders, we will get them," said Detective Inspector Hanson.

"Yes," said Petra. "One thing I didn't want was for any of them to commit suicide before I kicked their arses though. I also want every one of Sydney's hired law men rounded up like chickens and locked up for so long their flesh will rot and fall. I want people to know about the wicked acts they have done. By the way, where is your car?"

Hanson smiled. "I asked my brother to drop me off here as I knew you would give me a lift home. We can get a Chinese and then go to bed after I discuss something important with you."

Petra looked at Hanson hard and said, "Get the hell out of my way."

Hanson laughed saying, "I was joking. You should see your face."

Petra laughed. "Why are you really here?" Her face showed that she was glad to see him.

"To ask you to marry me, you know I love you. Petra, will you marry me?"

"Why?" She smiled and looked confused.

"Damn you Petra. I love you and I am asking you to be my wife."

"Hanson I love you, but I can't be your wife. Now let's go to my house," Petra said. "With a Chinese, but you're buying."

One month later Petra and Detective Inspector Hanson got married in St Peter's Church and the reception was held at the Swan Wings Hotel. At the table Hanson asked Petra, "Why did you marry your biggest enemy?" She whispered in his ear, "To kill him, but someone beat me to it instead."

They had a big wedding party with nearly the whole force and many other guests present. Large blocks of ice were carved out in the shape of a bride and groom and a daughter and son. After the party was over, Petra kissed Stanley, Faith, Jenny, Elizabeth, Martin and her brother Arden. She then said goodnight to everyone before her brother-in-law Paul drove them home and Petra's mother took Mrs Woods home with her for a week.

When Petra and her husband walked into their bedroom, she had the surprise of her life to see her white satin embroidered bedspread initialled with S, E, F and J, signifying her best friends' names Stanley, Elizabeth, Faith and Jenny. There was also a twin sets of white dressing growns from Ira and his fiancée Ellie and a set of white bath sheets embroidered with 'Mr and Mrs Hanson' from Detective Aaron.

On Hanson and Petra's wedding night while making love, Hanson took her panties from under his pillow and said, "Honey, since the day you shoved your beautiful panties in my mouth I knew you were the one for me. I love you so much Pet." He put on a CD of God Bless the Day I Found You. He then took Petra in his arms and they lay in bed listening and drinking brandy.

Two weeks later it was Christmas day. Petra, Hanson, Madame Stall, Dr Sean, Loretta, Arden, his girlfriend, Hanson's mother, father, brother Paul, Petra's mother and Grandma all spent Christmas together. It was a very happy gathering with plenty to eat and drink all accompanied by beautiful Christmas music. After the family left, Hanson and Petra bathed together and made love.

Just after New Year, however, WPC Bratcher went to Superintendent Peterson with vital information from Petra's mother, saying that Petra had killed her stepfather.

"Officer Bratcher, get the hell out of my office and stay out," Superintendent Peterson bawled at her.

Officer Bratcher then went to Judge Clews telling him what she'd told Peterson then said, "I went to the newspapers stating that Petra had murdered her stepfather six years ago but they refused to print the story."

Judge Clews asked her what the newspaper had said. She replied, "The putty-head man said that without solid proof they couldn't print the story. Also they didn't believe me."

"Well Officer Bratcher, the newspaper editor was very sensible, as was Superintendent Peterson. You best be careful with what you say. As for you

Officer Bratcher, it would pay you to keep your bloody mouth shut and get back on the street and do your job properly."

Officer Bratcher's eyes dropped to the floor.

"If I hear you say anything to anyone else, you will be looking for another job. Superintendent Jackson has earned her promotion by being a damn good cop and not even in a hundred years would you be second to her. I wouldn't dare blame her for my brother committing suicide. Superintendent Jackson has brought my brother to justice for doing everything that was wrong and I bear no resentment towards her. She swore to clean the filth out of the force and elsewhere and that's what she's doing. Now get the hell out of my face and stay out. And Officer Bratcher, if anyone comes to me with this, you know the answer."

WPC Bratcher hung her head in shame and tears flowed down her face. She left blowing her nose and drying her eyes and almost bumped into Petra running out of the building.

"Good morning Officer Bratcher," Petra greeted her. Officer Bratcher did not answer but rushed past. Petra pressed her lips tightly, wondering what could be the matter with her.

Petra went to see Judge Clews herself. Although his door had been left open she knocked.

"Oh, please come in and take a seat Superintendent Jackson. Or is it Hanson?" Judge Clews smiled.

"Petra would do, sir," she said.

"Well Petra, you've brought crime to its knees. I'm very proud and satisfied with what you have done and are doing for the community. In my twenty-seven years of being a high court judge, I've never experienced such magnificent work as you've done. Superintendent, you are really very special and important to the force and to the decent citizens in the land. Now that you're a very wealthy lady, I do hope you won't let your wealth stand in the way of your job. Superintendent Jackson, I can't afford to lose you, I need you more than ever; so do the people. I know you're now a superintendent and you have earned it and should be working in your office, but, I would be also very grateful if you could do me a favour."

"Judge Clews, I want nothing of what Sydney had. All he had now belongs to charity. And just to put the record straight, I knew when I married him he would fall under my spell, and his crooked followers would fall with him. Anyway, what favour would you like me to do?"

"I would like you to work on the streets, especially on Market Street, once again. I understand there are sacks of drugs delivered there regularly and cars filled with kidnapped youths under the age of sixteen. But I've no idea where the dropping or picking up point is. I also understand that some of these youths' parents have been paid very well with money and drugs. Some parents have said that their children have run away from home. There have also been five of our officers murdered due to their investigations. I want the sick-minded bastards who are responsible for killing my officers caught. I feel that you are the only capable one who I can trust. You do also have the right to refuse to work on the street as you're now above that; you are not under any obligation whatsoever. If you can help me out by working on Market Street, however, I'll give you four of the best men in the force."

"Judge Clews, I would like to help, but I would also like to discuss this with my husband. Incidentally, you have told me about Market Street but haven't you any clues of whereabouts in Market Street the drugs and these youths are posted to?"

"No Super. I have no idea where to tell you to start looking, but I was told a Mr Blimps is behind both the drugs and prostitution racket. Superintendent Jackson, have you heard of this Mr Blimps?"

"Yes Judge. I've heard about him and his kind. Well I'll try my hardest to find him. I understand he's Sydney's half-brother. But as I said, I would like to talk with my husband first."

"I understand Superintendent, but I would like your answer soon. If I don't hear from you within a week, I'll take your answer as no," Judge Clews said.

"Judge, whether my answer is yes or no, you'll have it."

"My sincere thanks to you, whatever you decide," Judge Clews said.

Petra got up out of her seat. Judge Clews stood up out of respect and shook Petra's hand showing her a lovely smile. "Well, goodbye Super."

As it was Petra's half day off, she went down to the Bullring in town and bought some fresh fish for her mother and herself. Before she went home, she stopped at her mother's and asked her to clean the fish.

Petra's mother gave her some fried fish for her and Hanson's tea and some raw fish to put in her freezer. "Pet, I've parcelled the fish into small portions so that you won't have any problem dividing them when you want to cook. You just take from the freezer what you need."

"Thanks Mum."

After Petra had spent another half an hour with her mother and Grandma, she kissed them both on their cheeks and said goodbye before she left. On her way home, she popped in to see Julia and the children. She gave her goddaughter a gold bracelet and two dresses she had bought for her birthday. "For you Master Todd, I bought a car," she said.

"Petra you have already given her more than enough, you are spoiling her rotten. You always bring her something when you come. It was only last week when you bought her lovely gold chain."

"Shut up Jul!" Petra joked.

"But Pet, apart from the large amount of money, you are still buying her so many gifts."

"Julia, I told you to shut up, she is my Goddaughter and it's my duty to help you take care of her. Anyway, I'm not staying."

Petra was about to leave, but Candice climbed up into her arms and kissed her giving a tight hug.

"Pet, you really are spoiling her."

"She is my godchild, haven't I got a right to buy her gifts?" Petra asked.

"Yes Petra," Julia said. "But really you don't have to give her anything else. You have already given her a fortune at the age of four and a half years old. You have made her one of the richest children in the country."

"Julia, I've fixed Candice's money so that you'll get the interest until she becomes eighteen. It is up to you if you want to take it monthly, quarterly, half-yearly or yearly. You could explore the world with the children and your husband at least once a year or when you please. You'll be drawing very good interest from the money for you to do whatever you want. Julia, I am speaking to you, you seem to be miles away."

"What was that you said?"

"Are you all right Jul?"

"Oh, yes Pet. I'm fine," Julia said looking lost.

"Julia you look so distant. Is having another baby worrying you?"

"Oh, Pet. I really don't want another child."

"Julia, you have no problem with money. You have a very nice supportive husband and loving family. I'm sure three children won't be too much. I could take Candice some weekends if it's all right with you. I'm also sure Irene would be happy to help you with them. So honey, I shouldn't worry if I were you."

"Pet you're so soothing."

"Well, I hope when my time comes, you'll give me a few comforting words. By the way, I will soon have another Godchild from my very good friend Elizabeth. We've been friends from an early age. I think she has about two weeks left."

"Pet, now you are married would you like to have children?"

"Sure Julia, at least one of each. But the truth is, sometimes I really get angry with my husband. When he comes near me I sometimes shiver and regret I married him."

"Why is that Pet, don't you love him?"

"Sure, I love him very much. But because I was raped it still affects me. The truth is that marrying Sydney Black was only a proposition deal so that his empire would go to the orphans. If I didn't marry him his wealth would have ended up in the wrong hands. Julia, I didn't ever let him near me."

"So you didn't sleep with Sydney?"

"No Julia, I didn't even let the bastard near me when we got married. As for Hanson, we have been married for three months but we have been sleeping in separate beds for five weeks. I'm so scared to let him take me again."

"Pet, I realise what you've been through and I haven't forgotten what you said to me six years ago either. Yes, when I first gave myself to Todd it was very painful. I had to press my lips together and grunt bearing the pain until making love became pleasurable. I used to even picture you in my thoughts when Todd was making love to me. Pet, I know it would be very painful for you, but try to think what Hanson must be going through. You are a very beautiful young woman, but youth goes very quickly. You'll have to take yourself to your husband. If you don't do that soon, you might lose him. Hanson wouldn't want your money; he's also rich in his own right. Remember he is a lawyer and a murder detective. Pet my friend, I had no idea you were raped."

"Julia, you are a really good friend to me. Do you want a couple of fish?"

"No thanks Pet. I bought some last week and most of them are still in the freezer," Julia said.

"Well, I have to go now. Goodbye Jul." Petra got up and faced Julia smiling. She then hugged her saying, "Thanks." After she parted from Julia, she kissed the children on their foreheads. Julia walked her to her car, watched her drive away and then went back into the house to be with her children.

Petra walked into the house to meet Loretta sitting in the kitchen drinking tea.

"Oh Petra, Sean was called to Miami to be godfather to his brother Zak's child, so I brought Mum home and thought I'd stay with you for a while."

"Have you any idea when he'll return?" Petra asked.

"Well, he's gone for a week. He said he'd be home next Sunday. You don't mind me staying here?"

"No Loretta. This is your home whenever you care to come and stay."

"But what about Hanson, would he mind me being here?"

"Don't be silly, we're practically family and this means we've become more than friends. So no, Hanson won't mind you staying with us. Besides, your room is still unoccupied. Anyway where is mum?" asked Petra

"Oh, I think she is taking a nap. By the way what's for dinner, I'm starving!"

"My mother gave me some fried fish. Luckily, I bought more than Hanson could eat. You can cook a bit less than a pound of rice while I go and change. Don't forget to wash the rice!" Petra joked.

"Don't be cheeky!" Loretta laughed.

After Petra changed her clothes she returned to the kitchen to put a bottle of wine on the table then helped Loretta with the cooking. While the rice was cooking Petra and Loretta were exchanging jokes and talking about their husbands Hanson and Sean and about how much they were in love.

The rice was cooked, the sauce was made and the salad was prepared and taken to the table. Loretta woke Mrs Woods telling her dinner was ready just as Hanson walked in. Petra met him in the hallway and kissed him.

"What's the matter with you?" he asked.

"Nothing. If I can't kiss my husband then who shall I kiss? Look darling, I know you've just come in from work and you might be tired but I've something important to show you upstairs. She held his hand leading him to their bedroom. She then got undressed and began kissing him on his face and neck. He undressed himself and kissing her, laid her on the bed and made love to her. After they showered together they went down to have dinner. At the table Loretta looked at Petra smiling to let her know that she knew that she and Hanson had just made love. Petra looked hard at her saying, "I would love a daughter, then a son."

"Then Hanson, it's up to you," Loretta said.

Hanson smiled.

After they had eaten, Hanson went to the Red Lion pub to have a drink with some of his friends and work mates.

When Todd returned home, Julia told him, "At the clinic today I stopped the nurse telling me what sex baby I would have. But the baby's fine."

"That's marvellous honey," he said looking very happy.

"Another daughter I think I might have," Julia replied.

"I would rather a son," he replied.

"Well, we will have whatever God gives us," Julia said.

"That's my girl," Todd said then went to have a shower.

When he returned from the bedroom Julia was sleeping. He didn't wake her as it was past midnight.

Meanwhile, Petra was working out the best way to tell her husband that she had had a talk with Judge Clews. Hanson was just singing softly to himself in deep thought as he looked down on her in bed. When Petra noticed the strain and expression on his face, she asked, "What's the matter darling?" As he didn't answer she kissed his lips then said, "Hanson, I had a very serious talk with Judge Clews."

"What did you talk about?" he asked seriously.

Petra recalled the conversation she had had with Judge Clews. "I told him I'll give him my answer within a week and that I'd like to discuss the matter with you first. Hanson, I would really like to help."

"Pet, you are my wife now. You can't always play the almighty God. It is time you stepped down from the high pulpit. Honey, I'm afraid that one day you'll not come home alive and I don't want to go to the morgue to identify you. I've seen many officers put in black bags and then taken to the morgue. When I first saw you, I fell in love with you. And as you were such a wild tiger, I thought it was going to be impossible for me to tame you. I don't want to lose you. I can put up with you refusing me in bed, but I cannot bear the thought of losing you. I want you to tell Judge Clews that he'll have to deal with the problem the best way he can."

"Hanson, those youths need help."

"I know honey, but you alone can't take on an army. You were lucky to succeed with those ruthless Blacks, but Johnny and his brother Daniel Blimps are just as dangerous, if not more so. Pet, I would like to have at least two children with you and not for you to be end up a cripple or dead."

"I'm sorry Hanson but those poor bastard youths need me more than you do. If you try and stop me then I'm going to divorce you."

"Damn you Petra! I don't want a divorce. I want you to stay my wife and have my children. I love you too much. Only God knows how much I love you," Hanson said.

"I know you do honey, but please try and understand. After I have helped these youths, I promise you I will only be the very best housewife, have your children, run your bath then wait on you hand and foot. Oh Hanson, I didn't think it was possible for us to be together either. I promise you a daughter and for me, a handsome son just like his father," Petra laughed.

"Pet honey, I really don't like the idea but I do respect what you're doing. What about your back-up?" he asked her very concerned.

"I will speak to my mates tomorrow, my own men," Petra said.

"You'll have to pay them well."

"Yes I know. Judge Clews will pay each of them well and please keep what I've told you to yourself. We don't want this operation broadcast to anyone, including my fellow police officers," Petra said.

"Who's your back-up?" her husband asked again.

"I can't tell you, but please trust me as I have a marvellous idea."

"What idea, to marry Johnny or his brother Daniel Blimps, the worst two of the lot?"

"Hanson, that's not fair. Don't push my head down into the mud. All I want from you is a little support to give me some confidence and determination. That's all. At least you could wish me good luck," Petra said.

"Pet, it's very hard for me to wish you good luck when I know you will be out there with the risk that you'll end up being connected to a life support machine or in a body bag. I'm really afraid for you Pet," he said.

"I'm afraid for myself too, but Judge Clews is depending on me to get those youths back to their homes," Petra said.

"For the past six years you've been living for those children. Don't you think it's time you started living for yourself and let someone else take over?"

"Hanson, you're being selfish. Those youths are going through the same agony as I did. I'm very sorry but I'm going to help Judge Clews find the youths even if it costs me my life."

"I see," said her husband as he swallowed some brandy. He shook his head, smiled, then poured some brandy into another glass and gave it to her. He then wished her good luck being that she was so determined.

Two days later, Petra rang Judge Clews on his private line at his home.

"Who's this?" Judge Clews asked.

"It's me, Petra."

"Go ahead, Pet."

"I'll do the job. I'll get in touch with my boys. But you'll have to pay them a quarter of a million pounds between the four of them. For me, I want nothing but to go in and rescue those youths and take them home."

"Superintendent, I'm willing to pay whatever you demand. I can now tell you that my sister's little girl was kidnapped three weeks ago because I sent three of the Black villains to prison five months ago, before you married that dog."

Petra laughed. "Judge Clews. May I ask you how old your niece is?"

"She will be sixteen in four months. She was kidnapped on her way home from school. After hearing she was a prisoner at the Black's resident, I had the whole place searched but she wasn't found. I would like you to find her and keep this private. I don't know who to trust in the force."

"Okay Judge Clews. No one will hear this from me. If she's there or anywhere in this country and alive, I will find her and I will bring her home to you and your sister."

"Thanks Superintendent, I appreciate this very much. I'll never forget you or what you're doing for the people. Her name is Anika. Please do your best for me."

"Okay I will speak to my boys later and we'll carry out our search Monday morning. I have a feeling where to find her if she's there," Petra said.

"Okay sup., God bless you and your team," Judge Clews said.

"Thanks," Petra said smiling then hung up.

On Sunday morning Petra and her husband invited both their families to have breakfast. While they were having breakfast the phone rang. Petra asked to be excused and she went into the living room to answer the phone. "Hello."

"Petra Jackson, I'm Marsha," she said crying.

"Well hello Marsha, what can I do for you?" Petra asked curiously.

"Petra, I didn't mean to kill old Mr Dean. I did point the gun above his head and fired, as I thought it was empty. I'd only wanted to frighten him to stop him meeting you," Marsha cried. "I didn't know someone had put a bullet in the gun. I swear to you Petra, I didn't know the gun was loaded. As I said, I only wanted to frighten the old man. Petra you've got to help me. The Blimps brothers are looking for me after I went to Judge Clews and told him everything. And about Sydney's money, you only received part of it. His bastard half-brother Johnny Blimps has at least a billion pounds of drugs money that Sydney never got. Oh Pet, you have to help me," said Marsha crying bitterly.

"Why should I help you?" Petra asked harshly.

"Cause I can tell you where they are holding Judge Clews' niece."

"Marsha, tell me where you are so that I can come and get you."

"I'm hiding in an old house on Shad Street next to an old factory."

"I think I know where. I want you to stay there and out of sight. I'll be there in about half an hour. I'll be in a dark green Land Rover," Petra told her.

"Okay, but please hurry. I'm feeling so scared about spending another night here," Marsha whispered.

"Marsha, just try and relax until I get there. And to put your mind at rest, you didn't kill Mr Dean, Haley killed him."

"Petra, I'm so frightened."

"I'm scared too Marsha. I'll be there soon." Petra put the phone down then she got back to her family to tell them. "I'm sorry but I have had an urgent call and I have to go."

She got changed into a pair of jeans, long sleeved shirt and black knee-length boots then grabbed a piece of toast as she was just about to have her breakfast. She noticed that her husband and his brother Paul had left the room. She looked in her handbag for her gun and saw it was there, and then she left. On her way outside she met her husband, his brother Paul and two of her husband's work mates Robin and Bruce.

"Where're you off too?" her husband asked.

"Oh I'm going to see someone. I'll be back soon. Hello Bruce, hello

Robin. Please boys make yourselves at home. I have just put a pot of hot coffee on the table."

"Thanks Mrs Hanson," Bruce and Robin said.

"But Pet darling, we've got guests."

"Hanson, they are not guests, they're close friends and family. Look honey, I can't stay any longer. When I return I will explain. Can I borrow your Land Rover?"

"Of course you can, but please Pet, if you find yourself in trouble, I want to know."

"Please Hanson, don't look so worried. I will be back soon."

"On the other hand, why can't you take one of the other cars?"

"Hanson, I would if I'd wanted too, that's why I asked to borrow your Land Rover as it is much darker."

"Okay Pet, but you might have to put petrol in it," Hanson said.

"Well, in that case, can I have some money?" Petra asked.

"Pet, I've already given you your allowance."

"Honey, the Land Rover is yours. I think you should keep it full."

"I agree," he said and gave Petra thirty pounds.

Petra kissed his lips. He pressed the fob to open the garage, gave Petra the keys then led his brother Paul and his friends Robin and Bruce into the house.

Petra drove the Land Rover to the nearest petrol station, filled up, then continued her journey to where Marsha was. As she got near to the old derelict factory, she parked up behind some hangover tree branches on the other side and walked about ten yards crossing debris from old buildings to get to Marsha. When she got to the doorway of the derelict factory she looked around very carefully to make sure that she wasn't followed. From where she stood, she could hardly see the Land Rover as it was well hidden by the overgrown and thick branches. She entered the crumbling dusty building. As the dry twigs cracked under her boots, Marsha called out. "Petra, is that you?"

"Yes Marsha, it's me."

Marsha showed herself.

"Petra, I'm really sorry. I'd only wanted to frighten old Mr Dean." Marsha paused then tears welled up in her eyes. "I was sure I had emptied the gun. Brad, cousin of Johnny, must have put the bullet in the gun when I put it on the table to change out of my skirt into a pair of jeans. I told him the gun was empty and that I only wanted to frighten Mr Dean to stop him from talking to you. I've known old Mr Dean for a long time. He didn't like what was going on any more than I did. I really wanted to go to the police about Sydney and his brothers, but knowing how crooked some police are, I didn't. I also got jealous when the bastard married you. Now I realise the reason why you married the evil bastard. You still have a hell of a lot of money to collect as he has a private place stocked with money no one knows about. I will take you there. I just wanted to tell you how sorry I am for throwing that drink in your face and I just hope you will forgive me so we can put it all behind us."

"Marsha, I don't want that man's money. But I'd like it to be shared amongst charities and to compensate those youngsters who have suffered under the monster hands. I know the money cannot make up for what the youths have been through or bring those that died to life again, but it could help their families to build a better future and to make living more comfortable. Marsha, you didn't kill Mr Dean. It was Officer Haley, Devine Ed's woman."

"Petra, telling me this, I now can breathe easily. But what are you telling me? With so much money that should be yours you don't want any?"

"That's correct Marsha. I don't even want to hear that bastard Black name ever again!" Petra was calm.

"But Petra, you could be a very rich woman," Marsha said.

"Marsha, I'm rich in my job doing what is right and trying to save people. Anyway, when was the last time you had a bath?" Petra asked.

"Three days ago when it was raining," said Marsha looking shameful and raised her left arm, sniffing her armpit.

Petra held her breath then put the palm of her hand over her nose. As soon as they got into the Land Rover Petra said, "Buckle up please will you Marsha."

Marsha buckled up. "I'm all yours, Petra."

Petra looked Marsha in the eyes and said, "I'm taking you to my home until you find a place."

"I understand."

Petra drove away. On the way home, she noticed a dark green Jeep following them. She took her gun out of her handbag and rested it on the seat underneath her left leg; she slowed down. The Jeep passed them at about sixty

miles per hour and was shaking violently going around the bend, then it came
to an abrupt halt. Petra drove past.

"I could swear that Jeep was following us," Marsha said.

"Yes, I'd thought so too as he seemed to be in a hurry. Hold on Marsha,
the road is too narrow if he decided to follow us. I'm going to drive faster
until I get past those trees," Petra said. Then she sped on passing the trees where
the road widened and then slowed down. The male driver passed them, then
did a U-turn moving behind Petra again. Marsha looked nervous and scared.
Petra looked in the rear mirror to see the young black driver closely behind
them. As Petra reached for her gun, the driver blew his horn, smiled then
shouted gorgeous! Petra smiled then put her gun back in her handbag. Marsha
nodded off to sleep and Petra looked at her smiling. Soon she was driving into
her gateway. She poked Marsha lightly in her side. "We're home."

Marsha winked her eyes open. "Petra, why did you give away all the
money Sydney left to you and turn his mansion into an old folks' home?"

"It was an old folks' home in the first place. The money and the mansion
weren't Sydney's."

"But you were married to him. Surely you were entitled to what was
his."

"It wasn't a marriage. I only agreed to marry him so that the family of
the youths he viciously abused and assaulted would share part of what he
robbed them of. I think they deserve to get what they're entitled to. Don't
you agree?"

"Oh yes, I do agree. But didn't you want any of his money really, not
even a small amount for the work you've done?"

"I see where you're going. You thought I bought this house with Sydney's
money, don't you?"

"Pet, I didn't say or think that!"

"But it's what you're thinking. Am I right or wrong?" Petra asked Marsha
looking upset.

"Well I was wondering why you have such a big and beautiful house
when you only got your promotion a few months ago."

"Marsha, you really know a lot about me. It's a pity that while you were
studying me you couldn't dig the ground to find water and have a wash. Well
this house isn't mine. Anyway, I might need your help to bring Matt Blimps,

his brothers Johnny, Daniel and the others into the open so that the world can see their ugly faces and know the wicked things they have done. It's time those germs were exterminated."

"I'll help. I'll do whatever I can to make up for Mr Dean's death. By the way how is Mrs Dean?"

"I think she's okay now. Her husband's death did really shake her up though. Marsha, while you are staying at my home I don't want you to phone, accept any calls or see anyone."

"I will not phone anyone, I give you my word."

"Okay, here we go," Petra said as she turned the key into the front door. She flung it open, walked in and said to Marsha, "I want you to march right upstairs into the bathroom and have a bath. I'll be up in a minute to help you with some clothes."

While Marsha was going up the stairs Petra approached her husband. "Honey, I brought Marsha here because she needs our help. Please treat her with kindness."

"But isn't she that woman who killed Mr Dean? And what is she doing out on bail?"

"She did not kill Mr Dean. Hanson darling, she explained to me that she thought someone had loaded her gun with the bullets. But I've gathered strong proof that Officer Haley Devine shot Mr Dean."

"And you believe her?"

"Yes. She only wanted to frighten Mr Dean. Anyway, Haley was picked up and she confessed to killing Mr Dean but accidently as the bullet was meant for Redd Black. Bullshit! I said. Anyway, could you loan me two hundred pounds as I haven't had time to go to the cash machine."

"What for?" her husband asked.

"I saw a black suit that I would like to buy to wear to Mr Dean's funeral." "But you have black clothes in your wardrobe that you could wear."

"I know, but I like this suit," Petra said.

"Okay, I'll write you out a cheque."

"Thanks, but I'd prefer cash," she replied.

Smiling, her husband took his wallet out of his jacket pocket and gave Petra the two hundred pounds. "I want it back."

Petra kissed her husband's lips and told him the kiss was worth two hundred pounds. Her husband took her by her hand and led her into the kitchen, pushed her against the fridge and kissed her passionately, fingering her until his penis got hard.

She pushed him away. "Now I've got half my money's worth until tonight, then I'll claim the other half," he said smiling.

"You'll be lucky," Petra laughed.

"Well in that case, I'll be more than very nice to your friend you just brought home," he joked.

"Don't push your luck mate!" Petra left him in the kitchen and went into the dining room and said to the rest of the family, "I'll be with you in about ten minutes." As they looked at her inquisitively, she smiled then went upstairs to be with Marsha. She knocked at the bathroom door.

"I brought you some clothes. After, you come down for some breakfast. Oh, and I put a pair of pyjamas, some clothes and panties on your bed. Tomorrow we can go shopping for clothes."

"Petra, thanks."

Petra smiled, watching Marsha getting into her bath.

After Marsha finished she went downstairs to have breakfast in the kitchen. As the door was closed, Hanson's mother knocked.

"Who is it?" Petra asked.

"It's me, Hillary."

"Come in," Petra told her.

"Petra, I'm leaving now. Paul will give us a lift home. Thanks for a lovely breakfast. I hope you and Hanson can make it over to my house next Sunday for lunch."

"Did you speak to Hanson about it?"

"No, not yet. I'll ring him Wednesday after work. Anyway, if I don't, will you tell him? "

"Hillary, I think it's best that you tell him now so that he won't get tied up with his friends. Oh, this is Marsha. Marsha, this is my husband's mother Hillary."

"Nice to meet you, Mrs Hanson," Marsha said politely. But Hillary was very rude and turned to leave. "Hillary, I know you have an attitude, but I didn't know you were so nasty," Petra told her.

"I know you try to help everyone, but do you have to drag in every piece of dirty rag into my son's home?"

"As much as you are my mother-in-law, I expect you to keep your insults to yourself. Furthermore, what I do in this house is none of your business."

"How dare you speak to me like that, you second-hand nothing! After your stepfather bedded you, then the drug worm Sydney had you, my son took your black ass in out of pity!" Hillary's eyes looked wild.

"Only now I see your true colours, mother white hog. You should be the last foul-mouthed person to talk about anyone. You put your first daughter in a children's home when you found out she was either your half-brother's child or your husband's brother. On top of that, you gave Paul to your husband when really he too is your half-brother's child or your husband's brother. So you see Hillary, your secrets are not only dark but also blacker than me. As for me, I've told the world and your son that I was raped by my stepfather before he married me. And your son begged me in tears to marry him and I have because I fell in love with him. Well, I got my revenge on my bastard stepfather before he died for what he did to me. As for Sydney the worm, he was the most descent man to me. He treasured me as if I was his child and he respected me and did not bed me. So, by telling me about my stepfather you're a long way behind. As for you my dear, you're so ripped through the flesh and near to the bone and blood, you leave me wondering if your husband is in fact Hanson's dad. Now I want you to take your crooked old arse out of my house, and don't come back till you find your manners!"

"This is not your house my dear, this is my son's house. If he had any sense he would leave a viper such as you well alone and find a decent woman."

As Hillary turned to leave, Petra pushed her out of the kitchen door and she almost fell on her face. She didn't even look back but went to her son Paul and her husband telling them she was ready to go home.

Marsha looked sadly at Petra with tears in her eyes. "Oh, Pet I am so sorry I came here."

"Marsha, you shouldn't be sorry. I'm very glad I brought you here. The fine white lady has turned out to be nothing but trash blowing in the wind."

Petra left Marsha in the kitchen and went into the living room to hear Hillary telling her husband, "Come on." She then took her husband by his left hand telling him, "Petra doesn't want us here." Her husband looked in her eyes then asked her, "Did Petra say she doesn't want us here?"

"The woman our son married told me to get out of our son's house. Are you coming home with Paul and me, or are you staying to be insulted?"

By this time everyone's eyes were on Petra. Petra faced Hillary with her mouth open. "I'm very sorry. I had no right to speak to you the way I did. This makes me even lower than you."

"What the hell is going on between you two?" Hanson asked. He faced his mother for an answer.

"Your wife just told me to get out of her house."

Hanson faced Petra. "Did you tell my mother to get out the house?"

"Yes, I did," Petra admitted.

"How dare you!" he said and slapped her hard in the face.

"You should not have done that," Petra said and left the room. Paul asked Hanson into the next room and said to him, "What were you trying to prove? Petra could have crippled you where you stood."

"Just let her try. She kicked me once in my testicle and I let her get away with it. Well, I'm not one of her play toys."

"Brother, she really loves you. Still, she just acted as a coward. Brother dear, you just made a mistake. For your own sake, don't ever hit her again until you dig deeper into the matter. Did you even bother to find out why Petra asked our mother to leave her house?"

"No Paul, I didn't."

"Well, it wouldn't hurt you to find out," Paul said.

"Okay," said Hanson. "I guess you're right, maybe she did have a good reason to ask mother to leave. I don't know. I'll ask her later."

"You do that! And always remember that Petra really loves you."

Hanson nodded his head. Paul touched him on his shoulder saying, "Brother, you have a good and honest wife." Hanson smiled then they both went back to their family and friends. After a little while, everyone thanked Petra for a lovely breakfast. Madame Stall and Loretta went to sit on the veranda with ice-cold lemonades.

At lunch, Petra took Marsha's meal up to her as she'd left her breakfast on account of Mrs Hanson's insults that hurt her. "I don't think I have the appetite to eat." Tears welled up in Marsha's eyes.

"Look Marsha, what that woman said, don't let it bother you. She's a nasty piece of work. You eat your lunch, as you didn't have breakfast. I will collect the dishes in a bit, in the meantime you should rest."

"Okay," said Marsha and thanked Petra. Petra then went to do the dinner, but being so mad, some chicken gravy splashed over her blouse and face when she grabbed the dish out the oven so she went to have a bath.

While she was in the bath, Hanson walked in and sat on the edge of it. "Pet, I'm sorry I hit you. I lost control," he said regretfully.

"Well, I forgive you this time. But never hit me again in the presence of your family, especially your mother. She told me you should never have married a viper such as me and that you told her my stepfather bedded me. Hanson, I told you my stepfather raped me before you married me. I'm not ashamed of the wickedness he did to me, but I'm so annoyed with you for telling your mother. How can I trust you again? Why did you tell your mother? It hurts so much when you confide in the one you love and think you can trust him or her then only to find out how wrong you can be and that your words are used against you as ammunition."

"Oh no," replied Hanson, then tears suddenly came in his eyes. Feeling hurt and betrayed by his mother he punched the basin, damaging two of his knuckles. When Petra saw blood dripping, she jumped out of the bath and took his bleeding hand and holding it over the hand basin ran the cold water to wash the blood away. She then reached for the Dettol and cleaned the wounds, then smoothed a light coat of antiseptic cream over his cut and bruised knuckles. As she reached for a plaster he said, "I will be okay." She looked in his eyes and kissed him.

"You poor fool but I love you so much."

"I love you very much too," he smiled.

"Now if you get out, I can finish my bath, return to my cooking and then do my ironing," she told him.

He smiled, took his wedding ring off and deliberately dropped it. He reached in for it and said, "Oh, I dropped my ring in your bath."

"Don't bother," said Petra. "I know what you are up to."

He smiled, then, pretending to feel for his ring slid his fingers between her thighs and they gazed into each other's eyes.

"You can forget it," she said "You're on punishment until I'm ready to surrender to you."

He smiled in her face, still sliding his fingers upwards to her navel and circling his fourth fingers tickling her making her laugh. Then he stripped naked and got into the bath with her.

"Get out!" she said.

"No," he replied, and as she was getting out the bath, he pulled her back, kissing her. She lay back while he put his mouth on her pointed hard nipples sucking them in turns. She felt a warm sensation inside her, and closed her eyes, hugging him around his neck and shoving her tongue in his mouth. She was ready to give in to him by throwing her legs on his shoulders when his brother Paul shouted up, "Hanson, you left your keys at Mum's and I let myself in."

"I'll be right down. I'm just changing my clothes," Hanson shouted down. "Help yourself to a drink."

"Well, you better get dressed and get down to your brother before he comes up and I give him what you were supposed to have."

He got out of the bath, showing her his erection, then burst into laughter. "Damn brothers!"

Petra stood up teasing him and he fingered her. "I shall carry on later where I left off." He put his ring on.

"Hanson!" Paul shouted up to him again.

"I'll be down soon," he shouted down, then got dressed and waited till his erection went down before he went to Paul.

Petra got out of the bath, wrapped her towel around her and went into her room to get dressed. While she was combing her hair, Hanson shouted up to her saying, "Pet, have you left some food for Paul?"

"Yes, I dished his out, it's in the oven."

Paul took the food with him and shouted up to Petra, "Thanks. I'll bring your plates back tomorrow."

Petra shouted, "Okay." And he left with the food.

Petra went to make some tea when she saw Hanson buttering a cob. "I'm a bit hungry. You want one?" he asked her.

"I thought you were going out?"

"Honey, I'm too tired. All I need now is to have this ham cob and then a nap with you by my side," he said.

"I'll make you your ham cob. Would you like some tea?"

"No, a cold beer would be better with my cob," he said.

After they had eaten their ham cobs and drunk tea and beer, Hanson went upstairs, took his trousers off, leaving his T-shirt and boxer shorts on, and climbed into bed. When Petra heard him snoring, she poked him in his side, he turned over and his snoring stopped. She smiled and went to Marsha to see what she was doing, but she too was sleeping. She quietly picked up the dirty plate and cup then left the room. As she closed the door and was going downstairs, she saw Loretta just about to walk up the stairs smiling. When she got to the bottom of the stairs, Loretta took the plates and cups from her, took them into the kitchen and washed them while Petra started the ironing.

After supper, Petra showed Marsha around the house. When she asked Marsha, "Do you like my place?" Marsha stared in astonishment to have seen how exquisite the whole place looked. When Petra saw the jealousy in her eyes, Petra hugged her saying Marsha, "You'll be fine."

As Petra and Marsha stood by the stable door, Marsha said to Petra, "Pet, you're blessed with beauty, wealth, luck, strength and a very handsome husband. I really envy you. But at the same time, I'm so glad you chose me to be one of your friends. Pet, I honestly thought you were a hooker and wanted Sydney's money, but I was so very wrong. Will you ever forgive me?"

"Marsha, you've done me no wrong, so there is nothing for me to forgive you for. You were simply under the influence of that bastard. Now let's get back into the house. Oh tomorrow we'll go shopping for clothes for you as I told you, or we could go to your home to get some."

"Pet, I have no money and I'm scared to go home as I was living with my uncle and when he found out about me, he threw me out," Marsha cried softly.

"Look Marsha, I think you should get at least twenty million of Sydney's money and you can help yourself to some of his stashed away money too." Petra opened the secret safe Sydney gave her to reveal bundles of fifty, twenty, ten and five pounds notes. "I'll still do the spending and buy you some clothes," Petra told Marsha. "Oh, the two horses were Sydney's. By the way, Hanson doesn't know I have this money. I will give it to you and my four helpful boys. The horses will be collected by someone next Friday."

The next afternoon, just before dinner, Petra went to wake her husband, who had gone for a nap. She slapped his bottom. "Hanson, dinner is ready."

"What time is it?"

"Four thirty. Your dinner is on the table. And your brother phoned to say he would be here for dinner. I'm going down, and don't take too long," Petra told him.

"Okay honey, I'll be right down after I have freshened up. Oh Pet, do you need my help finding the kids, as you might be up against more than you can handle?" Hanson asked. "Remember you promised to go to New York with me next week."

"I know honey, but only after I get those defenceless children back to their homes safe and sound."

"Pet, I don't think that I can wait that long. I do love you and I would like you to be with me on holiday," Hanson said looking stressed.

"I want to be with you, let's talk about this later. Please come and have dinner," Petra said to him.

"Well, I'm going to work with you from now on," Hanson was determined.

"No no Hanson! One of us has to stay alive. If you die working with me, I'd never forgive myself. But I promise you, I will come back to you safe and sound to kick your balls once more, and then we'll have two children, Milk and Coco!"

As they were sitting down to dinner, Paul knocked on the door and Marsha opened it. He walked in and gave Petra a bottle of wine and a bunch of flowers.

"Paul, you didn't have to bring anything. Anyway thank you. This is Marsha. Marsha, this is Paul, my husband's brother. Now let's eat." Hanson popped the wine open, served the six of them then said, to Madame Stall, "Hello Andrea".

At the table, Madame Stall said, "You all make me feel so happy."

Petra was looking at Paul, who was looking at Marsha and smiling. Paul stayed until nightfall. As he and Marsha got engrossed in conversation, Petra and Hanson said goodnight and left them in the living room. Petra had a shower, then saw Madame Stall into bed before she went to bed herself.

"I'm going down to get some water," Hanson said.

"You can turn off the lights when you get back," Petra said.

"Sure," he replied, then he went and took a bottle of water from the fridge then returned with a glass and the bottle of water asking Petra, "You want some?"

"No thanks."

He switched the lights off then slid under the quilt. Petra fixed her head on his arms. They kissed and made love.

The following morning Hanson woke up and did not see Petra beside him. He jumped out of bed and rushed downstairs in his pyjamas.

"If you're looking for your wife, she's out riding," Madame Stall said. "Your breakfast is already cooked and keeping hot. Why don't you sit down and eat?"

"No, no. Was she alone?" Hanson looked worried.

"Yes," Madame Stall said. "And don't look so worried, she will be all right."

Just then he saw the horse come trotting towards the stable with Petra lying on its back. He rushed into the stable and lifted her off the horse. He twirled around to face him. "Pet, I know you are capable of looking after yourself, but I don't want you to go riding alone as you are just learning. Do you hear me! I never, want, you, to ride, alone!" He took his time to tell her then said. "Looking at you lying on the horse, I thought you were hurt."

"Sorry H, but really, it's nothing to fuss about. I fell and hurt my arm but not badly," Petra said.

"Damn it Pet! You're never to go riding alone again," Hanson told her again as he was furious. "And I will be happy to see them go."

As they walked into the dining room with arms around each other's shoulders, Madame Stall said to them, "Marsha has cooked breakfast and yours is still hot." Petra thanked Marsha then said to her husband, "You go and get out of your pyjamas and into some clothes while I wash my hands and change into something more comfortable." Hanson smiled then they went and had a quick shower, got dressed then went down to have breakfast.

As Marsha was sitting nearest to the cooker, she asked Petra and Hanson to take their seats so that she could serve them. But as she was eating, Petra told her she would serve her and her husband. Loretta smiled. Madame Stall hadn't eaten much as she was complaining that she had wind. She asked to be excused and left the table, went to her room and lay down after taking milk of magnesia. Some time later, Madame Stall was feeling better and she sat in her rocking chair on the balcony taking in the fresh air.

Loretta also asked to be excused and went to make a phone call to her husband in Miami. After she spoke to him, she went back to Petra and Hanson and said, "Sean said hello to you both." She smiled then went into the library to get a book to read leaving Petra and Hanson eating. After they had eaten,

Petra puts the dishes in the dishwasher, then went and sat on her husband's lap. He kissed her just as Loretta walked in on them.

"I'm sorry," she said.

"What for?" Petra asked.

"To walk in on you while you're having a snuggle," Loretta said.

Petra laughed. "Don't be silly. I don't mind you seeing my husband kissing me."

"Well, I will have to wait for my husband to come home to get mine," Loretta said jokingly.

Hanson smiled.

"Oh I didn't want to say anything until my husband comes home, but as you both will be aunt and uncle, I might as well inform you of the good news. I also have to break the good news to Madame Stall as she is my mother now. I'm so very fortunate to have nice people as family and close friends."

"You are going to have a baby?" Petra asked anxiously.

"I'm six weeks pregnant. Isn't this lovely for Sean to hear when he arrives tomorrow?"

"I am sure he will be delighted with the news. I never thought I would have a child after being married for three years to my first rat of a husband. However, I am so happy with my consultant Sean and our new baby. I am sure he will be as very happy as I am. Pet wouldn't you like to have a baby?"

"Very much, Loretta. As a matter of fact Hanson would like a daughter, me a son. Once my husband and I go to New York for a week and return, then I'll squeeze that daughter out of his balls."

"Then Hanson, I guess it is up to you. Prove to the Mrs, how good a detective you are when you both get home from your holiday," Loretta laughed.

Madame Stall came into the room. "Any of you girls have any washing out? If you do, I think you should take it in as we might be getting some heavy rain, possibly thunder and lightning," she told them.

"No Mum, none of us have any washing out," Loretta said. "But I'll be having a baby in eight and a half months."

"That's wonderful Loretta. I'm looking for at least two each from Pet and you. This calls for a celebration. We'll have a nice cup of tea and one of Petra's cherry cakes," Madame Stall said and then went to fetch a full bottle of red wine and five glasses filling four with wine and one with milk. Just then rain began to pour down. "Well here is the rain," Madame Stall said with thunder and lightning following.

"Oh, how I like this kind of weather, especially when I'm with my husband," Loretta said. Madame Stall giggled while Marsha smiled.

Petra walked in with four cups of tea on a silver tray and saw them drinking wine. Passing the tea to them, she said, "I thought you all wanted tea."

"It was Mum that suggested tea, but changed her mind and got the wine instead," Loretta said.

Loud thunder cracked like a whip and lightning flashed frighteningly between the heavy rain which was beating hard against the window, bringing with it darkness. "It's so romantic, especially being with the man you love," Loretta said again.

"Well honey I have to go to work now," Hanson said.

"What work are you talking about? Today is Sunday," Petra said.

"Yes, I know. But I have to get to my office to study some evidence."

"It's Redd Black you're going to defend, aren't you?" Petra asked.

"No, it's Matt Blimps. But I asked my friend Cassie Thompson to take his case as she's a good solicitor and she said she would. I just have to fill her in with the final details as the case is tomorrow."

"Oh darling, why did you ask her to take his case when you know full well Matt Blimps is a rapist a kidnapper and a murderer?"

"Pet, who are you to say if he is guilty or not?" Hanson asked coolly.

"Well, I say he is guilty. Honey, I don't want your friend to defend that bastard no more than I want you to!"

"Pet honey, I'm sorry. She has already taken the case and has been paid."

Hanson, please tell me you will tell Cassie not to defend him. I will double what they paid her not to defend any of that family. Matt, Redd and Johnny are Sydney's half-brothers; they are rapists and murderers. Right now I don't think I want to discuss anything more concerning those bastards."

"Petra, I know you hate them, but I don't think Cassie can go back on her word by not defending Matt Blimps."

"Go on! Defend them and get them their freedom so that the evil pricks can rape and kill again!" Petra sounded very angry.

"They have already paid Cassie fifty thousand pounds."

"Hanson, we're talking about three fifteen-year-old youths that were raped and murdered by those maniacs. Also fifteen-year-old Tina was raped and badly ripped inside and is lying in some hospital right now but her parents refuse to say which one. Hanson, you help get any of those maniacs off and your hands will be smeared with those youths' blood. But I can promise you I'll finish them off. The son of a bitch Matt Blimps is far worse than his brother Sydney. Every one of their dicks and testicles should be ripped away from them and the dogs should be set on them."

"Petra, you're my wife. But I will take you in if I have to," Hanson said.

"Hanson, you hit me once and got away with it because I let you. But you hit me again for what I stand for and is the truth and I won't be responsible for my actions. You go and defend Redd and his brother, but if they get away with it I'll make them wish they had been sent to prison for a life sentence."

Petra walked away leaving her husband in thought. When she was halfway up the stairs, she turned and shouted down to him. "You better go and study your evidence with your woman for tomorrow. But remember, if you get them off, they'll lose their lives to me. Go on, go and meet your woman as you both had planned before she thinks you've changed your mind. Her poor husband has to sleep on what you let out?" Petra laughed. Hanson's face immediately looked pale white as if his blood had been drained out of him. He grabbed files from his desk, shoved them in his briefcase then stormed out of the house into the pouring rain. Petra rushed to the open door and watched him drive away. When he was out of sight she closed the door and leaned against the bottom stair railings puffing with anger.

"What's the matter with you and Hanson?" Loretta asked.

"Oh, he has a chip on his shoulder," Petra said.

"That's because you refused him. The poor man must be in pain from stiffness," Loretta said laughing.

"Loretta, shut up. He's not starving of sex because he gone to get some," Petra said, but couldn't help herself bursting into laughter as Loretta was laughing so much. Then they both sat on the middle of the stairs still laughing.

The phone started ringing. Marsha answered the phone while Petra and Loretta were still laughing.

"Any of you ladies named Loretta Sean Gresham?" Marsha asked smiling.

"You had better take the call before your husband runs out on you," Petra said jokingly.

Loretta took the phone from Marsha. "Hello my love," Loretta said smiling widely.

"Hello honey," said Sean, sounding very happy.

"Honey, are you still in Miami?"

"No Lo, I just left the airport and I'm on my way home. How are you, did you miss me?"

"Very much. We missed you so much."

"We?" he asked in wonder.

"Yes darling, we. I had a week of morning sickness so I went to see Dr Manners and he told me that I'm six weeks pregnant. Plus I had a pregnancy test. Isn't that marvellous darling?"

"Loretta honey, you have just made me one of the happiest dads-to-be. Are you still at Petra's place?"

"Yes honey. You can come and fetch me. Shall I prepare you something to eat?"

"That would be nice. I'll be with you soon."

"See you soon honey." Loretta put down the phone and faced Petra with a bright smile saying. "Sean is on his way here to take me home. Would you mind if I fix something for him to eat?"

"There's plenty of food left."

"Thanks Pet. As soon as my Sean gets here and he's eaten, we'll go home."

"Good! At least I will get some sleep," Petra said.

"Have I been disturbing you?" Loretta asked.

"Yes Loretta, you disturb me from my sleep all the time. Oh by the way, the garden is full of flowers. Why don't you have a couple of bunches?"

"Oh no Pet, Sean asked a florist to send me two bunches a week."

"How thoughtful of your Sean," Petra said smiling.

"Don't tell me you are jealous?"

"I am very jealous," Petra replied smiling.

The phone rang again. Petra answered while Loretta watched her curiously wanting to know if it was her husband Sean again. "The call is for me," said Petra. Loretta smiled and took Marsha into the game room where they played a couple of games of snooker and billiards before Petra joined them.

"What was so important that you spent twenty minutes on the phone?" Loretta asked looking confused.

"Ah, don't tell me you are jealous because my husband was talking to me," Petra said smirking.

"Oh, I'm so very, very jealous, my dear sister Petra," Loretta said giggling.

"Hey you two, have a little consideration for a poor lonely woman like me," Marsha said, giggling.

Loretta went to the drinks bar and poured herself a Martini. As she took a mouthful she pointed at the bottle to Petra and Marsha. Petra shook her head but Marsha nodded. Loretta gave her a drink.

As Petra picked up the snooker cue the phone rang again. Petra answered the phone. "Hello?"

"Pet honey, I have found out where the children have been taken," Hanson said.

"Look Hanson. I would like you to come home early so we can talk. Oh, mother wants us to have dinner with her and gran tomorrow; she said it's a fish dinner. She also told me to bring Marsha, Loretta and Mum. So I think you should give your mother a miss tomorrow. Hurry home," Petra told him.

"Look honey," said Hanson, "I don't think I will be able to have dinner with your mother as I have lots of paperwork to catch up on."

"Okay, I'll let my mother know. Can you bring me home some milk chocolates if you find a shop open?"

"Sure honey. Is Loretta still there?"

"Yes. Sean phoned from the airport to say he's on his way home," Petra said.

Half an hour later and Dr Sean arrived at Petra's gate. As Loretta was looking out for him, she saw him and let him in. "Sean, you go wash your hands while I heat your dinner," she told him.

He went to the bathroom to freshen up then returned to the living room and took his seat talking to Petra and Marsha while Loretta went to heat his dinner. "Sean, this is Marsha my friend. She's staying with me till she moves on. Marsha, this is Sean, Loretta's husband."

"I'm very happy to meet you Sean."

"Same here Marsha."

Loretta took her husband's dinner to him on a silver tray. After he'd eaten he presented Petra with a lovely pale blue cardigan. "Thank you so much," Petra said.

"Where's Hanson?" he asked.

"He went to see someone," Petra told him.

"Well, Petra, sorry I have to eat and run but I'm feeling a little tired and I would like to get home and sleep. Goodnight."

Loretta went upstairs and said goodnight to Madame Stall. "Sean is here to take me home," she said.

"Goodnight Loretta. You say goodnight to Sean for me."

"I will but I'll be here at the weekend to take you home," Loretta said then went down to be with her husband, Petra and Marsha.

Half an hour later, Loretta and Dr Sean said goodnight then went home.

Hanson came home an hour after with two boxes of chocolates. He gave one to Petra and one to Marsha. "Thanks," Marsha said while Petra kissed his lips.

Chapter 17

On Monday night Hanson got home just after nine o'clock. Petra was already in bed. "Pet honey, I bought you a present," he said. Petra did not answer him as she thought he had been with Cassie, which is why he couldn't be with her at her mother's to have dinner.

On Tuesday night he got home even later, at eleven o'clock. Petra had a good go at him and told him to take his clothes and move in with Cassie and her husband.

"Petra, I was working in my office until eight and then went to have a drink with my brother and friends."

"I don't believe you!" she bawled at him.

"Why don't you phone Paul and ask him?"

"Oh yes, as if your brother would tell me the truth."

"Pet, I don't want another woman. I love you."

In the end Petra slept comfortably in his arms. The next morning Petra phoned work and told them that she was taking the day off work, then went back to bed with her husband until nine o'clock. At two o'clock that afternoon Judge Clews phoned her and told her that Officer Dalton had been found in his car with a bullet wound in the right side of his head.

"Oh no," said Petra. "Judge Clews, it's time I moved in on those creeps. Officer Dalton was helping us. He told me he was asking some people about the missing youths."

"Well someone did not like him asking," Judge Clews said.

"Judge Clews, does Officer Dalton have a family?"

"Yes Petra, he had a wife and two daughters, Iona who's nine and Demy who's seven."

"Judge Clews could you give me his wife's address please? I would like to speak to her."

"Petra, I don't think it would be a good idea right now," Judge Clews insisted.

"And why not?" Petra asked.

"I think I know who murdered Officer Dalton."

"Where is his murderer now?".

"I can't touch him and I'm only going on what I heard," Judge Clews said.

"Why can't he be arrested and questioned?"

"Because news just came to me that the man I think murdered Officer Dalton has also been found shot dead. Are you still willing to help me find the children and my niece?"

"Yes, of course I am," Petra said. "I promised you that I would find the children and your niece and take them home and that is exactly what I intend to do. Goodbye Judge Clews."

"Bye superintendent." Petra put her phone down.

On Saturday morning Petra went to visit her mother before she and Marsha went shopping.

"I thought you would have brought Loretta."

"Mum, Loretta went home with her husband last Sunday. She was only spending a few days with us while her husband was away. Hanson is taking me and Marsha to the pictures tonight, so can Madame Stall stay with you and Grandma?"

"Of course she can stay the night with us. Where are you going after the pictures?"

"We're going to the midnight movie to watch a horror film. Hanson has been asking me to go since last week."

"Well, you have a nice time and I'll come over and fetch Madame Stall."

"Mum, she said to tell you it's time you called her Andrea. You can come and fetch her about six and I'll give her dinner before you arrive. You don't mind her spending the night with you and Grandma do you?"

"No Petra. Your Grandma and I always enjoy her company."

Petra phoned Madame Stall saying, "I've passed your message on to mother that she is to call you Andrea from now on."

Madame Stall giggled, "Thank you Pet."

Petra took Marsha shopping in Matter Land and then to her store and Marsha ended up with a wardrobe of designer clothes including underwear, pyjamas, three pairs of shoes, two pairs of sandals and bed slippers. When Petra and Marsha returned home they met Paul sitting in the living room drinking coffee.

"Where is Hanson?" Petra asked him.

"Your mother phoned to ask him to take Madame Stall over to her."

"Have you eaten?" Petra asked Paul.

"No, have you anything nice? I'm starving." He smiled, looking at Marsha.

"Well, you're in luck. I've cooked rice, chicken and corn. Are you coming to the midnight movies with us?" Petra asked him.

"Hanson asked me if I would like to come and I said yes."

"Good, I've asked Marsha," Petra said. "Let's go into the kitchen."

While they were eating Hanson walked in. He washed his hands and then dried them. After he and Paul had eaten, they raced down a cold beer then went into the living room to relax with another couple of beers watching football before they went to the midnight movies to watch a crime film. The film in fact was written by Petra and was called Bitter Desire.

None of Petra's friends or her family had known that she had written Bitter Desire until Paul noticed, 'Written by P. J. Hanson'. When the movie ended, Petra was so amazed and happy to see the cinema packed with people and many had said that the film was fantastic. On their way home, Hanson smiled. "It's a long time since I saw a great film like what we just saw." Petra giggled, but didn't tell them that she'd written it. When they got home, Petra said, "Seeing that film made me think how lucky I am."

"You are very fortunate," Hanson said. "I would like you to back out of searching for the children. Let Judge Clews and the police do their jobs now; you've done the mucky part."

"I just can't do that," said Petra. "I promised Judge Clews and I will keep my promise."

After Paul saw Marsha inside, he kissed her, said goodnight then drove himself home.

In bed Petra told Hanson, "I like the way Mimi stabbed the needle in her stepfather's neck then dragged the point of the needle into his wicked vein, knocking him out before she killed him and hacking off his dick then ramming it down his throat. As for Ace, she was good pulling the detective's gun out of his holster and shooting him and his mate for raping her. You see my love, never hesitate to kill your rapist," Petra said.

Hanson looked in wonder then said, "How about you trapping me between your lovely legs and making passionate love to me before killing me," Hanson joked.

"I was about to do that darling," Petra said rolling over onto his tummy then kissing him from his eyes down to his toes. She moved upwards towards his dick, taking it in her mouth until it got hard, then she spread her legs over his, taking the full length of his dick in her pussy and working her beautiful body. Hanson rolled her onto her back, kissing her all over right down to her pussy and shoved his tongue in, then slid it all the way up into her mouth. "I love you Pet," he whispered to her. As they were both coming, he dived into her fast until they both came together. He rolled off her and they bathed together.

In bed he said to her, "Honey, I know it is none of my business but I saw one of your bank statements. I knew you were rich but I didn't know you were Andrea's heir. Tell me Petra who are you really working for? Are you working for those poor defenceless children or for Andrea, better known as Madame Stall or Mrs Woods?"

"Hanson, I did not plan it to work out this way, or to work against you. Yes, she made me her heir only because she has no family. Hanson, we argue all the time but let's not argue over her. If I didn't care for those children I would not have bothered. I have taken an oath to try my hardest to get the children back to their families and put an end to the Black's wicked doings, permanently. As brave as I might be, I am still scared knowing it won't be easy fighting them. I don't know that if and when I get to those children I will get out alive. Hanson, I love you and I don't want to make you a widower at the age of twenty-two. I have put your name on my account so we have a joint account as I've told you. Hanson, I don't think we should have married to each other; I should have married a priest," Petra joked.

Hanson burst into laughter. "I'm seven years older than you my love." He slapped her face and kissed her.

"What was that all about?"

"You smart arse Mrs Hanson. Why didn't you tell us you wrote the film you took us to see? Petra I love you so much."

Petra laughed, "Old man, I'm in love with you. But if I find out for sure you're cheating on me, I will pull your dick out by its root."

Hanson laughed. "At least when I can't find people to arrest, or get a client, I have a rich wife to support me," he said joking. This made Petra laugh even more. "Honey, I've combined my money with yours. I turned to writing as I will soon no longer be working as a police officer. Anyway, how did you find out that I wrote the film?"

"You had a call from your agent saying the film was a hit and he'll ring you tomorrow morning around ten."

"Oh Hanson, I so wanted to tell you. Anyway, I almost forgot to tell you that my brother Arden and his wife will be coming home to spend some time with Mum and us. They want to live here for a while as their studies have finished; they both passed out to work together in their own office. And before I forget, Todd and Julia want us to have Christmas dinner with them. What do you think?"

"I think family should have Christmas dinner in their own home. I don't mind going to have a drink with them on Boxing Day though, but I want to be with you my wife if possible," he said.

"Well, it's nine weeks away. I'm going to sleep now," Petra said.

"Yes, I'll join you soon. I just want to write my reports."

"Okay, goodnight," said Petra, then kissed his lips. Hanson went to bed an hour later at one o'clock to find her sleeping. As he switched the headboard lights off, the phone started ringing. Hanson answered the phone.

"Hanson it's me Loretta. Is Petra sleeping?"

"Yes, she is."

"Hanson, will you tell her Sean and me will be coming over for lunch tomorrow," Loretta said.

The next morning over breakfast, Hanson told Petra that Loretta had phoned her last night to say that she and her husband would be coming for lunch.

"Why didn't you wake me?" Petra asked.

"Because you told me you were very tired. Besides, I didn't think it was important. Anyway, I always come home to a sandwich for lunch, why can't they," said Hanson in a jealous manner.

"What did you say?" Petra asked.

"I said that most of the time I come home to a sandwich. So why don't you do the same for them?"

"I thought you liked sandwiches."

"Well, I don't. When I was single, I had no choice."

"But H, remember I go to work as well. I have to eat sandwiches as well."

"Pet, honey you don't need to go to work. You know I will treat you right. Besides, you have more money than you can spend."

"I know that honey, but I want to work."

"I know it's none of my business, but I think a wife should be at home to cook, clean and take care of the husband and children," said Marsha, who was also having breakfast.

"Yes, my loving Petra, I agree with Marsha," Madame Stall said.

"This is between me and my husband. I don't remember inviting any of you into our conversation," Petra moaned.

"I'm sorry that I interfered," Madame Stall recited.

"Okay, three against one. As of now, I will cook my husband's meals," Petra said as she laughed and kissed Madame Stall's cheek.

Before Hanson left for work, he kissed Petra. Petra watched him drive away till he was out of sight before she went into the house and closed the door. When she sat at the table she admitted to Madame Stall and Marsha that they were right and that she would cook her husband meals instead of feeding him with sandwiches. She smiled.

"I'm happy to hear so. If you're not careful someone, somewhere will cook him his meals and you just might lose him. He's a very handsome young man," Madame Stall said with a nice bright smile.

"I know," Petra said, "But my husband loves me too much to mess with other women. Besides, he's a good cook. That was his job before he joined the police force."

Madame Stall smiled, so was Marsha's.

That morning Petra went to her local meat shop and bought pork steaks, beef, lamb chops, chicken, bacon, sausages and eggs. Then she went to the fish department and bought four different kinds of fish. She then went home and cooked dinner for six of them: Madame Stall, Marsha, Loretta, Dr Sean, her husband and herself. When her husband got home he was happy eating his meal, but was not at all surprised because he thought that Petra had only cooked because Dr Sean and Loretta asked her to. After everyone had eaten, they told Petra she should cook more often. Petra realised they had liked her cooking.

At five o'clock Petra went to her bedroom and made a phone call to her friend Ira and told him about her plan and about her four friends Marlon, Blake, Drake and Craig. She explained that it was time she brought out the criminals from under the rocks and into the open and that she had to go looking for those poor kidnapped children to take them home.

"Did you speak to your husband about this?" Ira asked.

"Yes. I don't think he likes the idea. He's afraid I might be killed," Petra said softly.

"Pet, your husband is concerned about you. He loves you. You shouldn't blame him for not wanting you to put yourself in danger."

"Ira, I'm not asking you to assist me in any way. Whichever way, I will keep my promise to find every one of the kids and take them home. By the way, how are you?"

"Pet my friend, I'm okay now," Ira said.

"Well I'm glad. Goodbye Ira and give my regards to your fiancé," Petra said.

Chapter 18

Three days later Petra went to see Blake. She told him what she intended to do, showed him the list of names and told him she wanted to nail the rapist bastards, even if it cost her her life. Blake told her he would get Drake, Marlon and Craig. Petra told him that they should make their move on Sunday morning very early when Matt and his brother Johnny Blimps least expected them. Blake agreed. Petra told him that she would get in touch with him on the Saturday night; Blake agreed with that too. Petra offered him ten thousand pounds in advance.

"No Pet. What I'm doing, it's for the youths. Besides, I'm still on the detective's payroll and you've given me a hefty one million pounds and your loyal friendship."

That Saturday night Petra phoned Blake again to find out what their intentions were. "Well," Blake said, "I've spoken to Drake, Marlon and Craig and everything is okay." On Petra's way to her mother's that same Saturday night, she saw her friend Martin just closing up his father's chemist.

"Well, hello Pet. That Tuesday when you called out to me, I was coming to you but I had to rush away when I saw the crowds and the police as I had to take a bottle of special medicine to a very ill patient. Her life had depended on the medicine. If you should need me to assist you in any way, you only have to call me. I'm always working in father's chemist."

"Thanks Martin," Petra said. "Anyway, it's nice seeing you again."

Petra patted him on the shoulder before going to see her mother and Grandma.

"Pet, there's some fried chicken and gravy in the dish on the side and some rice is in the pot."

"Thanks mother, but I've already eaten. I only came to see you and gran. Mother, I don't know how to handle my husband. I really love him, but I just can't stay married to him anymore."

"Pet honey, why don't you try to meet him part of the way?"

"Mother, I have tried, I really have. Since I decided to help the children, we are always fighting. If it was over another woman, I could fight her. But I don't know what to do. All I asked of him is to bear with me until I get the children to their homes. Mother, am I asking for too much?" Petra cried, then went on to say, "Mother, I know the horrible pain those children have suffered and still are. I was there mother. Oh God! Don't any of you care about those children? Well, I do! My God! I don't care if I have to give up my husband. I'll give whatever it takes to help those children."

"Pet, your husband may be right. He doesn't want to lose you. Pet honey, you must try and understand him. I don't think he ever wants you to go to work. Hanson is a well-paid lawyer as well as a private detective. He's not really a poor bloke; he can look after you. Pet honey, I know just how you feel about wanting to help the kids, but I think you should leave it to the police. Honey, please try and hold onto Hanson. He's such a nice husband to you and a very handsome looking six-foot sea-blue eyed brute."

"Mother, you do not have to remind me what a nice husband I have. I know and I love and care about him. Anyway, I also came to see Grandma too," Petra said. And as her mother looked hard at her, she said to her, "Mother, you've told me what you think and I respect you for your opinion."

"Anyway, your Grandma's sleeping."

"Well, will you tell her I was here, and mother, I love you."

"Sure, I will let your Grandma know and I love you honey, but you think about what I said. And remember, Hanson loves you and the sooner you give him a family the better you and him will get on. And don't look at me as if you don't know what I'm talking about!"

"Oh by the way, Hanson likes my earrings. What shall I get my brother for his Christmas present?"

"Pet, I don't think he would mind; I'm sure he would appreciate anything. Pet, don't look so worried. Your brother knows that you can't afford much, so anything will do. And don't think you can win me over by changing the subject to your brother."

"Mother, I will be a good wife to my husband. So let's postpone talking about my husband and me for a while and go on to my loving brother. Do you think he would like a car?"

"How on earth can you afford a car Petra? You've only just got a pay rise and I don't think your husband would lend you the money. A new car is at least six thousand pounds, for a decent one anyway."

"Mother, I have no problem buying a car for my brother. Money wouldn't be a problem. Please, I don't want you to tell a soul about this. Mother, Madame Stall has made me her heir."

"So that's why you want to give your life to finding her granddaughter's killer? And forsake your husband? Pet darling, I know you're trying to do well, but go home to your husband and try to understand him. No money in this world is better than your happiness and your health. Hanson wants children."

"Mother, I've got to go now; I've left a friend at my place. By the way, when Grandma's house is finished being repaired, what have you decided to do with it?"

"Your gran said it's yours. But with Arden and his wife coming home for Christmas, I think they can stay there until they decide what they want, whether they want to go back to Holland or Canada or to stay here?"

"Mother, I appreciate Grandma giving me the house, but I really won't need it. Anyway, I'm going home now," said Petra and she kissed her mother on the face and left.

When she got home Marsha said, "Petra, your husband came home and he said to tell you that he's at his parents."

"Good!" Petra said then made a phone call to Drake. She told him that she had tried at least three times to get in touch with Blake but she couldn't.

"Well, if you give me the message, I will get it to him," Drake said.

"I will need you as well," she said to Drake.

"Well, fire now sister," said Drake in a broad accent. Meaning, let's hear what you have to say.

She told Drake that she wanted them to get ready and prepare for the following early Sunday morning, about four o'clock, so that way they might meet all of their enemies sleeping.

"You mean Matt Blimps and his fellow members? Petra I know it won't be a smooth ride and I'm even prepared to lose my life for these youths if it comes to that. However, with a tiger like you, we're bound to conquer the baddies," Drake said.

"I phoned Marlon and Craig to let them know the situation and we'll meet up with them next Tuesday evening. But, as I couldn't get hold of Blake, I would like you to try and give him my message."

"Okay sister, I'll see Blake later."

"Thank you my friend, we'll leave in my Land Rover about three o'clock next Sunday morning."

"Petra, I'm glad I met you when I was chasing that young girl. Sister, you're the best. By the way, I came across the chick many times. I don't think she has any family or anywhere to live and I was told she's sleeping in an old house on Cherry Street. She's also looking rough. Petra, looking back on what you stopped me from doing, I really feel sick. Petra, I really would like to help that girl. I want to make up for what I was intending to do to her. Will you help me? I really meant what I've said. I would like to look after her like she was my own sister." Drake's tears dropped.

"Drake, are you sure that she's the same girl?"

"I could never forget her face. She's not a bad looking girl. She's working in the fish part of the market cleaning up. I see her every evening but I don't let her see me."

"Okay Drake, I can't do anything for her now until we do what we're going to do. Afterwards, I'll see if she would like to live with you, but I honestly think you should get married before thinking of adopting her," Petra advised Drake.

"Pet, I think I'll take your advice. Thanks," Drake said.

"Well you do that and don't forget to look up the lads and tell them what I've said."

"Petra, have I ever let you down?"

"No Drake, but there's always a first time. Anyway, thanks again. Well goodbye Drake." Petra hung up and then faced Marsha saying, "I'm starving."

"There is some cold meat and salmon in the fridge," Marsha said.

"I think I'll have a salmon sandwich," said Petra.

"I could do with a thick sliced-bread sandwich as well," Marsha said. "Anyway, I heard you speaking to Drake and I want to help. I want to come with you. I know every inch around the Matt Blimps territory. I could get us in secretly. I also lied to you about not seeing Lieutenant Gladstone. I saw him take money from Matt Blimps and Sydney. I know every policeman that took the youths to Sydney and claimed money; Petra you don't need any list. You take me with you and I'll give you every one of them. I'll give you judges, policemen, businessmen, priests, actors, lawyers and the ordinaries!"

"But Marsha, why didn't you go to the police?"

"Pet, I thought you had better sense than that. Going to the police? I might as well have put a loaded gun to my head and pulled the trigger. Those five brothers owned half the force. Most of those bastards are on the Blimps' payroll and were on Sydney's as well. Pet, I had to pay one of Sydney's men Andy with my body to get away: he was one of the gatekeepers. He stank more than an unwashed dog, but he helped me to escape once I let him have me and promised him I would be his woman. I heard after that that Redd cut his throat. Pet, I only went there to work as a nurse for the women and I was held a prisoner. The state some of those young girls were in sickened me. They have been used by some of the ruthless wicked bastards at least three to five men times in one day or night. Oh my God! When I attended to those girls, the smell that came from some of them was so disgusting it nearly knocked me out. Well, one good thing came out of it all, none of them had AIDS or V.D."

"Okay Marsha, but I don't want my husband to know anything about what we're going to do and what you just told me. We'll leave about three o'clock in the morning next Sunday. Do you know how to use a gun?" Petra asked her.

"Sure I do," Marsha said looking seriously.

"That was silly of me to ask you. Come on let's eat then I'll give you a gun," Petra told her.

After Petra and Marsha ate, they went to Petra's bedroom. Petra gave her a loaded revolver and told her to put it somewhere safe until they were ready to leave on the Sunday morning. Marsha went to her room, cocked and checked the revolver before putting it on a shelf in her wardrobe, then returned to be with Petra. She told Petra that she lived with Matt Blimps after Sydney had finished with her. She also told Petra that Sydney's house had at least eight bedrooms, a huge kitchen, two indoor swimming pools for him and his brothers and one for employees and his working girls, three bathrooms, four showers, a sauna room, an enormous wine bar, an indoor tennis court and a large workout room. The bastards had it all. What isn't in that gym they haven't made yet!"

Petra smiled and said, "I know. Well, Sydney was a very rich and powerful animal, but now neither he nor his kind owns anything, nor will his brothers."

"You're absolutely right. They are rich, powerful, vicious animals. Oh, and Matt has a poker room in his bedroom. Those bastards Matt and Johnny Blimps have earned billions by selling drugs, women and young men," Marsha said. "Oh, and most of what Johnny and his brother owns is from your first husband Sydney. They robbed Sydney even though they were partners and half-brothers."

"Marsha, I didn't marry that rat Sydney because I loved him. It was purely an agreement so that his fortune would be distributed amongst the needy and his victims, such as children's homes, old folks homes, hospitals, etc. etc. Now, what would you have done if you were in my position? Also, just for the record, I had no interest in what Sydney had in his trousers or his home."

"Petra, I had hated you for all of the wrong reasons, but now I understand your reason for marrying that wicked bastard! Pet, do you think your husband's brother really wants to marry me?"

"Listen to me Marsha, if Paul didn't love you, he wouldn't have asked you to marry him. He knows about you, take it from me. He told me he loves you and he doesn't care about your past."

Marsha smiled and tried to ignore what Petra had said. "Pet, what are you going to do about the Blimps brothers?" she asked.

"Well, they did own so much. Now they soon own nothing as I said! Look Marsha, I have to make a couple of phone calls before my husband comes home."

"Yes, of course," said Marsha. "Oh he enjoyed his dinner by the way."

Petra made a call to Martin asking him to assist her with some poison. Martin was glad to assist her with enough poison to wipe out a small village. He then asked Petra when she needed it by.

"Anytime next Saturday," Petra told him.

"Okay," Martin said and they both hung up. Petra then phoned Drake telling him to remind the boys that she would need them next Sunday at three o' clock in the morning and that they should meet at Johnny's petrol station on Lime Street, so that they could be at the Blimps place by four o' clock.

After Petra spoke to Drake, she phoned her godfather Johnny at the petrol station telling him what she intended to do and that she wanted to hire two of his Land Rovers.

"Petra, that's no problem. You come and get the Land Rovers with my blessing."

"Thank you my friend," Petra said and rang off.

Meanwhile, Drake got in touch with Blake, Marlon and Craig and told them what Petra had said.

Petra also made a phone call to her friend Detective Ira and asked him to get her about twenty pounds of meat in ten pieces and told him what she intended on doing. Ira thought it was a splendid idea and he told Petra he was going with her even though his wounds weren't quite healed.

"Ira, all I need from you is the meat. I only asked you because your father sells it. If it's inconvenient for you to do so, I'll get the meat from another meat shop."

"No, Pet. I'll get you the amount of meat you need," Ira said.

"Thanks," Petra said. "You get the meat for Saturday and I'll collect it in the afternoon."

"Okay. I'll have it ready for you and I'll be there by your side to bring down those rats," Ira told her.

"Thanks again. Anyway, how's your brother Aaron doing?"

"Pet he's getting better. Thanks for asking."

Petra put the phone down.

Ira's girlfriend asked him, "Was that Pet, am I right?"

"You're absolutely correct," Ira answered with a straight face.

"What did she want?" she asked.

"Just some meat," he replied.

"Ira, do you love her?" she asked.

"Yes, I do but like a sister. She's like the finest crystal and yet so strong; she's so beautiful. Yes, I love her but in a different way to you. Anyway, she's a very happily married woman with a very handsome husband whom she loves very much," Ira said.

"I like her too."

"Ellie, will you marry me?" Ira asked her.

"Do you... really mean that?" She gasped for breath.

"If I didn't, I wouldn't ask you. Will you be my wife and nurse me back to health on your tender breasts?" Ira asked Ellie with a lovely smile.

"Oh yes, Ira Lucklyn, I will marry you anytime," she said happily smiling with those big brown glittering eyes.

Meanwhile Petra's husband Hanson and his brother Paul walked into the house. Paul shouted up to Petra saying, "Petra, I have brought your loving husband home. We got caught up with a couple of friends and your husband has had a couple of drinks too many, so I brought him home to you, his loving wife."

"Well, you best take care of him," Petra said.

"Pet honey, I'm sorry," Hanson muttered.

Petra got out of bed, threw her housecoat around her and marched down the stairs.

"We're very hungry," Hanson muttered and he began to sing Kiss Me Honey Honey Kiss Me.

"Shush, mother is sleeping, you'll wake her up. Just look at both of you. Drunk. I'm disgusted with both of you. Paul, why did you let him get drunk? You both could have ended up in a nasty accident or even been killed," Petra said turning to her husband's brother Paul.

"Petra he's not that drunk."

Just then Marsha came downstairs. "I'll fix them something to eat," she said.

"No, you go back to bed. I'll fix them some strong black coffee," Petra told Marsha.

"We'd like something to eat," Paul announced.

"Then let me help," Marsha said.

"Okay, you slice some roast beef and I'll butter some cobs and make some strong black coffee," Petra said and she and Marsha washed their hands and made Hanson and Paul something to eat.

As Petra and Marsha watched them eating they too had some coffee. After Hanson and Paul had finished, Petra helped Hanson up to their room, stripped him down to his boxer shorts and helped him into bed.

"What about his brother?" Marsha asked when she saw Paul flagged out on the settee.

"As much as I would like to do the same to him, I couldn't," Petra said.

"Then I will," Marsha said. "After all we are both free, single and adults."

"Are you sure you want to do this?" Petra asked Marsha.

"Yes, I'm sure," Marsha said.

"Okay, but don't get too comfortable or tempted. I hate rapists - any rapists," Petra said with a straight face.

Marsha smiled as she thought Petra was joking. But Petra seemed not to be joking and she went to bed with her husband leaving Marsha helping Paul up to a spare room. Marsha pulled Paul's trousers off, leaving him in his shorts. But as she was leaving, Paul took her hand and pulled her in bed into his arms and kissed her.

"You shouldn't have done that," Marsha said to him.

"Why, don't you like me?" he asked her.

"Yes I do, but we must respect ourselves," she said.

"Marsha, I came here because I fell in love with you the first time I saw you. Marsha, will you marry me - again?" Paul asked her.

Marsha's eyes immediately filled with tears as she said to Paul, "Yes, I'll marry you."

"Then let's get married next week. Just you, me and my brother as a witness," Paul said.

"I've neither family or friends, oh, except Pet and her family," Marsha said.

"You also have me now. I'm your friend and your family if you will have me," Paul said.

"Yes, Paul. I love you and I will marry you," Marsha said.

That night Marsha and Paul had sex. At two o'clock the following morning Petra made love to her husband.

On Saturday evening, Petra, Marsha, Paul and Hanson had a great time watching TV, drinking wine and eating. On Sunday morning Petra sneaked out of bed leaving her husband sleeping. She had a quick shower and got dressed into a pair of jeans, khaki long-sleeved shirt with her knee-high boots and her long dark brown hair tied with a black ribbon. She then went to Marsha's room to call for her but Marsha was with Paul. She quietly opened Paul's door and saw Marsha in his arms naked with their lips almost meeting. She poked Marsha to wake her. Marsha lazily turned her head around and prised her left eye open looking up at her.

When she realised where she was, she opened her eyes wide staring at Petra. She tumbled out of bed. "I shouldn't have been in bed with Paul, should I?" Her face shuddered with shamefulness but also showed a faint grin. She then left behind Petra and closed the door very quietly.

"I'm sorry Pet that I slept with Paul. He asked me to marry him again and I said yes."

"Tell me all about it later. Right now you should have a quick shower. We have to be out of here in fifteen minutes," Petra said.

"Okay," said Marsha and she had a quick shower then got dressed into green jeans, a beige coloured top and knee-length boots just like Petra's. Both Petra and Marsha puts bullets in their revolvers and they took a box of bullets each then they left the house quietly leaving Hanson sleeping. Petra drove Hanson's Land Rover out the garage and told Marsha get in. "Petra, I hope you asked him to lend you his Land Rover."

"Marsha, what's my husband's is mine. Get in and let's go and meet our friends before they think we're not coming."

Marsha got in next to Petra and they drove to her Godfather Johnny's petrol station to meet friends Blake, Marlon, Drake and Craig. When Petra saw her other friends Stanley, Martin, Jenny, Faith, and Officer Joan Bradley in their cars waiting, she said to them, "I don't remember inviting you lot here."

Martin hugged Petra then said, "Petra my friend, when you told me your plans, I phoned Stanley and told him what you intended to do."

"That's right Petra my dearest friend." Stanley smiled in her face saying, "You don't think we would let you fight those skunks alone did you? Sorry Liz can't be here but she's almost ready to have the baby."

"I know Stan my dearest friend and thank you for being with me." She hugged him. "I love you Stan."

"Pet, we are one, just like the old days. We live together as friends and if we're to die at the hands of those good-for-nothing brutes, we die together as friends," Jenny said.

"Pet, I'm with Blake," said Officer Joan Bradley. "When he told me your intentions, I told him I would come with him. Pet, I'll fight with you. When I first met you I thought we would never be friends but you're everything I have always wanted in a friend. I will never forget that first day when we first met in the conference room."

Petra turned to her. "Look Joan. We might get killed. Frankly, I don't think you should be here. I know you're a good cop, but right now I think you should go home."

"Right now if I had enough money to support myself, I would quit the stinking force. Knowing about some of my fellow officers makes my stomach turn when working with them."

"Joan, it's not the job that stinks, it's the bad policemen who swore under false pretences that they would abide by the law and don't. Well, we will clean out the force eventually," Petra said.

"Thanks Pet, I'm really glad I met you. If we come out alive, Blake and I might be getting married on the twentieth of April next year," Officer Joan Bradley said. "Petra, now that we're getting to know one another you may call me Joan."

"Call me Petra. I'm glad to have you as a friend."

Then Martin asked Petra, "Where's the meat? We have to dose it now."

"Oh, Ira will give you the meat," Petra told him.

As Ira heard Petra, he took Martin to his Land Rover and gave him the meat. Martin injected the ten pieces of meat with poison then closed the door. Johnny the garage owner walked up to Petra and her friends.

"Well my friends, here's your transport." He then led them to the Land Rovers.

"Well my friends, I want you all to leave your cars inside my garage so that I can keep an eye on them. Park them over here in this clear space.

Petra said to her friends, "Our friend Johnny will look after your cars until we return – if we return." She smiled.

"We will return," Ira said. They drove their cars inside the garage and parked them side by side. Johnny covered them with plastic sheets. Ira divided the meat into three portions before putting a portion into each Land Rover. Johnny gave them extra revolvers and bullets.

"Go and get those rotten bastards and kill them with my blessing." Johnny then opened a bottle of mineral water, filled some plastic cups and passed one to each of them and smiled saying, "Good luck."

After they swallowed and found it was mineral water Marsha said, "I could do with some gin straight from the bottle."

Petra looked at Marsha smiling, then as Petra took in a mouthful of the water she screwed her face up. Her friends laughed at the look on her face as if the water had been tainted with paraffin. "What sort of water tastes like this?" Petra asked.

"Its mineral water laced with a drop of the finest gin," Johnny said laughing. "It was pure good luck juice. When you remember the taste, it will give you strength to fight those bastards and keep you thinking that you'll have to get back to get some more of this magical juice."

Petra looked at Ira, Ira looked at Marlon, Marlon looked at Faith, Faith looked at Martin, Martin looked at Stanley, Stanley looked at Craig, Craig looked at Officer Bradley, Officer Bradley looked at Blake, Blake looked at Drake, Drake looked at Marsha, they all looked at Petra and then at Johnny and burst out into hearty laughing.

"Seriously my friends, as you go with my blessing, I want you all to return with my blessing and my Land Rovers," Johnny said as he helped them to put the meat into the three Land Rovers and watched them drive away. He then went into his office and made himself a cup of coffee while Petra and her friends were on their way to the Blimps' estate.

On their way Petra was thinking about her husband. Then suddenly flashes of her being raped by her stepfather came into her mind. She shivered as tears rolled down her face. They drove for at least twenty minutes before they came to the road that would take them to the foot of Matt Blimps and his brother's estate. They stopped to park their Land Rovers behind tall thick trees and hedges to hide them. Blake, Craig and Martin carried the meat in three black carrier bags. Even though the meat was already poisoned, Martin still carried poisonous injection needles in case the dogs ignored the meat and attacked them.

As they were climbing up the stony path, they met stray dogs, cats, rats, squirrels and rabbits roaming the roads, but none of these animals interfered with them.

As Petra and her friends were getting nearer to Matt Blimps' estate, Craig spotted Matt and his brother Johnny Blimps as they closed their front door. Petra and her friends got near to the mansion. Then running up the long pathway that would lead them to the main gate, they came into contact with two of his dogs barking and growling. Martin flung a piece of meat to them and they grabbed each end of the meat, growling and looking ferocious.

Another two large aggressive bull terriers appeared and Martin tossed two pieces of the poisoned meat and the bull terriers grabbed a piece each and ate, then all four dogs went slowly down onto their sides, making long horrifying growling noises. Stanley and Ira dragged the dogs into the hedges hiding them. "Are they dead?" Petra asked.

"Yes I'm afraid they are," Stanley said, then he and Ira proceeded to catch up with their other friends. As the two of them walked on rustling the bushes, they succeeded in killing three other dogs by tossing a piece of poisoned meat to each of them. Petra warned Stanley that someone was coming their way and as a few of their friends were some distance behind, Stanley went back to warn them. As they hid behind the thick hedges Ira discovered at least four graves and one looked recent. Ira beckoned Stanley and Blake to come and look at them. After they did so, the three of them moved on to catch up with the others with Ira taking the lead through the tall hedges, but he stumbled on a ton of piled rubbish and cut down hedges. While getting up, he discovered the bodies of two dogs and a female. Ira marked the spot.

Meanwhile, Matt Blimps' men had noticed the dogs were missing.

"Hey Mike, have you seen any of the dogs this morning?" Matt asked thinking.

Mike thought for a while then said, "Come to think about it, no, I can't say I remember seeing any of them. Not even Rust, who is always the first to wander around the grounds. I wonder what has happened to them? Since the fucking bitch married the fool Sydney and covered my cousin's dick in baked beans and let the dog yank his dick off, I hate all fucking dogs."

"Look Mike, even so, you search the low grounds and I'll search the top," said Matt and then they both began to wander around the grounds whistling for the dogs to come to them.

As Mike was walking close to some tall hedges, he saw Marsha and went for his gun. Ira saw his move to shoot Marsha, so he quickly threw his knife into Mike's right leg and then knocked him out cold. Ira looked around to see if anyone else was coming his way. Then as he moved further into the woods he saw Jack, Burns and Mel: three men that worked for Matt Blimps. They were standing in a clear spot smoking and talking. Carefully Ira moved behind some taller thick hedges and threw a stone, then howled like a dog that was wounded. The three men set off in different directions searching for the dogs. As Burns was drawing nearer to Ira, he spat his cigarette out and stubbed it out with his shoe then called Darkie the dog saying, "Here boy, come on." When he did not see or hear the dog, he walked on shouting his mates' names, "Archie, Jimmie," but no answer came. He put his gun back in his waistband, tumbled through the hedges and came to a halt when Ira broke a dry twig under his shoe making a crackling noise. Ira kept his shoes on the twig and stayed still. Then after staying in the spot for some time and not seeing anyone, he moved off and came face to face with Archie.

Then Detective Aaron showed up. "Hi mate, the boss asked me to take over while you boys get back to the fort," he said.

"Well Jimmie, Simon, Mike and I were searching the grounds for the dogs; Jack and Mel are searching the other side. Did you happen to see any of the dogs?" Archie asked.

"No, I can't say I have," Aaron said. And as Archie turned to leave, he saw Ira and threw his knife at him, just missing him. Aaron pushed Archie against a tree and injected him with a sleeping dose in the back of his neck. He watched him fall to the ground, then tied him to the tree and went in search of Jimmie and Mike, but caught up with Petra and Marsha. As they moved further into the woods, they came across Mike and Jimmie. Jimmie went for his gun, but Petra kicked up dirt in his eyes and knocked him down with a blow to the side of his head with her gun butt. Ira threw his knife into Mike's right arm stopping him as he was going to shoot Marsha, then Martin injected Mike with a sleeping dose and Ira bound them to a tree.

"I just feel like lighting the field," Marsha said and when Petra looked at her, she said, "Those bastards don't deserve to live."

"I know," Petra said, "But, I'll make sure they get what's coming to them."

"Look Petra, there's Erika standing at the door. She looks like she's crying. I'm sure she's Judge Clews' niece."

When Tina saw Marsha and Petra walking to her and Erika, she whispered to Erika, "Dry your tears." Petra stood still and beckoned Tina and Erika to come to her. They trotted over to her and Tina showed a shameful smile. "Tina, Erika, you don't know me but I know you. This is Superintendent Petra my friend and Detective Ira. We are here with other friends to help you and the others. Honey, would you like us to take you two away from here?" Marsha asked.

Erika nodded then tears welled up in her eyes.

"Look honey, I want you both to get back into the house and stay there. Say nothing to anyone," Petra told them.

Tina replied, "I was actually kidnapped from of my father's gate about two months ago and I was a virgin, but now I'm no one." Tina cried louder and Petra comforted her. A little while after, Tina told Petra that she had heard Matt Blimps speaking to a Detective Porter many times and he had handed over thousands of pounds to him and other officers.

"Tina, do you want to be home again?" Petra asked her.

Tina replied quickly, "Yes, I want to be home. I want to be with my family."

"Are there any more children as young as you here?" Petra asked her.

"Yes," Tina replied. "There must be at least eight others as young as seventeen like Erika and me. Some police officers brought them here. Most of us screamed out in such agony when we were sexually assaulted. I watched two young girls being beaten up when they refused to go with an overweight man named Drew, but he still had them in the warehouse. I was so frightened that I swallowed my pain when I was first sexually assaulted just to stay alive. I have been used by a dozen men as much as four men in one hour including Detective Lewis and Judge Peters." Tina tightly closed her eyes and swallowed her saliva deeply and cried.

"So how did you know it was Detective Lewis and Judge Peters?" Petra asked.

"I've heard their names being called many times." Tina cried more. And Detective Lewis has a full greyish beard.

"Tina, we are going to take you and Erika home. Now Erika please get in the house and pretend everything is okay," Petra told her again.

"Okay," said Erika crying with snot dripping out of her nose. Marsha pulled paper handkerchiefs out of her jeans pocket and gave them to her and Tina. Erika wiped her eyes and Tina blew her nose then they both walked back into Matt Blimps' mansion leaving the door open.

Petra signalled to the others to move inside the mansion. As Blake was hurrying to get inside he got caught rushing over the barbed wire fence. While he was freeing himself, one of Matt Blimps' men saw him and fired a warning shot to alarm Matt Blimps and his fellow members that there were trespassers around.

In a matter of seconds, the grounds were swarming with Matt and Johnny Blimps' men. One of the men saw Marsha walking towards the gym and fired a shot at her, but Petra saw him and called out, "Hey, you pickled-faced bastard!" He turned, and Marsha hit him with her gun butt on the back of his head, which sent him to the ground face down. She kicked him in his mouth and two front teeth fell out. "You bastard, I knew I would get even with you," she said. He lifted his head, looking at Marsha with one eye open aiming his gun to shoot her, but Petra kicked the gun out of his hand, then stamped on the back of head. She then yanked his head up and held her knife to his throat, saying, "I ought to end your stinking life, but you know what, I want you to be a bitch for some thugs in jail." She then put her knife in her boot and injected him with a sleeping dose, dragged him by his hands and tied him to a pipe railing inside the barn.

With the door wedged shut, she and Marsha walked into a green building that looked like a storage room. Inside she saw two white females dressed in grey trousers and white short-sleeved shirts sitting with guns in their holsters; they were kissing. As the glass was misted up, she wasn't sure if she knew who they were.

Marsha and Petra hid themselves behind something looking like a boiler. From where they were they could see three black men standing in front of the garage door. One of the men was smoking while the other two were standing quietly. Petra left the stockroom, picked a pebble up and threw it, hitting the tallest man on his back. He turned to see Petra walking towards them, and then Marsha showed herself.

The three of them walked up to Petra and Marsha armed with knives and revolvers.

"I'm going to cut you both into little pieces and feed you to the wild foxes and birds. Hey, you bitch, haven't I seen you before?" the chubby one said, staring into Petra's face.

"Yes Mon, she's the same bitch that tried to fight Pete in the casino," his tall friend said standing in front Petra.

"Oh yes, now I remember her and that old bitch. Well bitch! You owe my boss twenty thousand pounds plus your body," said David. "But since you killed him with a deadly poison, you owe yourself to me now and I'm ready to fuck you here and now!"

"All I owe you is to see you in jail and to know that some thugs will shape you into a bitch," Petra blurted out.

"Hey you, you half-breed bitch!" David addressed Marsha. " I haven't seen you around since the last time you sucked my dick clean."

"You smelly old stale armpit bastard, are you referring to me?" Marsha asked him.

"Well, I see only the same half-breed cocksucker. The other one will soon be sucking my dick until I come. Her complexion is nice but she's rotten right through. However, you bitch Petra will have to wait until I fuck your half-breed friend once more, then you can suck my dick clean," David said and flicked his knife open while his mate Steve cocked his gun and pointed it at Petra's chest.

Marsha faced Petra trembling with her lips open from fear. Petra pushed Marsha out of the way and kicked Steve onto David's knife. David laid Steve on the floor face down with the knife stuck in his left shoulder blade then faced Petra with staring eyes and said, "I'll slit your guts open."

He pulled the knife out of Steve's shoulder. "Argh!" Steve cried out.

"Steve, you're fucked now," Marsha laughed. Steve moaned and groaned in pain.

"Trust me. You've done the wrong thing by pulling the knife out of your friend. He might end up bleeding to death," Petra said.

"He's already dead. Fuck him!" David said, swiping the knife at Petra's face. Petra jumped backwards each time he tried to cut her. He was persistent in trying to cut her face and she was so angry, but each time she backed away.

"I'm going to kill you, like you killed my friend!" David said. As he got nearer to Petra, she kicked him in the head sending the knife flying out of his hand, and then he stumbled over a rock and fell backwards cutting his forehead. He tried to get up but fell again. Petra left him on the ground to go to feel Steve's pulse but found him bleeding badly and seeming weak. She radioed for an ambulance telling them where to come.

Matt Blimps showed up and laughed in Petra's face and said, "I own half the police force. You married my fucking fool brother Sydney and he ended up dead. You take me in; you'll be laughed at. They'll just let us go you cheap sweet stepfather's slut. I know what you are. Ha-ha-ha!" he laughed.

Marsha walked up behind him and said, "Oh that's where you're wrong.

Matt Blimps, you remember me. I'm Marsha and you turned me into a harlot for your kind. I'm going to see that you're stuck in jail until you're old and grey and shitting yourself."

Matt pulled a gun from under his shirt and aimed it at Marsha, but she shot him in his forehead. He staggered backwards and fell dead.

"Marsha, at least you could have read the slug its rights before you killed it!"

"The slug was disintegrating anyway, so I've done it a favour by ending its life," Marsha said. "He and his brother Redd used me like a piss bucket."

"Well, if that's the case, I'm a key witness that this was how the slug had wanted to go," Petra said.

"The slug was already dissolving. I didn't want him to leave any more of his nasty trail behind," Marsha said.

Petra smiled then faced Steve. "Well, as for the rest of you dogs, you know my rules; it would bring disgrace upon me to end your nasty lives. Therefore, David, both you and your friend's arses will rot in jail serving some fagots."

"Fuck you!" David bellowed.

Aaron then came marching along with Jack, Burns and Mel in shackles.

When Petra heard the ambulance siren coming towards the location, she said to Steve and David, "I'll deal with you two in my own time. Now I have to show myself to the paramedics to get you to the hospital to make sure your arses are tight when the faggots penetrate you." After Petra witnessed the paramedics take Steve and David away she got back to Marsha and the girls.

A few minutes later, Judge Hall and Superintendent Thomson came on the scene. "You two fucked me then laughed in my face like I was a piece of clay," young chocolate-colour skinned Tina said to them then grabbed Superintendent Thomson's gun out of his holster then shot him and Judge Hall in the head.

Petra jumped with fright, then turned around looking at Tina. "Give me the gun now Tina," Petra said.

"They hurt me so much!" Tina cried.

"Look honey, please give me the gun," Petra asked her nicely. Tina then passed the gun to Petra.

Petra walked her from the bodies to the mansion gates leaving Erika with Marsha. Petra's friend Jenny rushed up to her and asked, "What's going on?

Where are you going? What happened?"

Petra replied, "We're going for a walk to get some fresh air. Everything around here stinks." Petra then put her arms around Tina's shoulders and then she looked back at the bodies. She walked Tina a little further away from the mansion gate to meet the detectives: her husband Hanson, his brother Paul, Todd, Robin, and Interpol Bruce, Superintendent Peterson Officers Hodge and Kelly.

"You little fool," Petra's husband said to her. "You could have been killed. I'm taking you home and you're going to quit the force. One family working in the force is enough. Pet, I want you to have my children. If you carry on chasing criminals, you might as well divorce me. I'm so frightened for you. Honey, I'm so frightened that I'll have to identify your body one day. Pet, I love you very much, but I'm really scared that you might be coming home to me in a coffin."

"Okay Hanson, I promise you I'll quit the force," Petra said and she hugged him.

Hanson's brother Paul hugged Marsha. "I love Marsha."

Just then Superintendent Peterson and five of his officers walked over to Petra with seven of Johnny Blimps' working men, all with their hands cuffed behind their backs. I heard you captured Johnny and his brother," said Superintendent Peterson.

"Yes Matt, he's dead. I've trapped most of your slimy slugs but the biggest of them all now to be caught is your precious villain friend Superintendent Bell. You'll find him with his mistress Linda Fenton at 172 Crescent Avenue," Petra told Superintendent Peterson.

"Superintendent Jackson, Bell shot Inspector Saunders and then shot himself. Now will you both excuse me while I go and radio in for a couple of ambulances," Superintendent Peterson said and he went to his car to radio for two ambulances to come and get the dead and the wounded.

While Petra's husband was helping her to his car, Superintendent Baldwin tumbled over to her and her husband. "Superintendent Jackson or Hanson, whatever the hell your name is, I was told that you've being warned by Officer Manners and Lewis not to interfere in the Blimps' and Blacks' affairs. And you deliberately disobeying their orders," Superintendent Baldwin said looking very annoyed.

"Baldwin, go fuck yourself then crawl into your shell. It took a fifteen-year-old girl to grow up to clean out dirty holes and this is how you assholes thank her! Well as from now, you assholes can get out of her face. As, of now, she's just quit the force," Hanson said.

Petra tossed her badge on the ground at Superintendent Baldwin's feet. Her husband took her to the hospital to have stitches in her arm and then took her home. For the rest of the day, her husband and Madame Stall looked after her. Marsha and Detective Inspector Hanson's brother Paul took young Erica to her home with best wishes for the future from Petra. Judge Clews and Erica's mother rang Petra and thanked her. Marsha rang Petra telling her, "I'm going to spend some time with Paul."

Craig drove Hanson's Land Rover and parked it on his forecourt as Hanson had asked him to.

Two weeks later Petra's brother Arden and his lovely wife Anita arrived home from Canada to live with his Grandma and to start his career as a doctor and hers as a senior bank manager.

The following Wednesday afternoon, Arden took his wife Anita to visit Petra. As it was his wife's first visit to Petra's house, Petra showed them around. Each room Anita entered, her lips stretched wide open as if the rooms were taking her breath away. She faced her husband Arden and said, "Oh Arden, I would like to own a house exactly like this one day."

Arden said nothing but smiled and went to speak to his sister Petra.

Later that evening Dr Stanley visited Petra. "Well Stan, thanks for your visit and kiss Liz for me." Petra saw Stanley out and closed the door then she fainted and fell. Marsha flung the door open and ran outside calling, "Dr Stanley, it's Pet, she's just fainted! Help me get her upstairs." Stanley slammed his car door shut and ran quickly to Petra.

"I'll be okay. Just help me into the living room," Petra said.

Her husband rushed to her and carried her into the living room and laid her on one of the settees then knelt down in front of her asking, "Honey, are you feeling pain?"

"No Hanson, I only fainted. I'm just a little dizzy, maybe it is because I haven't been eating properly for a couple of days."

"Okay, as from now you're going to eat properly," her husband told her and kissed her lips.

"Honey, will you send in Dr Stanley?" she asked him.

Hanson looked at her, then went to get Dr Stanley. He entered the room smiling and asked, "How are you feeling?"

"Well a little shaky." She smiled.

"By the way, I can't thank you and the rest of my friends enough for your support."

"Pet, my friend, that's what we decided to do as friends – be there for one another. Oh by the way, I was compensated half a million pounds. I'm going to use it to help buy some new equipment for the hospital."

"I'm very happy about that," Petra said, heaving slightly.

"Pet, would you mind if I examine you?" asked Dr Stanley.

"Why?" Pet asked.

"No reason. Only that you look a little pale. Besides, I would very much like to have a look at your stitches."

"Okay," Pet told him.

"Would you like your husband to be with you while I look at your stitches?"

"No. I would rather Marsha was," Petra said.

Dr Stanley called Marsha in and closed the door. He then carried out his examination on Pet. He smiled and said, "Pet my friend, your stitches look okay, but I'm happy to tell you, you're going to be a mother in about seven months. Well my friend, congratulations." Dr Stanley smiled.

Petra smiled then tears came into her eyes. "I could have killed my baby."

"Pet, this is probably not the right time to ask you, but when you married that Sydney Black, did he, did you let him..."

"No Marsha. And how can you ask me that when you know how much I hated the bastard? I didn't even let him see above my knees. Besides, Hanson and I have been married for three months now and I'm nine weeks pregnant."

"Pet, I'm glad. You have a good husband," Dr Stanley said.

"Would you like me to tell your husband the good news, or would you like to tell him yourself?"

"Thank you Stan, I'll tell him myself," Petra said.

"Then I will send him in," said Stanley and left Petra smiling then went to find Hanson for her.

He walked in smiling then sat on the settee beside her taking her right hand into his and looking into her eyes.

"Hanson darling, you're going to be a father," she whispered.

His smile was wiped off his face and he took his hand away from hers and got up. Petra turned her back to him and her tears fell heavily. He walked to the door.

"I would be happy to give you a divorce," she told him. He stood firmly at the door, closed his eyes tightly for a second and then opened the door and went to his bedroom for a large glass of whiskey. He then flung himself onto the bed with tears running down his face.

Stanley touched Petra on her shoulder. "Pet my friend, I'll look in on you tomorrow." Then he left.

Meanwhile, Marsha filled her glass with whiskey and swallowed the whole lot in one go then asked Petra, "Are you having a baby?" Petra nodded her head with her back to Marsha. Marsha smiled then she kissed the back of her head.

Petra faced her. "Oh Marsha, I'm so ashamed that Hanson didn't meet me as a virgin and it's now three months since Hanson and I got married," said Petra sadly.

"Pet honey, you've told him what had happened to you in the past and I'm sure he understands what you went through. You were only a weak child when your stepfather took advantage of you."

"Marsha, I don't remember that I told you that," Petra said.

"No honey, Loretta told me. I didn't want to put it to you so bluntly, but you're so loving and caring and it slipped out. Will you please forgive me?" Marsha asked.

Petra was so furiously upset with Marsha that she asked her not to say anything to her husband, but instead Marsha went to see him upstairs in his room.

"Now what do you want? And don't you believe in knocking and waiting to be asked in before you enter?"

"Yes, I do. But the state you're in right now, even if I'd knocked you wouldn't have invited me in anyway." Hanson looked hard at her.

"Hanson, what I have to tell you will only take a minute."

"Well say what you want, then get the hell out of here as I am not in the mood to hear anything," Hanson blurted out, then he swallowed another mouthful of whiskey.

"Hanson, Petra's child is yours and don't you think any different. She told both Dr Stanley and me that Sydney Black didn't even see her knees and she doesn't tell lies. Besides, you already know the reasons behind why Pet married that dog Sydney Black. Hanson, please don't let Pet go through this alone, she needs you. Please don't make a big mistake and then regret it for the rest of your life. At least wait until the baby is born and then decide. Hanson, it won't be difficult to judge if the baby is yours or not. Sydney Black was black; you're white and Pet's black. Am I asking for too much?" Marsha pleaded.

Hanson said nothing. He rested his glass on the bedside cabinet and told Marsha to leave and to close the door on her way out.

Marsha turned to leave then said, "Pet is as honest as the day she was born. I would hate to see you make a big mistake, you're very lucky to have Pet. I honestly think that she deserves a better husband that will worship her for having helped those defenceless youths out of their agony."

Marsha paused. "Hanson, she has put her life in danger to help people. She got Judge Clews' niece home when you assholes failed."

Marsha walked out of the room leaving the door open.

Hanson got up and said, "At least you could have closed the door on your way out."

Marsha looked back at him and said, "Most animals use their feet, I'm sure you're capable of that." Hanson pushed the door shut and Marsha went to her room for a few minutes before she went back to Petra in the living room and said, "Petra I spoke to your husband about the baby."

"Marsha, I'm going to call my lawyer. I'm going to give Hanson a quick divorce, as I want him out of here by tomorrow. I love him, but that's the way it has to be."

"Pet, he deserves a kick up his arse, but I don't agree with you about divorcing him. You should give him some time."

"I really love him. I don't want us to be apart, but if we have to be, then, I will have to accept that."

Then Hanson came into the room and said, "Oh darling, I've been so selfish to you, our baby and to myself. Will you forgive me?" he asked with tears in his eyes.

"There's nothing to forgive. I love you so much," she said pressing his hands over her breasts.

Marsha smiled and kissed Hanson on his cheek before she left him and Petra to go and see Hanson's brother Paul in the library.

"I love you Hanson," said Pet, "And I'm going to be the lady of the house from now on."

Hanson smiled, "I don't want you to do too much."

"I won't. Marsha will always be here to help me. Will you ask her to come to me?"

Hanson kissed Petra's lips, then went and sent Marsha to her. As the door had been left open, Marsha walked in. "Did you want to see me?"

"Yes Marsha. As you understand what I did for the youths, I'm really happy to have you as one of my friends. Marsha, I'm very sorry for the way that things have turned out. But the way I see it, only caring parents and a few of us others really do care about every child," Petra said.

Marsha smiled. "Well, all of this is behind us now and we will put it down to experience."

"Yes," said Petra whispering softly.

"How about a nice cup of coffee?"

"I would love one."

Marsha went to make Petra some coffee, then Madame Stall entered the room and hugged Petra lovingly. "Petra my dear, I'm very happy that you're going to have a baby. That will bring a lot of happiness into this home. Pet, this is for the baby. I would like you to keep this safe until he or she is born. I know that I am not you or Loretta's real Grandma, but I couldn't love both of you more. I gave Loretta a share for her baby."

"But Mum, baby doesn't drink champagne! Anyway, you will be just as real a Grandma to my baby as my blood Grandma!"

"Pet, I was saving this for this very special moment. This bottle contains eight rubies and four uncut diamonds. They are at least sixty years old and were worth a fortune then. I believe they are worth much more nowadays. Anyway, I'm going to make us our favourite chicken soup, as you will need your strength; we want a healthy baby. Oh, you screw off the bottom of the bottle," Madame Stall said.

"Thanks," said Petra and she gave Madame Stall a tight hug and started to cry. Hanson opened a bottle of champagne and filled six glasses and two cups of coffee. He passed the champagne to his brother Paul, to Petra's brother

Arden, his wife Anita, Marsha and Madame Stall, and himself. Then he gave coffee to Dr Stanley and Petra. When Dr Stanley asked why coffee for him and Hanson replied, "You'll need a clear head for when your godchild is born."

Everyone laughed and Petra and Dr Stanley laughed together.

When Dr Stanley, Arden and his wife left, Hanson cooked roast lamb to follow the chicken soup for Petra, Madame Stall, Marsha, his brother Paul and himself.

Long after dinner, Pet phoned her friend Amelia, Jenny, Faith, Julia, Liz, her mother and Grandma and told them of the good news.

The following day, Petra's brother came to see her. She told him that Madame Stall had given her the house and over two billion pounds and the Hot Leg Store. Arden looked startled. "Petra, I'm really happy for you."

Petra put a cheque for a hundred and fifty million pounds in his pocket. "This is for you little brother."

Much later that day, Superintendent Peterson called to see her and told her that all who had helped to catch the Blimps brothers and their men would be rewarded well and given a job if they wished. As for the youths that were kidnapped and taken to Sydney Black's residence to work as prostitutes, they would be compensated very well, including Mrs Dean for the death of her husband. Judge Clews' niece Erica was back at home with her family, and she too would be compensated, as well as the parents of the murdered children and Hans, who had had his hand chopped off.

"Without you, none of this would have been possible," said Pearson. "Thanks again, Petra."

Pet was so relieved to hear this that she asked Marsha to get Pearson a cold beer. Marsha left and returned shortly with the beer. Peterson thanked Marsha. She smiled and then left the room. After he had finished his beer he told Petra, "You should take things easy for a while."

After he left, Detectives Sinclair and Walker called in to see Petra. When they saw Detective Inspector Hanson, Detective Walker said, "We've come to see Superintendent Jackson."

"She is no longer Superintendent Jackson. She's my wife and she's Mrs Hanson," said Hanson.

"Well, we would still like to see her as we have a case we would like her to help us with," said Detective Walker.

"You're both detectives. You crack the case, and I don't want to see either of your faces except at work."

"Come on Hanson, let us talk to your wife."

"Walker, I ought to crack your stupid face. You and your detective get the hell out of my house and stay out."

Petra heard the voices while she was getting dressed. Her husband walked into the bedroom and she asked, "Who was that?"

"No one special, just a newspaper boy asking if we would like the Evening Mail delivered to us. Don't worry about it honey, you get some rest."

Detective Sinclair knocked on the door again while his mate Walker waited in the car. Marsha answered the door and asked Detective Sinclair to wait outside while she went to get Detective Inspector Hanson.

As she was going up the stairs to Hanson he was walking down. "Hanson, I think Detective Sinclair wants to speak to you again. I asked him to wait outside while I fetch you."

"Thanks Marsha," said Detective Inspector Hanson and closed the door in the detective's face and walked away. Detective Sinclair knocked on the door several times before Detective Inspector Hanson eventually opened the door looking vexed.

"What the hell do you want from us?" Hanson asked Detective Sinclair.

"Will you please tell your wife that I would like to speak to her?"

Hanson fisted Sinclair in his face then said, "Happy Christmas to you, arsehole, when it comes." He then closed the door and went into the kitchen, pulled the ring off a can of coke and drank deeply.

Although Detective Inspector Hanson had hit Detective Sinclair, he still knocked on the door again at least five times. Marsha looked at Hanson with pleading eyes. Madame Stall was out in the back garden cutting some flowers for the living room. Hanson was so annoyed that he went and yanked the door open.

"What the fuck do you people want from my wife? She's done your dirty work while your lazy asses sat comfortably and laid down the rules; my wife was that someone. Now I'm warning you if you ring my bell or knock on my door again, I will not be responsible for my actions. Now get the hell off my property and stay off!" Hanson flung the door shut in Sinclair's face. But the detective insisted on seeing Petra and wanted to speak to her, although she was sleeping. No one answered the door again, but Detective Sinclair was so persistent in ringing the doorbell that it disturbed Petra. Detective Hanson got so annoyed that next time he answered the door with his revolver in his hand. "Why don't you get in your car with your friend and both of you get the hell out of here and leave us alone!"

"Look, I know that your wife is in a class of her own; one of the best. May I just speak to her for a minute?" he asked, feeling the side of his face where Detective Inspector Hanson had hit him.

"You really are a fool. My wife is finished with the force. Done, left, quit, packed in her job. She doesn't want to have any more to do with the force and especially with your kind."

"Well, let me speak to her then she can tell me that herself."

"My wife is sleeping from exhaustion after chasing and capturing all your rotten druggies and rapist maniacs and saving the children that you lot kidnapped and took to villains to be used as whores and bitches. After doing your work, you could at least manage to respect her by letting her get some rest. Instead, you'd rather pound on my door every five minutes disturbing her," said Detective Inspector Hanson.

"Well, she can sleep after I speak to her. I want her on a case to help catch a drugs gang."

"Sinclair, my wife is pregnant and I won't have you putting her and my baby in danger. As much as I respect you, you knock on my door again disturbing my wife and me and I will put you in hospital for Christmas." Detective Inspector Hanson grinned and closed his door. Detective Sinclair banged hard on his door again. Detective Inspector Hanson reached for his gun and opened his door and looked hard in Detective Sinclair's eyes.

"Just let me speak to your wife," he said.

Detective Inspector Hanson smiled in Sinclair's face and punched him in his eye, then fired a shot through his foot. "Now take your arse somewhere away from here. Your friend's more sensible than you by staying put. You knock on this door again or ring the bell and I will blast you to kingdom come."

"Tell me this Hanson," groaned Sinclair. "I've heard you were going to ask your wife for a divorce as you thought the child was not yours. So what suddenly changed your mind? Oh yes, she's rich and much better at her job than you!"

"Asshole, my wife just woke me up to realize that I'm working amongst creeps such as you. Like my wife, I've succeeded in seeing through maggots such as you. Now move your arse off my premises," said Hanson and closed his door.

Petra had heard the shot and she got out of bed and was looking at Sinclair through her window.

"What happened to you, Sinclair?" Detective Walker asked smiling, although he saw what had happened.

Detective Sinclair looked hard in Detective Walker's face. Walker laughed. Sinclair watched him hard. "What the fuck are you laughing about?"

"You mate, you got what you deserved, now let's get going," Detective Walker said.

"Walker, shut your black mouth and get me to a blasted hospital."

Detective Walker looked at him and shook his head smiling.

"I'm in fucking agony! The son of a bitch punched me in the eye and then shot me in the foot."

"Yes Sinclair, I can see that. To the hospital we shall go," Walker said grinning.

Meanwhile, Madame Stall took a vase with flowers into the living room and asked, "Hanson, were you cleaning your gun again?"

"No Mum."

"I thought I heard a gunshot," she said looking at Marsha. Detective Inspector Hanson smiled and went upstairs and sat on the bed beside Petra. "Who was at the door?" Petra asked.

"Sinclair, Cassie's husband."

"What did he want?"

"He came to congratulate us on our first baby."

"Why didn't you call me? I would have liked to meet him. I've been told he's very rough and doesn't stand for any nonsense from anyone."

"Well, you can forget about him. You're going to keep out of danger and give us a healthy baby."

"Oh Hanson, guess what?"

"You're going to have a son by any chance?" Hanson asked.

"No, we're having a daughter. Would you do me the honour of cooking supper for the four of us, only for today, as I'm feeling a bit run down. I really fancy some of your tasty tender beef like I had when I first met you," Petra said.

"Who's the four?" Hanson asked.

"Your brother Paul, Marsha, you and me."

"And what about Mum?"

"I've already made arrangements with my mother for her to have supper with them."

"You've really succeeded all the way," said Hanson and laughed.

Petra smiled happily and closed the door with the intention of making love with her husband, but as they were kissing the phone rang. She answered the phone.

"Hello sweetheart," her mother said.

"Oh hello mother."

"Now that the fantastic news about the baby has sunk in, I have decided that I will come over each day to do the housework and cook your meals so that you can rest. And Petra you made me cry making your brother a very wealthy millionaire."

"Mum, Marsha is doing the housework. She insisted that I should have plenty of rest. Also, Hanson is a very good cook and I have already chosen the godparents for my baby. They're Stanley, Martin, Jenny, Faith, Elizabeth and old Mr Parker. I'll speak to you tomorrow when you come over. Right now, I have an appointment with my husband."

"Pet, you're very lucky to have nice people to look after you, but I'm your mother and I should be the one to look after you."

"Mother, I'm not a child any more. I'm a happily married and pregnant young woman. I love you and the rest of my family. About my luck, it's because I believe in God and myself, and in doing what's right. Bye mother and give my love to Grandma," said Petra and put the phone down. She rested her head in her husband's arms.

"Sorry Pet my love, I have to go and cook what our baby fancies."

Chapter 19

Meanwhile at the hospital, Detective Sinclair told Dr Stanley that his gun had accidentally gone off while he was cleaning it and shot him in his foot. Dr Stanley had his foot X-rayed and plastered after having the bullet taken out.

"Well Mr Sinclair, I would like you to rest your foot when you get home for at least a week because of the swelling and take a couple of pain killers four times a day for six days."

Sinclair nodded. But the next day Sinclair he back to the hospital looking angry because he was feeling a lot of pain and his foot was badly swollen.

Much later that afternoon, Dr Curtis was working on the same ward. He recognised Detective Sinclair and went to him. "Well, well, well. What has happened to you now?" Dr Curtis asked, smiling.

"If I tell you, you won't believe me."

"Try me," Dr Curtis said, smiling broadly.

"I went to see Superintendent Petra Jackson and her husband shut the door on my foot."

"Did he hit you in the eye too and shoot you?" Dr Curtis interrupted.

"Yes, he did! I'm going to take him to the cleaners for all he has done."

"You must have really upset him for him to have done this to you."

"I need his wife," Sinclair groaned.

"So you're in love with his young wife?" Curtis laughed softly.

"No, no. I only asked him to let me speak to her as she's one of the best, or so I have been told."

"She's going to have a baby. I also heard she left the force to take care of it, then after the baby is born she might return to work."

"Is she really having a baby?" Sinclair asked, as if he didn't know.

"Yes, I believe she's about two months pregnant and she's very lucky that she didn't have a miscarriage with all the hard work she's done recently."

"Well in that case, she has my blessing, but we still want her in the force," Sinclair said, looking serious.

Dr Curtis shook his head and was about to walk away when Sinclair said, "I don't know what the hell she saw in that man she married. She's the only one that succeeded where we had all failed. We want her back even if we have to wait for five years, or even if I have to blackmail her because of her husband damaging my foot. Besides, I know some of the things she has done."

Dr Curtis walked away, shaking his head.

Back at their home, Petra and her husband were kissing passionately. Suddenly tears came streaming down her face as she remembered the first day she had met her husband. It had been love at first sight for both of them, and she shoved her panties in his mouth to shut him up as he was laughing so much and making fun of her.

"What's the matter honey?" her husband asked her.

She replied softly, "I'm so happy to have you."

"Honey, as I've said many times, I'm the luckiest man to have a wife like you."

"Well, we are both lucky and happy to have each other."

"Pet, this is a token of my love." Her husband slipped a diamond ring on her finger.

"And what's this for honey?"

"This ring is because you're going to give us our first beautiful baby. You'll have one of these for every child you bring into our lives."

"Hanson honey, I don't need another ring. All I need is God, Jesus, you and my family, as well as health and good people in my life. I'm really very happy and feel blessed." She put her husband's right hand on her tummy and smiled.

"Oh Petra, you remember the young girl you told me about and how you protected her from your men friends."

"Yes. What about her?"

"I saw her yesterday. She told me her name is Arlia Singleton. I told her you would like to see her and she said she'd come and see you tomorrow. I gave her our address. Would you like me to pick her up after work? I asked her about her family and she told me her mother ran out on her and her father two years ago to live with another man. She hadn't seen her mother since, her father died eight months ago and she was staying with her aunt and her boyfriend sometimes. Honey, she's really in need of help."

"Thanks for finding her. I'm really glad you spoke to her. Blake will be so happy. He wants to adopt her after he gets married. I have to buy myself at least five outfits, one for Ira's wedding, one for Paul and Marsha's, one for Joanne and Curtis', one for Kim and Officer Hodge's and one for Blake's."

"Who is Ira getting married to?" asked Detective Inspector Hanson.

"Ellie, you'll get to meet her soon. Oh by the way, how's your nuts? Sorry to have almost kicked them out of you." She burst out laughing.

Her husband smiled and then whispered in her ear, "Well, they did the job right, you're carrying the proof. They're also feeling great, in fact, exceedingly great and strong." He stripped naked standing in front of her laughing. Petra looked at him then burst out laughing.

"What's so funny?" he asked.

She replied, "Mr Handsome Dick is taking a nap!"

Hanson looked down at himself and burst out laughing too. When Madame Stall and Marsha heard the laughing coming from Hanson and Petra's bedroom, their faces lit up with happiness.

That Wednesday morning at seven o'clock, Hanson drove to the small factory at Walls End to see Arlia scrubbing the tiled floor. He hid behind some crates watching her.

"She works here every morning from seven to eight thirty then goes to school," the woman supervisor said.

"Thanks for telling me," Detective Inspector Hanson said still staying out of sight and listening to Arlia singing 'One day at a time sweet Jesus'. Her singing was so breathtaking that Hanson wiped tears from his eyes. At the end of her song, Hanson approached her saying, "Arlia, do you remember a young policewoman who stopped three young lads from chasing you?"

"Yes! So what about it, did she send you here to remind me?"

"No no! Nothing like that, but she would like to see you. I told her you were coming to see her," Hanson said.

"Well, I don't want to see her, you or those bastards again, ever!"

"I do understand what you're going through," Hanson said.

"No, you don't have the slightest idea what I'm going through. Right now I'm scrubbing tiled floors and packing milk bottles before going to school, then I'm going to people's homes after school and at weekends ironing clothes, scrubbing the fish market, just to get money, then searching for somewhere to sleep when my aunt and her man are high on drugs. So tell me if you still know what I'm going through."

"Well ... well ..." Hanson stuttered.

"Exactly, you don't know! So you can just fuck off back to your fine police lady and tell her that you haven't seen me!" Arlia said in a bad temper.

"Okay, I will tell her what you said. However, this is my card if you change your mind and need a caring friend to talk to."

The supervisor smiled looking at Arlia.

"Hey mister, thanks. I will see her after school."

"By the way, you have an excellent voice. You'd make a fortune singing if you were guided in the right direction."

"Do you really think so?" Arlia asked, interested. "I have a white friend Kira nearly the same age as me, fifteen. We sometimes sleep in old buildings. Her parents died last year in an accident. They were drunk going home from a party and their car collided with a lorry. She's like a sister to me. We depend on each other, so will it be okay if she comes with me?"

"Sure. Would you like me to pick both of you up?" Hanson asked.

"Yeah, that would be so cool."

"Would four o'clock be all right?" Hanson asked.

"We will be waiting by the market door in town."

"Okay, I'll be there," Hanson said.

While Hanson was talking to Arlia, Kira was walking the streets in town begging for money and picking sweets from shop counters before going to school. At four o'clock that afternoon Hanson met Arlia and Kira as planned. He took them to Petra's.

"You wanted to see me?" Arlia asked.

"Yes, I don't know how to put this to you. You remember those blokes that were chasing you?"

"Yes, how can I forget them?"

"Arlia, would you believe me if told you they are good people now?"

"Why did you ask me here?" Aria's eyes dropped to the floor.

"One of them would like to adopt you as his sister. He has really changed. He would like to have you living with him and his fiancée. He is engaged to be married. What do you say?"

"Thanks, but there's no way I'd live with any of those bastards that tried to rape me. Luckily for me, you saw them. You were the one who stopped them and now you want me to live with one of them! No way would I live under the same roof with any of them. Sorry, we've both wasted each other's time. I'd rather pack milk bottles, scrub tiled floors, do people's ironing and sleep in old buildings. Come on Kira, we're sorry we dirtied your home lady," Arlia said.

"Please wait Arlia, me of all people should have known better. I was totally out of order, but I do want to help you and your friend Kira. What if I asked you to come and live with us, my husband, Mum and me? Would you both like that?" Petra asked.

"I don't know."

"Yes, I'd like that," Kira said. "I need a home and a family."

"What do you say? You could have your own room and go back to school properly; you both look like bright girls. Let's put the past behind us; just say you'll try. If you don't like living here you can leave," Petra said.

"Okay, I suppose it wouldn't do any harm. Kira and I will move in, but any hassle from you and we'll be gone," Arlia warned.

"I will treat you both as family, but I won't stand aside watching you both doing any wrongs. You behave yourselves respectfully and I'll show you the same. If you have anything that is sentimental to you that you would like to keep I'll take you both to get them. Tomorrow we will go shopping for clothes."

"I have nothing worthwhile going back for. All I need is a hot bath and sleep after I eat," Kira said.

"Me too," Arlia replied.

After Arlia and Kira had eaten, Petra showed them to their rooms. That afternoon they showered and Petra gave them new nightclothes and panties to sleep in. After Petra saw the girls settled in bed, she rang Loretta telling her about Arlia and Kira and how happy she was to have them both staying with her and that they were both very pretty, Arlia being mixed race and Kira being white.

"I'd love to meet them," Loretta said.

The next day, Petra took Arlia and Kira shopping for clothes, shoes, trainers and whatever else they wanted such as a wristwatches, earrings and toiletries of their choice. That same day Petra and her husband filed for custody of Arlia and Kira.

A week later, Arlia and Kira went back to school and gave their friends and teacher a surprise by how nice they looked. Both girls were so happy living with Petra that they started to call her Aunt Petra, Uncle Hanson and Madame Stall nan. Petra picked the phone up and dialled some numbers.

"Who are you phoning now?" her husband asked.

"Loretta."

"Can't you phone her tomorrow? Right now, your dinner's getting cold." He took the phone out of her hand and placed it on the receiver. Whilst Petra looked at her food, he watched her and realised she didn't feel like eating. She asked him to take the food into the kitchen, but he insisted she should eat. He picked up some of her food on a fork and put it in her mouth then kissed her lips. Arlia and Kira smiled.

Petra took the fork from him and started eating. Over dinner, she said, "Hey Hanson, I thought Todd's mother had a daughter?"

"Yes, she has a daughter and two sons."

Chapter 20

The next Saturday evening, Hanson invited his brother Paul, detective friends Todd, Robin, Bruce, Ira and cousin Derrick, his wife, step Uncle Aldridge, mates Drake, Craig, Blake, Marlon, doctors Stanley, Curtis, Sean, Officers Hodge, Kelly, Rogers, Mr Jordan the night watchmen, Johnny the garage owner, Chief Superintendent Peterson and his friend John the estate agent all to celebrate his future fatherhood and he and Petra's new found family members Arlia and Kira.

Petra's brother Arden, his fiancée and Martin turned up and joined in the celebration. As Hanson was playing pool with Todd, the phone rang. Hanson's brother Paul answered the phone. "Can I help you?"

"My name is Mrs Phyllis Garnett. Can I speak to Detective Inspector Hanson or his wife please?"

"He is in the middle of a game. Can I take a message and he'll get back to you soon?"

"I'd prefer to speak to Detective Scott Hanson directly. He is a private detective isn't he?" Mrs Garnett asked.

"Yes, he is," Paul said.

"Then I'd like to speak to him straight away. It's rather urgent," she insisted.

"Okay, I'll get him. Just hold on," said Paul and went and told his brother that a Mrs Garnett was on the phone and would like to speak to him.

Detective Inspector Hanson passed the cue to Detective Todd and told him, "I'll be right back." He then left to speak to Mrs Garnett.

"Detective Inspector Hanson speaking. What can I do for you?"

"I'm Mrs Phyllis Garnett. My eighteen-year-old daughter was raped and murdered and I'd like you or your wife to find the man who did these dreadful things to her. Mr Hanson, my reason for asking you to find my daughter's rapist and murderer is because you and your wife believe in justice. Mr Hanson, I will pay you a very handsome fee."

"When was your daughter raped and murdered?" Detective Inspector Hanson asked.

"Two months ago. At that time, I was at a friend's house. When I got home at about ten past eight on the Friday night, I found my daughter naked on my living room floor and the state she was in was disgusting. Her legs were so bloody and, and Mr Hanson, I'm willing to pay you or your wife whatever. Please find the bastard who raped and killed my daughter!"

"Look Mrs Garnett, my wife and I were away at that time. However, I'll get back to you if you'll give me your telephone number and I'll call you some time tomorrow. Mrs Garnett, I'm really sorry about your daughter."

"I'm willing to pay you or your wife part of the fee now as I know she'll need some to work with. Detective, I'd really rather have your wife working for me."

"Mrs Garnett, she can't take the case."

"And why not? I'm a very wealthy woman who is desperately seeking her help to find that or those bastards that raped and killed my daughter. Detective Inspector Hanson, I will not rest until I know my daughter's murderer has paid for his crime. I'm offering your wife one million pounds, I'm sure this is an offer even you wouldn't refuse. Half now and half when you catch the ugly son of a bitch or bitches!"

"My wife is pregnant. That is why she can't take the case. But I have four of the best lads here with me. They're working with my wife and they've really proved to be the best. I'm positive they'll bring your daughter's murderer into the open."

"I want the son of a bitch in front of me, so that I can split his face open as he did to my daughter's legs."

"As I've already said, I'll get back to you. Just a minute, I'll get a pen and paper to write your number down."

"Would you mind if I come to your home instead? Say next Monday morning."

"Yes, that would be okay Mrs Garnett."

"Well, I'll see you then, Mr Hanson. I do hope those lads are really as good as you make them out to be." Mrs Garnett breathed out in frustration.

"Trust me Mrs Garnett, they're really the best you can buy," Detective Inspector Hanson said looking at Marlon, Blake, Drake and Craig as he was giving Mrs Garnett his address.

The following Monday morning at eleven o'clock Mrs Garnett went to see Detective Inspector Hanson as she'd promised him. She told him her daughter was seeing a young man by the name of Nolan. She paused and tears filled her eyes. She explained, "I never met the lad, but from what I heard about him, he sells women and drugs and he's cousin to your ex- wife's husband." Hanson looked hard at her. "Detective, I should have known better than to remind you of the past. Anyway, Graham's brother Earl threatened to kill Verna and her mother if they told anyone about him or Nolan being with my daughter."

"Where is Verna?" Detective Inspector Hanson asked.

"Her mother sent her away when they heard on the news Nolan had been found on Bold Street in his car murdered. I think Verna is in London or Leeds with family in a hideout. Her mother will not say where she is, but I reckon Earl took her to Leeds."

"Well, if Verna is in any of those two places, my lads will find her. Marlon and Blake will go to Leeds and Drake and Craig to London. They'll leave next Monday morning. I will need a photo of Verna. Can you get us one, Mrs Garnett?"

"Yes, I think I can. My daughter had taken a few pictures of them together."

"Good."

"I'll bring you a couple of photos with a down payment of five hundred thousand pounds. Mr Hanson, please don't look at me like I'm the criminal. If two million shocks you, don't be. I think my daughter is worth what I'm offering you to bring her murderer to justice. Detective Inspector Hanson, you and your boys find that bastard and you'll be greatly rewarded."

"Okay Mrs Garnett. You bring us the photo and we'll do the rest."

The following day Mrs Garnett took two photos of her daughter and Verna at a fair and gave them to Detective Inspector Hanson.

"Look Mrs Garnett, you're overpaying us. I've never charged any clients this amount. Not even for the toughest cases."

Mrs Garnett smiled. "Detective, what I'm going to pay you and your lads can never amount to more than what my daughter is worth. As I said, I'm a very wealthy woman. Even if I wiped my arse with a fifty-pound note every day for the next hundred years, my money would never run out. I once heard that Madame Stall said she'd pay a large amount to find her granddaughter's killer. Well, I'll pay ten times the amount to find my daughter's killer. Detective Inspector Hanson, you're not giving me a price on how much you want, so I'm giving you what I want to pay. I do hope your lads are as good as you and your wife."

"They might even be better."

"Well, I'll leave it in your hands."

"Have you any other family?"

"Why do you ask?"

"Because your life may also be in danger. I really think you should take a holiday to a secret location. But I would like to know where you are, just in case I need to contact you."

"Where do you suggest I should go for a holiday?"

"America, Canada, the Virgin Islands, the West Indies, anywhere you like. Provided you let me know."

"Well, how about your place? No one will have any idea I'm staying at your place. That's of course if your wife wouldn't mind."

"I don't think she would mind, but I'll have to speak to her first."

"You do that, Detective Inspector Hanson. You speak to your wife and then get back to me."

"I will," said Hanson.

By this time Paul and Detective Todd were listening to the conversation. Paul said, "Hanson, I know this is not my business, but with Pet being pregnant, don't you think it might be dangerous to protect anyone at your place? Especially in this situation. Of course I know that Pet can take care of herself, but with her condition, give her some space. Think about the baby. This is of course if you want the baby."

"Paul, you're my brother, but this doesn't give you the right to interfere into my private life," said Hanson.

"If you will excuse me, I think Paul's right," said Todd.

"The next time I hold a meeting with my clients, make sure you remind me to invite you two in," said Hanson.

"I'm sorry I spoke." .

Just then Petra's phone rang. It was Dr Stanley. "Pet, my dearest, Elizabeth has just given birth to a seven-pound handsome baby son, and we've named him Jackson after you. Mother and baby are doing very well. Pet, you must come over soon and see your godson."

"I will. By the way, what about Janet?"

"Oh she's doing very well. She's passed all her exams and she's going to university next term. She wants to be a doctor."

"That's great. So there will be three doctors in the family?" Petra asked.

"It looks that way. Anyway, I won't keep you any longer. And please have plenty of rest."

"Well, kiss mother and son and tell them I'll be coming to see them soon. Goodbye Stan."

Stanley smiled and put his phone down.

Meanwhile, Peterson was telling his detective son-in-law Todd and his family the good news that he had now been promoted to Chief Superintendent. He was so overwhelmed that he was almost in tears. He then said, "Without Petra, he wouldn't have been promoted." He hugged his wife Irene and said, "I'm going to ask Petra and her husband here for a celebration dinner with us next Saturday evening. Would you mind?"

"No honey, I would be happy to have them here. She deserves much more than a dinner. But being so young and wealthy, I think she'll pity you and accept a one-time invitation from an old man who has just been promoted because of her."

Peterson and his family burst out into laughter.

"Speaking about dinner, I'll have to phone Dorothy and ask her to come over and help me with the cooking. I believe there will be about thirty people coming to the party. I hope Petra and her husband will be able to come. She's so adorable. Detective Inspector Hanson couldn't have married a finer lady than her. Oh Rodney, I also hope Doris and Eric will be back from their holiday by then. Joanne, I'm so glad Curtis chose you for his wife."

"Speaking of wives, Kim will also be getting married two weeks on

Saturday. I also heard that she inherited half a million pounds," Julia said.

"Yes, we both have. Only neither of us can touch any of the money until we're twenty-five. We both have at least three years to go; Kim's five months older than me," said Joanne.

As soon as Joanne told Julia and Irene about the money that she and Kim had inherited, Curtis came and took her away.

"Did you know they had this amount of money?" Irene asked Julia.

"Yes," Julia replied. "Joanne told me."

"The one thing that puzzles me is how come Doris adopted Kim and Kim's daughter? Come to think of it, Kim's child resembles Todd," Irene said giggling.

"Because they're family."

"How could they be blood family if Kim was adopted?" Irene said.

"Well you don't go anywhere with this as we don't know the truth."

"My dear husband Rodney Peterson, what was said here is now forgotten," Irene said. "Still, I was told Doris' sister was having affair with a Ruben Malcolm and she got pregnant with Kim, then told her husband she had to work away for five months and went to stay with a friend until Kim was born. A month later she took Kim home and told her husband she'd promised her dying friend to take care of Kim."

"How come you know so much about Kim and Todd's aunt?" Julia asked.

"I can't tell you where I got my information except your aunt-in-law gave birth to Kim in a private home and had her family fooled."

"Well I don't think it's fair on Kim. She has a right to know who her mother is or was," Julia said sympathetically.

"By the way Rodney, Dorothy told me that you told her Curtis is twenty-nine years older than Julia. How could that be when Curtis is thirty-three and Julia's twenty-four? What were you thinking when you told her your children's ages?" Irene laughed.

"Did I tell her that?" Peterson laughed hilariously.

"Well, that's what she told me," Irene laughed heartily. "This means you had Curtis well before you were ten."

When Peterson saw the funny side of this, he laughed aloud.

"Truthfully Rodney, what were you thinking at that time?" Irene asked him again.

"I was thinking of you honey."

"Oh Rodney, I bet Madame Stall donated the two million pounds that was paid to the children's home six years ago. And since her granddaughter was raped and murdered, I heard she has been using her maiden name Woods," Irene said.

"So where did you get that information from?"

"I read it or heard it from someone. Besides, who else would have cared so much for those children to put up such a high ransom? Not forgetting Madame Stall's granddaughter was one of the victims."

"You really remember well. By the way, remind me to give Inspector Carson a ring. I want to invite him to Curtis and Joanne's wedding."

"But I thought you told him already," Irene said.

"Yes, I did. But he is so forgetful these days. I would still like to give him a call to remind him."

"Okay Rodney," Irene said.

In bed, Hanson told Petra about Mrs Garnett and her daughter and what he intended to do. Petra agreed with his decision and told him that she would help him in any way she could.

"No! I can't let you risk our baby's life. I know you're very good, but it might be too dangerous. I want you and my baby in good health. I really love you Pet."

"I know."

On Thursday evening Petra and Hanson had dinner with Chief Superintendent Peterson and family. Curtis invited the lads to a stag night, drinking on the Friday evening. On Saturday morning two of Irene's friends helped her and Julia do the cooking for the wedding. Joanne and Curtis were married at two o'clock and by ten o'clock the party was over, as Joanne hadn't wanted a big do.

Two weeks later, Hanson had looked into the rape and murder of Mrs Garnett's daughter. He suspected Graham Vincent, one of the Blimps' cousins, had done it, but without Verna, who was a key witness, Detective Inspector Hanson told Mrs Garnett it was impossible to arrest Graham Vincent. Three days later, Detective Inspector Hanson summoned, Blake, Drake, Marlon, Craig and Detective Aaron to his office. Hanson told them that Graham had raped and then murdered Mrs Garnett's daughter but he had no proof.

"You don't need proof to arrest the bastard," Blake said.

"Well we still have a problem. I heard the brute fled to Leeds or London," Hanson said.

"Hanson, if he's in hell, we'll find him," Marlon said.

"Mrs Garnett is willing to pay you fellows a large amount to share between you."

The five of them looked confused.

"Look lads, I have summoned you here because I need you."

Blake giggled.

"My friends, this is no joking matter. I'm serious as can be. Blake, I need you and your friends to be in London and Leeds to find Vincent Graham. Are any of you interested?" Detective Inspector Hanson asked.

"We'll need money," Blake said.

"We all are very interested," Detective Aaron said.

"Good! But I will need you here with me and Ira," Hanson said.

Without hesitation Blake said, "We'll take the job."

"Speak for yourself," Marlon said.

"Ok, if you boys don't want the job I have others who would appreciate a wealthy pay packet of one hundred and fifty thousand each," Hanson said.

"Look Hanson, we'll take the job. But we'll need spending money, if we have to travel from one city to another to find this Graham Vincent. We'll need a couple of thousand each for paying hotels, getting information, you know things like that," Craig said.

"Well boys, after this job you might be richer than me. Mrs Garnett has already paid us a down payment. The rest of the money will be given to us when the job is done, when we have Graham behind bars. I want you to meet me here Tuesday morning to get your tickets, money and instructions of what to do. Any questions boys?" asked Detective Inspector Hanson.

"Just one," Craig said.

"Shoot," said Detective Inspector Hanson.

"After we find this Graham Vincent, can I fight you for Pet?"

Blake, Marlon, Drake and Detective Aaron burst out into laughter, while Hanson's face suddenly went pale and looked serious before he burst into laughter too then said, "You four get the hell out of my office, but be here on time Tuesday."

After they had all left the office, Hanson began twirling himself around in his chair, saying, "Boys, we're in big business! This is just the beginning of your undercover work. Whoopee! Pet honey, you've made it possible for us all. I love you."

Just then Paul went to Hanson and said, "And why shouldn't you love your wife's brother, after all, you had at least eight phone calls from some of the richest folks asking for you or your wife to find their missing families."

"Paul, how would you like to work for me privately?"

"Hanson, I'll give you my answer later," said Paul and left Hanson in deep thought. A bright smile came over Hanson's face then he said, "Pet honey, I couldn't love you any more if I tried."

Four days later Marlon, Blake, Craig and Drake turned up to see Hanson as he'd asked. Hanson gave them the keys to two brand new cars, an M-power BMW and a Mazda RX8. "I want them back in the same condition as I gave them to you in," he said. The lads looked at each other in surprise, then smiled. Craig chose Drake to go with him to London leaving Marlon and Blake to go to Leeds to find Graham Vincent.

In Leeds, Marlon and Blake were making enquiries about Verna Somers and Graham Vincent; Craig and Drake did the same in London. In Leeds Marlon and Blake drove past a gang of scruffy-looking youths sniffing cans of glue and puffing out smoke from smoking drugs on Chapel Town Road. "Blake, turn the car around. We will go back and ask the gang we just passed if they know this Graham."

Blake looked hard at Marlon before turning the car around and driving back to the gang. Marlon wound down the car window, "Hey lads, do any of you know a Graham Vincent or a Verna Somers?"

"Who wants to know?" said one of the lads as he walked over to the car puffing his drug-infused rolled-up cigarette.

"I want to know," Marlon said.

"Man, hook me up with a cock and hen," the lad said blowing his thick smoke into the car. Marlon fanned the smoke away and said, "Come on, why would I want to hook you up?"

"Man, I can help you get what you're looking for," the lad said.

"And how do you know we're looking for something or someone?" Blake asked.

"You asked if I know Graham. I man know about everything that goes on around here. That's why they named me Know-it all." He smiled and said, "I know a Graham Vincent and his buddy Earl. You see, Earl has told me he accidentally killed a rich woman's daughter so he decided to come here to Leeds instead of giving himself up. He had sex with her but the second time around he was tipsy and could not get it up. She laughed at him and he strangled her. She was a virgin too. Graham was blamed for hers and the Nolan murder. I believe the girl's mother is called Mrs Garnett."

As Know-it-all turned to walk away, Marlon grabbed him by the back of his stained shirt collar. "You take us to Vincent and you could have ten cocks and hens."

"Let me go tell my peeps that I'll be gone for a while and I'll be back soon," Know-it-all said.

"Okay, be quick. Remember you have ten crisp tenners waiting for you," Blake said.

Know-it-all trotted back to his mates and said, "I'm going somewhere with my two cousins, I'll be back soon."

Meanwhile, Blake was making a call to Detective Inspector Hanson. "We have information and strong leads that Vincent and his brother are living somewhere in Leeds," he said.

"And what about Verna?" Hanson asked.

"Well, we have nothing on her yet, but if she's in Leeds, we'll find her. We'll get back to you soon. By the way, call Drake and Craig and let them know they're wasting their time in London."

"Okay. You two be careful with those brothers and if you should need help, let me know."

"Right boss," Blake said and closed his mobile phone.

Know-it-all returned to Marlon and Blake and sat in the back of the car and directed them where to go and told them to stop in front of a big house on Chapel Town Road. "Vincent and his brother Earl live here. Now give me what you promised."

"You'll get it when I'm satisfied," Marlon said.

"Look at you mans, shining up to the nines, dressed to the nines in the latest crises garms and driving the latest top new car, no man, this must have cost you at least thirty grand and you mean to say you can't pay me one hundred quid?"

"Know-it-all, you give us Vincent and you'll never look scruffy or beg again. You might even stop your bad smoking drugs and sniffing glue habits," Blake said.

"Okay, you so much want this Vincent I'll give you him roasting hot on your lap. I'll take you to his favourite nightclub tonight, Club Exposure, but I'll need something decent to wear. You know what it's like."

"Okay Know-it-all, we got the message," Marlon said.

"We need fresh outfits too," Blake said.

"Then let's go shopping! It's Friday night, we've got two hours late shopping before the shops close," Know-it-all said.

So they went shopping for clothes, and Know-it-all changed into the outfit Blake bought him. Know-it-all was very humorous and commanded a lot of respect from people in the area. He was very tall at five eleven with a fit body and dark skin. He had very short Afro-Caribbean hair, which was wavy when washed and relaxed with Brylcreem. His complexion was very dark but this brought out the whiteness of his teeth and eyes. Not quite Wesley Snipes, but very close. He stood in front of the mirror smiling and admiring his sparkling gold tooth, looking up and down at his reflection in the stylish light blue Armani two piece suit and navy blue shirt he was wearing. He grinned. "Yeah man, I could get used to this," he murmured.

When he got back to his friends, one said, "You look like you even had a bath."

Another friend said, "It's a shame about your shoes."

Know-it-all looked down at his shoes and said, "Bollocks. That can be fixed."

Kate was one of Know-it-all's closest friends; she was at least five foot seven. Just by looking at her, you could tell she was living a rough life. You could see also that if she cleaned herself up, she would be very beautiful. Her skin was of a caramel colour with scattered freckles on her face and her hair was rusty brown, which complemented her skin.

As Know-it-all looked deeply into Kate's bright big brown eyes, he said, "I haven't had a bath but a shower at my two cousins' hotel. I even shampooed my hair." He laughed.

"Those two guys are your cousins?" Kate asked, interested.

"Sure, I almost forgot I had cousins like them," he said laughing.

"How can that be, when one is white?" Kate said.

"Well the white one is married to my cousin, you get it?"

"Sure, know-it-all, I get it. So he's your cousin-in-law?" Kate asked.

"Well if you put it that way," said Know-it-all and laughed.

"Put in a good word for me, your other cousin is kind a nice," Kate said playing with the chewing gum in her mouth.

"I'll see what I can do."

"Well the time has come for me to take my two long-lost cousins to the club. If you could borrow something to wear, you could come with us too," Know-it-all said to Kate.

"Yea, I'd like that. And I know just the person, my friend Verna."

"Verna?" Know-it-all asked in shock.

"Yes, Verna. Why are you sounding so surprised?"

"Well Kate, you've just soothed the spot that hurts. Will Verna be at the club tonight?"

"Why are you so interested in Verna?"

"What do you think?"

"Well I don't think you'll have much of a chance with her tonight as her man will be with her, Graham Vincent, and you don't stand a chance against him."

"Kate you know what? I love you! I'll tell you what, why don't I ask my cousins to buy you something to wear instead. You can give your friend Verna a surprise. Let me see." He looked at his cheap, half-broken leather watchstrap. "Yes, we still have some time left before the shops close. Let's go and see my cuz."

He took Kate to see Marlon and Blake.

"You'll like hearing what she has to say, but first she needs some clothes to wear to the club tonight. We'll take her with us tonight; she won't be any trouble. She knows something we don't."

"What's she doing here?" Blake asked.

"Take us shopping now, as we don't have much time left and I'll tell you after."

"Are you trying to blackmail us?" Marlon asked.

"No cuz, but you know what it's like ... nothing is for free," Know-it-all said.

"Cuz?" Blake asked looking surprised.

"You know how it goes?" Know-it-all said smiling.

"Okay, let's go and get your lady friend some clothes. But you both better make it worth my while or you won't want to meet me again," Marlon said.

"In other words," Blake said, "You'll regret meeting us. Get me?"

"I get yah!"

Blake and Marlon took Kate shopping in City Plaza. The shop was full of late shoppers looking classy in the latest trends. As Kate walked into the shop, heads turned as she looked out of place amongst the people. The shop assistant looked at her scornfully and did not want to serve her. Instead, she asked her to leave. Marlon heard and said to the shop assistant, "Have we got a problem here? She probably looks scruffy, but I'm sure the money is smooth. Okay lady, you might want to refuse her, but I'm sure you'll want the money and I want to buy my cousin some clothes."

"Please sir, why don't you take your cousin somewhere else."

The manager was listening. She walked over to Kate and looked hard at her saying, "Your beauty is hidden under that roughness. Let's see if we can explore it to the surface." She smiled and asked Kate to come with her and choose what she would like. Smiling, the manager looked back at Kate and Marlon. Marlon said to her, "We'll pay for every outfit my cousin tries on."

Kate tried on four sets of clothes: a pale grey trouser suit with matching silver vest, a lovely floral short flared skirt and pale lemon off-the-shoulder blouse and one of each short black and off white thin strap dresses. She kept the black dress on but before she walked out, the manager went and grabbed a selection of cosmetics, which were on the sample display for her to try on. While the manager was applying the make-up, she said, "I knew something beautiful was hidden under all that. Now, let me see." She then took a brush from a packet and brushed Kate's hair in a style that suited her good-looking face then gave her the brush set. "Well..." The manager stopped herself speaking because she thought Kate might take it the wrong way and was insulting her. "Now, all you need is a pair of shoes." She then took Kate to the shoe department, where she tried on a pair. "They look good on you," said the manager.

"I'll keep them on," Kate said.

Then Know-it-all and Blake showed up. Know-it-all was wearing a new pair of black shoes, a silver bracelet wristwatch and a smile big enough to brighten up the whole shop.

"All you need now is a nice watch and gold chain," Marlon said to Kate. She smiled but her eyes moistened with tears.

The manager took her to the jewellery department and Kate chose a gold chain, wristwatch, a handbag and perfume. Marlon looked hard at her and smiled. The manager walked back to the clothes department and said to Kate, "Now you're polished up like a diamond. Now go out there and give them something worth looking at." Kate walked out of the changing room carrying her new clothes. People's heads turned again, but this time in surprise. The manager took the clothes from her and took them to the sales counter. Marlon said, "Please, we'll take the lot." As everything came to seven hundred and ninety-four pounds and seventy-nine pence, the manager asked Marlon, "How would you like to pay sir?"

Marlon answered, "In cash madam."

Marlon smiled and took eight hundred pounds from his wallet. The manager counted the money and gave him the change. Marlon put ten pounds in the charity can.

"Well thank you sir," she said shaking his hands with warmly. Smiling she said, "It was a pleasure doing business with you. Please come again." Marlon smiled saying thank you once again before he and his friends left.

As soon as they had gone, the manager said to her staff, "In future, don't make any customers feel as though they're not welcome. In other words, never judge anyone by their appearance. If for any reason you're not sure about them, please see one of the managers. Do you understand?"

"I'm sorry Mrs Bates," the young assistance apologised.

"Yes, we almost lost a good sale. However, some of us learn the hard way," the manager said.

Meanwhile, back in Birmingham, Hanson's mother went to see Petra.

"Look Hillary, if you have come here to give me another lecturing, I'm really not interested," said Petra.

"No, I've come here to apologise. I was out of order. I've never seen Hanson so happy in a long time. Paul also speaks so highly of you. It makes me sometimes wonder which one of my sons is married to you. Please don't shut me out Petra. I would like to share in the upbringing of my grandchildren."

"Okay Hillary, I accept your apology."

"Well, I have nothing to do, so why don't you let me help you with whatever you're doing for the rest of the day?"

"I'm okay, really Hillary, I'm okay."

"How about let me help you with the housework, cooking, dusting or ironing."

"All right, I suppose you've twisted my arm. I have plenty of clothes that need ironing," Petra said.

"Well, I better get cracking with that then," Hillary said and started ironing the basket of clothes. When she had almost finished, Hanson walked in and saw her, he smiled. "Hello mother."

"Hello son. I'm helping Petra with the ironing."

"I can see that," he said smiling as he looked at Petra. Petra smiled and he shrugged his shoulders.

"Well Petra, I would like all the family to come two weeks on Sunday and have dinner with us. It's Eric's sixty-fourth birthday," Hillary said. "Please say you'll come."

"Hillary, I wouldn't miss Eric's birthday for anything," Petra said.

"I know it will be hard at first, but it would be nice if you could call me Mum. I like you a lot you know, I really do."

Hanson looked into Petra's eyes and was ready to burst into laughter. And as Petra shook her head, he covered his mouth with his palm and went into the kitchen to have his lunch.

Meanwhile back in Leeds, Marlon, Blake, Know-it-all and Kate were on their way to the club. Marlon kept looking at Kate.

"Why don't you ask Blake to stop the car and we can swap places? That way you can look into one another's eyes," Know-it-all said.

"I agree," Blake said.

As they got to Club Exposure, they parked their car under a lamppost then walked towards the club door to meet a well-built door attendant. "Four of you?" he asked.

"Yes," Blake said.

"Eighty pounds mate," the doorman said.

Blake paid the amount and the doorman let them through. Know-it-all's eyes glittered with excitement to see the overcrowded dance floor with so many people of different ages, especially when the beautiful white dancer walked off the stage and kissed him. The DJ announced, "This is for all lovers." Then he played Save The Last Dance For Me. Marlon took Kate in his arms and led her onto the dance floor. As they were dancing he kissed her. As she felt deep love for him tears came into her eyes and she held on tightly around his neck. Verna saw her and walked over to her smiling. "Kate, is that you girl! You look so beautiful, why only now do you decide to shake off your old look?"

"I'm tired of my old self, so I've decided to clean up and go forward, maybe find a decent man to fall in love with and settle down. Get married and have children," Kate said.

"Girl, you really are trying to make an impression. Whether, it's for someone or for you, you sure look good. Ever thought about taking up modelling?" Verna asked.

"No," Kate answered. "That's the last thing on my mind. Besides, I'm not too keen on cameras."

"Well, it was just a thought," Verna said.

"Would you excuse me while I go and see some friends?" Kate said, then left. As she looked back at Verna, she thought she saw Graham Vincent pulling her by the hand, but it was his friend Hugh wearing the same jacket. Verna was struggling to pull away when he slapped her face and shoved her in a room. Marlon joined Kate again.

"That's Graham," Know-it-all said. "That's Graham Vincent and his woman Verna." Know-it-all pointed them out to Marlon.

"Okay, Know-it-all, you stay out of the way while Blake and I deal with the mighty Graham Vincent," Marlon insisted.

"Don't get killed, I want my money," Know-it-all said. Blake gave him three hundred pounds. He smiled, then kissed the money before putting it in his inside jacket pocket, then he took Kate onto the dance floor while Marlon and Blake went after who they thought was Graham Vincent.

Marlon knocked at the room door. "Who's there?" Hugh asked.

"A friend. I came to give you a message," Blake said holding his gun.

"What message? Get your arse away from my door," Hugh said.

"Are you opening the door, or shall I kick it open?" Marlon shouted.

Verna quickly opened the door. Hugh hit her hard in the face, busting her lips. She cried out as she held her hand under her lips catching the dripping blood. Marlon and Blake burst into the room with guns, but by then Vincent had realised that Marlon and Blake were after him and fled, leaving Hugh in the room holding onto Verna. As Marlon and Blake hadn't met Vincent before, they thought Hugh was him.

Blake read him his rights. "Graham Vincent, you are under arrest for rape and murdering fifteen-year-old Jersey Garnett. Anything you say may be used against you in the court of law. If you need a lawyer and can't afford one, one will be appointed to you."

"What the fuck are you talking about? Hugh said. "I haven't raped or murdered no one and you want to take me in? Well over my dead body!" Hugh didn't explain who he was.

"That's okay by me. Whichever way, dead or alive suits me," Marlon said while Blake looked on.

"You go fuck yourself," Hugh said. He jumped out of the three-storey window and ended up dead on the spiked railings. Marlon looked out of the window, shook his head, saying, "Vincent boy, you had enough blood to fill a bucket, but you chose to go that way."

Marlon walked back to Kate and said, "You stay here and enjoy yourself." Kate held his hand and he kissed her, saying, "I'll be back." Kate smiled and went dancing while Marlon and Blake went outside to look at Graham's body. Then Blake went to call Detective Inspector Hanson, telling him, "Graham Vincent threw himself out of a three-storey window and he died instantly."

"Well, I hope to see you and Marlon soon then. Drake and Craig left London and are on their way home. You boys take care," Hanson said and rang off.

Blake said, "Oh wow! Such a bloody waste, I hate to see blood."

"That makes two of us," a policeman said. Blake smiled leaving the police to deal with the body. The music was still playing while people flocked outside listening and looking at the police and the ambulance men taking the body.

Just before the dance finished, Blake and Marlon went to their hotel to checkout. They said goodbye to Know-it-all and Kate and gave Know-it-all a couple more hundred pounds and told him, "Take care, we might meet again." Know-it-all was looking sad and so was Kate.

Suddenly, Know-it-all glimpsed Graham Vincent and belted out, "Rassclart! Vincent!" Blake stopped talking and smiled broadly. Marlon and Blake looked at him once more before getting into their car. And as Marlon looked into Kate's eyes, she asked him, "What about Verna?"

"She's no longer wanted," Blake said. "She's free to do whatever she wants. Well guys, as I said, we might meet again."

By this time Marlon was sitting in the car watching Kate and looking downhearted. When Blake looked at him, he smiled, then asked, "Why do you look as though you have just been pulled out of a tonne of molasses?" Marlon made no reply. Drake drove off looking at him and after driving about fifty yards Marlon was still looking back. As Blake looked at him he pulled a tissue from the box and gave it to Marlon. "Dry your eyes mate, don't fall to pieces on me. If you want Kate, go and get her." Marlon smiled. Blake turned the car around just to see Kate and Know-it-all sitting on a park bench looking sad. "Hey, you two come over here," Blake said.

Know-it-all and Kate quickly jumped up and went to the car. "Jump in," Blake said. Know-it-all climbed into the car while Kate was standing by the car chewing her gum and holding her carrier bag with the clothes Marlon bought her. Marlon got out of the car and asked her, "How would you like to live with me?"

Kate said nothing, but ran into his arms. Marlon kissed her. Blake gave Know-it-all one of his cards saying, "We're looking for recruits, how about you let your friends know and you could come and check us anytime. My number and address is on there as well. And mate, stay out of trouble and give up the drugs man, I want you to be clean."

Know-it-all looked at the card and smiled. He then put it in his jacket pocket and took the weed out of his pocket and threw it in the street bin. Smiling, he looked up at the sky saying, "Oh my God, one step at a time," as this was his favourite tune.

Meanwhile, Kate saw Verna. "Verna, I'm so sorry for what happened," she said.

"Girl, don't be. You have no idea how long I have waited for this day. Now I can go home to my family. Graham and his brother, I knew they would come to a bitter end. I don't even want to see his body. He was a dangerous brute, but at least there's no chance of him coming back. As for his brother, time will catch up with him." Verna didn't realise that it was Hugh that had fallen and broken his neck. Know-it-all however went and saw the body and found out it was Hugh that died but didn't say anything to anyone, especially Verna, Marlon and Blake.

Blake got out of the driver's seat to sit in the back. Kate got in the car and sat at the front with Marlon driving. "I will phone my friends later to let them know I will be spending time in Birmingham," Kate said.

"Yes and the rest of your family," Marlon said.

"Well them too, my two sisters, but I'm taking us to let my mother know I'm going with you," Kate said as she gazed into Marlon's eyes, smiling.

Back in Birmingham, Hanson told Petra, "I received a message from Blake saying that Graham Vincent is dead."

"Oh, but I'm not so sure. He's one of the smartest bastards of all," Petra said.

Hanson kissed Petra. "You're my wife, my life and everything else. I love you so much."

In Leeds, after Kate spoke to her mother and sisters, Marlon drove back to where he had asked Know-it-all to wait. At one time Know-it-all thought he'd seen Vincent Graham walking amongst a crowd of people but said nothing. As he was leaning against Marlon's car, he sank into thought. Flashes of Vincent came haunting him as he remembered Hugh was wearing Vincent's jacket. Know-it-all smiled again and walked away from the car whispering, "Graham Vincent, you may fool my two cousins and your woman Verna, but not me. Just remember I'm Know-it-all and you and you're brother's arses are mine when I'm ready for you."

Know-it-all walked back to the car smiling from ear to ear. "What's with the sentimental smiling Know-it-all?" Marlon asked him.

Know-it-all stopped smiling and said, "Night runs till day takes over." Marlon and Blake looked at each other's eyes, wanting to know what Know-it-all meant. Blake said to him, "You just keep clean and if you're interested in working for us, a home will be ready and waiting for you or for anyone else who's interested. Just call us."

Know-it-all shook his head and Marlon drove away with his newfound girlfriend and his mate Blake and headed back to Birmingham.

Marlon took Kate to stay with him and his mother for the time being and promised her he would soon get them a place of their own.

Early the next morning, Blake, Marlon, Drake and Craig took the cars to Detective Inspector Hanson. "You boys keep the cars, you have earned them," Hanson told them and threw two sets of keys to them saying, "Now you each have a brand new car and one hundred and thirty thousand pounds. Thanks lads, you have a job as of now and twenty thousand is for your newfound friend Know-it-all."

The boys grinned widely and took off in their new cars.

Back in Leeds, on Tuesday morning, the postman knocked at Know-it-all's door.

"Who the fuck's knocking at my door this early in the morning?" Know-it-all watched his mother eating her scrambled eggs breakfast.

"Well, you only have to go and find out," his mother said, "As I'm sure it's not for me."

The postman knocked again.

Know-it-all went to the door holding his fork. "Who's there?" he asked.

"The postman. I have a letter for you that you have to sign for."

Know-it-all opened the door. The postman gave him two registered envelopes. "Please sign on these two lines."

After Know-it-all signed, the postman said, "Thank you," and left. Know-it-all closed the door and walked to the table and stood over his breakfast looking hard at the envelopes. He asked himself, "Who would send me these?"

"Open them and find out," his mother said. He looked hard at his mother before opening the envelopes to find a diamond ring and two thousand pounds in fifty-pound notes. He laughed so loudly that his mother looked hard at him. Reading the note, the ring dropped and sounded heavy. He picked the ring up. "Rassclart, real gold." He laughed. Reading the note it said, 'Thanks mate for not giving me and my brother up.'

"I know it's from you Graham Vincent. I know I man was right about you and your rassclart brother Earl. But little do you two know; you both jumped out of the frying pan and into my fire," Know-it-all mumbled. He opened the other envelope to find a cheque for twenty thousand pounds from Detective Inspector Hanson and a note saying "Thanks for helping my officers".

Then the phone rang. Know-it-all jumped and picked it up.

"Know-it-all, you keep my secret about me and my brother and you'll be getting more money than you can spend. The ring is only the beginning of our friendship. I'll get in touch soon." Graham Vincent closed his mobile phone.

"That's what you think, rassclart. I man know you bastard's are on the run and I man will track you and your brother down when I man is good and ready. Meanwhile, I man will keep your secret till the time is right," Know-it-all said laughing till he was in tears. Then, looking at the cheque, he said, "Kate, thanks for giving Detective Inspector Hanson my address."

Chapter 21

Two months later Kim sent a wedding invitation to Julia and family stating that she and Officer Hodge were getting married on 14th November. Julia replied that she, her father, Irene and her family would gladly attend. Later that evening when her husband got home, she said, "Todd, Kim invited us and the family to her and Officer Hodge's wedding."

"Oh," Todd said, "Hodge told me."

"So you will be going then?" Julia asked.

"Well, I wouldn't miss it for anything. I do hope she's marrying him for love and not for the wrong reasons."

"You know Todd, I hope her next baby looks like Hodge and not like you, otherwise she will have people wondering and asking questions."

Todd smiled. "What's for supper Jul?"

"Roast beef with mash and roast potatoes, string beans, carrots and cherry pie with custard."

"No Yorkshire pudding?"

"Yes Todd, put what you want in the oven for five minutes. I've already eaten and the kids are sleeping, and I'm going to have my bath. Are you going out tonight?"

"No honey, it's nearly eight o'clock. I'll be up later," he said.

Julia went to have her bath while Todd heated his supper and ate.

The next afternoon Petra went to visit Julia. As they got talking, Julia said to Petra, "Kim sent me and the family an invitation to her and Hodge's wedding."

"She sent us one. I think she means well. Will Todd be giving her away?"

Julia burst into laughter.

"I wonder what she's up to," Julia asked.

"Well my friend, if we don't go, we'll never find out," Petra said.

"You know what Petra my friend, you're so right. Are you sure you will be able to go as you'll nearly be ready to give birth around that time."

"Yes Julia. If I have to go into labour at that worthless bitch's wedding, so be it. The one I'm feeling sorry for is Officer Hodge."

"Do you think my husband's still having affair with the bitch?"

"No Julia, Todd made a mistake and I'm sure he regrets it. Todd loves you honey, and I'm quite sure he has stayed well away from the bitch as he doesn't want to lose you and the kids."

"Petra, I saw Todd in Kim's daughter, do you…"

"Julia, just forget about Kim. The child's family and Todd and family do look alike sometimes."

"Thank you Petra for making me feel good," Julia said.

"Petra, are you trying to avoid what I asked you?" Julia asked.

"Well honey, I really can't say. All I know is that Todd loves you. How are you and he getting on? Does he act like he's having an affair?"

"Well, he has been here for me and the kids all the time. Petra, I love him so much," Julia said.

"Julia, I'm happy for you. Todd's a lovely bloke. Oh Julia, I have to rush home as I'm feeling pain under my tummy. I have just over three weeks left now."

"Will you be okay to drive home?"

"Yes, I think so. Well I'll see you soon," Petra said and Julia hugged her. "Drive carefully," Julia said.

"I will," Petra said.

Later her husband got home from work and found her sleeping. He tried to leave the room quietly, but Petra opened her eyes and saw him. "Hanson, I'm sorry I couldn't cook you anything but I was having pains."

"Are you still having pains honey?" he asked.

"Yes, but not as much as before," she said.

"Are you hungry?" he asked her.

"No, but whatever you do for you, I'll have a little."

Hanson cooked Petra's favourite meal of fish in butter sauce, mash and carrots and watched her eat. Later, Paul phoned him. "Are you coming for a drink?"

"No mate, Petra's not feeling well and I have to be home in case she needs me."

"Okay bro, I'll see you tomorrow," Paul said.

Three weeks later, just as Detective Inspector Hanson left for work, Petra went into labour. As Julia lived near to her, she phoned her, her mother and Hanson's mother and told them. Julia was the first to get to Petra, then within minutes Hanson's mother was there.

"Are you ready to have the baby?" Hanson's mother asked.

"Well, I have been having pains for the past three days, but from this morning the pain has been constant and for an hour or so now the pain is very strong and I had a show in my pants," Petra said.

"Young lady, I think you should be in hospital. Would you like me to call Hanson?"

"No, let me have the baby first," Petra said.

Julia phoned for an ambulance and as soon as it came Petra's mother drove into the yard. She saw the ambulance and ran to Petra. "How's the pain honey?" she asked.

"Bad. It comes almost every eight or ten minutes."

"Well I'm coming with you," her mother said.

"Me too," Mrs Hanson said.

Julia kissed Petra's forehead. "Well, you have more than enough people to accompany you to the hospital. I'll stay by my phone. Let me know when you have the baby," Julia said.

Petra nodded. Mrs Hanson climbed into the ambulance with Petra while her mother followed by car. Within twenty minutes, Petra had had a baby daughter.

The midwife cleaned it up and put it into Mrs Hanson's arms. She rested the baby in her cot, then phoned Detective Inspector Hanson and broke the news to him saying, "Petra has had a little girl." He said nothing but his face saddened and he closed his mobile phone.

Later, he asked Paul to the club to have a couple of pints with him and told him Petra had had a daughter. Paul was looking as happy as if he was the father himself, but he saw the gloom on Hanson's face.

"What's the matter?" he asked.

"Nothing," Hanson said.

"Well, I think we better get to the hospital to see our family," Paul said. As Hanson took his seat, Paul asked him. "Are you coming?"

Hanson got up and they drove their own cars to the hospital. When Hanson saw the baby, he smiled to see how beautiful a mixed-race baby it was with blue eyes and a flat dark mole to the left side of her upper lip like his mother's. Tears came into his eyes and turned his face away as he remembered what Marsha had said to him, to wait till the baby was born to know if it was his.

He dried his eyes and his mother took the baby out of her cot and put her in Paul's arms. After Paul had had a good look, he put her into Hanson's arms. Petra looked hard at Hanson and said, "She's our baby." He said nothing, but leaned forward and kissed Petra's lips. Then he asked, "Did she give you a hard time?"

Petra smiled. "She's like her father. She gave me a lot of pain before she decided to come out."

He whispered into Petra's ears, "That's because you kicked her father in the nuts."

Petra smiled. "She's beautiful. Would you go and tell Julia she has a goddaughter and I will let my other friends know. Oh Hanson honey, I might be out tomorrow if the baby and I are okay. I will let you know tomorrow and you could bring Arlia and Kira to see their baby sister. Oh don't let them stay up too late even though they're not at school tomorrow."

The following day was Saturday. At ten thirty in the morning Petra rang Hanson to let him know that she and the baby were coming home. Hanson took the girls to the hospital and as they saw Petra they ran to her. "Are you okay Mum?" they asked.

"Come here you two," Petra said and she hugged and kissed them. "There's your baby sister sleeping in her cot." Then Hanson walked up to her and asked, "Are you and my princess ready to go home?"

"Yes we are, but she's sleeping."

Then a doctor and a nurse went to Petra and said, "You take care. Do you have a baby seat?" the nurse asked.

"Yes," Hanson said. Petra went and said goodbye to her room-mates and left holding hands with Arlia and Kira while the nurse carrying the baby walked with Hanson.

After the nurse made sure the baby was secured in her safety car seat,

Hanson got into the driving seat with Arlia next to him while Petra and Kira sat in the back with the baby. "Drive carefully, take care and a nurse will see both of you tomorrow Mrs Hanson," the nurse said.

"Thanks for your help," Petra told her. The nurse smiled and Hanson drove his family home to meet Loretta with her baby son and the rest of her family.

For five days a nurse visited to look after Petra and her baby until the baby's cord dropped off on the fifth day. She took a sample of blood from the baby saying, "This is my last day but if there is anything wrong, we'll let you know. Goodbye Mrs Hanson."

"Goodbye nurse and thank you for looking after us."

Chapter 22

Three months later, Kim and Officer Hodge were married. At the reception, Kim left her husband and led Todd onto the dance floor and whispered in his ears, "I still love you Todd and I have feelings for you. We also have a daughter and I'm not sure this second one inside me is for my husband. But I'll keep your name free. I don't love my husband as I love you but I married him to keep the press off your back."

Todd grinned and kept calm, danced her into her husband's arms then went to dance with his wife Julia. "I saw her whispering in your ear," Julia said.

"Oh she was saying how happy she is." But as Julia looked at him, he showed guilt on his face. "I think we should take the children home as it is past their bedtime," he said.

Julia went to Petra and told her Todd was taking them home.

"I think I should ask Hanson to take us home. It's after ten and my mother must have had enough of the baby by now."

Petra went to Hanson. "Honey, I think it's time we took the girls home."

"Go get the girls," he said.

Petra went to tell Marsha that Hanson was taking her and her girls home. "Oh Petra, Paul asked me to be his wife for the fourth time and I said yes. But we haven't set a date yet."

The following Monday morning Petra sold her first wedding ring back to the jeweller's for five million pounds, the same as Sydney Black bought it for. "Mrs Hanson, I'll give you what the ring cost as I knew your reason for marrying that bug Sydney Black." The manager smiled.

"Well thank you Mr Holden." While the manager was making out the cheque, Petra said, "Please make it out to Marsha Daniels."

The manager looked at Petra smiling, then handed over the cheque to her.

"Thank you very much," Petra said and left.

The following morning Petra gave Marsha the cheque. Marsha looked hard at the cheque and then at Petra. "Thanks, but I wasn't looking for any of this."

"Well Marsha, it's yours my dear. I sold the ring, which I think should have been yours in the first place, and this is how much it had cost. Also this is for the time you were working for that bug." Marsha looked on the second cheque and saw it was for two hundred million pounds. She cried hugging Petra. "Petra, I don't know what to say."

"Say nothing. Joanne is pregnant and Curtis is so happy," Petra told her.

"Petra, I think I'm pregnant too," Marsha said happily. "And Paul is so happy too."

"Oh Marsha I'm happy for you and Paul. He's a really nice bloke," Petra said.

"Let's drink to our happy family," Marsha said and she and Petra toasted with a glass of orange juice. Hanson walked in and said to Petra, "By the way honey, we rounded up Johnny Blimps and most of his disciples and have recovered at least a billion pounds in money plus drugs."

"Well Hanson my love, let's leave those poisonous vipers in their cages for now, hey?"

Hanson smiled. "By the way honey, Arlia and Kira promoted us from aunt and uncle to mum and dad."

"Is that so bad?"

"Petra honey, I love those girls like our own," said Hanson, smiling.

"They're our own, Mr Scott Brett Hanson, they're our precious daughters," Petra replied.

Printed in Great Britain
by Amazon.co.uk, Ltd.,
Marston Gate.